THE TEN THUNDERBOLTS

R.A. CRAWFORD

R.A.CRAWFORD

ACT I

THE LIGHTNING SITE

"I wish that strife would vanish away from among gods and mortals, and gall, which makes a man grow angry for all his great mind, that gall of anger that swarms like smoke inside of a man's heart and becomes a thing sweeter to him by far than the dripping of honey."

"The Iliad, right?" Kang was quick to add citation. The epics were his specialty. Homer. Virgil. Quintus. He's been able to recall entire chapters from any of their pages since we were eight years old. Of course, those were just myths. Stories told by poets to bind meaning between fiction and organised religion.

"Come on, Zeke," he said. "Give me something that's at least slightly obscure."

"Alright." I had something in mind. I'd had it since the moment we'd boarded the plane, nearly five hours ago. The flight from Heathrow to Larnaca wasn't particularly long, but we would be landing just an hour before the exhibition and needed to keep our minds sharp for when we arrived.

"Thus fell one house, but not one house alone deserved to perish; over all the earth ferocious deeds prevail,—all men conspire in evil. Let them therefore feel the weight of dreadful penalties so justly earned, for such hath my unchanging will ordained."

Kang looked dumbfounded. The colour from his cheeks drained till they were pale, while he thumbed his upper lip in the same way he always did when he found himself disarmed of knowledge.

"How long have you been waiting to hit me with that?" he asked.

I shrugged, feigning disinterest while I enjoyed his obvious attempts to buy himself thinking time. Kang's mind was like a library, where the shelves were lined with books that varied from ancient Roman texts to last month's issue of Green Lantern Volume 6.

"Fine," he eventually said, after another thirty seconds of silent contemplation. "You got me." I'd been trying hard to conceal the smirk I could feel tugging at the corner of my lips, but finally, I raised my eyebrows and grinned at him. He was ready to admit defeat.

"There's no way I could be prepared to recall some obscure piece of text from one of Ovid's poems." My heart sank as Kang continued and I quickly realised his expression wasn't one of defeat, but relief. "It's probably something like book one, paragraph two-hundred. If I had to guess, that's the Nineteen-Twenties translation. Cornhill publishing? At least, that was the version my grandmother kept in the attic."

I slammed shut my laptop and whispered, "I hate you." Kang, of course, was already stretching across me, reaching an arm to the centre aisle to get Xiao's attention.

"Hey," he said. "Did you see that? He actually thought he had me."

Xiao didn't seem to care enough to remove her flight blindfold, instead, plucking one headphone reluctantly from her right ear.

"What?" she said, not bothering to conceal her exasperation. She never did. "This better be about the exhibition being cancelled. Or this plane going down. Otherwise, I doubt you have any reason important enough to wake me while we're still in the air."

"It isn't important," I said. "Ignore him."

"Gladly," Xiao replied. "Couldn't you have just let me enjoy the last--" she lifted her blindfold to check the screen on the headrest in front of her. "Fifteen minutes of this journey, without having to hear you two argue about nothing."

"Oh, we weren't arguing," said Kang. "To argue, we would both have to be experiencing a feeling of injustice or mistreatment. But all I feel is triumph. I think this puts me back in the lead."

Before I could unleash the full extent of my wrath and lay into Kang about the fact that it was impossible to keep track of the scores, the fasten seatbelt sign above our heads flicked on. As the plane began its descent, I snatched the pair of headphones from the pouch of the seat in front and slotted them over my head. The time for games was over and it was important I get myself in the right state of mind. This wasn't a holiday, it was a business trip. We would only have fifteen minutes from the second we landed to make our forty-five-minute journey to arrive at the exhibition on time. Scratch that, the exhibition already started an hour ago. But the talk we were cutting it so tight to make it for, was the only part that held any interest to us.

Scratch that, too. There was nothing about this exhibition that was of any interest to me, Xiao or even Kang. The only reason we were attending was because our benefactor had instructed us to.

Doctor Pierceson. I usually stop there whenever I mention his name. Working for the world's foremost expert in archaeology had more perks than you could imagine. Name-dropping Pierceson had seen me into more A-list galas, artefact unveilings and restricted access auctions than I could recount. Historians who had studied for decades and spent years in the field hadn't been privy to the kind of global freedom of access we three enjoyed. And we were only nineteen. Did that make me a little arrogant and headstrong? Hell yeah. But even those were qualities demanded in one of his students. Plus, there was something tremendously satisfying about being asked to valet somebody's car, only to laugh and fast-track my way ahead of them into an event.

 Even I wasn't sure what age the old man was pushing these days, but he certainly wasn't capable of jet-setting around the globe week-in, week-out to follow up on leads. That left it to us, his apprentices, to perform the bulk of the legwork. In the past season alone we'd been knee-deep in the snowy streets of Reykjavik, riding funiculars in the Buda District, and hiking past the Skakavac Waterfall in Perućica. Without us, he ran the risk of being beaten to every new potential discovery. Sure, most ventures would end relatively fruitlessly, but it was that level of persistence that led to the biggest scores of his career. And it was the level of determination that he sought to instil in us, his proteges.

 This wasn't the first time he had saddled us with a last-minute destination like this, and it wouldn't be the last. But even I had to admit that, lately, it felt more and more as if we were being sent off to investigate dead-ends. Our last six trips, though admittedly enjoyable in their own right, had left us empty-handed. Though Kang would prepare for every outing as if we were tackling the Temple of Doom, it wasn't like we were expecting to stumble across some ancient artefact. But it would be nice if, for a change, we could uncover some new text, or translation or a new take on old-myth. Something. Anything. We just wanted a discovery of our own. I just wanted a real story of my own.

 I was unlikely to find it sitting in the Cyprus Museum listening to one of Pierceson's former students talk about some obscure excavation he and his team had been undertaking on the shores of Paphos, a city on the southwestern edge of Cyprus.

A few minutes later we touched down and were ushered off the plane, before the rest of the passengers.

"What's going on?" I looked accusingly at Kang as we were led down the aisle, between the rows of infuriated passengers forced to remain in their seats. Kang was more guilty of abusing Pierceson's resources than any other and undoubtedly it had been him that arranged this treatment.

"I may," he started, with an unconvincing shrug. "Have arranged for a private transfer, direct from the runway, and all the way to the museum. I also may have called ahead and asked them to delay things by an hour. Or two."

"*You* asked them?" Xiao raised a sceptical eyebrow.

"I *may* have said that Doctor Pierceson had specifically requested it."

"Man." I slung my carry-on luggage over one shoulder. "All we're going to get is negative attention when we arrive now. They'll be expecting Pierceson. Not three students."

"Whatever." Kang pulled his red-lensed shades from his shirt pocket and dropped them over his dark blue eyes. "You love when people underestimate you. Besides, I didn't rush over here on the only available overly-cramped flight just to miss the whole damned thing." Neither I nor Xiao replied, instead just exchanging the usual glance of repulsion we felt whenever we were forced to admit that Kang was right. "I'll take that as a thank you," he said.

The drive to the museum was uneventful. Minutes after taking her seat in the rear of the luxuriously-spaced people-carrier, Xiao was asleep. She slipped in and out of consciousness so easily it bordered on narcolepsy. And no matter how much she slept, no matter how many hours we afforded her, she was ready to pass out once again. Still, neither of us dared tease her about it. Xiao's sense of humour was... questionable, on a good day. And any jokes at her expense usually ended with, at best, a days-long cold shoulder or, worst, an untimely knee in the groin. Not that I would know, Kang was the expert in receiving her penance.

As we navigated the streets of Nicosia, the capital city, Kang kept ducking his head to get a look at the tall buildings that lined the roads.

"What is it?" We had visited Cyprus before, a few years earlier. Albeit when we were young enough to require an escort. But the city streets themselves were unfamiliar to me.

"I'm trying to find that hotel we stayed in. The Imperial Atlus."

"Don't think I'd recognize it. It wasn't so memorable, was it? Maybe it doesn't exist anymore."

"It better." Kang smiled suggestively. "They took my booking for a room in it."

"And what's so important about this hotel, in particular?"

"What's so important?" Kang waved a questioning hand in my direction, then cut me off before I could respond. "Nothing. Nothing at all, old buddy. But I'm not spending my night here pouring over textbooks or history blogs. I'm going out and making the most of whatever Nicosia has to offer. And the one thing I remember from our visit here is that old Mr. Edgerton kept an eye on us the whole time. In particular, to make sure we didn't stray across the road from our hotel and into the university campus. You know, the one with all the European undergrads."

Of course. There was only one thing Kang cared about more than mythology and popular culture. The opposite sex. He craved the attention of anything with a pair of legs and X chromosomes. Annoyingly, he always seemed to get it.

"Fine. Do whatever you need bro. But don't end up in a state that leaves me at the second part of this snoozefest tomorrow by myself. Or worse, with just her." I gave a wary nod in Xiao's direction, suddenly uncertain whether she was truly asleep or not.

"Be easier if you just came with me." Kang slipped an arm over my shoulder.

"And have you throw me to the wolves again?" I drove an elbow into his ribs. "No chance. Find another wingman."

I ended our last night out in Budapest sneaking through the rear delivery exit of the city's most raucous bar. Kang had long since abandoned me, absconding with a member of a travelling university volleyball team, and leaving me with the other ten or so members.

Suffice to say, our appetites weren't exactly aligned. After spending hours watching their drunk and disorderly conduct and rejecting what felt like the hundredth request to return to their hotel, I made my escape and spent the rest of the night in an overpriced all-night tea-house. Better that, than returning to whatever sordid affair Kang was up to back at our hotel.

"Whatever you get up to, leave me out of this time." I wanted to make sure Kang knew I wasn't joking. "Or I'll tell finance to take a closer look at your expenditure. You wouldn't want to get cut off, would you?"

"You wouldn't dare." Kang's hand was on my shoulder this time. "That would make me unhappy. And if I'm unhappy. You'll be *very* unhappy."

An hour later, and in remarkable time, we arrived at our destination. The Cyprus Museum of Nicosia.

If I remember correctly, the construction of the museum was supervised by George H. Everett Jeffery. We Brits have a knack for finding our way around Europe and a tendency to leave behind a legacy, for better or worse. The entrance had been architected to mimic a classical temple entrance too. Four columns plus an undecorated frieze and pediment. I meant to visit the last time we were in Cyprus, but we'd ended up having to leave early to meet up with Pierceson in Athens.

The exhibition was over.

Kang pre-empted the barrage of questions I had for him. "Don't even try to blame me," he said. "I was the only one trying to get us here on time."

"What happened to delaying by an hour?" Xiao took a threatening step towards him. "Or two?"

Kang was quick to restore the distance between them, backing towards the entrance. "At least I tried. All you two did was complain.

Besides, what are you so pissed about? If anything, we lucked out." He rubbed his hands together eagerly. "I say we head back to the hotel, asap, drop off our things and make the most of the day."

As much as I was annoyed at having missed the whole event, we had bothered to make the journey after all, there was a part of me that couldn't help but share Kang's sentiment. Still, as much as I would've liked to leave, the Pierceson-taught apprentice in me couldn't leave entirely empty-handed. "We can't go yet. Let's at least ask around and find out what was on show."

"You're right." Kang nodded and gave me an over-zealous pat on the back. "*We* should totally do that. Tell you what, you ask around here, while I head to the hotel and find some wifi to email the organisers. Maybe I can arrange a meetup for tomorrow or something."

"Really? You're just going to leave me here?" Kang was already inching away. "Xiao? You with me?"

"Sorry, Zeke. This has been a waste of time." She didn't even bother whispering. I'm not sure Xiao knew how. Nor did she seem to know, or care, how to conceal her displeasure.

"Alright, fine. I guess I'll do all our jobs."

"Seriously, chill." Kang looked to the skies. "There's next to nothing to see here."

I waved dismissively back at him before dragging my bag over my shoulder and turning away.

"The only thing noticeable about it is that it wasn't noticeable at all," I said.

"Don't quote Pierceson-isms at me and walk off." Kang's voice grew quieter behind me.

I didn't bother looking back as I entered the office labelled, 'Press Signups', opposite the library.

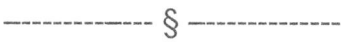

Inside the office a somewhat striking middle-aged looking woman sat at a semi-circular desk; her eyes locked on her laptop. There was something alluring about her broad shoulders and the almost Viking braid of long hair that reached over her shoulder and fell onto the desk by her elbow.

"Hi," I started. "I'm Ezekiel Lewis. I missed the exhibition due to some travel issues. I was wondering if there was a summary available?"

"Sign-up for the private sessions." She didn't look up, instead nodding her head to the left. "Form's there."

After a few moments of hesitation spent searching the page, I tried to speak with her again. "How come Mr. Ealing isn't on here?" The only names listed were Miss Vinter or Mr. Kincaid."

Ealing was a former apprentice of Pierceson, once holding many of the responsibilities that now fell to us. After working directly for our benefactor for several years, he had since embarked on his own journey and carved out a successful niche as a Mediterranean Historian. Ealing, I assumed, was the reason we were asked to be here in the first place. This was *his* project after all.

"He's busy. Take a seat in the back hall. The sessions will start in a minute."

"Okay." I slid my bag off her desk and headed away.

It took every ounce of professionalism I could muster not to spin around and lay into the woman for being so terse. If there's one thing I can't stand, it's when someone decides they don't have time for me, without bothering to figure out if I'm worth talking to. I wanted to tear her down and lambast her on how negligent it was, especially in our profession, to dismiss a fellow archaeologist without giving them the time of day, then throw Pierceson's name in her face and walk out.

However, apart from satiating my need to vent, that probably wouldn't get me far either. Instead I just continued out of the room, without looking back. Pick your battles and choose which fights to walk away from. Advice my mum had always given me.

In her words, 'Son, you're black and you're British. Grow some thicker skin and toughen up.' Good advice. She was full of it. 'If I wanted you to be a sap, I wouldn't have named you–"

"Ezekiel Lewis." The strident and unpleasantly familiar voice of the only person ahead of me in the waiting list knocked me from my thoughts. "As I live and breathe."

I stopped dead in my tracks and panned my head up from my size ten boots to a chair on the left of the corridor where a woman sat, one leg crossed over the other, with her head cocked to one side and a malicious smile curving across her lips. "Camilla."

I used her name like a curse. In most ways it was. As Kang would say, every hero needs a villain. Iron Man has The Mandarin. The Flash and his Reverse. Reed Richards had Doctor Doom. For our benefactor, Doctor Pierceson, it was Professor LaGuerre. He was regarded as the world's foremost expert on classical civilizations and made himself consistently available to scrutinise each and every one of Pierceson's discoveries over the past few decades. And like we acted on the behalf of Pierceson, Camilla carried out LaGuerre's bidding. That put her in direct competition with us on an almost daily basis.

"How the hell did you find out about this?"

"It's called being good at my job." She rose from her chair and stood uncomfortably close to me until we were face to face. "We can't all rely on handouts from our master."

"Mentor. I don't have a master. Though if I did, I'd serve him *loyally*."

"Oh, Zeke." She reached a hand towards my face, from which I recoiled. "It's always the same thing with you. You really mustn't hold such a grudge."

"I don't. The past is the past. It's when my present intersects with yours that's upsetting." I used my bag to gently ease her aside as I stepped further down the corridor and slumped onto one of the benches.

As she slid into the seat opposite, with all the poise and grace of a monarch, I couldn't help but be reminded that there wasn't a single thing about Camilla I didn't hate. The way she grinned whenever we made eye contact, knowing how it got under my skin. The way her narrow eyes scanned me up and down from behind her dark mascara. But most frustratingly of all, the way she was forever showing up in the exact same place as us and managing, all-too-often, to beat us to the punch.

In Cumbria, she had arrived a day earlier than us to the unveiling of three new Roman texts at the Hadrian's Wall Emporium. She nailed exclusive looks at each text long before the event had started. Exclusives we had promised to secure for our Institute. It was the same thing again in Luxor when new mummified remains were discovered in the tombs at the Valley of Kings. Despite Pierceson being the first in the know, and dispatching us the same day, we arrived to find Camilla skulking around trying to persuade several of the discovery team to allow her entrance. And succeeding.

Even now, at this exhibition I could barely pretend to care about, she had somehow managed to worm her way in and end up ahead of me in the queue. How did she do it? Coincidences were one thing. Bumping into one another at the same event. But she was always there. At every expo and every press conference. I was convinced she had someone on the inside. A rat working for Pierceson, feeding her information. But there was no way to prove it.

"How's Kang?" she asked. She almost looked sincere.

"Like you care."

"Oh, for goodness sake." Her eyes rolled up at the ceiling. "Do you always have to be so pugnacious, Zeke?"

"Don't call me Zeke. That's reserved for my friends. People who have my back, not the ones who stick a knife in it."

Camilla merely shrugged, interlocking her fingers and sliding them over one knee. "I'm sure Pierceson wouldn't want us at the throat of one another. Just because we're now rivals, does that mean we can't be civil?"

"Yes. That's exactly what it means." I tried to ease away the intense frown I could feel burning across my forehead. "But it's not because we're rivals, Camilla. It's because you're a snake. No, a scorpion. And I know exactly what you do."

A smile stretched steadily across Camilla's mouth, until her immaculate white teeth parted and she chuckled aloud. "A scorpion?" she said, apparently amused by the accusation. "I like that. And what are you, a frog? Maybe a swan? You really do think the world of yourself."

"Whatever." Her laughter only worsened my mood. "Are you done?"

Before she could answer, one of the doors on her side of the hall swung open, and a bald-head dipped through the frame. "Camilla Winnett?" The senior-looking man flicked his eyes towards her.

"I guess I am," she said, her eyes lingering on mine for a second before switching to him.

She disappeared into what looked like a laboratory, as the door swept shut, affording me only a brief glimpse inside. Chaotic was one word I could use to describe it. There were at least four other people in the room and plenty of chatter being shouted back and forth while the door was open. To my own surprise, my disinterest had been replaced by curiosity. Why was the backroom so much busier than the stage area? All that the slides showcased were photographs of weathered jewels found somewhere beneath the Mediterranean sea. Yet, clearly, there was more story to accompany their findings than had been revealed. And it irked me to no end that I was forced to sit idly by, outside, while Camilla soaked up the details ahead of me.

"Ezekiel Lewis?" I heard my name called in the same distinctive Scandinavian voice that had offloaded me at the signup desk. I glanced up to find the woman's eyes locked on her phone as she stormed down the hall in my direction.

"That would be me," I said, rising to greet her with a handshake. She never even saw my hand, as she yanked open the same door Camilla entered and beckoned me to follow with a nod of her head.

I didn't have time to be insulted, instead, rushing after her as she disappeared inside. I quickened my pace to keep up as we bypassed several workstations, including one Camilla was perched by as she listened to the bald man, who must have been Mr. Kincaid, lecture her on the method by which they conducted the deep sea dives.

She looked bored. To me anyway. I doubt many could spot the signs. After all, she was naturally talented at feigning interest. She flashed her eyes wide whenever Kincaid addressed her and let her almost-too-perfect smile do the rest as she nodded along with his story. But it was the rest of her body-language that told the real story. The way her foot tapped incessantly and she clicked the pen in her palm repeatedly without writing a single thing down. And the way she ever so slightly jumped the gun with several of her 'I sees' and 'fascinatings.'

Camilla's biggest tell was how whenever Kincaid glanced down at his laptop, her eyes would dart inquisitively around the room, pouring over every detail, no matter how subtle, absorbing the scene to examine later. Kang could remember pretty much every word he had ever read, like an encyclopaedia of knowledge, but Camilla's memory was photographic. She only had to see something once to add it to her collective, making her perfect for stealing information not meant for her.

As the Scandinavian woman headed further into the lab, I lost sight of Camilla and switched my own attention to the surroundings. What was most likely meant as some kind of storage room had been converted into a makeshift laboratory. There were numerous brands of chemical agents used for cleaning and sterilisation scattered about, while dozens of books and computer screens were open on pages detailing everything ranging from doric order architecture to Sophocles' tragic tale of Oedipus. Undoubtedly, an investigation of some sort was underway here. Camilla, too, would be aware of that fact. And no doubt using every deceitful and underhanded weapon in her armoury to uncover their goal for herself.

There was so much going on, I'd hardly considered just how little attention my guide was paying me as she weaved between workstations. "Excuse me," I finally said. "Vinter, right?"

The interjection seemed to startle her, as she turned to regard me with wide-eyes like she had forgotten I was accompanying her. "Yes," she eventually said. "Ezekiel, wasn't it? Sorry. It's been a busy day. And we still have a lot to do."

"Not a problem. Although, with all due respect," I fashioned the most sincere smile I could manage. "The exhibition details didn't exactly scream, 'big discovery.'"

"The exhibition is a formality." She waved her hand as if wafting away a bad odour. "Fundraising for our board and continued sponsorship. The real discovery here has only just begun."

"Then why the sessions? It's not like I had to pay extra for them."

"Michael's idea." She rolled her eyes. "He said anyone determined enough to come see us afterward might be the kind of person who could offer useful insight."

"Ealing?" I took a step closer to her. "So he is here. Maybe if I could speak to him directly?"

Vinter was shaking her head before I'd even finished speaking. "He's far too busy. Completely absorbed in the work."

"Right." I nodded. "If you're talking, then you're not concentrating on your work. But, if you're not talking, then nobody knows what the hell you're working on." I stared, deliberately, at Vinter, hoping for a reaction.

"That's the exact same shit that Michael says." Her arms came to rest akimbo on her hips. "Who are you?"

"Just another student of Doctor Pierceson, Ma'am." I reached out my hand again.

This time she shook it. "Alright, fine. Come with me. He'll never forgive me if I turn you away."

She led me out of the lab and around several corners till we passed through a large storage room lined with more modern replica sculptures of different mythological heroes. Heracles, caped in the skin of the Nemean lion. Theseus, wielding the head of Medusa. Jason, adorned in a golden fleece. There were dozens more. The museum had long since reached capacity and held far more treasures than it could possibly display at once, leading to the impressively crowded store rooms. When we reached the end of the left-hand wall, a sharp turn took us into a spacious office where even more equipment was set out and a ponytailed man presided over the remains of a heavily corroded statue.

"Michael," said Vinter, as we entered. "I have a guest for you."

"Oh?" said Ealing, not turning around to face us.

"He says he's–"

"Zeke." I took the incentive and barged my way across the room. "It's been a while Mr. Ealing."

Ealing panned around and lifted the pair of magnifying glasses he had over his eyes till they rested on his forehead. "Zeke?" He sounded unsure.

"We only met a handful of times," I replied, trying to maintain the bass in my voice amidst the nerves that were now building. "In London. You were visiting Doctor Pierceson during his event on the categorization of Hellenic myth." Still he eyed me warily. "You gave a speech on the value of poetry in ancient and modern mythology. I was the one you practised with beforehand."

Suddenly, and to my relief, his eyes brightened with recognition. "Zeke. Pierceson's prodigy. The old man was really fond of you, I remember. How's he doing?"

Prodigy? I wasn't aware he'd ever referred to me as such, but it was enough to boost my confidence in dealing with Ealing. "Pretty much the same," I said.

"Stubborn and self-serving, you mean?" Ealing smiled.

"That's one way to put it."

"Trust me, that's the only way to put it. I do miss his lectures. He was always... wait–" Ealing gave me a look from head to toe. "Did he send you here? I mean, of course he did. But what did he tell you?"

I shrugged. Honestly. "Nothing much. Literally, we were only told to attend your presentation and report on the results of your dive."

"That man." Ealing shook his head and smiled. "He knows. How does he always know?"

"Knows?" I looked at each of them. "Knows about what?"

Ealing seemed to eyeball Vinter for a second, checking before he spoke. When his attention finally flicked back to me, his smile was gone and his eyes had grown intense. "The Lightning Site."

Both Vinter and Ealing were silent for a moment, staring me down, no doubt checking for some kind of reaction.

"I have no idea what that is," I said, breaking the deadlock. "Look, if Pierceson knows something, he sure didn't pass it on to me. Last I heard, you were digging around in Arabia. So I'm curious to know, how did you end up here in Cyprus? What did you find out there?"

Ealing breathed a long sigh, then swept his finger over the trackpad on his laptop. "Alright," he said, dispatching several screens of information before pulling a map, bordering the Arabian Peninsula, central on his screen and plunging his index finger against it. "Lebanon, actually. In Beirut. We were digging there, on a site, more hopeful than expectant. There were reports of a local historian having dug up the remains of some... statue. Certainly, it wasn't Arabian. Or at least, it showed signs of Hellenistic influence. The pieces he had recovered suggested it was at least seventy feet tall."

"Seventy feet?" I immediately found myself sceptical of Ealing's tale. There weren't too many constructions of that scale in the ancient world beyond the Colossus of Rhodes. "That seems unlikely."

"Exactly," Ealing nodded. "We didn't believe it either at first. For weeks we helped trudge up every inch of the place. We found nothing. So instead, we focused on the pieces he already had. It was definitely humanoid.

From what we could tell, a knee or a shoulder. But more interesting was the type of damage. I had an expert examine the cracked piece. It wasn't caused by weathering or collisions. It was pressure damage."

"Pressure? As in water pressure. You think the piece came from the ocean?"

"I did. And I was right. Turns out the owner of the site had dug his own sewage line to the sea. He thought it was a good idea, given his proximity to the coast. But more often than not it just ended in oceanic waste clogging his waterworks. So I sent our diving team down to scour the seabed there. Our findings were huge. I had to call in a favour from a friend with a cargo hauling service, out on the coast of Paphos. We brought bits and pieces here, to Nicosia, to study. The rest of what we found is still sitting out there on the boats." Ealing's eyes went to Vinter once more.

"So what *did* you find?" I asked her.

Vinter sighed and reluctantly tapped on the large touchscreen monitor behind her until a sculpture filled the screen. It wasn't fully intact, there were fractures throughout and dozens of pieces were missing. But it looked like she had attempted to extrapolate the shapes of the missing pieces using whatever software she was running, with a grid-like mesh filling in wherever there was a gap. "This," she said.

Again, the pair left me to decipher their findings alone. It felt like one of Pierceson's famous pop quizzes, where we would turn up to class one day only to be presented with an obscure case study from his past and left to retrace his train of thought and rediscover his findings.

I identified the obvious parts first. It was indeed a sculpture, nearly ten feet tall from the scale that bordered the screen. There were two figures, both men judging by the beard on one and the genitalia on the other. The more elderly figure was sitting in a chair and looking proudly up at the taller man. At first, I couldn't identify the standing man, but the seated figure. Him I knew. It was almost a carbon copy of Phidias sculpture at Olympia, or at least how I had seen it depicted.

A wreath of olive leaves, sceptre in the left hand supporting an eagle, and sandals perched upon a stool. Even the chair, no, the throne upon which he sat was familiar; adorned with what was likely to have been precious metals and jewels. This was Zeus, God of Thunder and ruler of Mount Olympus. Only... never as I'd seen him depicted before.

Zeus looked... weary. Old. Sure, he was sculpted as an aged figure throughout most historical and modern-day art, but here it seemed as if he was nearing the end of his days. His limbs were thin and wiry, his skin wrought with wrinkles and the eyes sunken in fatigue. More tellingly, he was injured. Or at least he had been injured in the past. A thick scar ran over his forehead and down through one missing eye while his right hand, often held high above his head and grasping a mighty thunderbolt, was instead a stump from the wrist onwards.

"I'm not sure this is a Greek sculpture after all." I took a seat in one of the computer chairs and gave it a kick, spinning three-hundred and sixty degrees. "I've never seen Zeus like this before. Non-mighty, that is. Thinking about it..." The gears in my head started to turn some more. "I don't know of many events in Greek mythology that end with the King of the Gods being left in a condition like this." I raised a finger to the screen. "Who is the other figure supposed to be? I'm guessing you know."

"Interesting one," said Vinter, offering information without resistance for once, as she nodded at the monitor. "This is only speculative, of course, but the first thing we noticed is the size of the man. Even if Zeus were to stand, this man would dwarf him, on this scale, by about two feet. Then there is the scar on his chest. Like Zeus, we assumed he had been through some kind of attack or battle. But then we thought more about the position." Vinter drew her index and middle finger across her own torso. "Upper right portion of the abdomen, just above the stomach." She tapped her fingers on the position she described. "The liver."

"The liver?" I knew instantly what she was inferring. "You think this is Prometheus?"

"You don't have to say it," said Ealing, with a lopsided smile. "It doesn't make sense. These two. Together. Zeus looking up at him with... affection. There's no narrative to support this."

"I suppose you want to show him the stones, too," said Vinter, pulling around a chair for herself.

"The stones?" I scanned the image once more. "What stones?"

"See the throne." Ealing circled the chair upon which Zeus sat, in particular where it was decorated with jewels. "These were precious stones. Nothing remarkable in composition. Pearls, Emeralds, Garnets. What *was* remarkable about them was their condition. They were all stained in some sort of black... ash. The compound itself, we can't identify. But it does contain traces of carbon."

"That's what your team is doing downstairs." I thought back to the stock of chemicals I'd walked by.

Ealing nodded. "So far, nothing removes the black marks. The parts of the stone in contact with the sculpture are carbonised to an extent we've never seen. Do you know what would have to happen to cause that?"

"Yeah." I did. And I was starting to see what Ealing was getting at. But it was almost too ridiculous to say aloud. But clearly, he was expecting me to, and I wanted to keep him engaged. "It would have to be struck by lightning."

"Or?" Ealing smiled. And I sighed. "Indulge me, son. I know it's against the old man's philosophy.."

"Or. A thunderbolt."

Ealing clasped his hands together and shook them as if he were thanking me. "A thunderbolt. Through the statue of the God of Thunder himself. Poetic. Isn't it?"

"Okay." I bit my inner cheek with my right molars as I suppressed the need to voice my scepticism. "I'll play along. Just for a moment. You want to believe that this statue, of a friendly Zeus and Prometheus, was struck by a thunderbolt. From Zeus. Right?" Vinter and Ealing looked at one another but didn't reply. "But like much of what you've got here, there isn't a single myth to explain any of it."

Vinter smiled, as she crossed her arms and leaned back in her chair. "That you know of."

"What's that supposed to mean?" I asked, wondering exactly what I had said to amuse her.

"Well, I'm not telling him," she said, nudging Ealing with her elbow. "It's your theory." Ealing looked back at her, apparently slightly uncertain, for the first time. "Besides, I have to admit, he's good. He reminds me of you. Just tell him about it."

"About what?" I asked again, more impatiently this time.

Ealing glanced quickly around the room before clasping his hands and raising both index fingers to his lips. "Alright, he said. I'll tell you, Zeke. About The Ten Thunderbolts."

ACT II

THE BENEFACTOR OF FIRE

'Your speech is pompous sounding, full of pride, as fits the lackey of the Gods. You are young and young your rule and you think the tower in which you live is free from sorrow: from it have I not seen two tyrants thrown? The third, who now is king, I shall yet live to see him fall, of all three most suddenly, most dishonored. Do you think I will crouch before your Gods, -so new-and tremble? I am far from that.'

I slammed the book shut. Pierceson often quoted Aeschylus, and in this case it only served to further conviction in my belief. Ealing's story didn't make any sense.

To the point where I was irritated at myself for having stayed behind to listen to it. There were so many glaring holes in his hypothesis, I was having difficulty keeping track of which parts he had said and which parts I might have imagined, to fill in the gaps. And yet, despite it being three in the morning, there I was, sitting in a twenty-four hour library with my nose in one of Pierceson's texts.

I don't know why, but I just couldn't get any of it off my mind.

First, there was the statue. It was, literally, the biggest question mark. Everything about it was a mystery concealing a greater mystery. What was a sculpture of Zeus doing out on the coast of Lebanon? Even if it had been appropriated by some other archaeologist and lost in transit, where did a monument that large come from in the first place? Then there was Zeus' condition. Why depict the King of Gods in such a debilitated state? Was it supposed to show weakness? That even their society's most powerful mythical figure could suffer? Or was it meant to eschew triumph? After all, his expression in the piece wasn't one of sadness, but something closer to joy or pride.

The most head-scratching part was the second figure in the sculpture. Ealing's logic here was sound enough. It could be Prometheus, the Titan. But that scene alone would require remarkable imagination to fashion.

As I'd just read, written poetically in the words my own titanic mentor, Zeus and Prometheus were not friends. Prometheus was one of the few Titans spared the fate of being banished by the lightning God. But that didn't stop the pair from eventually coming to conflict. Prometheus, famously, stole the invention of fire from the Gods. Spiriting it away from Hephaestus' lab and into the hands of Humankind. In doing so, he became almost a benefactor of the entire Human race, propelling us forwards in science and technology while spearheading culture like never before. As punishment, Zeus had the immortal Titan chained to a rock where an eagle would spend each day pecking out his liver, only for it to grow back by the following dawn.

That was how the myths went, anyway.

Betrayal was an act unforgivable by Zeus and I couldn't find any evidence that would make sense of an aged Zeus looking up with pride at one of his greatest nemeses.

Ealing had his own explanation, of course. 'The Ten Thunderbolts.' That was his tale. And it was ridiculous. He spoke of an event, so cataclysmic in scale that the very existence of the Gods came under threat. And that Zeus brought an end to the conflict by striking the heavens with a thunderbolt. Ealing's myth suggested that only ten Gods survived Zeus' outburst, his thunderbolts hurling them across the seas and striking ten separate sites around the continent. Of course, when I probed into the origins of this fantasy, he was far less forthcoming with the details.

Nonetheless, he believed his sculpture's original location to be one of those sites.

"Bullshit," I said under my breath, annoyed by the entire thing.

"I'm sorry?" said a distinctly feminine voice.

It definitely surprised me. My shoulders jolted and a surge of heat ran through my chest.

I didn't think there was anybody nearby. There had been one man at the security desk. Middle-aged and a native Cypriot, judging by his accent. It was a little more melodic than the Greeks normally sounded. He was only there to take my name and wave me inside. And I hadn't seen a single other person on any of my trips to collect books up and down the various aisles.

I tried to pretend she hadn't startled me, relaxing my shoulders and shuffling more comfortably into my seat. But as I looked up, ready to issue her with a retort or a dose of sarcasm, I was surprised yet again.

Staring back at me, was indeed a girl. And she didn't look like any librarian I had ever seen. Dark brown hair flowed over her shoulders, complementing the ocean-blue silk of her blouse and matching trousers. The questioning look on her face did nothing to detract from her beauty, instead pushing her full, cherry-blossomed lips into a half-pout while one immaculately painted eyebrow arched up towards her forehead.

I'd seen attractive women before, but none had left me as speechless as her. At first I couldn't understand what it was about her that proved so instantly alluring. Only as I stared, still silent, did it hit me. Her eyes. They were golden. Not like a sunset or the glow of a warm fire. Like real gold, melted into spheres and staring back at me from behind a pair of rectangular black and yellow frames.

"Did I disturb you?" she said. It was a good thing she spoke. I hadn't said anything for an embarrassing amount of time.

"No. Well. Yes. Actually. I'm kind of in the middle of something." I wish I could've thought of something more interesting to say. But it was late and my brain was desperate for sleep. Still, I didn't want her to leave. "What are you doing here in the middle of night?"

Her neck retracted and her brow furrowed as she tapped a plastic tag pinned to her chest that revealed nought but the name of the library.

"Me?" She looked bemused. "I work here."

"*You* work here?" I hoped she could detect my scepticism.

"Yes." She smirked. "Is that a problem?"

"No. Uh... no problem." An attempt at a nonchalant shrug was all I could manage.

"What are *you* doing here in the middle of the night?" she replied.

"Working." I wasn't in the habit of sharing the details of my work with strangers. No matter how attractive they were.

"On?"

"Nothing you'd be interested in. Trust me."

"Try me." All of a sudden her arm was pressed against mine as she rested both palms on the table and scanned the books I laid out, before flipping one open. "Maybe I can help."

Though she had seemingly little respect for personal space, maybe it couldn't hurt to bounce a few thoughts off her. I couldn't exactly talk to my team at this time of night. Xiao was undoubtedly back at the hotel, snoring too loud to hear her phone ring. While Kang was likely off somewhere doing something I'd rather not conjure an image of. Besides, she was just a librarian. Hardly likely to spill the embarrassingly vague details to the press.

"Well." I shifted the feet of my chair to put a little distance between myself and the librarian as a bead of sweat traced its way down my armpit. "I'm trying to find out if there are any records for commissions of colossal sculptures of Zeus. Ten, in fact."

She didn't reply straight away. Instead, turning the pages of the book in front of me a few times. "Why ten?" she eventually said.

"Not important."

"Seems important to you."

I sighed and rubbed my tired eyes. "The guys who found one of the sculptures think it's related to something called 'The Ten Thunderbolts.'"

The librarian's head swivelled like an owl. "The Ten Thunderbolts?" she repeated, mulling it over as she tapped her pink nail against her matching lips. "Never heard of it. But if you're researching Greek myth, why all these Pierceson books? All you'll find here are dates and classifications. You're not going to find your myth in one of these boring statistics books."

For the first time in the conversation, I found it easy to forget I was talking to an attractive young woman, as I slammed the hefty book shut again. "I'm not looking for myths."

If she was startled, she didn't show it, instead flashing an almost belittling smile my way. "Why not? You want to know the meaning of your statue. And the story it's trying to tell."

"No. I want to find out when it was sculpted and by whom." I could tell my voice had grown stern and my manner cold. "You start with the facts. And let the media write the story." It was another old Pierceson quote. Clearly one that went over her head, as she returned only a blank stare.

"Okay..." She adjusted her glasses and lifted the book to examine the spine. My directness hadn't appeared to deter her one bit. "Well, do you want me to at least bring you some of the newer editions. We just got a whole bunch more of this Pierceson guy's stuff. It's in aisle..." She trailed off as she consulted her phone. "L. Section-three."

"No thanks." I pulled my jacket from around my chair and slipped my arms through. "It's already later than I planned. I think I'm just gonna head."

"Oh." She almost sounded disappointed. "I'm sorry we don't have whatever you're looking for. Although, you know you can probably just google it, right? The internet is really great for finding old myths and stuff."

"I'm not trying to find–" I bit my lip before I got any angrier. "Look, it's fine. I came here because I wanted to be alone. I don't actually need the books. I *work* for Doctor Pierceson."

Truth be told. The internet was full of distractions. I knew I'd end up searching for football transfer rumours and reading the latest chapter of some obscure manga if I dared open my laptop. The library was a place free of distractions. Or at least, it was supposed to be.

"That makes sense." She smiled again and leant closer to my ear to whisper. "You know, maybe you do work for this Pierceson guy. You kinda sound like a textbook." Before I could reply, she started stacking the volumes atop one another. "My dad knows a lot about books and history. He always said, 'All tales, be they fact or fiction, have a story behind them. Everything worth knowing starts with the narrative.'"

How I had ended up in a library at three in the morning being lectured by some librarian, who couldn't even remember which aisles the books came from, was a mystery to me.

"Listen, lady. You're a librarian. And I'm an archaeological researcher. I do this for a living. So why don't you let me do my job, and you can get back to yours."

"Ouch," she said, her eyebrows raised. "Anyone ever tell you, you're kinda rude?"

"And you're kinda–. Nevermind. Have a nice night. And those are from aisle H-two by the way." I nodded at the books she cradled.

Her eyes shot down to her phone once more, where it rested on top of the books.

"Hey, you're right." She gave me a smile I, admittedly, was surprised to receive. "Thanks. And good luck with your thunderbolt thingy."

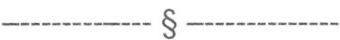

It took me a while to get back to my room at the hotel. Kang had managed to give me both a misspelt address and incorrect room number. Which, considering his perfect memory, must have been sent in haste. Not that it was a surprise, he was probably too busy throwing around chat up lines he'd read online at the most raucous group of undergrads he could find.

After hailing a cab that eventually got me to the right location and an excessively long and arduous conversation with the receptionist to convince her to give up Kang's room details, I finally got hold of a room key. I swiped it at the door, dumped my bag in the corner and collapsed onto the bed in exhaustion.

Still, sleep didn't come. I tossed and turned for a few minutes before rolling out of bed, grabbing my laptop from my bag and opening it on the nearby desk. The battery was still at sixty-eight percent. I'd forgotten my charger and used up some of the battery during the flight to Cyprus. After a moment's hesitation, and berating myself for even thinking about it, I opened the browser and started typing.

'The Ten Thunderbolts.'

Yes, I'd taken the librarian's advice and resorted to googling for clues on the obscure myth. As I'd expected, the results were full of nonsense. Google was great for one thing, telling you what other people already knew. And I *knew* that this myth wasn't real.

I tried again, this time typing 'Largest Zeus sculptures.'

Nothing. Well, there were lots of things, but nothing that I hadn't seen before. The statue at Olympia featured prominently as I clicked through each page and already I was lamenting having given into aimlessly searching for an answer. I went through pointless phrases, one after the other. 'Zeus's Thunderbolts.' 'Ten Greek Gods.' 'Prometheus.' 'Zeus and Prometheus.' Each one proved as fruitless as the last.

I was just about ready to call it quits, wishing I was still in the library so I could tell that librarian, 'I told you so,' when a line of text caught my eye.

I was on the eleventh result page, far beyond the boundaries of where any sane person would venture. It was nearing five in the morning too, so I was hardly in the best shape to process anything other than short words and phrases displayed in the small text. But somehow, a word caught my eye.

Thetis.

I recognised the name. Thetis was a Nereid, a sea Nymph. But that didn't make her particularly special, she had forty-nine sisters after all. No, there was a particular prophecy associated with Thetis. It was foretold that should one of brothers Zeus, Poseidon or Hades, court Thetis and see her sire an heir, that heir would be powerful enough to bring about an end to their reign. Not that this was the only time the Gods were warned of their own demise. What really made the myth standout right then, was the individual that divined it. Prometheus.

There had to be some connection between whatever battle Ealing claimed to have taken place, that led to Zeus supposedly hurling his ten thunderbolts, and the sculptures of him embracing Prometheus. Maybe this was it? I should have seen it before, I'd been on the right lines. The very book I'd had at the library, part of Pierceson's analysis on Aeschylus' Prometheia trilogy, went on to detail a lesser myth of Prometheus earning his freedom on account of this same prediction.

Prometheus warns Zeus about pursuing Thetis, but gets himself imprisoned for betrayal. Zeus seduces her anyway, and ends up fulfilling the prophecy. Things go bad for the Gods, so Zeus ends up calling on the one person who saw it all coming. Then, somehow, Prometheus saves the day and gets himself immortalised as Zeus' new best friend in statue form.

It didn't quite get me all the way to the The Ten Thunderbolts. If Prometheus had come to the rescue, why would Zeus still have to use his thunderbolts to separate the Gods? That was part of the problem with anyone relying on mythology to prove a point. It was easy to rearrange the details to fit whatever story you were trying to sell.

Pierceson would be disappointed. I was clutching at straws like some first year novice? Just as I knew it would, resorting to google had me chasing wild gooses that I would usually never consider. I flipped the laptop shut and threw myself back onto the bed. Sleep. That was the answer. Tomorrow, I'd take Kang and Xiao to see Ealing. They'd hear his story and remind me that it was all a waste of time, then we'd be on a flight back to London by sunset.

The next thing I remembered was wiping the drool off my pillow as the irritating sound of my alarm drummed against my ears. I rolled over and saw Kang shaking my phone like a maraca as he did the closest thing he could manage to dancing beside my bed.

"What time is it?" The words felt laborious as I reached for a bottle of water to quench my dry throat.

"Nearly midday," he said, swiping away my alarm as he handed the phone over. "I think you've missed at least five of these."

"I had a late night."

"Come again?" The next thing I knew, Kang was dragging me up and wrapping one arm around my shoulder. "*You* had a late night? Without my help? Give me all the details. Now. I want to know every sordid, ill-intentioned and downright per–"

"Not that kind of night." I shoved him hard enough to push him off my bed. "I was working. At the library."

"Oh." Kang just about kept his balance as he slid off the bed and stood upright. "You mean an actual late night. How... disappointing."

"I take it *you* weren't out studying?"

"Oh, I studied alright." A grin almost too wide for his mouth stretched across Kang's face. "Two of the students from Nicosia University taught me everything they know."

"You're gross, man." I headed into the bathroom and grabbed my toothbrush before leaning my head back around into the bedroom. "Seriously. Two?" Kang nodded smugly. "Unbelievable."

I could never figure out how he did it. Kang wasn't ugly, that much I could begrudgingly admit. But where he had learned the social skills to win so many women over was a mystery. For the lion's share of our childhood, he had been the most socially inept human being on the planet. He could barely order a cup of coffee from the opposite sex without spilling it down his trousers or miss-pronouncing his own name. More often, he would embarrass himself by getting into a conversation about his name.

"Kang," he would say, when they asked him what to scribble on his cup.

The barista would respond with a curious stare. It happened each and every time. They would squint at his pale white skin, eyeball his long brown hair and listen to his 'raised-in-south-london' accent, before they usually sought confirmation.

"Kang? Is that a nickname or something?"

"Yes." He was always delighted to respond, never realising that he was the only one who found the story even remotely interesting. "I'm the namesake of Kang the Conqueror." He would usually get a shrug or a "who?" in reply. "The Marvel villain." His voice would grow quieter. "Rama-Tut. Immortus?" Nothing, as always. "The time traveller? Leader of the Anachronauts? Sworn enemy of the Avengers and Fantastic Four?"

I could count on one finger how many times someone responded with even the faintest clue of who he was referring to. What I couldn't recall was just how many times he had sauntered away red-faced and downtrodden with a cup that had the name 'Kong,' penned on the side.

Often, I would have to intervene on his behalf, to break up the unbearable awkwardness of it all. Which is why it was so frustrating that, at some point, our roles seemed to have reversed without me realising until the metamorphosis was complete.

After an over-zealous knock at the door, Kang let Xiao into our room. Though we'd known her for years now, I preferred it when Xiao's room was separate. The problem wasn't hers. She was comfortable sharing a room with us. Way too comfortable, if you asked me. The regular boundaries of Human privacy didn't seem to concern Xiao.

But being cooped up in the same small space for days on end during previous expeditions had, on occasion, led to more than a few... awkward situations. Needless to say, I had no desire to repeat bumping into her as she crouched topless and rifled through her case in the communal living room in search of a bra. And I definitely didn't care for her telling me to 'man up,' whenever I voiced my discomfort.

This way was far less complicated. "Did we miss breakfast?" I asked.

"No idea," Xiao replied. "I woke up, had a shower and came to get you."

"Seriously." It never ceased to amaze me. "Do you have any idea how long you've been asleep?"

"Not long enough." Xiao yawned and stretched her arms above her head. "I take it you two had a late one. I saw this one leave early." She pointed a thumb at Kang. "And probably not come back. What's your story?"

"He had a late one alright," said Kang. "At the library."

Xiao's eyes were raised in expectation. "That means you've got a lead on something?"

I smiled back at her. At least Xiao was perceptive enough to read my behaviour without mocking me. "Easier if I show you," I said, taking a seat at the desk.

My laptop was still open. I thought I'd closed it, maybe I forgot, but the power-saving should have kicked in and put it in standby. Strangely, the screen refused to power on as I tapped at the keyboard. After watching me swipe at nearly every key possible, Xiao elbowed me in the shoulder.

"Battery's dead genius," she said. "Again."

"That doesn't make sense," I replied, turning to Kang. "Dude. You better not have been playing DOTA on here while I was sleeping. You know I hate when you use my account."

"Seriously? You always do this, then try and pin the blame on me," Kang replied. "It should be me questioning what you're doing on this thing at night when nobody else is around. Just plug in and light it back up."

"Can't. I forgot my charger at my mum's place. Forget it, I'll explain on the way."

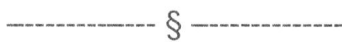

"Never heard of it," said Kang. I'd just finished explaining Ealing's theory about the sculpture to them, along with his myth, 'The Ten Thunderbolts.' "You know how many poets I've studied, man. How many myths and legends I've written case studies on. I've never come across anything even remotely resembling what you're talking about."

Most people would wonder why Kang not knowing the myth was different to anyone else. But I knew better. His father had been reading him textbooks on the very subject since he was only a toddler. His head contained more information on ancient mythology than scholars thrice his age. If he hadn't heard of it, it meant there were likely few that had. Even more likely, it didn't exist.

"Well, Ealing has." Xiao turned back as she neared the entrance to the museum, having gotten slightly ahead of us. "So let's roll with it until we can take a closer look at his findings for ourselves."

She was right. She often was. Sure, Xiao was headstrong, not unlike me, but she was far more capable of humbling herself or feigning ignorance than I. "Right." I shook off Kang's protests and headed for the entrance, only to stall once more when I saw a woman by the entrance.

I might not have paid her any mind, were it not for the stack of books she carried. Four or five thick texts that I might've struggled to lift myself. That, and the fact that she was as out of place as Kang in a celibacy support group. Her bright purple yoga pants and grey tank top weren't exactly common attire for the kind of people we were coming to visit. At first glance I didn't recognize her, but the moment her eyes fixed on me I was dumbstruck. Again.

"Hey," I said, taking a few steps closer. "We meet again. I wouldn't have picked you for the museum type. You come here often?"

She looked up at me, her bright golden eyes meeting mine, and smiled. "Yeah. But this is a business trip. We sometimes loan books to the museum. I'm just collecting these." She strained as she lowered the weight of the books onto one knee.

"Right." I nodded, buying a moment to fashion a few more words to share. "By the way, I'm sorry if I came across as a bit of dick last night. I do that sometimes when I'm working."

"Oh. No problem." She looked at me like a teacher does a student who has just given a stupid answer. "Have we met, by the way?"

"Huh?" I returned the expression. "Are you serious? I was at the library last night."

"Oh, I see." She flashed me a dismissive smile. "I see a lot of faces there everyday. Sorry about that."

"We were the only ones there." I could tell the softness in my voice had dissipated, but her refusal to acknowledge me was frustrating. "It was three in the morning." Her expression was as blank as the first page of a new notebook. "I told you about the sculpture. And the Ten Thunderbolts." Still, nothing. "You really don't remember me?"

She shrugged. "Sorry, but I really have to go."

"Alright." Clearly, she wasn't going to accept that we had met. "Do you want me to call you a cab or something?"

"I was just going to walk actually. The museum was on my morning running route."

"You're going to carry those back to the library? You're still over a kilometre away."

"Yeah, I know. Didn't think it all the way through I guess. Anyway, bye." And just like that, she pressed a headphone into each ear and shuffled away.

I didn't need to turn around to feel the hole that Kang was burning in the back of my head with his eyes. "What?" I demanded.

"What?" His voice came out so high-pitched I could have mistaken him for a young girl. "Is this the research you were doing last night?" He mimed inverted commas as he said 'research.' "Zeke, you little snake."

"It wasn't like that. She's the librarian. Nothing happened. We just talked."

"I can believe that," said Xiao. "From the sound of things, your way with words had the usual effect on her."

Even Xiao was taking snipes at me.

"Whatever. Can we just go inside, please?"

Xiao was already through the doorway when Kang put a firm hand on my shoulder. "So, for future reference, which library was this again?"

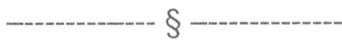

We ended up having to wait another couple of hours for the closing day of the exhibition to run its course and the last of the press to leave before we could get any time with Ealing and his team. As Vinter finished her final summary they disappeared one by one, until there was just a solitary notebook wielding woman left waiting. She turned away after a brief exchange, a disappointed frown crossing her familiar shaped eyebrows. It looked like she'd been dismissed along with the rest of the press.

"Camilla." Xiao almost snarled. "I didn't know they were studying reptiles here? Did they need a skin sample?"

Camilla looked as if she were stifling a retort. Somehow, she always resisted Xiao's insults, never exchanging the jabs. She was, of course, more than happy to take shots at Kang and I. Frequently. I'd put it down to some kind of weird mutual female respect thing, only Xiao obviously hadn't received the memo. My teammate held nothing but contempt for Camilla.

"Xiao," Camilla nodded. "If you'll excuse me." She barely broke stride and would have walked into me if I hadn't sidestepped out of her path.

"That's it?" I said. "What's up? Did beating us here not get you what you want for a change? I guess it's a shame they only let professionals have access to the real discovery."

She didn't turn around, instead continuing on her route out of the building, until she reached Kang, who blocked her path. He didn't move immediately, and Camilla had to come to a full stop. A few seconds passed, with them eyeing one another, before Kang finally stepped aside and let her leave.

"Time to get to it I guess," said Kang, as he sauntered over in not-quite his usual stride.

"What was that?" The words slipped almost accidentally from my mouth. At this point in our relationship, I could tell when Kang was hiding something. But I hadn't really meant to question him on it right there and then.

"What was what?" he said. The response of a guilty party, if ever there was one.

"Nothing. Dude, come on. Let's get this over with." I glanced over at Xiao to see if she'd noticed. She was already pointing back at me and introducing herself to Vinter, paying no mind to the two of us. Fortunately.

Camilla's back had been towards me when she stopped in front of Kang, so whatever brief exchange they had shared, vocal or otherwise, I hadn't been privy to. But clearly, something had happened between them. I didn't want Xiao involved because she would immediately jump to conclusions. She would slam Kang's head against the nearest wall and ask him if he was working with Camilla. It wasn't an entirely crazy idea, in fact. But I knew my friend better than that. He wouldn't betray us. Especially not with Camilla. It was something else, and I had to admit I was curious as to what. But not as curious as I was about getting to the bottom of Ealing's damned discovery.

The next two hours passed by in a blur of unspectacular and circular recounting of events. It was nearing ten o'clock and after the latest round of lectures and an exchanging of theories with Ealing, Vinter and Kincaid, Xiao finally lost her patience.

"Show us the stones," she said, her humble facade having evaporated. It wasn't quite an order, she was hardly in charge, but her demand was clear. Vinter immediately looked incensed, whispering in Ealing's ear as she eyed us suspiciously. Whatever caution she suggested didn't seem to bother Ealing, who gently shook his head and agreed to take us into the lab. Fortunately, Xiao's forthrightness hadn't triggered them into kicking us out, as it had done more than once in the past.

They led us over to a crate, protected with a digital numpad, into which Kincaid tapped at least 15 digits. When the light went green, he used the back of his hand to wipe several droplets of sweat from his bald head, then lifted open the lid.

"That's it?" said Xiao, unmistakably unimpressed.

I probably wouldn't have said it out loud, but I can't say I wasn't thinking the same. All that was inside, resting atop a layer of protective foam, were a dozen or so gems. They didn't look particularly rare or precious, not by modern standards anyway. A few rubies, emeralds and sapphires. There was little about them that could be deemed special.

Vinter rolled her eyes. I'd made some headway winning over Ealing's teammate last night, but that seemed to have been eviscerated during Xiao's outburst, leaving her more openly hostile than before. Clearly, she didn't see much value in our continued assistance. "Just examine them or leave."

Ignoring the 'this is a complete waste of time,' look that Xiao was giving me, I reached into the crate and pulled out a red gem. On the desk beside me were a couple of flashlights, the nearest of which I grabbed and clicked into life. Under the blue light, there were definitely some abnormalities on the gemstone. Like Ealing had said, at first glance it just looked like dirt. But rubbing it with my thumb and scraping it with my nail did nothing to dislodge it.

"It doesn't come off," said Kincaid. "We've tried everything."

"Carbonization," I said. "This is what you meant."

I placed the gem under one of their microscopes and asked Xiao to take a closer look. She was the expert in archaeometry after all. In the meantime, Kang and I helped ourselves to several of the other gems, sorting through them as we discovered much of the same damage or marking or whatever it was, on each.

"Weird," I said.

"The dispersal pattern?" Kang added, ever on the same wavelength.

"Yeah." I pulled two gems out and held them side by side, rotating them slowly.

"They're similar. Only, the angles don't match."

Kang sorted through several of the precious jewels, before emerging with two more and setting them down on the table opposing one another. I spread them a metre apart, then placed my two down, above and below, each gem like the pole of a compass.

"Ealing," I said. "Have you seen this?"

Both Vinter and Ealing peered down at the table. Each stone had a similar mark of damage, starting with a wide blackened smear nearest the centre of the table then fading out until they were almost unblemished at the edge.

"Something," I wondered. "Perhaps... your lightning, struck the centre of wherever these gems sat. The carbonization fades the further you get from the origin point." My eyes flicked to the crate of jewels then back towards the large empty monitor on the desk. "Vinter, can you show us your rendering of the sculpture again?"

Vinter swiped at her tablet, causing the monitor to flicker into life with a small-scale diagram of their colossal finding. "But what are you expecting to find? We've been over this a hundred times."

I stepped closer to the monitor and tapped my finger repeatedly on the glass until Vinter started to zoom in. "These rubies look to have been close to equidistant from the origin point. I want to know their whereabouts on the sculpture. More importantly, I want to know what was in-between them."

Vinter pinched the screen on her tablet causing the image to gradually enlarge.

"Stop." Kang stepped beside me and drummed his knuckle on the corner of the monitor. "Check out the throne."

On each handle of the throne, upon which the weakened Zeus sat, were a pair of rubies. My eyes darted between them, before following one arm of the chair up to the shoulder where I locked onto a third. And a fourth on the opposing arm.

I traced my finger down the screen from the top of the chair to the middle, until it rested around the Thunder Gods abdomen.

"There." In the centre of the sculpted body, fastening together the robes of the King of the Gods, was a clasp. A relatively small zigzag shape, a thunderbolt, with an empty round slot at its centre. "Vinter, do you know which gem was in that slot?"

"No," she replied. "They were mostly dislodged. Those rubies were amongst the few still in place."

"Stands to reason," said Kang, his hands diving immediately into the crate. "That it was something unique." The jarring sound of gemstones scraping against one another went on for over a minute until Kang was interrupted by the buzz of static as the room went black.

It had to be nearing midnight, and so the sudden death of lighting left us in almost complete darkness, save for the ghostly white glow of a few phones, laptops and tablets.

"The hell is this?" Xiao demanded.

Kincaid let out a heavy sigh and I caught a reflection of the light bouncing off his bald head as he looked to the sky. "It's the bloody generator again. It happens if we overuse the labs. They're not designed for this kind of intensive work. But, the backup generators should kick in right... about..." He paused for a few seconds. "Now."

Nothing happened.

"That's odd." Kincaid sounded genuinely perplexed. "The system is automated. It should have come online by now."

"Maybe this is a sign that it's time to call it a night." It was Xiao's voice in the darkness, recognizably monotone.

"Could be. But I'll check the power grid first. Shouldn't take a minute."

Kincaid shuffled between us and slammed the door clumsily behind him, as a bright light appeared next to me, shining directly into my eyes.

"Sorry," said Kang, turning around and directing the light from his phone's flash away.

"What is it?" I asked, noticing him still fumbling with a gem in his hand.

"Nothing. Not in this lighting anyway."

"Put the stones back in the box." Vinter's flashlight focused sharply on the crate. "I don't want you losing anything."

"She's scary," whispered Kang, as he headed to the crate and the sound of something precious nestling on top of the other gems followed.

Another five minutes passed as we waited, some of us more patiently than others, in uncomfortable silence, before Ealing finally spoke.

"Something's not right," he said. "He must be having trouble."

"Ugh." Vinter sighed. "I'll go find out and what the problem is."

"I'll come with you," I said.

"Just stay here." There was no mistaking the hostility in Vinter's voice now.

"Hey, take it easy," said Kang. "We're just trying to help."

"We had power before you started to help," she hissed. "Now, conveniently, our research is blocked."

"You're accusing *us* of having something to do with that?" Xiao's tone was even fiercer than Vinter's. "Believe me, lady, we don't give a shit about your cheap stones and meaningless sculpture. We'd rather be off chasing *real* leads."

"Xiao!" I had to cut her off before she said something we couldn't recover from.

"Oh, really?!" shouted Vinter. "I know what you people do. Pierceson's disciples. You're thieves carrying out his dirty work. Why do you think Michael quit? He got tired of stealing for a living. And–"

"Enough!" It was Ealing that yelled to intervene this time, before his voice grew quiet once more. "Let's all just calm down. Nobody is trying to steal anything here. Go and help Kincaid. Zeke can go with you, he might be helpful. In the meantime, I'll make sure these two pack things up for the night. I think we could all do with some rest."

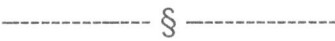

It was an uneventful walk down to the basement with Vinter. Despite it being almost pitch-black, I felt like I could see the glare in her eyes. She'd turned completely passive, not saying a word as she navigated the corners and steps. I was as uncomfortable with small-talk as they come, but even I felt the need to say something.

"We're really not trying to steal anything here. Ealing just sent us to find out anything we can. If you want us to leave, we will."

"Then go," said Vinter. "But not before I search you. And your friend."

"Kang? Trust me, he's no thief. We once took home a twenty-pound note that fell out of an old lady's bag. He wouldn't even let us spend it. The guilt was too much."

"Whatever."

Vinter was being unreasonable. But one thing she said had stuck in my head. Something I felt compelled to clarify before we left the museum. "Did Ealing really not like working for Pierceson anymore?"

"Damn right," Vinter replied. "He said the only reason the old man is successful is because he has eyes and ears everywhere. You're like his network of spies. Stealing puzzle pieces so he can put them together and stamp his name on the big discovery. Michael won't say it to your face. You're young. You're getting off on the lifestyle Pierceson provides for you. I'm sure it must be irresistible. But one day you'll realise, same as him, that maybe you'll actually want to discover something for yourself."

I didn't reply right away. Not because anything Vinter said had shocked me. I've bumped into the same accusations a dozen times before. Only, I'd never heard it from one of Pierceson's former disciples. I still hadn't. Vinter's paraphrasing didn't sound like mild-mannered Ealing at all. But one thing was for sure, I needed to ask him about it. Directly. Working with Pierceson had been my whole life. But that didn't mean that, occasionally, I didn't find myself wondering what the future would hold. And if I would ever hear my name, Ezekiel Lewis, shared on the lips of the rich and famous.

"Well, let me help you get this generator on and we can leave you to your work in peace."

"Works for me. Would have preferred if you just stayed with your friends, of course." Vinter stopped and pointed her flashlight at me. "Let me guess? You think because I'm a woman I can't get it done for myself? I have a masters in mechanical engineering."

"Whoa. I don't even–" How had my offering to assist her ended up with me as the misogynist? "Look, that's good, because I don't know a thing about engineering or power generators. I'm just here to hand you and your buddy tools while you fix this thing. Jeez. You know, you'd be right at home on my team."

"And why's that?"

"Because you like to fly off the handle at the slightest provocation. You and Xiao could be a tag team." I held up a hand to quiet Vinter before she could reply. "No, not because you're women. Because the second she thinks someone is discriminating against her for being asian, she goes off like a grenade. I don't even think she–"

I wasn't sure if I was still talking or not, but my mind went blank as the beam from my flashlight panned away from Vinter's face and down to the shape at her feet.

"Well? You don't think she what?" Vinter demanded.

"Don't move." I motioned down with my light, which finally made her turn, look down and fall equally silent.

I could see more clearly now, as both our lights shone through the darkness and circled on the same position. The staircase ended three steps below Vinter, each one coated with a deep crimson puddle. Blood. At the end of the trail was a body. Her teammate. Kincaid. His bald head was about the only thing I could use to identify him. Because from the look of his contorted limbs and lacerated skin, he was very, very dead.

ACT III

THE HOUNDS OF GERYON

To fear death is nothing other than to think oneself wise when one is not. For it is to think one knows what one does not know. No one knows whether death may not even turn out to be the greatest blessings of human beings. And yet people fear it as if they knew for certain it is the greatest evil.'

No offence to Socrates, but I'm guessing he'd never seen a dead body like this before. There were bones and muscles and blood, so much blood, but so little of Kincaid remaining beyond his head; the face still paralysed with a look of pain and horror. The eyes wide open. Staring. Searching for help. Help that hadn't come. The whole thing seemed pretty evil to me and I'm not sure anyone could describe it as a blessing.

"What... What..." The beam from Vinter's flashlight shuddered as she spoke. Indomitable until now, the sight of her friend's tattered corpse had left her visibly shaken. "What could have done this?"

I tried to sound calm and reassuring, but the only words I could manage were barely a squeak.

"I have no idea."

I wanted to crouch down. Take a closer look. But a corpse, in real life, it's not like the movies. It's undistilled fear and panic in physical form. I was more likely to run a thousand miles in the opposite direction then take even a single step forward.

My hand shot over my mouth as my stomach twisted and turned, but vomiting wouldn't help. "We... we should get out of here. Now."

Vinter raised her hand; her fingers stretched, reaching out for Kincaid, like she wanted, no, needed to embrace him. To touch him and see if he was real. Then suddenly she recoiled.

"What was that?" she muttered.

I was already on edge. The last thing I could stomach was Vinter further losing her nerve and jumping at every shape, shadow and sound that rustled in the darkness. If only I hadn't heard it too.

A rumble? Like an engine running in the distance. No, it was far more natural than a motor. Breathing? Like a heavy-set man snoring out of sight. No, it was too raw to be a person. My teeth clenched and my grip around the flashlight tightened as the sound finally formed a clear picture in my head. Growling.

It was quiet. It was low. But it was near.

"That." Vinter turned her flashlight on me. "Tell me you–"

Before she could say another word, I rushed into her, put my palm over her mouth and backed us against the wall. Her eyes widened, probably surprised by my sudden force, but I stared her down with equal ferocity before slowly pulling my hand away. Tapping my flashlight, I clicked the off switch and waited for her to do the same.

Vinter might have been in shock or otherwise, but she still had enough of her wits about her to understand. Her light went dead and she flattened herself against the wall by my side, as both of us peered down the corridor. The growl came again, sending an icy wave down my spine. It was louder this time. Closer. But still invisible.

"There," I whispered, pointing out the storage cupboard standing opposite us with the door wide open.

Our faces were just inches apart now, united by mutual terror, so Vinter should have been able to see my outstretched arm. She glanced back and forth, at the cupboard, then me, then back again, before finally nodding nervously.

I wasn't sure if she could see me silently counting to three with my fingers, but when the count expired we leapt across the corridor together and tumbled into the cupboard, where I eventually fumbled the door shut with a faint but heart-tingling thud. Shit. It was all I could think. Did it hear us? Did it see us?

As the seconds ticked by uneventfully, I was ready to breathe a sigh of relief. But it was premature. Something was edging closer, not growling this time. Silent, but for a soft tapping. Like feet. No. Like paws. My jumper tightened around my shoulders, Vinter had a hold of me around the waist, trying to grab my attention. I backed, more delicately than ever before in my life, away from the door and rested against the rear of the cupboard with her.

I don't think I took a breath for over a minute as I eyed the slatted door of the cupboard, peering through the gaps. Something was there. It stood just a metre or so from us, outside the tiny cupboard that had quickly become our cell. Or tomb.

Still, I couldn't see it. It was completely devoid of light in the small confines of the cupboard. Were it not for Vinter's hand on my arm, and mine on her shoulder, I wouldn't have even known she was there with me. The creature was moving, that much was certain. The slow, almost methodical, scratching of its feet was so loud it could have been walking on top of me.

I wasn't sure if it was looking at us. I figured at least the whites of its eyes might become visible at this range. Regardless, it knew we were there. But what was *it*, exactly? If it were an animal, wouldn't it have smelt us by now? If it were some nocturnal predator, wouldn't it have seen us?

Another thirty seconds dragged by in agonising silence. Vinter's heart must have been racing as her hot breath on my neck increased in frequency. My fists were wound so tightly I thought I might draw blood as I strained to focus. To keep still.

Then the sounds of its feet echoed once more, as the dark shadowy presence rolled away from the door. I wanted nothing more than to cry out in relief, but we were hardly out of trouble yet. Part of me thought about waiting it out here, for as long as it took. Until help came or until we knew the coast was clear. Then it hit me.

Kang. Xiao. Ealing. They were all vulnerable. If this thing found its way upstairs before we could warn them, they'd end up like Kincaid.

"We have to move," I whispered to Vinter. "We need to warn the others."

Vinter took a few seconds to reply, as I stared intensely into the darkness wondering what kind of expression she was pulling.

"Right," she finally said. "We have to chance it."

Bravery. Stupidity. Whichever trait had suddenly overcome the two of us, I was already reaching forward and placing a palm on the cupboard door.

"Ready?" I asked. "If it's clear, we run for it."

"I'm ready." Vinter's voice lacked conviction, but I felt about as nervous as she sounded.

Tentatively, I applied pressure to the door, easing it open just an inch or two then stopping to listen. Nothing. I pushed again, gently bringing it to what I hoped was a third of the way open, before gulping. It was a tough swallow, my mouth as dry as the Sahara. Nonetheless, I edged my head through the opening and panned left and right down the corridor.

Admittedly, it was too dark to see anything without a flashlight. But there were no footsteps and, more to the point, nothing had noticed us.

"I'll go first," said Vinter. "I know the way. On my mark."

Vinter slipped in front of me as we prepared to escape. Again, the hall fell dead silently as I waited for her signal.

"Go!" she finally said, a half-whisper half-shout.

Vinter's presence vanished from in front of me. Immediately, I gave chase, following the sound of her footsteps. Before I knew it, I was regaining my balance as we ran into a flight of stairs and I had to thrust out an arm to the railing to prevent falling flat on my face. In the brief pause, I searched for Vinter. Not with my eyes, but my ears. She hadn't stopped, her feet were still pounding the steps as she ascended. But she wasn't all I could hear.

The familiar sound was back. The smacking of animal paws on the hard floor pulling my attention from above, back to the basement level. And for the first time, I caught sight of it. Drawing towards me, faster than I could imagine. Growling wildly, louder and more ferocious by the second. I froze. I thought about moving my legs, but they wouldn't obey. And it wasn't the gnashing of teeth or the closing distance that had me so paralyzed. It was the eyes.

Giant ovals, fixated on me. Consuming me. Like they bored into my head, into my thoughts, into my very soul. Wide eyes, piercing me like a sword. Eyes begging my attention. No, demanding it. They weren't Human. They weren't even animal. Nothing could be more supernatural than their emerald glow. It was like staring into a well as I fell, never reaching the bottom.

"Lewis!" Vinter yelling my surname at the top her voice jolted me from a statue back to a terrified mess, like a teacher had just scolded me for letting my attention wander. "Run!"

Not needing a second invitation, I took off up the stairs after her, rounding the flights as fast as I could until I bundled through the door Vinter was holding open for me and knocking the both of us to the ground. She kicked the door shut behind me just as the creature slammed against the glass and wood, clawing and scratching at the only barricade between us.

"What the hell is it?" Vinter was already back on her feet, shining her flashlight down as she extended her arm towards me.

I grabbed her by the hand and pulled myself up. "I don't know. But we have to get out of here."

Vinter led the way back through the storage rooms, each of us knocking over artefacts and equipment as we fumbled and rushed through the darkness, all the while hoping the gnawing and scratching somewhere behind us continued to grow distant.

"Guys!" I shouted, as Vinter kicked open the door to the lab. "We're getting out of here."

"About time," said Xiao, her head resting on one hand behind a laptop screen.

I headed straight for her, clamping her by the elbow and dragging her out of her seat "Now."

"Zeke? What's wrong man?" asked Kang. "You sound out of breath."

"No time to explain. Just get up!"

"Where's Michael?" said Vinter, her light panning around the room at double speed.

"He went to put the stones away," Kang replied. "What is wrong with you two? And where's Kincaid?"

"Nevermind." Vinter sped across the lab and pushed open the door on the other side. "We need to find Michael. It's not safe here."

My friends finally seemed to get the message as I headed after Vinter, falling in line behind me as we cleared the door and stepped into the hall. We were bunched so close together, there was no time to notice Vinter had stopped dead in her tracks. I slammed straight into her, bashing my lip on the back of her head.

"Why are we stopping?" I asked, pinching my busted and bloody lip.

"Michael!" Vinter screeched.

I stepped around her and waved my flashlight at whatever she was screaming at. Ealing was dangling, both his feet twitching in the air, as a dark silhouette held him aloft. Whoever it was, they were impossibly strong, gripping him by just the neck and holding him up with one arm. Ealing was clutching at his throat with both hands, right before they fell limply at his side. When his body stopped moving, he slipped from the grasp of his attacker and slumped down to the ground.

"No!" Vinter lunged, only to be yanked back as Xiao grabbed her by the wrist.

"Don't," Xiao said calmly.

I wanted to say something. Something practical, or reassuring or even sympathetic. But I couldn't. My attention wouldn't leave the dark figure in front of us, no matter how I tried. Not because of what she had just done to Ealing. And not because I thought we might be next. It was because she was staring straight back at me, locked in focus with those same emerald eyes. They were smaller, less ferocious and more Human. Though, no less supernatural. But the look, the look was the same.

The attackers hand shot out once more, flexing their fingers towards the crate by the motionless Ealing's side. The same lid that Kincaid opened via combination, burst free and slammed across the hallway. Seconds later, the crate was awash with wisps of jade light, twisting and turning around its open top. One by one, the stones leapt from the crate nestling into a bag the attacker held open at their waist. I must have been wearing the same look of bewilderment painted all over Xiao and Kang's faces as I tried to make sense of what was happening. The stones clinked and clashed as they landed inside her bag, until the crate was empty and the strange light faded.

"You bitch." Vinter lunged once more, slipping free of Xiao's grasp and arrowing towards Ealing's attacker. The mysterious figure thrust up a hand and Vinter stopped dead in her tracks.

And she hadn't just stopped, it was as if she had *been* stopped. Her head still leant forward, and one arm still stretched out in front of her while the other was spread out behind. She was in mid-sprint, and then suddenly, she wasn't.

Paying little attention to Vinter, the attacker dipped their hand into the bag and rifled through its newly acquired contents. I could see them more clearly now, standing beneath one of the large rectangular windows where the starlight poured in and cast a ghostly white light over them. They were slight, their slender body adorned with a tight-fitting robe that covered them from head to toe. Even their fingers and face were wrapped in some dark cloth, leaving just those hypnotic green eyes to identify them. Eyes that quickly narrowed in anger.

"Where is it?" they said, the voice smoky. Feminine. "What did he do with it?"

"Go to hell," Vinter shouted. "Those don't belong to you."

"And to whom *do* they belong? Him?" The green eyed woman cast her bright eyes down to Ealing. "A dog digging for bones in their neighbour's yard. I seek to return them to their rightful owner."

Be it fear or rage, I finally found the words to confront her. "You have what you wanted. Just go. And leave us alone."

"No," the green eyed woman cursed. "It isn't here. This one." She looked disdainfully at Vinter. "Or the dead ones. They've hidden it. Kept it for themselves." She stretched the fingers on her gloved hand and bubbles of green light bloomed across her fingertips. "You can tell me what you've done with it. Or I can teach you pain. Ineffable pain."

The green-eyed woman cycled her fingers, drawing the green energy into a circle on the ground from which a shape began to sprout. Like an artist painting a canvas, her carefully woven construct became real. It had four legs, a mouth full of jagged teeth and a pair of piercing green eyes. I knew it instantly. The creature from the basement.

"Your bald friend could attest to what you're about to endure, if only he still drew breath. So, unless you want Orthrus here to snap your limbs with his jaw and peel the flesh from your bones with his teeth, you will tell me– Where is the Thunderbolt?!"

While the green eyed woman yelled, her beast barked and gnashed, straining to break free from her one fingered grasp of its collar.

"Go. To. Hell," said Vinter.

"You first," said the green-eyed woman, slipping her finger free from the collar.

The beast leapt at Vinter, landing just short of her as it unleashed a howl so chilling it felt like someone had just poured a bucket of ice down my spine. It was undoubtedly canine, though its proportions were unnaturally distorted. Its head seemed slightly big for its lean torso, while its legs were so thick and muscular they defied the subtlety and grace with which it had moved through the basement. It was the most terrifying and nightmarish sight I had ever laid eyes on, leaking at the mouth and its eyes vicious and bloodthirsty. It's pulsating jade eyes. But it didn't attack. Not Vinter, anyway.

The beast half-circled her, making its way to her rear where it fixed its attention on us. The green-eyed woman, too, strode past Vinter and cocked her head to one side as her poisonous eyes widened.

"You," she hissed. "You have the bolt. Orthrus." She pointed a finger towards us. "Bring it to me."

"But we don't–"

Kang grabbed me by the arm before I could protest. "Run you idiot!"

He was right. There was no time to argue. No time to figure out what the hell this woman even wanted. No time to help Vinter. The creature had bounded halfway down the corridor, growling hungrily as it neared. Xiao was already through the lab door as Kang dragged me inside and I slammed the door shut behind us.

"Help me with this!" shouted Xiao. The blue light of the monitors reflected in her eyes as she drove a shoulder into one of the work benches. Kang was quickly beside her, as I followed suit and pushed from her other side, slamming the bench up against the door just as the beast rammed its head against the glass in the door frame. It shattered instantly as a pair of green eyes lit up the room. Again it rammed, sending more glass showering down on us.

"It can't fit through there," said Xiao. "Let's go."

I wasn't about to test her theory, turning and dashing out through the back entrance and back down towards the basement.

"Is it safe down there?" asked Kang, his voice panicked and desperate. "Weren't you two just running from this direction?"

"Yeah," I replied. "Running from that thing."

The green-eyed woman had somehow summoned the creature to her through– what exactly had I seen? Magic? It couldn't be. Could it? No. Regardless, there was no way to be sure the creature couldn't somehow find its way back down here.

"But there has to be a way out of here," I said, hoping I didn't sound as devoid of confidence as I felt.

When we hit the bottom of the stairs, I pulled my flashlight and searched left and right.

"Holy crap," said Kang, angling his phone downwards. "Zeke, what the hell–"

"Don't look." I pulled him away. "It's Kincaid. And you don't wanna see it."

The frantic clatter of furniture being overturned and a ferocious growl nearing in proximity made sure neither of us had time to focus on the body anyway.

"This way," said Xiao, already at the left end of the hall. "Hurry."

I had no idea if she knew whether we were heading into a dead end or not, but Xiao's instincts were usually spot on. I trusted her, implicitly, and there were few people I'd rather have at my side during a crisis. I rounded the corner, Kang hot on my heels, and found a door flung open against the wall. My shoulder slammed against his as we both attempted to push through the doorway. I turned to one side, letting him slip through, before turning back to slam the door behind me.

The heavy wooden door, more sturdy than the office glass, bolted from the inside, so there was little I could do but hope it might keep the creature out for a few moments at least. The cool evening air pricked my ears as I turned to find my friends up against a seven-foot metal gate, forged of thick metal bars. And it was the only thing barring us from the ramp that led up and out into the night.

"No. No. No," said Kang, hammering a red switch labelled 'Up.' "It won't open."

"The power is still out," Xiao lamented, her eyes examining every inch of the bars, then darting to Kang and I.

"What?" said Kang."What are you thinking?"

She didn't reply, instead raising one leg and slipping it between the bars. There couldn't have been more than seven or eight inches between each iron bar, but her petite frame slid easily through the gap as she hopped out on the other side.

"Come on." Xiao waved an urgent hand.

Kang's hands gripped around two of the bars. "Are you for real? We'll never fit through there."

I was ready to join in his protest when a sudden slam at the door behind made me leap almost out of my skin, as I instinctively raised one leg towards the gate. The growls of our feral pursuer were all the motivation I needed to push every inch of my six-foot frame through that gap.

My shoulder slipped through easily enough, but I could feel the pressure on my chest as the weight of the bars crushed against me. It felt like trying to bench press an unliftable weight as I pushed against the metal, rocking my body back and forth, trying to eek my way through. Then just as it felt like my lungs were pressed so tight that there wasn't room for air, and that my ribs would cave into my chest at any second, the pressure was suddenly gone and I was stumbling onto my knees on the other side of the gate. I sucked in a desperate gust of air, relieved to be free, when Xiao again barked at me.

"Zeke." Her voice was strained. "Get up and give me a hand."

Her feet were planted wide and she had Kang by the arm as she desperately tried to drag him through the narrow gap. Kang was hardly overweight, he and I ran a few kilometres together most mornings, but his penchant for alcohol and fine-dining left him heavier set and the extra inch or two around his waist was wedged tight between the bars.

I leapt immediately to my feet, grabbing hold of him by the arm and heaving back with all my strength. Kang yelled in pain as we pulled on his arm like a rope in a tug of war.

"Stop," he cried. "I'm not gonna make it. Just go."

I let go of his arm and placed my hands on the bars, futilely trying to push them wider. "We're not leaving you man."

"You have to," Kang said, looking me dead in the eye. "I don't want you to see me get eaten."

"Would you just shut up," said Xiao. "Suck it in and we pull again on three. You ready?" She eyed me this time as I nodded uncertainly. "One. Two. Three."

Kang closed his eyes as Xiao and I yanked back on his arm. For a second, he didn't budge, and I wondered whether my last memory of him really was going to be watching him torn apart by some pet monstrosity, his flesh and bones carved up just like Kincaid. Before the fear could set in, I went tumbling onto my backside as first Xiao then Kang crashed down on top of me. Again the air was forced from my lungs as the weight of each of them crushed down on my chest.

"Yes!" yelled Kang, throwing his arms into the air. "We did it."

"We?" said Xiao. "You nearly–"

"Not now!" I gave them both a shove as the door blasted open and the creature came thundering out of the museum. The three of us scrambled across the floor, putting as much distance between us and the gate as we could while the beast teethed and snarled at the bars.

"What is that thing?" asked Kang, backing further up the loading ramp as he spoke.

"You want to stay and find out?" I replied.

"No. But, it can't get through the bars. Right?"

The creature was gnawing at the iron, its jagged teeth scratching and grating until the thick bar finally creaked and bent under its might.

"Wanna bet?" said Xiao, backing into me before turning and fleeing up the ramp herself.

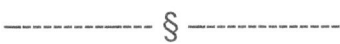

We raced out into the street, where a thickening mist rolled through the air, finding nothing and nobody to turn to. I glanced down at my watch, it was nearing two in the morning.

"Fog?" said Kang. "In Cyprus? In mid-September?"

"Who cares!?" Xiao shouted. "Which way do we go? We need to find help."

"What about Vinter?"

"You want to take your chances with that green-eyed killer bitch, be my guest."

"She's right," I said. "There's not much we can do. We need to get somewhere safe."

"Everywhere is closed." Xiao reached for her phone, then looked perplexed as she tapped the screen. "And something is screwing with the networks. I've got zero signal."

"Me too," said Kang, as he gave his phone a couple of frustrated swipes.

It had to have something to do with the bizarre mist quickly filling the highstreet. And at this rate, we'd be blind to any attack from the creature at our backs. There had to be some kind of all night bar or club that we could–

"The library!" My previous night's antics finally caught up with me as the idea blossomed in my head. "It's open twenty-four-seven. And there's a security guard there too. He's got to have a working phone or a gun or something. It's straight up the highstreet. We can run it."

It didn't take long for my friends to agree and a minute later we had sprinted away from the museum. I managed to keep a half decent pace going, though I was sweating like a pig and my feet were cramping up in my boots. Kang managed to keep pace behind me too. He panted heavily, his breathing was always his weakness, but he was pushing it far harder than I'd ever seen. Still, I had to yell at Xiao not to get too far ahead. I'd bet she could run all day, her fitness was incredible. But if she didn't slow down we'd lose her in the mist, which by this point was so thick I could only just make out the front of each building as we passed.

Five minutes later, I was on the verge of collapse. My legs were so heavy each stride was barely more than a few inches and the heat around my neck and chest was unbearable. We must have covered at least a kilometre and a half, as Xiao drew to a halt in front. She had stopped on at least four of five occasions, but this time she put her hands on her head in a recovery position and waited for me to arrive.

"Is this it?" she said, letting me lean on her for support.

I half-walked half-limped over to the side of the road with her.

"Yeah!" I shouted, still short of breath.

Glancing back to make sure Kang was still visible a few dozen metres behind, Xiao and I leant on each other for support as we descended the steps then crossed the courtyard to squint at the fogged glass windows. Switching my weight from Xiao to the window, I rubbed the glass with my forearm, grinning with anticipation as I peered through at the books and desks inside.

But Xiao wasn't smiling. "Why does it look closed?"

She was right. There was nobody on the desk and the automatic doors didn't slide open as we approached. Kang finally jogged up behind us and backed against the doors.

"What's the deal?" he said, sliding down to the ground. "Don't tell me it's closed. I've been let down by a lot of things in my life, but never the library."

"I don't get it." I moved from window to window, irritation fueling my body. "It says twenty-four-seven."

"We have to keep moving," said Xiao.

"I can't," said Kang. "I don't even know if I can get up."

"Then stay here and get eaten."

"Wait!" I shouted, focusing on what I thought was movement somewhere near one of the back shelves. "I think there's someone inside. I saw something. Hey!" I started to bang frantically on the glass. "Hey! Can you hear us? Hey! We need to come in."

Xiao, too, took to hammering on the window and Kang somehow found strength in his legs as he appeared on his feet next to me shouting and slamming his palms on the library entrance. There was definitely someone inside, moving from row to row. Only, they couldn't hear us. My hands were throbbing and red from drumming on the heavy window. It had to be two or three panes thick and might have even been soundproof. If it was, we were screwed.

But I couldn't give up. We kept at it for at least another minute when a head finally emerged from behind a stack of books and looked me dead in the eyes. I thought I'd been delighted to see those bright golden eyes the night before, but I couldn't put into words the relief, the warmth, I felt from her confused golden stare.

"It's the librarian," I shouted, as she stumbled over and dumped the tall stack of books she carried on one of the desks. As she marched over towards the security desk, I couldn't help but beam a wide and expectant smile at her. There was a buzz of static as her finger touched the desk controls and a green light appeared above our heads.

"Hello?" she said.

"Hey. Hey!" I could barely contain my enthusiasm. "You have no idea how glad we are to see you. Can you let us in?"

"Uh…" the librarian hesitated. "Have we met?"

Never before have I flipped so instantly from elation to rage in my entire life. "Are you kidding me?! I was here last night. With you. And again at the museum this morning. We spoke. You were collecting books."

"I see," she replied, not sounding convinced. "Well anyway, we're closed."

"You can't be closed." I couldn't help yelling. "You're open all-day-everyday."

"Yes," she nodded. "But Giorgos, the security guard, is off sick today. And I can't let anyone in at night without security. Sorry."

"Okay, fine." I raised both hands in frustrated appeasement. "But you don't understand. We need to get in. There's some... thing, chasing us. We're in danger."

"Some...thing?" she replied.

"Yeah." I nodded.

The librarian seemed to be considering as she took her hand off the desk and twirled the strands of her hair. "If you don't leave, I'm going to have to call the police."

"Yes!" shouted Kang. "Do that. Call the police. Just let us in first."

"Lady." Xiao shoved me aside and slammed the base of her fist on the glass. "If you don't open this door, all the police are gonna find are ours, and maybe your, freshly chewed corpses when they get here. Open. The. Door."

"Seriously," Kang said. "There's this thing after us. It's like a... a–"

"Dog?" The librarian asked.

"Yeah." Kang and I looked at each other.

"Like that one?" The librarian pressed her index finger against the window.

My head whipped around so fast I risked getting whiplash. Stepping out of the fog, where it was thickest in the middle of the road, the four-legged creature perched at the top of the steps. Before anyone could say another word, I threw a finger to my lips and swung on each of them, urging silence.

In particular, I leant my head against the window to make sure the librarian understood.

She frowned, maybe wondering just what we were all afraid of. From where she stood, behind the glass and in the misty night, it probably just looked like a regular dog. But if she pressed that intercom button again, I was certain she'd find out it was something far worse.

I'd been contemplating, amidst the frantic run towards the library, why the creature hadn't found Vinter and I in the basement. My only hypothesis was that, despite its peculiar eyes, it had poor sight. It hadn't smelt us either, suggesting it depended on its ears to track down its victim.

So if it couldn't hear us, it didn't know where we were. It was hardly the most ideal circumstances to test my theory, but we were only a few seconds from becoming a chew-toy anyway and I didn't see anyone else coming up with fresh ideas.

Kang, Xiao and even the librarian fell dead silent as the creature took a few more downward steps. It stopped, five or six steps from the bottom, turning its head keenly from left to right. By this point, I wasn't breathing, let alone talking, as it's eyes fixed directly on us.

Kang eyed me nervously, shrugging his shoulders as if I had asked him to rescue us from this predicament. Xiao was still staring the beast down, likely readying herself to take off at her quickest pace if the creature made any sudden moves. There was a lump in my throat that I dared not swallow, as I focused intently on keeping silent as my eyes fell searchingly on the librarian.

Her olive skin had fallen pale and her eyes were wide with distress. I knew exactly why. At this much closer distance, the creature's abnormal and terrifying nature was bared for all to see. Blackened saliva dripped from its teeth and its barbarous green eyes pierced through the vanishing mist.

I nodded, trying my best to calm her and acknowledge that we were seeing the same monstrosity. And we were all terrified. But still I kept my finger to my lips. She had to stay quiet. She nodded back at me. She nodded so hard it looked like her head would roll off of her shoulders, as she chewed at the nail on her thumb.

A nudge in my abdomen brought my attention back around, as Xiao nodded in the direction of the creature. It had taken two steps back towards the street. It took another step. Then another. Up and away from us until it was near the top of the stairs once more.

Watching the creature retreat felt like someone had just lifted Thor's hammer from my chest, as I finally started to breathe freely again. Which made the blaring klaxon of a ringing phone catch me completely off guard. I slammed my head back against the glass as I fumbled around searching for the source of the noise.

"Shit!" said Kang, as he slipped his phone from his pocket and silenced the ear-piercing tone and flashing screen.

But it was too late.

The creature had already turned on its heels and was glaring down at us on high alert, its growl amplifying and ears pointed like arrowheads. As it took two quick steps forward, the intercom buzzed behind us.

"Get inside!" yelled the librarian as the doors slid open.

Xiao was already through the doors before they fully parted while Kang, back on all fours, dragged himself inside.

"Close the doors!" All three of us yelled, as I charged inside and collapsed next to Kang. "Close them now!"

The glass doors swept shut as the creature came thundering towards us and crashed against the doors. It felt like the entire building shook, but the glass held firm.

"It can't get in here, right?" said Kang.

"Right," said the Librarian. "It's security glass. I think."

Back went the creature again, across the courtyard and towards the steps, stamping and kicking its paws, before it burst towards us again. It's head blasted against the doors, this time really knocking several books off the shelves. But again, the glass held firm.

"I think we're okay," I said, pulling Kang up off the ground with me.

"What the hell is wrong with your dog?" asked the Librarian.

"It's not my dog. Does it look like my dog? Would my dog be trying to kill me?"

"Then why is it following you? And why did you bring it here? And what is wrong with its eyes? Just who are you people anyway!?"

I placed a hand on her shoulder in an attempt to reassure her. "Just try to calm down."

"No." She brushed my arm aside. "Tell me what's going on. Now."

I paused, searching for the words to begin with. Something, anything, I could use to quickly win her to our side, but Xiao drew my attention back to the doors.

"Guys," she said ominously. "What's it doing?"

Outside, the growling was no more and the creature had ceased its assault on the glass. It had withdrawn, midway across the courtyard, but I couldn't tell what it was up to. Its front paws were bent and its head was tucked in towards its chest.

"No idea," I replied. "But this is our chance. Let's call the police."

"Kang can do it," said Xiao, her face twisted in anger. "We know his phone is working."

"That wasn't my fault," he replied. "We didn't have any signal before. It must have been that weird mist." He looked down at his phone. "Anyway, I guess it's back now."

While Kang headed towards the back of the library to make the call and Xiao slumped into one of the chairs, I couldn't help but approach the doors and keep an eye on the creature.

Something was wrong.

"Hey," the Librarian whispered behind me. "Zeke? Right?"

I smiled. "So you do remember me?"

"Kind of," she grimaced, before putting her head in her hands. "What is going on here?"

Just thinking about it made me sigh. "Honestly. I'm not sure. But we're not safe until the police show up." The more I spoke, the harder it seemed to find the next word. There was just something about this librarian that seemed to draw out my social ineptitude. "So. Uh. Thanks for letting us in by the way. I'm pretty sure we'd be dead otherwise."

"It's okay," she said, dropping her hands. When she looked up at me, with those grand and golden eyes, it was as if, just for a moment, the horror of our situation didn't exist. Like it was burned away by the warmth of her gaze. Like everything would suddenly be okay.

It didn't last.

The creature's growl returned, only this time it was more of a howl. Its head shot up as it looked to the stars, green eyes pulsating and limbs twitching. Then, like a scene from an exorcism, its head snapped to one side, like the neck had been broken. It was still alive, that much was certain, as its head began to shake. Slowly at first, from side to side. But it got faster and faster, until it was almost vibrating; its head rattling back and forth from left to right. The eyes were like headlights, swerving down a wet road, flickering back and forth as if there were a thousand of them.

Then, it stopped.

And when it did, there were not a thousand lights. Neither were there two. There were four. Four lights. Four eyes. Two heads. Each bearing emerald eyes staring hungrily back at us.

ACT IV

THE METIS HEADACHE

'We can easily forgive a child who is afraid of the dark; the real tragedy of life is when men are afraid of the light.'

I never thought a Plato quote would be the last thing that ran through my head before I died. Kang was probably thinking of some cool Rorschach line like, 'What's one more body amongst foundations?' But there was an image I simply couldn't shake. Those eyes. Those four menacing green eyes glowering through the glass as the creature reared back, preparing to ram the doors once more.

In milliseconds, it was across the courtyard as both heads crashed against the front of the library. "Shit," I cursed, recoiling from the vociferous blast of the impact and chilling creaks that followed as a thick jagged line traced its way from the centre of the glass. "It's going to break through!"

I swung around to face the bookshelves that paved the way to the back of the building, looming over us like an audience at an execution. I turned to the librarian.

"Is there another way out of here?" Beit the shock of what was unfolding outside, our likely and imminent deaths, or just the usual lack of wits and awareness she had continued to display, the librarian didn't respond. "Hey!" I could feel the rush of heat in my head, panic and fear, but that didn't stop me from grabbing her harshly by shoulders. "Can you get us out of here or not?"

"Zeke!" Xiao shoved me with enough force to break my hold on the librarian. "Let go of her. You were just screaming at her to let us *in*."

The building rattled once more as the beast outside collided with the glass again.

"Do you have a better idea?" asked Kang. "Because we're like a minute away from forgetting about Zeus and worrying about Hades."

"Give me a second." Xiao spun away, leaving us to wait impatiently as the back of her head angled from left to right, then back again.

I rubbed my face with both hands as I stared down the creature, kicking it's heel and readying it's next assault. "We are out of seconds, Xiao."

"Hey," it was Xiao's turn to stare demandingly at the librarian. "Does this place have sprinklers?" My teammate put an arm on the librarian, accompanied by an expression more gentle than any I had ever seen her foster. "Think."

"Yes," the librarian replied.

"Can you turn them on?"

"I can try." In seconds the librarian was behind the security desk once more; a look of determined concentration carved across her brow, as she attempted to decipher the system. She screamed when the creature hit the door once more. The glass resembled a spider's web, circling around as the fractures grew away from the centre.

"Xiao, what are we–"

She cut me off before I could ask. "Help me with this."

Xiao pulled something from her pocket and dropped to her knees without further instruction. I knelt down next to her, as Kang set down beside me. Xiao was wielding a butterfly knife. I'd seen it before. Caught her playing with it in fact. Flicking it open and closed by the black grip with the golden flowers. But this was the first time I'd seen her put it to use.

She had the blade in between the floor and the carpet, digging up the grey material and yanking it away. I remember exchanging a brief, 'what the hell are we doing?' glance with Kang, before simultaneously taking hold of the carpet and tearing it away. The floor housing was at an incline, I assume to help disabled guests up into the slightly raised flooring inside. Already, Xiao had her knife in a floor panel, prying it open as what sounded like a pipe bursting overhead distracted each of us.

Before I could look up, water spilled over my face as the sprinklers kicked in.

"Got it!" shouted the librarian, but Xiao wasn't paying attention.

She already had the floor panel open and was cutting into a thick section of cabling.

"Are you crazy?" said Kang, his hair plastered across his forehead by the deluge.

"I'm just exposing the wiring," Xiao replied, carefully sliding the rubber away and dropping the cables. "There. Now, back off you two," she barked, grabbing one of the wooden chairs and placing it down beside the cabling.

"You've lost your mind," said Kang, clambering atop one of the desks and shaking his head frantically.

"Maybe," Xiao replied. "But I'm not just gonna stand here and wait to die like you guys."

I leapt on top of the table beside Kang, as the water filled the lowered area at the base of the ramp. "Xiao," I said, extending a hand to help her over.

She shook her head and dragged her unravelled hair away from her face, causing me to shudder as I saw that familiar dogged intensity in her eyes.

"Bait," she whispered.

I hardly took a breath. The seconds felt like minutes as time all but stood still. I looked towards the creature, now certainly just inches from crashing through the glass. I saw the librarian, pressed up against the corner of the security office, standing on the corner console with her eyes firmly shut. I glanced at Kang, standing beside me, suddenly checking his pockets and sporting an epiphanous look I didn't have time to fathom. In those split seconds, and surely aided by the adrenaline in my veins, I reacted.

I launched myself off the edge of the table towards Xiao, just as the beast leapt through the glass window. Razor-sharp shards whistled through the air, grazing my cheek and nicking my jacket as I flew shoulder first into Xiao, tackling her off the flimsy chair supporting her.

I landed atop her on a table on the other side of the ramp, slamming our heads, amongst other things, together while ignoring the pain as we both craned our necks to look at the beast.

It too had landed; it's four legs thigh deep in the water, each straight as a pole. It's head had snapped back and angled towards the sky, and it's top teeth had bitten clean through it's lower lips. Its body convulsed only slightly, but the electricity had taken hold and was undoubtedly coursing through every cell in the creature's body. But still, it was the eyes that drew my gaze.

Their emerald light brightened at first, like a car flicking its high beams on in the dead of night. They shone so intensely, I shut my eyes in fear of blindness, but still found the chilling jade light boring its way through my eyelids. Finally the light faded, but when I opened my eyes it still wasn't over. The room went bright again, but this time it was the building lights, followed by the TV monitors, the computer screens and the blinking indicators on every piece of machinery. The library lit up like a firework display, darkness one second and blazing colour the next. Even the creature's eyes flickered, until finally they went black. Along with the rest of the building.

Silence, dead silence, followed as I, and I assume everyone else, waited to see if the creature would move again. It did. But only to slump down into the water, lifelessly.

I breathed a heavy sigh of relief. "We did it."

"Get off me," said Xiao, pressing her forearm into my chest.

"Ow." I shuffled to the other end of the table and only then felt the ringing in my head from our collision. "You're welcome."

"I didn't ask you to do that. I don't need rescuing, Zeke."

"Okay. I get it. I'm sorry." I wasn't. Just because Xiao thinks she has everything under control, doesn't make it so. And asking your friends to watch you risk your life is pretty selfish if you ask me. Regardless, now wasn't a good time for an argument.

"Are you two okay?" asked Kang, from across the room.

"I'd be fine if your boy hadn't headbutted me," Xiao replied, checking her head.

"Good. Then get up and take a look at this."

Kang was perched on the edge of his table, getting as close a look at the creature as he could. I did the same, kneeling down until my head hung over the edge of the desk.

"There's no power," said Xiao. "If you're so interested in this thing that nearly killed us, you can get in the water."

"You first," I said. She didn't reply. Nor did she test her theory. Ignoring her, I stared at the creature in disbelief. Laying in the water, was a dog. No more, no less. It had four legs, a short tail and one perfectly normal head.

"You did see what I saw before, right?" said Kang. "Some kind of multi-headed chimaera hellhound thing with laser eyes?"

"Yeah." I nodded. "We all saw it."

"So, what's this?"

Usually I'd have something to say. Something clever. Something ironic. Something... well something. But, what *was* it?

"One of you really needs to tell me what's going on here," said the librarian, tiptoeing across the security consoles with her arms stretched out wide for balance and one of her three-inch heeled boots in either hand. "What was that thing? Who are you people? And who is going to pay for all of this? I'm calling the police."

"Did that," said Kang, helping the librarian down onto his table. "Not sure they believed me. Either way, with all this noise someone will show up soon. Can we find somewhere dry to discuss this? Away from the electricity and water."

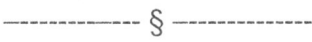

"What was all that?" I asked.

"What do you mean?" said Xiao, her arms crossed. The librarian had led us into the foyer, where a flight of stairs led to the upper level, before ducking into one of the back offices to grab her valuables. "You mean me saving your life?"

"Not that. You were going to let that thing eat you."

She rolled her eyes. "Of course I wasn't. I was going to move if you hadn't jumped all over me. Anyway, it was all instinct. Survival or whatever. I do *not* want to die on some bullshit assignment in Cyprus. More importantly, why was that thing chasing us to begin with?"

"I don't know. Loose ends, I guess."

"The museum was a massacre. There were loose ends everywhere. She wanted something."

"The lightning bolt." I paused after saying it aloud. "That's what she said. 'Where is the lightning bolt?' She seemed to think Ealing had it. Or Vinter. But they're both dead. And she's still looking for it."

"Well, we don't have it." Xiao threw her hands in the air.

"Uh, about that," said Kang sheepishly. His head hung so low his beard must have itched his chest as he reached inside his jacket and felt around. A few seconds later his hand emerged clutching a small oval stone between his thumb and index.

"Are you kidding me!?" yelled Xiao.

I managed to catch her by the elbow as she tried to step forward. But that didn't mean I wasn't just as furious. "Dude, what were you thinking!?"

"I forgot I had it." Still Kang refused eye contact. "I was just…"

"You stole one of the gems. Why?"

"I wasn't going to steal it. I put it in my pocket when the lights went out. I wanted to take another look with the two of you when they were busy. I was never going to take it from the museum. But then things went crazy and people started dying and I… I just forgot."

"That doesn't change a thing," I said. "Don't you see? You've made us thieves. Exactly like Vinter said."

"Forget that," said Xiao. "You nearly got us all killed. I…how…what…Urgh!" Xiao growled almost like a bear, as she stomped up the stairs complaining. "I need a minute. If I look at you again I'm going to punch that stupid expression off your face."

Finally, Kang looked me in the eyes. "I'm sorry man."

I put a hand on his shoulder. "I know."

A flicker of the usual brightness appeared in his eyes as he rolled the stone into the palm of his hand. "But check this out."

It was a deep golden colour, almost like amber, perfectly preserved and smooth on every edge. Except for the same carbon blemishes that blighted the rest of the collection. But Kang was right, there was something worth looking at on this particular stone. It bore the same black marks, yes. But as Kang placed his index finger atop the mark and traced the shape in a firm zigzag, I knew we were both considering the same explanation.

"It's shaped like a thunderbolt," I said. Kang's eyebrows raised as he nodded. "This could have been the gem set in the clasp. On the belt of the

Zeus statue. If that gem were struck by lightning, it would explain the dispersal pattern."

Kang waved the stone closer to my face. "That crazy murder-death-kill lady. She took all the gems from the crate. But none of those had markings like this. *This,* is what she was looking for."

I struggled to gulp the thick saliva in my throat. "We... we have to get rid of this thing man."

"Yeah." Kang clasped the stone tight in his fist. "Or... we get it back to Pierceson."

"Kang–"

"Here me out bro. This could be exactly what he sent us here for. He'll know what to do with it. Turn it into a huge discovery. And we were the ones that found it."

"No, we didn't. Ealing found it. He and his team died for it man. And we're gonna die for it too, if we don't ditch that thing and get back on the fastest plane home."

"I know. But if we ditch it, what did Ealing even die for? Come on, Zeke. Don't you want to see this through. Don't you want to tell the world about what we saw here?"

"We didn't see anything man."

"What?" Kang's head snapped back and his eyebrows nearly touched his hairline.

"Look, I don't know what we thought we saw, but all that's back there is a crazed dog. That lady, maybe she dosed us with something. An airborne toxin or hallucinogen."

"You can't *actually* be serious, Zeke?" Kang's nose wrinkled in abhorrence. "You want to write all this off? Pretend we didn't see that monster? And that magic the woman did?"

"Monsters and magic are myths. There's got to be something that explains all this. What we need to do is throw that thing away and get back to our hotel so we can get our heads straight. Now, gimme the stone."

"Why?" Kang's hand flew behind his back, the stone still within.

"So I can throw it as far away as possible."

"Hell no. Did Frodo give Sam the ring?"

"This isn't a movie Kang!" I held my hand out in front of him. "Give me the gem."

"Lookout!" Xiao's voice thundered above us.

I turned my head just in time to see the two headed creature, back on its feet and charging towards us. I shoved Kang as hard as I could, falling to the ground as he tumbled onto the staircase. The creature passed between us, before swivelling to face me.

Who knew how it was still alive, but as it stood not inches from my face, it had clearly returned to the same ferocious and terrifying appearance as before. Its thick midnight-black skin swallowed the light and its heavy spike tipped paws clawed at the ground. Two giant heads snarled and dripped saliva on my boots as its piercing and paralysing eyes shot through me. But it didn't attack.

Instead, it turned, waving its long anaconda-like tail over my head as it faced the staircase.

"Run!" I shouted. It wanted Kang. It wanted the stone. And it knew he had it. To his credit, Kang didn't freeze like I had. He launched himself up the steps, clambering as fast as he could on all fours. In one leap, the creature was behind him on the staircase, cracking the steps beneath it with its weight as it bounded up after him. As Kang rounded the top of the stairs, he and Xiao found themselves backed into a corner with no escape.

"Kang!" I screamed, as the creature smashed through a bookcase at the top of the stairs. "The gem. Throw it to me!"

Without a second of hesitation, Kang lurched towards the balcony and the stone came tumbling through the air towards me. I reached up a hand to catch it, but thought twice when I sensed the enormous shadow looming over me. The creature had followed the flight of the stone, diving from the balcony and cannoning towards me.

I ducked and rolled out of its way, hearing the stone hit the wall and bounce away. The creature's hefty paws scratched the ground where I had been, as its four haunting eyes glowered at me. Again, it didn't pounce. It still wanted the stone. The creature and I both turned to my right, where the stone lurked enticingly in front of the glass door to the back office.

Neither the creature nor I could make our move before the already ajar door opened fully, and the turquoise heeled boot of the librarian stepped out. "What's going–"

She never finished her sentence, though it wasn't for the shock of the dual-headed monster that stood ready to devour her. No, the librarian's eyes and tongue were still, as she fixated on the glistening amber stone between her feet.

"What's this?" she said, her voice both serene and somehow excited all at once. As if she were somehow unaware or unconcerned by the chaos unfolding around her.

"No!" I shouted, when I saw her fingers outstretched and her arm reaching towards the stone. "It's after the gem!"

My warning fell on deaf ears. She must have heard me, I was barely two metres in front of her. But I might as well have been two miles away for all the good it did. It was like she was drawn to the stone. Her golden eyes locked hungrily upon it as her knees bent.

Then, the creature pounced.

The coward in me wanted to look away; not ready to see an innocent girl torn to pieces right before my eyes. I fought the urge, not just to turn away, but to run in the opposite direction. I wish I could call it defiance or bravery, but it wasn't. It was the librarian. As her painted nails curled around the stone, the amber came to life.

Its centuries old glisten became a fiery golden blaze as light burned from her palm and the stone hummed like a laser from a science-fiction movie. Her eyes, too, shone brighter than before; the whites turning to sun-fire and lashes like mid-summer rays. It was like her entire body ignited, turning the dark power-sapped library into a dazzling light show.

The creature didn't leave a scratch on her. As its claws threatened to tear down her radiance, the light grew in intensity. The monster's claws turned to dust and its skin to ash as, in an instant, the light burned straight through it and left nothing but a scorched outline across the floor.

For a further moment, she continued to shine, like a star in the night, her skin glowing brighter by the second and forcing me to avert my gaze. I didn't want to look away. I fought against it, in fact. Just as she seemed compelled to touch the stone, I felt the need to watch her. To witness what was happening. To be mesmerised by it.

Then, just as quickly as she burst into magnificence, she faded. The library was thrown into darkness once more as the librarian's knees buckled and she collapsed in a heap on the floor. It might have been my imagination, or the blinding light, but just an instant before she fell, I could've sworn I saw her smiling.

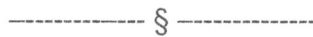

"Okay Zeke, tell me, what the hell was that?" Kang had his hands on his head and was pacing back and forth. "How do you plan on rationalising that one? This mild mannered librarian just went full-on Jean Grey Phoenix. Tell me again how I'm hallucinating."

"I saw it too," said Xiao. "She touched the gem and shot lightning at that thing. Unless I'm losing my mind?"

I didn't have an answer. My first instinct was to rush over and check on the librarian. But caution grabbed me like a steady hand on my shoulder. What had just happened? Did she mean to do... whatever she did? Did she even know she could? Was she dangerous? Of course she was dangerous. Again, the thought crossed my mind.

Run.

But as I looked down at her limp body, her golden eyes obscured by eyelids firmly shut, I knew I couldn't just leave her here.

"I don't get it," said Kang. "I've been holding that thing all evening and nothing happened."

"Well, something sure happened when she picked it up," I said.

"Alright, forget that thing. We leave it and get it out of here. Back to London. Asap."

"A minute ago you wanted to take it with us."

"That was before I knew it was cursed. Wait, what do *you* want to do with it? Take it with us?"

"Yeah." I nodded. "We can't just leave it here and let someone get hold of it. What if it's a weapon? Like you said, Pierceson will know what to do with it."

"Fine," said Kang, nudging me forward with his shoulder. "But I'm not touching it. Who knows what she's activated."

As I eyed the stone laying an inch from the librarians fingertips, I had to admit I didn't relish the idea of handling it. Who knew what it had done to her? It could have cooked her alive from the inside out. Maybe it was radioactive or time released. The fear of a thousand deadly scenarios streamed through my head.

"For goodness sake," said Xiao. "You two are such cowards."

I grabbed her by the wrist as she reached for the stone. "Wait. I don't think a woman should do it."

Xiao scowled. "Excuse me?"

As I realised the taboo nature of the phrase I tried never to use in her presence, I let go of her hand and stepped between her and the stone.

"Not like that," I raised both hands in appeasement. "I meant because Kang touched it and he's fine. But she touched it and now she's unconscious. It might be activated by the touch of a female.... Or something."

Xiao's eyes were like daggers, but, eventually, she softened and dipped her head in agreement. I reached into my jacket and pulled out a handkerchief. My mum insisted on reinvesting much of the money I gave her back into my wellbeing. Buying me fancy attire along with gentlemen's jewellery and accessories. None of it really suited me, but I at least entertained her efforts by always carrying around one of my overpriced handkerchiefs. I placed it across my palm and, gently, wrapped my hand around the stone. Quickly, I covered the whole thing and slipped it into my pocket before vigorously shaking my hands, as if they were doused in some contagious liquid.

"You alright?" asked Kang, eyeing me suspiciously like I carried the black plague.

"I'll live," I replied.

"Good, then let's get out of here. The police could show up any second to check out my call, remember? And without that creature chasing us, our cover story isn't looking too good right about now."

"He's right," said Xiao. "Several journalists can place us at the museum, which is a bloodbath right now. No doubt we'll be linked to Ealing's death by morning. And when they arrive here, all they'll see is a heavily vandalised library and us standing around one of its employees."

"Then let's get a move on," I said.

"What about her?" Xiao tilted her head in the librarian's direction.

I'd been contemplating that myself. "We take her with us."

"What?" said Kang. "Are you crazy?"

"We can't just leave her here." I was already crouching down and placing one hand beneath her head.

"Why not?" Kang had backed away towards the entrance. "We have no idea what's going on here. For all we know, she could be in on it. Using some kind of magic or whatever, just like the woman at the museum. Even if she isn't, she'll slow us down."

There wasn't time to argue with Kang. Instead, I looked to Xiao and fashioned the most intense stare I could manage.

"One vote each. It's your call."

Xiao folded her arms and looked down at the librarian, whose head I had raised onto the crease of my arm.

"Fine," she said, with an exasperated sigh. "We take her."

Kang growled in protest. "I can't believe we're doing this."

"Stop complaining," said Xiao, as she helped me pull the librarian to her feet in between us, and rested half the weight on her shoulder. "Just call a cab to meet us further down the street."

"Fine. But where do you expect to take her?"

"To the hospital," I said. "We should make sure she's alright."

Kang placed his head in hands. "Dude. How many hero-fugitive movies have we watched? Every time they go to the hospital to patch themselves up, the bad guy finds them. Public places are a stupid idea."

"Do you have a better idea? We can't go back to our hotel. We checked in with our passports. If anybody comes looking for us, that's the first place they'll go."

"Okay, okay. Everyone relax." Kang was actually the only one still pacing back and forth, before finally heading towards the exit. "I'll take care of it."

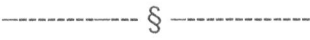

An hour later, we were safe in a hotel room. Or as safe as a trio of potential fugitives could be at least. Kang had called a cab to meet us down the road. A little further down than we had anticipated actually, leaving Xiao and I to ferry the librarian nearly a kilometre without his help. I panicked the entire way; the streets now miraculously free of the thick fog that swept through the city earlier.

Fortunately, our Cypriot cab driver asked few questions. We told him the librarian was drunk and bundled her into the back, while Kang directed him from the front. Kang was talking so much, I couldn't follow half the instructions, and or questions, he was firing at the driver, but it seemed to be enough to get the car moving further away from the scene of the crime.

As we twisted and turned through the Nicosian streets, the librarian's head kept rolling back and forth between Xiao and I, who sat either side of her.

"Just hold onto her," Xiao had said, thrusting her back towards me.

Nervously, I wrapped one arm around her and pulled her tight. It was all still quite surreal, for me anyway. I probably should have been more concerned about the other wild ongoings of the night, but at that moment I couldn't escape my thoughts about this girl I barely knew. The wind from the cracked window kept blowing her dark hair into my face and, though she was unconscious, I could feel the warmth of her skin as her hand brushed repeatedly against mine.

Truthfully, it made me feel like a creep. I hadn't met her till last night, and yet I was as close as I'd been to a girl in longer than I'd care to admit. And she wasn't even awake.

Xiao shook her head.

"What?" I asked.

"You're as bad as him." She pointed to the seat in front of her.

"I didn't do anything."

"Yeah but you're thinking about her."

"Am not."

"Uh huh."

"Whatever." I turned my attention to the window for the rest of the journey. Away from Xiao's malice.

Twenty minutes or so later, Kang was ushering us out of the cab and into an unglamorous hotel. At the reception, they didn't even bother asking for ID, so disreputable was the accommodation. And despite our circumstances, Kang was practically grinning as he rattled off a set of card details from memory instead of using his own. 'Benjamin Ecclestone,' was the name he used. Another of Pierceson's apprentices with whom we occasionally shared assignments. Clearly, Benjamin hadn't been wary enough to conceal his card when paying for one of Kang's coffees.

Now, the librarian laid passed out on one of the twin beds in a filthy room whose purpose I dared not imagine.

"We need to get out of the country," said Xiao, kicking off her boots. "Back to London. And back to Pierceson. So we can offload this gem and forget any of this ever happened."

"We can't do anything without our passports," I said. "Ours are in the safe in our room, back at The Imperial Atlus."

"Same here." Xiao cracked her knuckles in frustration.

"We have to go get them. Just two of us maybe. With the librarian safe here, we could be in and out of there fast. As long as no police are already investigating the place."

"Or that woman," Kang added.

"Alright," said Xiao. "I'll stay here with the girl. You two go back and get our stuff."

"Hmm." I rubbed my nose in contemplation as I carefully considered my next words. "Maybe... you should come with me."

In my head it was simple. If something happened while I was gone and the librarian needed to be moved, Xiao might not be strong enough to do it. Or she would struggle at the very least. Kang was much bigger and stronger, though admittedly less spontaneous and cunning, than our petite female friend. To avoid a black eye of course, I wanted to forego saying that directly to her.

"You're a lot faster and more subtle than he is. The two of us can be in and out much quicker. Besides, do you want to trust him with the combination to your safe? What else do you use those numbers for?"

Xiao only took a second to consider, before reaching for her leather boots and sliding them back on.

"Well, hurry up," said Kang, shoving his phone towards my face. "It's just past four-thirty. I'm guessing the museum staff arrive pretty early in the morning. And we need to be airport-bound before they can link us to any of it."

"Alright," let's go.

After getting the receptionist to call us a cab, Xiao and I were in the backseats and on our way ten minutes later. Surprisingly, she hadn't dozed off yet. Though I found myself repeatedly looking back and forth to check on her.

"What?" she asked, when she finally noticed my attention.

"Nothing." I smiled. "Just thought you might be catching a quick nap while you had the chance."

"Is that supposed to be funny?" she said, clearly unimpressed. "In a few hours we're going to be fugitives, Zeke."

"Ssshhh." I gave her a shove as I attempted to quiet her. "He'll hear us," I said, pointing at the driver.

"He barely speaks any English," she said.

"Okay, whatever. Just keep your voice down. And I just meant that, you know, if you wanted to rest up this is probably a good time."

"Rest? How am I supposed to rest at a time like this?" She was at least half-whispering now. "I just saw a bunch of people get killed right in front of me, by magic. Then some kind of mythological beast chased us through the streets, which somehow nobody else saw. And after that, some girl turned into a human lightbulb and killed the thing. How am I supposed to rest after all that?"

"Xiao." I could see she was panting as she spoke, maybe only now allowing the frantic events of the night to catch up with her. Maybe she'd been acting on instinct up until now and finally the dam had broken. "It's okay. Calm down."

"I am calm," she replied. "You just patronised me and I didn't hit you. I'm very calm. And why are you so laidback all of a sudden?"

I shrugged. "I'm not. I just think that there has to be an explanation for all this. You don't really believe it's magic do you?" It was Xiao's turn to shrug. "Listen, I don't know what's going on. All I know is we were in danger. And when you're in danger, your mind tries to rationalise things in order to process them and have you react accordingly. Just like the classical writers and poets wrote down their version of events in an attempt to understand things they couldn't explain."

Xiao took a sip from the bottle of water she had taken from the hotel. "So you think this is what? Science? Some kind of cover up? Have we been drugged? What?"

"I don't know. But we'll get to the bottom of it."

"Alright. But Zeke, even if my mind is lying to me, that doesn't make it any less real. We can only deal with what's in front of us."

"Yeah." I gave her a more playful shove this time. "Good thing I got you keeping me safe, right? What was all that Xena, Warrior Princess, stuff back there?"

"I dunno. Just a rush of blood. I really didn't want to die."

"Me neither."

Xiao's eyes went back to the windows. "It's getting busier outside. The early birds."

She was right. There still wasn't much light, but people had begun to appear on the streets. Vendors grinding coffee, stocking paper stands and oiling public transport motors.

"You think the police have been to the museum or library yet?" I wondered.

"Hmm. The library maybe. I wonder what they think happened?"

"You might be onto something." I reached into my pocket, pulling out the phone inside.

"Zeke," said Xiao, with a loathing I had already anticipated. "You took her phone? That is *not* okay."

"Yeah, yeah. Scold me later." I readied my finger to tap the screen of the small, hot-pink covered phone when Xiao snatched it from my hand.

"At least let me do it," she said. "You can't just go through women's things. How do you even know the code?"

"There isn't one. It's unlocked."

Xiao swiped at the screen, and the screen unlocked just as I said it would.

"Wow." She rolled her eyes. "She really is an idiot, isn't she? What am I looking for?"

"I don't know. A shift rota. An emergency contact. The name of the manager? Someone we can call to find out if they've heard about what's going on." Xiao thumbed through the phone's contents, holding it at an angle to ensure I couldn't see, when her eyebrows lowered in concentration. "What? What is it?" I asked.

"Holy shit," said Xiao. "This is her, right?"

She spun the phone around and held up a picture of the librarian. It was a photocard of some kind. Maybe her work ID.

"Yeah," I said, wondering what the problem was.

Xiao edged the phone closer to my face.

"Zeke, she isn't a librarian. She *is* the manager."

I snatched the phone to take a closer look at the image. It was a selfie of the librarian holding the ID up and smiling.

"Avy Pendragon. Library Manager," I said aloud as I read. "This can't be serious. She's in charge of the whole library? She didn't even know where any of the books went."

"That name though," said Xiao.

"Yeah," I replied. "Avy. I didn't picture her as an Avy. But it is a nice name."

"No, you idiot. Pendragon. That sounds fake. Like 'Arthur Pendragon.' Nobody has a name like that."

"You're right. It does sound fake."

"We need to question her when she wakes up."

"Agreed."

Before we could find anything else in the phone, the cab pulled up outside of our hotel. I paid the driver in cash and asked for him to wait here for us. He didn't understand, and pulled away the second I handed over the money.

"Shit," I cursed, as I tried to wave him down.

"Forget it," said Xiao. "Let's just get in and out. Fast."

We walked as fast as we could through the lobby, while still trying to look casual and draw as little attention as possible. The reception staff greeted us with smiles as we passed by, while the three or four other people present ignored us. I thumbed the call button on the lift four times, attempting to hurry it down to us.

"Alright," Xiao whispered. "Once we're in the lift, get your keycard ready. When you get to your room, grab your valuables. Shove em' in a bag. Get out. Got it?"

"Got it," I replied.

Finally the lift chimed and the doors slid open. I expected to be relieved when they did. But then I had hoped the lift would be empty. And even if it hadn't been, I wouldn't have expected to recognise the person inside. Their long blonde hair. Their expensive designer heels. And their insidious frosted-white smile.

"Ezekiel," said the woman.

"Camilla." I almost choked on her name.

"I've been looking for you," she said. "And you should count your blessings that I found you first."

ACT V

THE STRAIT OF MESSINA

"The traitor moves amongst those within the gate freely, his sly whispers rustling through all the alleys, heard in the very halls of government itself. For the traitor appears not a traitor; he speaks in accents familiar to his victims, and he wears their face and their arguments, he appeals to the baseness that lies deep in the hearts of all men. He rots the soul of a nation, he works secretly and unknown in the night to undermine the pillars of the city, he infects the body politic so that it can no longer resist."

Had Cicero met Camilla? How else could he have described her so aptly? Sly whispers. Secrets. Infection. Those were her tools. Tools she was more adept with than any other. I knew it. Kang was supposed to know it.

And I thought Xiao would have known it by now. So why we were standing in a halted lift, even contemplating telling her a single detail about what had happened, was a complete mystery to me. And frankly, the four metal walls surrounding us were the only reason I hadn't snatched Xiao by the arm and dragged her far away.

"First," said Xiao, responding to the barrage of questions Camilla had opened with. "Tell us what *you* know."

Camilla sighed. "I don't *know* a thing. What I've *heard* is that a bunch of archaeology students who stayed after hours at the museum yesterday, are wanted for questioning about a murder today."

Admittedly, my heart damn-near stopped when she said that word. *Murder*. We were suspects in a murder.

"We didn't kill anybody," Xiao protested.

"I gathered that much." Camilla rolled her eyes. "So what happened? Ealing is dead. I got as near as I could to the scene before the police sent me away. It's like the set of a horror movie in there."

"It's a long story. And you wouldn't believe it anyway."

"Xiao." Suddenly I found myself back in the moment. "Don't tell her anything."

"Stop it." Xiao looked me dead in the eyes in retaliation. "We need to know what she knows." Before I could object, Xiao was back to addressing Camilla, who of course flashed a triumphant smile my way. "Who found them this early? And why are they sure it was us?"

"Cleaners," Camilla replied. "Apparently, they were first on the scene. They called in the police, plus the museum owners and event organisers. An hour ago. Many of them placed Zeke at the museum a night ago, and the three of you arriving late yesterday."

"Dammit." Xiao kicked the lift doors. "But they don't know where we are, right?"

"Not yet." Camilla leant her shoulder against the wall. "But if I found you, how long do you think it will be before they do?"

"Uh huh." I stepped in close to Camilla, with my arms still crossed as I tried my best to offer up intimidation. "And how did *you* find us, exactly?"

"Oh, Zeke." She tried to brush her hand on my cheek but I managed to lean back, just out of her range. "I could always find you anywhere. Now, are you going to explain this insanity or not?"

Xiao didn't answer this time, instead looking to me for... permission? A decision? Maybe she was just respecting my complete and utter reluctance to share anything with this serpent of a woman.

"Fine. We'll tell you." I was already shaking my head as I said it. "But let's get to the room first."

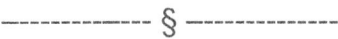

Camilla burst out laughing. "What do you take me for, a fool?"

"Quiet!" I stopped just short of placing my hands over her mouth. "You wanted to know what happened. Now you do."

"Complete and utter bollocks. A magical murderer? A demonic two-headed hound? A bolt of lightning? I know you don't believe in any of this nonsense, but even your poor imagination could surely conjure something more convincing than this?"

"Suit yourself." I went back to throwing as many of our important possessions into my backpack as I could.

Camilla sat on the bed and crossed her legs, in that attention seeking manner that she always did. "Alright. If you want me to believe you, show me this stone of yours. The one that turned a monster to ashes."

This time, I was the one to laugh. Not loud enough to draw any unwanted attention, but certainly enough to draw a frown from her. "Hell. No. I couldn't care less if you believe me or not. I'm not letting you anywhere near the stone. Ealing didn't, so why should I?"

"Zeke." She reached into her purse and pulled out her phone, pressing the black glass against her peach lips as if contemplating. "Show me the stone. Now."

The game had begun. One I'd played a thousand times before with her. The only question now was what each of us were willing to bet.

"Or what?"

"Or. I call the police and tell them where you are."

"You wouldn't." She wouldn't. There was no way the Camilla I knew would go as far as to deliberately leave us facing murder charges. She was an uptight, self-serving snake. A scorpion. A villain. But she wasn't a monster. Or at least, she wasn't before.

And yet, something was off. This threat was different. She hadn't offered it with her usual grin. That look of delight she took in taunting me, goading me, when she knew she had the upper hand. No, this time she looked... uncertain. As if she were unsure whether she'd overplayed her hand.

I often describe Camilla as my arch-nemesis. The Red-Skull to my Steve Rogers. But in reality, that wasn't truly accurate. We hadn't always been on opposite sides. Hadn't always had opposite goals. And we hadn't always been at each other's throats in an endless game of career-defining cat and mouse.

Once, we were inseparable. She had studied under Pierceson, side by side with Kang and I. We were a trio. Joined at the hips. Much like we were now, only with Xiao in her place. Well, that was if Xiao actually did care for us. It's often hard to tell. But it was different with Camilla. I'd known her since the day Pierceson had opened his programme to a promising batch of handpicked twelve-year-olds who had been discarded by a system that warned them they had no future. For a time we'd even been– Well, we'd been closer than just friends. Until she threw it all away.

No. Camilla was no Red-Skull. If I could liken her to one enemy, it would be Sinestro. Sinestro was once the greatest of all Green Lanterns. Their strongest, smartest and most revered hero. Until one day, it wasn't enough. He decided he was above the others. Better than them. That he didn't need them anymore. He fell from grace and found an opposing way, betraying his brethren and becoming their worst nightmare.

Camilla had soaked up everything Pierceson taught us, then abandoned him. Abandoned us. Accepting the offer from Professor LaGuerre was tantamount to betrayal. She never even told us why. But I already knew. The money. The position as his personal aide. The power. She had always been ambitious. Always hungered to be top of the food chain. I just never thought she would ever consider us her prey. Of course, I was wrong.

I dumped my bag on the floor and took her by the wrist, holding the phone up to her head. "Do it then. Call them. If you want to leave us in prison for murder, all to please your boss. Then do it."

She pushed me in the chest with her free hand, she was always so strong for her slight build, and slipped free of my grasp. "I thought you were innocent?"

"We are."

She swiped to unlock her phone. "Then you have nothing to fear."

Whether or not she was really about to go through with it, the knock at the door snatched our attention away. I rushed over and leant in close. "Who is it?"

"Me," came Xiao's reply. "Open up."

I pulled the door ajar and allowed her to slip in. She brushed by me and quickly crossed to the other side of the room.

"Are you ready?" Xiao looked out the window. "We should get going." It was then that she must have noticed the tension in the room; her neck craning between Camilla and I when neither of us responded. "Okay, whatever is going on between you two. Can we just drop it until we're somewhere safer. Zeke?"

Xiao looked expectantly at me.

"Sure." I didn't care how obvious the lie was.

"Camilla?"

I couldn't help but let my scorn linger on Camilla a while longer, as she nodded with far too much grace for someone who had just threatened to condemn us.

"Of course," she replied. "There's no reason we can't be civil–"

Camilla's previously unfurrowed brow wrinkled as her eyes darted towards the door. The stain of her threat was suddenly washed away as my concern narrowed on the entrance to the room.

"What?" I whispered.

Despite her attempt to hide it, Camilla looked nervous. Her calm breaths halted and she didn't blink. "It's uh... nothing."

"Nothing?"

"I dunno. I thought I heard someone."

Dunno? Camilla rarely abbreviated or failed to enunciate so obviously. So lazily. Something had alerted her and only seconds later, as we waited in near-silence with just the hum of the air-conditioning to fill the void, there was a soft knock at the door.

"Room service," said the husky voice on the other side.

"Who's that?" I whispered at Camilla.

"How should I know?" she mouthed back.

"Hey." Xiao pinched my arm hard enough to make me screech, though I managed to stifle it. "Stop arguing. Find out who it is and get rid of them."

She was right. It was no time to be caught up in an internal tussle. I placed my hands on the doorframe and spoke through the hinges. "No thank you."

"Room service," she repeated, in her Cypriot accent. I looked to Xiao for advice, but she only gestured angrily at me, which didn't help.

Taking a deep breath, I cracked the door. Outside was a woman. She definitely looked like she worked at the hotel; sporting the same burgundy uniform as the rest of the staff and wearing a nametag that read, 'Marina'. But there was something odd about her. Something almost... bewitching.

The glossy dark-skin. The extravagant long hair, braided only at the top. And something else. Something I just couldn't put my finger on.

"Hi." She smiled. "Is this Zeke Lewis's room?"

"Yeah," I replied. "We uh... we don't need any service though."

"No problem." She waved a hand in apology, before extending the other to me. "But we found this in the lobby. It's yours."

In her hand was a lanyard. And it was mine alright. From the exhibition. I must have dropped it on our way in. An unbelievably stupid move for someone who was currently a wanted man.

"Thanks."

My fingers brushed against hers as I took the lanyard from her, and though her touch was ice-cold, I didn't recoil. Instead, my hand hung there for a moment as she looked me in the eyes and winked.

I would have stayed longer, if I didn't feel the light tap of something brushing against my ear. Looking down, I saw a ball of scrunched paper rolling away, no doubt having been thrown by Xiao.

"See you around," I said, slowly edging the door shut.

"What the hell was that?" demanded Xiao, before I could even turn around.

"What was what?" I asked.

"Were you really just flirting with a maid?" Camilla joined in. "I thought your dilemma was urgent."

"No. I wasn't... It wasn't... She was just... nice."

"Give me that," said Xiao, reaching out dramatically and thrusting a palm almost into my chest. "The lanyard. Give it to me." As I started to raise my hand, she snatched the plastic card out of my grasp and scrutinised it. "Shit."

"I know. I can't believe I drop–"

"No." Xiao shoved the lanyard back into my hands. "Look. It says E. Lewis."

I felt like I should have known what point Xiao was trying to make or at least been able to bluff my way through. But I had to admit, I was a little disorientated by the whole encounter.

"So?"

"So?! She called you Zeke, dummy."

The fog in my head parted in an instant. "Crap. You're right. How could she know my name?"

"What did she look like?" asked Xiao, as her eyes searched the room in paranoia. "Was it the murder lady?"

"No."

"Are you sure? Sure you weren't too busy telling her how pretty she was to notice?"

"I told you, I wasn't– It's not her. I would have recognised her. Her eyes were different." Then it dawned on me. What it was about the maid that paralysed me. It *was* her eyes. They were hardly emerald green or glowing. But they were grand. Deep. Hypnotic. "We have to go."

"Go where?" asked Xiao. "She could be right outside. And she might not be alone."

I rushed over to the window and threw it open, eyeing a way to the ground. "Fire escape."

"Right." Xiao grabbed her bag and wasted no time pushing it through the window and clambering out behind it.

"Let's go." I nodded towards the open window as I stared Camilla down.

She took one look outside and snapped her neck back, unimpressed. "You *must* be kidding. I'm not climbing down there."

"Alright." I pushed my bag out. "See you around."

I was halfway down the ladder when I heard the clang of heels getting caught in the grate above me. As if she could resist pursuing us. By the time I reached the ground, Xiao was on her phone.

"What's taking her so long?" she asked, placing one had over the microphone.

"Camilla never rushes." I threw my bag back over my shoulder. "Ever. Who are you calling?"

"Pierceson. I'm done with this. We're getting the first flight out of here." Xiao's expression really was one of somebody who had reached the end of their tether.

"You're right," I said. "We have to go. Now."

"I'm on with one of his assistants. They're booking something in for us. Call Kang and check on him. Make sure he's ready to go."

"Right." I swiped as fast as I could to Kang's name as Camilla finally reached the ground.

"Urgh," she growled, brandishing a heel that had snapped away from the shoe. "Look at this. Do you have any idea how much these cost?"

"Quiet." Quickly, I turned my back on her. "Kang. How is everything?"

"All good here dude." Kang sounded remarkably calm, all things considered. "Under control."

"How's the librarian?"

"What librarian?" Camilla, as always, finessed her way into the conversation.

"Shhhh!" I hissed.

In her defence, I had purposely omitted the part of the story involving the librarian. Instead telling her that the stone alone had burned the creature to death. But if I were forced to share any more than that I'd be tempted to see if the stone would do the same thing to her.

"Dude," said Kang. "Was that *Camilla*?"

"Nevermind," I replied. "How is she?"

"The Starfire chick? She's still out cold."

"Still?" I was starting to think I should have ignored my friends and taken her to the hospital. "She's still breathing though, right?"

"What?" said Camilla. "I thought you guys said you didn't hurt anyone!?"

"Seriously. Shut up for a second." I had to bite my lip to stop from lashing out further. "Listen, Kang. We're getting on the next flight back to London. Make sure you're ready to go when we get back."

"Alright." Kang sounded confused. "But what about your friend here?"

"We'll figure that out when we get to you. See you soon bro." I hung up before Kang could say anything else, then turned on Camilla. "Can't you mind your own business for just five seconds."

"No," she growled. "Not when you're still hiding things."

"We don't have to tell you anything. In fact, we're done with this. All you've done is threaten to make things worse. And I'll be damned if I'm gonna stick around and wait for you to offer up another ultimatum. Hey." I shook Xiao by the arm. "Time to go. We get a flight?"

"Still waiting," Xiao replied.

"You're being stupid again," Camilla said. Heeding the advice of my friend for once, I didn't engage her. Instead, I ushered Xiao in the opposite direction. "Okay. Have it your way. But if you think your faces aren't going to be plastered all over the security screens by the time you make it to the airport, you're even bigger fools than I gave you credit for."

I wanted to keep walking, but my feet had already stopped. Gradually, Xiao's hand fell away from her ear too, as she hit the end call button.

"What're you doing?" I said, as if I didn't already know.

"She's right, Zeke," Xiao replied. "We can't get on a plane."

"Well we can't stay here either. We have to go somewhere."

"You know..." Camilla trailed off, dragging out the sentence until she had our full attention. "I could probably help."

Here we go. I should have known it from the start. When playing against Camilla, it was never a fair game. She rarely played the hand she was dealt, always bringing an extra card to the table. Whether or not she had been bluffing earlier, the scorpion had bared its tail, ready to strike once more.

"How?" asked Xiao. "You have a way through security?"

"Not through." Camilla seemed to take an age, that we didn't have, to get to the point. "Around. A private jet."

"*You* have a private jet?" Xiao scoffed.

"Of course." Camilla chuckled, as if access to a private aircraft were no different than owning a bicycle. "I guess my benefactor trusts me with far more responsibility than yours does you."

"And you'll really help us get out of here?" Xiao had taken the bait and now Camilla would reel her in.

"Why not? I'll even take you straight to London."

"What's the catch?" I asked.

There was, of course, no way on Earth she would offer something so vital to us without wanting something equally precious in return. And even though I asked, I already knew what it was.

Camilla smiled. "We take your precious stone to Pierceson, together. A joint-venture."

"The hell we will. And why are you even so interested in the stone? You don't know a thing about it."

"No." She shrugged. "But I know you're desperate not to let me see it. That means it's important. Rare. Special. And that interests me."

At the very least, listening to her terms made it easier to walk away. "Not happening."

"Zeke." Xiao pulled me around. "I know where you're coming from. But we need this."

"Seriously?" I couldn't believe Xiao was still buying any of this. "She didn't even lift a finger to find this thing."

"Neither did we. Ealing did. And he's dead."

"And we nearly died too! She doesn't deserve to be in on this."

Xiao sighed. "Is that even important right now? What are your priorities, Zeke? Your career? Or your life? In fact, if we end up stuck here, you'll have neither. Don't let her get in your head. If you end up in jail, what would that do to your mother?"

"Dammit." Xiao had me kicking at a stone in frustration. She was right. About several things. "The mother card is low. But alright. Let's just get this over with."

"Excellent." Camilla clapped her hands. "I know it's difficult. Rock, hard place. Scylla, Charybdis. Et cetera. But rest assured, this is in your best interests. Now, hurry back to... where are you staying again?"

"Nice try. Just call us with the details and we'll meet you. Do you still have my number? I know yours has changed."

"Oh? And how do you know that?" Camilla batted her lashes mockingly.

"I... I just meant–"

"Aw. Did you get lonely and try calling me? That is so sweet."

"Do you have my number or not?" I said, gritting my teeth.

"What do you think?" she said, giving her phone a shake. "It'll take me at least half a day to get the jet here. So stay hidden until then." She hopped over and did manage to pinch my cheek this time. "And don't do anything foolish."

"We'll try," I said, with my most obvious false smile.

"Oh," she started. "Before you go. Show it to me." At this point, she was just rubbing her victory in. "You don't expect me to lend aid without even seeing the prize. Do you?" I reached into my pocket and dragged out the stone, holding it up and away from her. Just in case. "How enchanting," she said, with a generous dose of sarcasm. "I'll have to take your word on its authenticity. Don't worry, I'm confident in your basic archaeological skills at least."

"Are you done?" Just hearing her voice was becoming too excruciating to bear. Yet somehow, she still wasn't finished, eyeing Xiao up and down, before fixating on her feet.

"What size are you?" Camilla asked.

"Six," Xiao cautiously replied.

Camilla waved her broken heel in Xiao's face. "Then I'll take those shoes too." Surprisingly, Xiao managed only to swear under her breath as she pulled off her black studded boots and handed them over. "Terribly out of season, but I suppose they'll have to do."

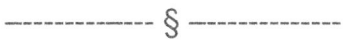

"What?" I knew Xiao must have noticed the intense scorn I'd been aiming at her since we got into the cab. Finally, it seemed to have irritated her enough to respond. "What is your problem?"

"This is a huge mistake," I replied, trying my best not to shout and draw too much of our driver's attention.

"Yeah, maybe it is." Xiao actually looked equally frustrated. "But I didn't see you volunteering any better ideas. As long as she gets us home alive, I'm fine with it."

"She won't. She'll sting us."

"You don't know that."

"I'm telling you she will. She's a scorpion."

"What does that even mean!?" she shouted, causing the driver to look back at us, eyebrows raised, through his rearview mirror.

"Nothing," I muttered. "Just something my mum used to warn me about."

Xiao crossed her arms and cocked her head at me. "I'm listening?"

Letting out a defeated sigh, I cast my thoughts back to my youth; tucked under my covers as my mum sat beside the bed, recounting stories. Poems. Myths.

"A scorpion sits at the edge of a river, looking for a way across. Not long later, it sees a swan swimming upstream. The scorpion asks the swan for a lift across the river, but the swan refuses. The swan says, 'if I let you on my back, you'll sting me.' But the scorpion explains that it can't swim. So if it stung the swan, it would only be dooming itself too. So, against its better judgement, the swan decides to give the scorpion a lift.

"Halfway across the river, the scorpion stings the swan.

"'Why did you do that?' the swan asks. 'Now we'll both drown.' And the scorpion replies, 'I can't help it. It's what I do.'"

Xiao didn't say anything, instead biting one of her nails as she seemed to contemplate the tale.

"My mum used to tell me that story." I went on. "About trust. About the nature of things. Camilla is a scorpion. And at some point, she's going to sting us. That's *her* nature."

"That's a good story," Xiao eventually said. "But she already got what she wanted from you guys, right? Just because she betrayed you once, doesn't mean she will again."

If Xiao was trying deliberately to make me angry, she was doing an incredible job. "Yes it does! Don't you get it? She's playing us. And as soon as she sees a chance to screw us over, she will. She was threatening to call the police on us just seconds before you came in."

"Oh, come on," said Xiao. "She wouldn't do that."

"Why are you defending her?" My patience had long since worn thin. "I thought you hated her too."

"I do. Just not for the same reasons as you. I hate her because she's a smug, superior, spoiled bitch. And because she's always beating us to the punch. But that doesn't blind me to the fact that we are out of other options."

"You have no idea what you're talking about. This is what she does, Xiao. Look how she's got us arguing. We're supposed to be relying on each other but here we are at each other's throats instead. It's exactly what she wants."

"Urgh." Xiao put her face in her hands. "You are so infuriating. And the worst part is, you two are so similar."

"Excuse me?"

"You are. You're exactly the same. You say she manipulates people. Uses them. But how is that any different to what you do? Aren't you using Pierceson just the same? And why are you even still mad at her? Is it because you can't stand that she left, and you miss her? Or is it because you're actually jealous of her?"

If we weren't in the worst predicament of our lives, trapped in a hostile city with the authorities after us, I would have stopped the cab there and then. I would have walked off into the distance and not looked back.

"You don't know what you're talking about," I said, as I felt my pulse racing. Seething. "And clearly, you don't know me at all. If you had been through what the three of us had, you wouldn't dare say that."

"Oh I get it." Now Xiao was as angry as I'd ever seen her, as the veins on her forehead started to bulge. "I'm not one of you. The magic trio. Pierceson's favourites. Well, I never asked for him to put me on this team."

"Neither did we." I regretted the words before they even left my mouth.

"Maybe we just shouldn't talk. Until we're back at the hotel," said Xiao.

"Yeah. Maybe."

As I watched the other cars whizz by outside the window, I knew I'd overstepped. Xiao didn't deserve that. She was a great student. As good as Kang or I, or anyone else in the programme. It had been difficult to adapt to working with her of course, after Camilla. But over the past two years, we'd grown into a great team. Great friends. I needed to apologise.

"And you know what?" said Xiao, beating me to any decision I might have come to.

"I thought we were not talking?" I replied.

"Camilla isn't the reason we're at each other's throats. You are."

"What?" Suddenly that apology seemed like a thought in the distant past.

"The only reason she can get under your skin so bad, is because you are so completely and obviously susceptible to it. You show her all your weak points. You paint a big target on your forehead every time you see her. And guess what, she never misses. You fall for it every time."

I thought for at least a whole minute on how to respond, but in the end I settled on just leaving it alone. "How about we just stick to the not talking thing?"

"Fine," said Xiao.

"Good," I replied.

The rest of the journey was as awkward a time as I had ever spent around Xiao. And awkwardness was already her whole raison d'etre. It was a sharp parallel to how open she had been on the drive here. Camilla strikes again.

As we arrived back at the seedy hotel, and I took a second to pay the driver, Xiao had already marched off into the lobby. I expected to see her at the lift, but all I caught was a glimpse of her bare feet as she stormed up the stairs. We were on the fifth floor, so I knew she must have been especially pissed.

By the time I arrived at the hotel room and knocked on the door, she was only just rounding the corner. Out of breath, she came and stood just behind me.

"Hey," I said. Finally remembering my original intention. To apologise.

"Don't," she replied. "Lets try and stay focused."

"Right." It was probably too soon to broach the subject again, but Kang was taking an age to open the door. "I just wanted to say I'm sorry. I didn't mean what I said. About not wanting you on the team."

"I know you didn't," said Xiao. "You would just prefer if it was *her*. Right?"

I hung my head in half-shame, half-frustration as I hammered the door again. "Kang! Open up."

"Just a second," he replied.

"What took you so long?" I asked, when he finally swung the door open.

"Sorry," said Kang. "It was our guest. She's awake."

As Kang led us into the room, I had to resist rubbing my eyes to make sure I was awake. That this wasn't some dream, hallucination or otherwise.

On the floor sat the librarian. But her hands were tied over her head, around the bedpost, with what looked like silk pantyhose used as binding. Over her eyes was a blindfold that had the words, 'Be Naughty,' printed across the front. And in her mouth was the type of ball-gag that gave me flashbacks of the weirdest scene in Pulp Fiction.

"Dude!" I slammed the door shut behind us. "What the hell is this?"

"What?" said Kang, with a look of somewhat genuine innocence, before looking back at the librarian and turning sheepish. "Oh. Oh! No. Come on guys. It's not what it looks like. I just needed to restrain her. These were all I could find in this place."

Xiao had obviously passed the point where she could even express her exasperation. All she did was wave a hand in my direction as she looked to the ceiling.

"Zeke," she sighed. "Talk to your boy. He's an idiot. And I'm going to bed."

As Xiao clambered up onto the deep windowsill and propped a pillow up behind her head, I pulled Kang aside. "What is going on? Why is she tied up?"

"I had to," said Kang. "She woke up kicking and screaming. She even—"

Kang was drowned out by the librarian's mumbling as she tried to protest something with the gag in her mouth.

"I'm taking that out," I said, as I leant down and reached around the back of her neck. "Stay calm. I'm taking this gag off. I'm not going to hurt you. Okay?"

The librarian went still as I unclipped the gag and chucked it under the bed, along with the blindfold. "Be careful," said Kang. "She bit me, you know."

"Because you put your hand over my mouth," said the librarian. "And said, 'if you want to live, you'll do as I say.'"

"Okay," said Kang, as I glowered at him. "I can see why that might be interpreted as hostile. But that's not what I meant. What I was trying to say, was that we're all in danger. So you really need to stay quiet."

"Danger?" she said. "What danger?"

"It's alright," I replied, eyeing the formidable knot that Kang had tied around her wrists. As eager as I was to untie her, perhaps it was time to start thinking things through properly. "I'm sorry about my friend. But you're not in danger. Not right now, anyway."

"Then why do we have to be quiet?" she asked.

"Trust me. I'll explain everything, Avy."

Though I was trying not to stare too noticeably at her, I flinched when her eyes shot up at me.

"How do you know my name?" she asked.

"What?" She had caught me off guard.

"My name. Who told you that?" Just like the maid had given her game away back at the other hotel, I'd slipped up and thrown away any reason she had to be comfortable with me.

"I uh…" I was lacking anything close to a reasonable explanation. "I have your phone," I said, pulling it out of my jacket pocket and resting it on the ground beside her.

"You went through my phone?"

"In my defence, you really should change your passcode," I joked. She didn't look impressed. "Help me out here," I turned to Xiao for help. "Xiao?" I should have been surprised that she was asleep already, but once Xiao had decided she was done, there was little to nothing that could keep her awake.

"And you expect me to trust you?! You have me tied up God knows where and you want me to just do what you say? Who are you people!?" Her bright golden eyes seemed to redden like fire as she expressed her contempt for us.

"Seriously?" said Kang. "She's completely forgotten us already."

"Maybe you have a concussion," I said.

"There is nothing wrong with me," she growled. "I remember you from the library. I meant *who* are you? What do you want with me?"

With all that had happened last night, I found it a little hard to believe she could recall anything at all. "Then what's the last thing you remember?"

"I remember *you* three." Her eyes were like daggers as she nodded at each of us. "You came to the library and started banging on the glass. I wasn't going to let you in, but there was some.. thing chasing you. So I opened the doors."

"And then what happened?"

The fire in her eyes dimmed as she looked, searchingly, from left to right, then back at me. "I... don't really remember. There was a dog. Only it wasn't a dog. And there was this gemstone. Only it wasn't a gemstone."

I contemplated leaving her to wonder what had happened. Maybe it was the safest thing to do. But I honestly still didn't know what *had* happened? We needed answers. *I* needed answers.

"You're talking about this?" I pulled the stone from my pocket and held it in front of her.

"Yeah." She nodded quickly. "That's it."

"You don't remember picking this up?"

"No."

"And you don't remember using it to burn that dog to ashes?"

"What?" she exclaimed. "No. I think I would remember something like that."

"Well." I put the stone away. "That's what happened. At least, that's what it looked like happened."

"Listen." The librarian rattled the bed as she shook her hands. "Untie me. Please? Just let me go? I promise I won't tell anybody anything about whatever you're up to. I don't even know anything to tell. Please?"

I really did want to untie her. She didn't deserve to be treated like a hostage, but Xiao said I should start using my head. And letting her wander off now, was not the smart move.

"I promise to untie you. And then you can go free. But I can't just yet. Pretty soon, our flight is going to be ready. And once we're safely on our way to the airport, you're free to go wherever you want and tell whatever story you want."

She looked terrified, as if she would weep at any moment. But there were no tears and no further eye contact of any sort. Instead, she looked resigned to whatever fate she thought she was in store for.

"Zeke." Kang backed away to the other side of the room and beckoned for me to follow. "So, what's the deal? When is our flight?"

"Change of plan," I said. "We're not taking a commercial flight. We're waiting on a private jet."

"No way?" Kang's eyes lit up like a boy who'd just unwrapped the present he had always wanted on his birthday. "Pierceson sent a jet? About time we started getting the exec level treatment."

"Nah. That's not it." I could barely summon the positive energy to correct him and tell the disappointing truth. "Not Pierceson. The jet is Camilla's."

"Camilla?" Kang didn't look as offended as I thought he should. "She's... helping us? Why?"

"The same old why. She wants in on the stone. And whatever it might lead to."

"Ah. Makes sense." Kang stroked the stubble that had started to show around his neatly groomed beard. "Seriously though," his voice went up an octave. "She uses a private jet?"

"I know right? We seriously need to start one-upping her one of these days."

"Xiao?" said Kang, as he bumped fists with me. "You up already?"

I turned to find Xiao pushing past me and opening the door. "Can't sleep with you two yapping. I'll be in the hall. Keeping an eye out."

The door slammed shut before Kang or I could persuade her otherwise.

"She seems angry," said Kang.

"I know," I replied.

"No. I mean angrier than usual. And what happened to her shoes?"

"Nevermind. It's Camilla's... Well. It's my fault. I'll talk to her later."

"So in the meantime, we're just going to sit here and wait? For Camilla? You're sure about this?"

"No. I think it's one of the worst decisions we've ever made. But it's all we've got."

"In that case." Kang laid down on the bed and pulled the cover over his head. "It's your turn to watch her. I'm getting some sleep."

It only took Kang a few minutes to start snoring, leaving me to slump down to the floor and sit opposite the librarian. Who in reality, had become our hostage.

"So," I said, determined to break the silence and hopefully restore some goodwill. "Avy. That's an interesting name."

"If I can make fire," she said, ignoring my statement completely. "Then why don't I just burn these off my wrists. Then do the same to you. And your friends."

"Ah." I laughed. "Well, first of all, it wasn't exactly fire. It was more like some kind of light. Or laser. Second, it happened when you touched the stone."

"Then why don't you keep your stupid stone and let me go. I can't hurt you."

She was so bitter now, she hardly seemed like the same girl who had helped me, or at least attempted to, in the library two nights ago. A cloud of disdain had descended over her bubbly demeanour and I could hardly blame her.

"For the record." I paused to make sure Kang was still snoring. "I don't think you're dangerous. I wanted to leave you in a hospital. But my friends are a little more suspicious. This whole thing with the museum, the dog, the stone. They're just afraid that whatever this 'Ten Thunderbolts' mess that we've gotten ourselves into is, it's going to get us killed."

"Wait." As she looked up, the cloud seemed to have parted and once again the innocent and bright-eyed librarian sat in front of me. "You said the 'Ten Thunderbolts?' I've heard that somewhere before."

I could hardly overlook the opportunity to raise an eyebrow. "No, you haven't."

"Excuse me?"

"If you had, you would have mentioned it when I asked you about this at the library."

Her face looked as if I had just tried to explain the Dichotomy Paradox to her.

"I told you," she said. "I don't remember what happened at the library."

There was no way that she could be this forgetful. Was there?

"Not last night," I explained. "The night before."

Still, she looked perplexed. "When did we meet the night before?"

I consider myself a patient guy. But this girl was really beginning to push my buttons for the umpteenth time.

"Nevermind," I said, squeezing my palms as tight as I could. "What do you know about it?"

"Not the details, exactly. It was in a book I have at the library."

"I really wish you had told me about this when we were there."

"No," she shook her head. "It's not a regular library book. My dad kept a bunch of old journals. He mentioned this in one of them." She jerked her hands away from the bedpost once more. "If you just untie me, we can go back and–"

"We can't go back to the library."

"Why not?" Her eyes grew suspicious, but this wasn't the best time to break yet more bad news to her.

"We just can't," I said.

"Then I can't really help you," she replied. "Can I?"

I was losing her. And I had to get some kind of information before she decided to shut me out again. If she knew just one useful thing about this stone, it could help us explain why the woman that killed Ealing was so desperate to get her hands on it.

"Come on. If you've read about it, you must remember something? Anything?"

I figured she wouldn't reply, but to my surprise, after a few moments of deep thought, she nodded at me.

"The only thing I remember from my dad's notes is how the story ends. The part after the Gods die."

"You mean, the Gods dying isn't the end of the story?" I asked. "Then, what happens next?"

"Like all undying things," she said. "They rise again."

ACT VI

THE WARMING OPHIS

'And there the children of dark Night have their dwellings, Sleep and Death, awful gods. The glowing Sun never looks upon them with his beams, neither as he goes up into heaven, nor as he comes down from heaven. And the former of them roams peacefully over the earth and the sea's broad back and is kindly to men; but the other has a heart of iron, and his spirit within him is pitiless as bronze: whomsoever of men he has once seized he holds fast: and he is hateful even to the deathless gods.'

Deathless. That's how Hesiod recited them. Gods and Goddesses so eternal that even Thanatos, the literal embodiment of death, could not claim them. But what is death to a God?

'Everyone dies, Ezekiel.' My mum made sure I knew that. 'They leave this life and, depending on their deeds, take the next step in their journey.'

I believed her, then. When I was a child. But life is a harsh critic on your beliefs. Still, there were few, if any, myths that chronicled the death of an Olympian. So even if this 'Ten Thunderbolt' sensation were true, about them being defeated, Avy could still be right about their resurrection.

And whoever was interested in staking a claim to this potential new myth was willing to kill Ealing, and all of us, to take credit for it. Admittedly, my curiosity in the subject was reaching its zenith, too. But my interest lay less in the stone. The Thunderbolt. Whatever we were calling the supposedly magic gem I kept harmlessly in my jacket pocket. No. What I valued was the myth itself. Myths were ridiculous sensationalism, make no mistake of that. And yet, they were invaluable in what they could teach us about the culture that believed in them. That invented them. So my concern laid in the question yet to be answered. Or even asked.

If the Gods weren't dead, where were they?

"I can't go with you standing there." Avy's voice interrupted my train of thought.

"You can't even see me," I replied, leaning against the outside of the closed bathroom door. "And I certainly can't see you."

"Doesn't matter. I still know you're there."

"Seriously?" I rubbed my eyes as I felt the claws of fatigue scratching at them. "It's been nearly five minutes. Aren't you finished?"

"Did you hear me pee?" she asked.

"Uh. No."

"Then no, I'm not finished. Am I?"

"Okay. Okay." I really didn't have the patience to go on fighting her. "If I go sit on the bed, can you hurry up?"

"No promises," she replied, as I dragged my feet over to the bed and sunk down. "Are you gone?" she asked.

"See." I threw my hands in the air. "You can't even tell. I'm on the bed."

"Good."

Even from across the room, I could still hear her peeing.

"Okay. Cuff me kidnapper," she said, as she emerged from the bathroom.

"Take a seat." I pointed at the hard leather armchair in the corner.

"Really?" There was a more familiar twinkle in her eyes. "No more bondage?"

"Stop calling it that. And yeah, no more. Just sit down and please don't do anything that means I have to tie you up again."

"I won't," she said, turning up her nose as she inspected the chair. "Don't suppose you have a black light?"

I smiled, for the first time in what felt like days. "Better off not knowing."

"Right," she chuckled. As she sat and stretched up high, free of Kang's sordid bindings, I tried my best not to stare. But really, she was undeniably attractive. Scratch that, she was hot.

"What?" she asked, looking back at me. Clearly my attempts at obstinance had failed.

"Nothing." I shied away, desperate to try and change the subject. "It's just, you said you worked at the library. You never said you owned it."

"I don't," she replied. "My dad does."

"But you're the manager."

She shrugged. "Yeah. So?"

"Again. That seems like important information."

"Maybe. But also, do I have to announce myself? My title? What difference does it make? Or is it that you only judged me on my looks and took me for some dumb student who is just in it for the paycheque?"

"No. Not at all. I literally just thought you were the librarian on a night shift. Believe me, as a young black guy, studying to be an archaeologist, and having to talk to a thousand old white dudes every week, I make a point not to judge people solely on their appearance. That would make me one hell of a hypocrite."

"I guess," she raised her eyebrows in what looked like contempt. "You still think I'm an idiot though. I can tell."

"Again," I said with a dismissive swipe of my hands. "I do not. But... you do seem to be a little... forgetful." Instantly, her expression fell from stern defiance to passive vulnerability. "Sorry. I didn't mean it as an insult."

"It's fine," she replied. "I *am* forgetful. But that doesn't stop me from being good at my job. I've run this library with my dad for years."

"That's incredible." I nodded. "Where is he now?"

"Retired. Back in Izmir."

"Izmir?" said Kang, as he shuffled out from under the covers and stifled a yawn. "Turkey, right? Aegean coast."

Turkish? I wouldn't have guessed that.

"Izmir? Is that where you're from?" I asked. "I can't really place your accent."

"Yeah. I've lived there with my dad for as long as I can remember. I'm not really sure why I don't have an accent like his. Dad thinks it's because we travelled a lot when I was young. I've spent endless hours listening to American and British experts drone on about the past. Also, western movies are great."

"You like movies? Which ones?"

"The classics."

"Like Clash of the Titans?" Kang replied. "That's my favourite. Or Spartacus."

"Original or TV show?" I asked.

"Original," Kang scoffed. "Still, Ben Hur is better.

"The Charlton Heston one, right?"

"Of course. The reboot was terrible. Bunch of pretenders," Kang said, deepening his voice to mimic the way Pierceson would voice his disdain for fantasy movies.

"Uh... I was thinking more like The Devil Wears Prada," Avy interrupted. "And Legally Blonde."

"Oh," said Kang, stepping out of the bed and pushing against the window frame to finish his stretches. "The *classics*. You should check out How to Lose a Guy in Ten Days. Hudson and McConaughey are electric."

Somehow, even at a time like this, Kang had managed to find an angle to flirt with her.

"I'd love to," said Avy, crossing her arms. "If you ever let me go, that is."

I can't pretend watching him fail didn't bring me at least a little joy. I'd certainly find an opportunity to rub that in later.

"Hey," I said. "Stay focused. And stay away from the windows."

"I'm checking for anything strange," Kang replied. "You want to end up surrounded before we realise it? This is hardly Nakatomi Plaza. There are only so many places to hide."

"Alright, alright. Good point." I joined Kang by the window. "See anything?"

"Nope. Looks clear."

"Zeke," Avy called out to me. "Do you have anything to eat? I'm starving."

"Uh." To be honest I hadn't even thought about food. And only realised how my own stomach growled now that she had mentioned it. "Kang?"

"When do you think I had time to pick up food?" he replied. "They don't serve fugitives at McDonalds."

"Can we order room service?" asked Avy.

"In this place?" Kang replied. "They'll probably just bring us a strawberry flavoured cond–"

"Okay." I put my hand over Kang's mouth before he could say anything vulgar enough to embarrass all three of us. "I think I saw a vending machine in the lobby. I can go get us some snacks at least. Anything specific you want, Avy?"

"Chocolate," she instantly replied.

"Just chocolate?" I asked.

"Well... whatever else they have." Her cheeks reddened as she broke eye contact. "But chocolate would be great too."

"Alright," I said with a smile. "Chocolate it is. Kang? How about you man?" Though I was speaking only a few centimetres from Kang's face, it seemed like he hadn't heard me. Instead, he was staring intently through the window at the rooftop opposite. "What is it?" Quickly I switched into high-alert as I half-ducked and surveyed the scene outside. "Police?"

"You have to see this," he finally replied. "Quick. Over there. On the gutter." His fingertip tapped the glass frantically as he pointed.

"What am I supposed to be looking at?" I wondered, squinting at the roof opposite.

"There," he stressed, as if whatever he was pointing out were obvious.

I took one final look before groaning in frustration. "I don't see anything. Just an empty roof and a bird."

"No, that's it. The bird. Doesn't it look weird to you? Bright blue feathers. Even the beak looks blue."

"What?"

"I'm being serious. Look at it. What species of bird is that even? I don't trust it."

I don't know if it was the exasperation or our predicament, the fatigue from barely getting any sleep over the past few nights. or simply the fact that a strange looking bird seemed entirely irrelevant in this or any situation. The only thing I know is that it was as close to punching Kang in the face as I'd been since we were about seven years old.

"Listen to me, Kang," I started, exercising the kind of restraint that deserved a Nobel peace prize. "I am going to go downstairs and get us something to eat. And I need you to watch out for things that are *actually* suspicious. Like magical killers, two-headed monsters or a police SWAT team. So unless you've suddenly become an ornithologist in the last few days, you better not mention anything about birds to me again. Otherwise, you're going to find out what having that gag in your mouth feels like. Got it?"

Kang nodded. Silently.

"Good." I started across the room. "And one more thing. I'm getting you a lime soda."

I couldn't find Xiao anywhere. Not on the couch in the hall. Not at the large window seats by the lift. And not even when I reached the lobby. There wasn't much reason to worry. Yet. She could have been in one of the public restrooms. Maybe she'd come down to the vending machines and I'd missed her while in the lift. She might even have gone for a walk around the building, just to blow off steam from our argument. I know my own harsh words still left a taste in my mouth that I was eager to wash away. Whatever the reason, Xiao was the last person who would do anything stupid to put herself at risk. If I couldn't find her in another ten minutes or so, then and only then would it be the time to panic.

Pushing her temporarily from my thoughts, I tried not to look too suspicious as I sped across the lobby towards the back corner. The only person around was the disinterested clerk on the front desk; too busy playing on his phone to even look up unless someone directly approached.

I searched my pocket for one of the nordic gold coins I'd stashed away, and eyeballed the machine for the first chocolate bar I could find.

"A Twix," I said aloud, my thoughts fading from my errand and being cast back to an altogether simpler time.

After a quick glance at my watch, I reached for my phone and swiped up to the number that I knew would reach my sister. After being kept on hold for a few minutes, I was finally transferred to the guest line where a hardened voice spoke for the first time.

"Bookz?" she said. "Is that you little bro?"

"Relle," I replied, unable to hide the grin that always accompanied hearing my sister speak. "Yeah, it's me."

"You're off schedule," Sherelle replied. "What's wrong? Is mum okay?"

"She's fine. Nothing's wrong. Sorry, I didn't mean to scare you. Just... saw a Twix and thought of you." It wasn't an especially good reason, but in my current predicament I honestly just felt compelled to talk with someone who knew how to navigate tricky situations better than most. "You used to steal 'em from Dad's bag and split 'em with me. Remember?"

"I remember that you would eat yours in a split-second then beg for half of mine too. I kinda miss the tubby little shit you were."

"Got no idea what you're on about," I replied with a chuckle. "What's poppin? Ya know, on the inside?"

"It's prison, little bro. It's proper shit. And don't 'what's poppin' me. You're an educated man, and I know you don't chat to your mates that way. So did you call me just for the small-talk? Not that I mind or nothin', but you usually only call me to brag innit."

"You love when I brag. You ask for it."

That wasn't an exaggeration. Sherelle really did ask for it. All she ever wanted to hear was the stories of where I'd been, what I'd found, and how brilliantly it was all going. She said it was the closest thing she got to being outside. That it made her feel free. And so I told her every detail, from the sublime to the mundane.

"So why aren't you doing it?" she asked. "What's wrong?"

Incarceration certainly hadn't dulled my sister's intellect. Her problem had always been that she wasn't 'book smart,' like she claimed I was. Something her nickname for me would never let me forget. But, contrary to what most people understood about her, including our mum, the reason she was in there and I was out here was because she was 'street smart.'

Still, after rushing into the phone call, I quickly realised I couldn't tell Sherelle what I had gotten myself into. If she knew I'd potentially gotten myself in trouble with the authorities, she'd never forgive me. Not after everything she'd done for me.

"Nothing," I replied. "Well, not nothing. It's just... this lead I'm following. Things aren't exactly going how I expected."

"So what?" Sherelle sounded unimpressed. "Listen Bookz, you're not at school anymore. In the real world, nothin' happens like you want. All this globetrottin' you're doin', when you gonna' learn to accept things that you can't control?"

"I guess I need someone older and wiser to keep reminding me."

Being locked up had changed my sister. Not fundamentally. She was still the same music-loving, wise-cracking, hard-headed girl she had always been. But she finally seemed less... angry. It seems that time had been the only thing that would ease the pain of what happened with Dad. If only she had been able to spend that time out here with us, instead of in there with nobody.

After a few more minutes chatting with her about nothing in particular, I decided to get back to the mission at hand before I let something slip that would cause her to worry.

"Look, I have to go," I said. "But I'll call again at the usual time."

"Alright," she replied. "But listen, don't be calling me up randomly unless summin' is wrong. You made my heart skip a beat."

"Understood. And I'll visit soon."

"No rush on that," she said after a slight pause. "Just... keep living your life, innit. You know that's all I ever ask you to do. You're this family's shining knight. So... shine."

"I know. Bye, Relle."

"Talk soon, Bookz."

I slipped the phone back into my pocket, feeling so much better for taking a moment to distance myself from the madness, then returned to my errand of fetching snacks.

"Sweet tooth?" said a voice from behind me.

Though it didn't sound familiar, I spun immediately wondering if I might find Xiao scowling back at me and looking displeased with my decision to venture out of the room alone, then spend time chatting away on the phone. Instead, sitting in a chair I was certain had been empty not seconds ago, was a woman. She definitely wasn't Xiao, but she *was* familiar.

"I'm more of a savoury girl myself," she said.

"You!" I cursed, when I realised who I was looking at. The maid from the Imperial Atlus.

"Why don't you sit down?" she demanded, when she realised I was already backing away.

"The hell I will." The only thought racing through my head was to run as fast as I could. To get back to my friends. To warn them that someone had found us. But as I pondered the fastest route back upstairs, I felt the rough material of the chair in the palms of my hands, gripping the armrests. Somehow, I was already sitting in the chair opposite her.

"That's better," she said, her voice perilously intimate. "Comfy?"

"How... how did you do that?" Something was very wrong. I couldn't remember sitting down. Or even thinking about the chair.

"Me?" she replied. "I haven't done a thing. Clearly, you're feeling tired. And a few minutes of relaxation are all you desire. Right?"

As she spoke, my vision began to darken and my eyelids felt as if they were being slammed shut.

"No," I shouted, shaking my head and regaining my focus. My voice echoed through the empty lobby, drawing my attention to just how vulnerable my position was. While the woman's chair faced towards the back of the room, mine was the opposite. Leaving me exposed in plain view of anyone who might waltz into the hotel at any moment.

"You alright?" I heard the receptionist say, as he leant over his desk and cocked his head at me.

"You're fine, right?" said the woman, just as I prepared to yell the complete opposite.

"I'm fine," I repeated, with deadpan delivery. I'd never been so confused. I'd formed the words perfectly in my head. 'No! Get help! There's a woman here trying to kill me.' But my own tongue had betrayed me, wrapping the words into sentences I had no control over.

"You were going to tattle on me," she said. "And I thought we were hitting it off."

"What are you?" I snarled. "Some kind of hypnotist? Suggesting thoughts into my subconscious?"

The woman burst into laughter, not so loud that the receptionist might overhear. But hysterically enough to really get under my skin.

"They said you'd do this," she cackled. "Said you didn't believe in us. All science and no substance, aren't you?"

"What are you talking about?" I said, willing my muscles into action but finding them disobedient.

"You still think this is some kind of trick." The woman leaned forward in her seat and cupped my cheek with her hand. "A scheme. A deception. But, little Zeke. We are everything you pretend doesn't exist. When you reach the end of the thread, where your facts and findings unravel. We are the invisible hand that pulls your yarn tight."

Only as the woman spoke, staring hungrily at me as if I were her next appetiser, did the wheels in my head turn and pull my memory back into reach.

"So you're with her," I said. "The woman from the museum. She did things I couldn't explain too." Still, my arms and legs wouldn't budge. "Are you going to kill me? Why didn't you just do it back at the other hotel? Posing as a maid, you could have taken me by surprise then, Marina."

The woman shook her head. "That wasn't me. If it were, you would be dead already. And my name is Kerrel."

While I pondered what she meant by it not being her, I noticed the feeling in my limbs starting to return. Warm blood in my feet and at my fingers. Sure, her hair was different. Dyed blonde and worn free, thick and curly. But her face was the same. Big brown eyes. Petite smile. Exactly the same.

"So, how are you keeping me here?" I asked.

"I told you," she replied. "I'm not doing anything. The only thing keeping you here, is you. You want to stay. All I have to do is ask."

For the first time, I knew what she meant. Each time I had felt my will sapped, my actions stripped from my control, she had asked a question. Regardless of what she implied, it was the power of suggestion. She was tricking me into doing as she wanted. All I needed to do was figure out how to ignore her. Or make her ask something she couldn't predict the outcome of.

"Then why aren't I sleeping?" I wondered. "I'm certainly tired."

Finally, the smug look on her face was wiped clean, though her eyes still twinkled with intrigue.

"Good question. I've never seen anyone with resistance quite like yours. Most of your kind wilt like flowers with just the slightest hint of inception."

"My kind?" Though I knew it's not what she meant, her complexion was as dark as my own after all, I'd heard phrases like that too often to like the way she said it. And regardless of why she said it, it usually implied the same thing. Superiority.

"Mortals," she continued. "Humans."

The moment the words left her lips, my trepidation began to lift. I had thought this woman, Kerrel, to be some kind of professional assassin, or part of some secret organisation of artefact collectors like in the Uncharted or Tomb Raider games. Instead, here she was claiming to be some kind of... what? Mythical creature? Fantasy monster? It was ridiculous.

"I see." It was worth playing her game until my willpower was restored. "You're not *my kind*, then? So, what are you?"

"They always ask that." Her eyes narrowed like a poisonous snake. "*What are you?* You aren't like them, so you're just a *thing*. Your kind were always so pious. It's the reason I have so little sympathy for what I'm going to do to you once you give me what I came for."

"And what did you come for?"

"The stone. Give it to me."

I smiled, for the first time knowing I had the upper hand. "No."

Placing a hand over each of my wrists, she yanked forward; jolting me and the entire chair towards her with ease. "You have it, right? Give it to me."

This time I shook my head, slowly. "Nope."

"Alright." She licked her lips. Not seductively. More like the way my 6 year-old nephew does while my mum plates up his next meal. "You still think this is a game. That this isn't real. Maybe you need a little more incentive," she said, rising from her seat and turning to look over the top of her chair. "You!" she shouted, towards the front of the lobby. "Come here," she beckoned, as the receptionist leaned forwards over his counter once more.

The pale-skinned man sauntered down to the back of the lobby, where he looked down at me. "Is there a problem?" he asked, switching his confused gaze between the two of us.

"Not at all," the woman replied, reaching behind her back. A second later, she was caressing a small six or seven-inch black tube, decorated with blood-red flowers. Only as she pressed her thumb against one end and began to slide it upwards, did I realise what she was cradling.

"Run!" I shouted at the man.

"You don't want to run," the woman promptly replied, wrapping her hand around the handle of a short blade as it slipped silently out of the tube-like sheath. "You're here to help, right? To do your job?"

"Yes," he replied, wearing the same look of puzzlement that I probably had when I found myself no longer in control.

"Good. Then stay right there," she continued.

In one lightning quick motion, almost too fast for me to follow, she zipped forward and thrust the blade into his neck, before snapping back to where she had been standing. For a few seconds, the man didn't move. He stared, emptily, back at her before turning back to me as his arm wearily clutched at the wound on his neck. Blood began to seep out, pouring through his fingers and raining down on the matching coloured carpet.

"No!" I shouted, as he fell, not guarding himself as he slammed headfirst into the ground. He didn't move again. "What have you done!? He had nothing to do with us. Or the stone!"

"Don't lecture me," she shouted, lifting her heel and slamming it down on my knee. "You got him killed. By not cooperating."

The sight of her, a murderer, already disgusted me. And yet her grotesque display was far from done. She lifted the blade, resting the tip between her lips, and swiping it along her tongue. Like a wine connoisseur, she swirled his blood around in her mouth, only to spit it to the ground, colouring my boots dark-crimson as it splashed.

"Yuck," she cried. "Anaemic. He needed a better diet. Now, unless you want to be next. Give me the stone."

"You're insane!" I shouted.

"No. I'm hungry."

"Zeke?" I was too busy recoiling from the vile woman to hear the hotel door swing open, ringing the bell in the process. When I looked up, Xiao was standing by reception; her eyes wide with shock as she surveyed the scene.

"What's going on?" she demanded.

"Xiao, stay back!" I yelled. Finally, I felt the freedom of my body restored, having resisted her questioning. Launching up from my chair, I speared into the woman's torso and knocked her back against the vending machine. Not bothering to check on how much damage I had inflicted, I sprinted towards Xiao and grabbed her by the hand.

"We have to move," I said. "She's another killer."

"Zeke." Xiao was still looking past me. "She's gone." I spun on my heels, searching the lobby. But it really was empty. "What's going on?"

"I don't know," I replied. "But we have to get out of here. Now. I'm going to get the others. Can you try and flag down a taxi?"

"Are you sure?" Xiao gripped my wrist tight as I tried to pull away.

"I'll be fine," I said, patting her on the hand before wriggling free. "Just make sure we have a way out of here."

Ignoring the lift, I sprinted up the stairs as fast as my legs could carry me. I had to get to Kang and Avy before she could. I didn't have the stone with me. That's the only answer I could think of as to why her suggestions hadn't worked on me. She was asking the wrong questions. But if she had figured that out, then the others were in danger.

Finally, I rounded the corner and burst out onto our floor. Sprinting past door after identical door, I skidded to a halt in front of the room at the end of the hall. The doors didn't have numbers or letters, just labels. 'Mistress Hera,' ours was aptly named, but I needn't have checked the plaque. The door was already wide open.

Panting, I barreled through the doorway and came face to face with the woman again. Her arm was clamped around Kang's throat as she pressed her blade against the side of his neck and scowled at me. How was she moving around so fast? She wasn't even short of breath.

Quickly, I scanned the room for Avy and found her huddled down by the bathroom door.

"Hey." I thrust my hand out towards her.

Avy leapt up and squeezed my fingers so tight I thought they might break as I dragged myself between her and this murderous woman.

"Let him go," I shouted.

In response, the woman ran the tip of her blade down Kang's neck, drawing blood then licking the fresh wound with her tongue.

"Much better," she said. "He's a keeper."

"Don't hurt him," I pleaded.

"Then get me the stone," she replied. "It's in here, right? You don't have it on you?"

As I tried to find the perfect words to divert her, it was as if there was a second voice in my head, searching for the truth. Forbidding me from deceiving her.

"Yes."

"And you're going to show me where it's hidden, right?" She lowered the blade directly under Kang's chin this time, threatening to slice his throat open.

"Yes. I will."

I didn't try to resist her questioning this time. And I didn't have to. She had just dangled the slightest hope of escape in front of us. Kang often warned against keeping close the very thing that made you valuable.

'Not having it,' he would always say, 'but knowing its location, was like wearing a suit of armour. They kill you, and it's lost forever.' I was happy to admit that on this occasion, he had been right. Now we just needed his meticulous preparation to pay off.

"It's in the safe," I said.

"And the code?" she urged.

Just before I answered, I chanced one final look at Kang. Not at his predicament - the blade against his neck. But at his eyes. And when he made eye contact with me, his single glance down, rather than at the safe, was all I needed to comply.

"One. Nine. Eight. Six."

"You wouldn't lie to me?" she asked, rolling her blade against Kang's skin. "Right? If it's wrong, he dies."

Any outward confidence I was portraying betrayed the dryness of my throat and trembling of my clenched fists.

"It's right."

Still dragging Kang along, the woman stepped over to the safe and loosened her grip on my friend.

"You open it," she ordered.

Kang didn't hesitate, punching in the numbers on the safe and waiting for it to chime. A second later, the door popped open and the quiet ding sounded in the silent room. As Kang reached into the safe, the woman released her grip on him and hurled him across the room. He flew like a ragdoll, slamming against the chest of drawers.

Despite my eagerness to rush to his aid, I held still waiting for her to inspect the contents of the safe. She reached in and quickly withdrew a closed hand. Only when she started to unfurl her fingers did I dart towards Kang and drag him up to his feet.

"What's this?" said the woman, as she inspected the contents. But it was too late. A puff of smoke erupted from her palm, wafting up into her face. She tried to turn away, but she was caught off guard and found herself shaking her head to dispel its effects.

"Let's go!" I shouted at Avy, shoving her out of the door as I pulled Kang along behind us.

"That wasn't your stone," shouted Avy, as we rushed down the stairs.

"Nope," said Kang. "Chloroform pouch. I switched it for the stone the moment Zeke left the room. Old trick of ours. Operation lime soda."

"Right... I wondered who on earth would want lime soda. But chloroform? I thought you were archaeologists? Not secret agents?"

"I love lime soda. And we are archaeologists. Apprentices anyway. And Pierceson gives these get out of jail cards to all his students. You never know who is out to rob you in this line of work. I just hope it knocked her out. We've never actually pulled that off before."

"What?! You two are just winging it!?"

"Can we talk about this later!" I said, as we rounded the last corner and hurried into the lobby.

"We can talk about it now," said an all-too-familiar voice as I looked up at reception.

It was impossible. The vial had burst right in her face. If she had inhaled even half of it she should be unconscious. Not to mention we had just sprinted down the only stairwell in the building. So how could this woman be waiting for us at the front desk? It was impossible.

"That was rude," she said, stepping towards me and placing her hand on my chest. A second later, I was flying over a table and crashing through a glass vase. As if I had just been hit by a moving vehicle. Though my leather jacket did a good job of protecting me from the shattered shards, I could feel dozens of tiny needles against my palm as I pressed myself back up.

"Where's the stone?" she asked again, dragging me up by the collar and flattening me against the wall. Gone were the subtle suggestions and teasing quips. Gone were the murderous threats and deadly ultimatums. All that remained was rage. A rage directed solely at me.

"Get off him," yelled Kang, leaping onto the woman's back. With a casual wave of her arm, she sent him tumbling across the lobby and slamming against the wall.

"Fine," said the woman. I could barely breathe as she leant more heavily against my throat, but I could still see her reaching around for the blade I knew she kept at her back. "Once you're dead, one of your friends can find it for me."

"Leave him alone." It was Avy rushing towards us this time.

The woman took one look over her shoulder at the slight librarian, then ignored her to focus back on me. She probably thought Avy was no threat. I was inclined to agree with her, given the unbelievable strength she had used to brush Kang and I aside. But as Avy approached her from behind, she thrust both arms out at the woman to push her.

The next thing I knew, I was gasping dramatically for air as the hands around my neck vanished. Avy was standing over me, mirroring my look of perplexion with her attention turned towards the back of the room. The woman had been tossed across the lobby, fifteen metres or so, and crashed through the vending machine glass where she lay unconscious.

"What did you do?" I said.

"Nothing," she replied. "I... I just tried to push her. And then... I dunno."

"But–"

"Hey!" shouted Xiao, her head poking through the front door of the hotel. "What's going on? Are you three coming!?"

"Yeah." I frowned once more at Avy before brushing past her and helping Kang up. "Let's get out of here while we still have the chance."

"Drive," said Xiao, as she hopped into the front seat of the cab and urged the driver to get moving.

In the back, Avy had squeezed in between Kang and I as she stared in bemusement at her own hands.

"How did I do that?" she said, more to herself than either of us.

"Nevermind," I replied. "Let's get as far as we can away from here before something else goes wrong."

"What the hell happened back there?" Xiao had twisted around in her chair to face us, even as the driver implored her to sit down. "Who was that woman?"

"Maybe we can talk about this later," I whispered with a nod towards the driver. "In private. Where are we even going?"

Xiao shrugged dramatically. "How should I know? I just told him we're looking for a new hotel on the other side of the city. Tell me what's happening."

"Later, Xiao. And where were you, anyway?"

"Excuse me?" Xiao went from irritated to insulted in a flash.

"Where were you? I came looking for you before that woman ambushed me. I could have used a little help."

"I was out getting some air. Away from you two and the trouble you seem to attract."

"Us?" said Kang. "How is this our fault?"

"You're the one who took the stone in the first place," I said. Apparently, he'd forgotten that part.

"Oh yeah? Well, you're the one who wanted to meet with Ealing to begin with. Xiao and I wanted to go home. Now I've got crazy dogs trying to eat me and women sticking knives in my neck."

"What knives?!" said Xiao.

"Can we just drop this for a second?" I couldn't hear myself think with the argument raging out of control. "We need to figure out where we're headed."

"I say we call Camilla," said Kang.

I rubbed my temples in frustration. Truly it seemed like there was no path that didn't lead to her at this point.

"Ah shit," said Xiao. She was facing forward again, only this time she was exchanging suspicious glances with the driver. Beyond them, where his phone was clipped to the dashboard, I could see a bulletin scrolling across his GPS app. It had each of our faces, Avy excepted, and though I couldn't read the non-English text, I'm pretty sure the translation was exactly what I thought.

Suddenly, the panicked driver started to shout in a language I couldn't understand.

"It's Turkish," said Avy. "He says we're wanted criminals. And he's... not happy. To put it mildly. I think he's going to kick us out."

"Sir." I wasn't sure if Xiao could understand him or not, but she was doing her best to stay calm and rational. "I promise you this is a misunderstanding." It was difficult to even hear her over the driver's frantic yelling. "We're not dangerous. If you could just– please– If we can. Hey!" she finally shouted, when he wouldn't let her get a word in. "Calm down. We're not going to hurt you. We just–"

"Lookout!" screamed Avy, pointing at the road ahead.

It all happened so fast, and so slow at the same time. There was someone on the road. The driver swerved. The car brushed just inches away from them. And as we skidded to the left and towards a lamppost, I was certain I'd seen the brown eyes and blonde hair of the woman we'd just left in the hotel.

"Are you alright?" I heard Avy's voice along with the brush of a silken hand on my face. "Zeke. Are you okay?" Gradually, I blinked away the darkness and shook off the daze. "Careful," she said. "You're bleeding."

I reached for a painful spot on my cheek. It stung when my fingers brushed against it, and a few specks of blood covered my fingertips when I pulled them away.

"What happened?" I asked.

"We crashed," said Avy, her voice growing more urgent by the second. "But we need to go. I think I saw that woman again. And I hear sirens."

My head was ringing so bad it was tough to focus on what she was saying.

"Okay." I reached for the door handle and pried it open.

"Ouch! Wait." I was slowly regaining my bearings when I heard Xiao's pained voice. "Slowly," she said.

Kang was in front of me, helping to pull her out of the front seat. Then I saw what was delaying him. Xiao's arm was badly swollen. Maybe even dislocated or broken. Either way, it looked horrific. Kang slipped her out of her seat and pulled her good arm around his neck.

"Okay," she said. "Now you can hurry."

I felt Avy wrapping a hand around my waist, hurrying me along.

"Come on," she said.

"What happened to the driver?" I asked.

"He ran."

"Why didn't you?"

Avy looked up at me, then shied away again. "I have no idea."

"Down this alley," said Kang, leading the way. "How did that lady catch up with us? How is she doing any of the things she's doing? And where is she now?"

"Questions later, remember," said Xiao. "Right now, we need to–"

The obnoxious blare of sirens cut Xiao short as a police car swerved into the end of the alley and blocked our path.

"Just do what they say," said Kang, as we stared down the collective barrels of several firearms being waved in our faces. He helped Xiao to her knees, as Avy too raised her hands above her head and slowly crouched down.

"Zeke!" Kang was whispering, though his voice was urgent. "Get down. Please."

Each officer was yelling something different, in incomprehensible Greek, and each weapon seemed to have found its focus solely on me. My head was telling me to be reasonable, to be smart. But my heart urged otherwise, reminding me of offences past. Injustices. Deaths. The police were no friends of the Lewis family.

But Kang was right. This time, *they* were right. As far anyone knew, we were dangerous killers. And provoking them was only going to get me killed.

"Alright," I said, reaching my hands slowly behind my head. "I'm surrendering." Kang gave me a nod, half 'thank-you' and half 'you-idiot,' as I settled down beside him. I gritted my teeth as one of the officers grabbed me by the shoulder and shoved my face into the concrete while cuffing me.

"Hey!" said Kang, just as another offered him the same treatment. "You can't treat us like this. We haven't done anything wrong." Xiao cried out in pain up ahead, as they manhandled her busted arm and forced her into a pair of cuffs. "Take it easy!" Kang yelled. "She's hurt."

"They're not going to listen," I said.

Kang ignored me as he shouted out again. "Hey! Leave her alone, she's got nothing to do with this."

This time I looked up and saw Avy being pinned against the ground.

"She's innocent!" I shouted.

"They decide who is innocent," said the officer behind me, as they pulled me up by the shoulder and spun me around.

My rage turned to fear when I saw who was looking back at me. The same brown eyes. The same dark skin. But the hair had changed, again. Black, braided and tied back beneath the police cap she was wearing. In fact, she was clad head to toe in uniform as she smiled back at me.

"Shut your eyes," she said.

I stared blankly back at her. Gone was her rage. Gone was her contempt. All that remained were a pair of soft-eyes, somehow imploring me to cooperate.

"What?" I asked.

"You hate the police," she said. "Do you want to be arrested? Or do you want to get out of this? Shut. Your. Eyes."

I'm not sure why, but I was strangely ready to trust her. I shut my eyes.

How long I was supposed to keep them shut, I didn't know. But I squeezed them tighter when she spoke, half expecting that blade of hers to pierce my throat.

"Gentlemen," she said. "Say cheese."

The dark inside of my eyelids lit up in a flash, like someone had just let off a firework in front of me. A rush of heat flushed against my cheeks as a buzz, almost like a wasp zipping by my ears, started and stopped just as quickly.

"Alright," she said. "You're good."

I assumed that was a sign to open my eyes, but I couldn't help but be apprehensive about what might be waiting for me when I did. My eyes sprung open involuntarily, however, when I heard Kang shout.

"What the hell just happened!?" he said, sitting up with his hands still fastened behind his back.

The officer next to him stood motionless. It took me a while to notice, but it wasn't just his feet or arms that didn't move. He wasn't blinking. His eyes were still. He didn't even breathe. As if he were completely frozen. I looked around at the other officers. Each was the same. All four of them stopped mid-whatever motion they were carrying out and locked in place as they stared straight at me. Then I realised, it wasn't me they had been looking at.

I rounded on the woman. "What did you do?"

"Nothing," she replied, with a somehow innocent smirk." They're just.... on a time-out."

"For how long?"

"Forever. If I want."

"Why are you helping us?" I demanded angrily. "You were trying to kill us a minute ago."

She rolled her eyes in exasperation. "That wasn't me, obviously."

"That was me." The click of heels along the stone sounded from further down the alley, as a second woman stepped out of the shadows.

I was tired. Hungry. Confused. And my heart had been pumping a mile a minute for some twenty-four hours. And yet, despite all that, I was fairly certain that there were two of the exact same woman standing in front of me. The only difference was that one seemed to want me alive. And the other *really* wanted me dead.

ACT VII

THE GORGONEION APOTROPE

'But still Penthesilea brake the ranks, and still before her quailed the Achaeans: still they found nor screen nor hiding-place from imminent death. As bleating goats are by the blood-stained jaws of a grim panther torn, so slain were they. In each man's heart all lust of battle died, and fear alone lived.'

As the bright-haired woman teased her blade from its sheath, verse after verse of Quintus Smyrnaeus poem cycled through my head. His account of the Amazonian warrioress, Penthesilea, painted her as a force of nature. A merciless death-dealer on the battlefield; feared by all. And while I'd grown up enjoying powerful female icons, like Buffy, Xena and Diana Prince, they often felt like the exception. Not the rule.

Physically, I don't know if I had ever truly feared a woman. Perhaps as a child, the belt of my grandmother and the iron grip of my mum. But those were threats. I feared the consequences. I never feared *them*. But in the past two days, the number of women who wanted me dead had doubled. One wished to snap my neck, through supposed magic. And the other sought only to run her sword through it.

Ironically, the only reason either of them had failed was because of the opposing women that continued to protect me. First, Xiao and her quick-thinking. Then, Avy and her still-inexplicable feats of heroism. And finally, a mystery woman protecting me from the police. And in the process, looking identical to the one I did fear.

"What are you doing here, Kerrel?" said the woman with the elegant dark braids coiling down over her shoulders.

"What does it look like?" the blonde replied. Kerrel. She hadn't lied about her name. "Someone has to punish these children. Clearly, it isn't going to be you. You were going to let them go, no doubt."

"They're not to be harmed. Mother's orders. You want to challenge her?"

"I don't care what mother said! Othrus is dead. Because of them. They killed him."

This time, the black-haired woman cut a far less sympathetic figure as she brushed a few braids from her eyes.

"We don't know that. Mother isn't sure what happened to him. Whatever it was, there's no way they could have done it."

"Of course they could," Kerrel erupted. "They have the thunderbolt."

"Which they can't use. No mortal can."

"For Hera's sake. Wake up, Kelis! They are more than they appear. Anyone who works for Pierceson is. And I don't care how they did it. If you won't avenge our brother, I will."

It was surreal. Listening to them argue. Like a scene displaced from my childhood imagination or an HBO fantasy. Both shock and intrigue pulsated through my head, as I soaked up the scattered pieces of their debate.

They spoke of both a mother and brother, which at least made them sisters. Kelis, my saviour, and Kerrel, my tormentor. Could this *mother* be the cloaked murderer from the museum? Why would she send anyone to protect us? And who was this brother they wanted to avenge? We certainly hadn't killed anyone. I had so many questions, but Kerrel didn't look like she was in any mood to provide answers.

"Are you really going to try to stop me?" said Kerrel, as her sister stepped across her path.

"You know I won't," Kelis replied. "But I'm asking you not to do this. Mother's wrath will be immeasurable."

"I don't care," said Kerrel, as she shoved her sister aside and marched towards me, her dark eyes narrowed like a starving wolf. "You first."

"Stop," said Xiao, attempting to step between us, only to be swatted aside.

Xiao hit the wall with such a sickening thud, I knew instantly something was wrong. My first instinct was to rush to her aid, but I was beaten to it. Kelis was already kneeling beside Xiao and checking on what looked like a broken arm.

"Have you lost your mind?" said Kelis. "What if you had killed her?"

"As if," Kerrel replied. "I barely touched her."

By this point, I really was confused. Kelis seemed even more concerned for Xiao's wellbeing than she had for mine earlier. Just what was her mission here? And why was her sister's goal so different?

"Zeke." I heard Avy's cautious whisper in my ear and turned to face her. She nodded her head once towards me. "The stone. Use it."

"What?" Though I understood the words she was saying, my mind took a while to catch up.

"You said it saved us before. Use it again."

She couldn't be serious. Could she? The stone wasn't magic. It was just that, a stone. Whatever happened back at the library, beit a power surge, a freak accident, or even some kind of hidden weapon inside the jewel, there was no way it was going to miraculously save us from this cut-throat murderer.

And yet, with no other option presenting itself, it felt as if there were nothing more to do but embrace the ridiculous. I reached into my jacket pocket and felt the smooth surface of the stone against my fingertips. I fidgeted around it for a second more, unsure of my next move, before clutching it firmly and dragging it out of the pocket.

Kerrel's brown eyes grew large when she saw it, yet she didn't break stride or sheathe her sword. Every step she drew closer brought the truth into better perspective. She was going to kill me. Whether I gave up the stone or not, she was going to kill me.

I squeezed the stone tight, not truly knowing what to expect. What to want. In truth, the outcome was exactly as I knew it would be. Nothing. The stone did nothing. As I expected, as I feared, it was just a stone.

Desperately, and against every logical instinct in my body, I thrust my hand out and up in front of me, pointing the stone at Kerrel as if we were a weapon. As if it would call down a thunderbolt from the heavens to strike her down. It didn't.

"You can't be serious?" Kerrel could barely contain her laughter, holding her torso as she chuckled. "You thought you could use the stone? You? A mortal? How precious."

I would have fashioned some smart retort, but quickly her hand was around my throat, followed by an indescribable sudden pain in my right shoulder. The stone fell from my grasp as my hand shot up to grasp at the sword that had been driven into my flesh. The pain seemed to multiply by the second, as the shock of being stabbed wore off and left just the hot and heavy sensation of fire in my shoulder.

While I writhed in agony, Kerrel stared deep into my eyes, not breaking focus as she swung an elbow at Kang to fend him off and topple him over into a pile of trash. I tried to fight back, but my arm slipped easily from her sword as it began to numb and lose strength. It felt like my vision was also darkening and I wondered whether I would soon pass out, when a bright light suddenly washed away the shadows. I felt the sword slip from my shoulder, as Kerrel was hurtled away from me and slammed against the far wall of the alley.

I don't remember falling, but as I laid on my back in pain and confusion, I cast a look back at Avy. She was amazing. She was beautiful. She was glowing. Literally, she was glowing. Golden light pampered her skin, illuminating the darkness like a star in the night. When she looked at me, somehow emitting both confidence and awe as she examined her own hands, I realised what had happened. She was holding the stone.

In one hand she held the tiny gemstone, her head tilted and brow furrowed as she looked ponderously upon it. Her other hand was clenched, then open and clenched again, as she tested some new found strength or sensation, apparently impressed with what she found. Strangely, she seemed unlike the distraught librarian I had spent the past few hours with. Gone was her sense of innocence, and perhaps ignorance. Gone was the questioning, the doubt, the fear. In its place was something... new.

There were only two things about Avy that now appeared familiar. First, those golden eyes of hers, now burning brighter than ever. When she glanced over at me, it felt as if I might melt under just the weight of her relentless gaze. Yet still there was something in them. A mystery. An allure. Something that I knew meant I needn't fear her. That she recognized me.

The second thing I belatedly perceived was the light now shining around her. Or on her? Maybe from her? It was hard to tell, but I knew it. Recognised it. It was the same light we had seen fleetingly back at the library. When she had first gripped the stone and turned the dog to ash. Shock and scepticism had burned most of that incident from being clear in my memory. But seeing her now, standing bold, if perplexed, in radiant glory. I had no further doubt that there was something special about Avy.

In the library, the touch of the stone, or its reaction thereafter, had been enough to knock Avy unconscious. This time, however, she was still on her feet as the light finally faded. The alley went dim, like a power outage as just the lamps from the distant roads at each end cast a faint glow upon us. Her skin returned to its natural olive hue, her clothes no longer appeared in shimmering white and her hair, which had flared up towards the sky, sunk back down over her shoulders. Her fire had died down, in all but her eyes. They still glowed like a pair of headlights in the darkness.

"Zeke?" she finally said, her eyes almost too bright for me to look at directly. "Something's happening."

"It's the stone," I said. I didn't know what I meant, I just knew it was true. "Somehow, it's reacting to you."

"What do I do?" Her voice trembled as she spoke, and I realised whatever strength and confidence she had used to send Kerrel spiralling away was fading as quickly as it had appeared.

"Drop it," I replied. "Throw it away."

"Okay," she said, reaching an arm behind her head as she readied to launch the stone down the alley. Only, the throw never materialised. Instead, she lowered her arm and focused once more on the stone in her palm.

"What's wrong?" I asked.

"I can't."

"Why not?"

"Because," she said, her voice growing steady again in a way that unsettled me. "I... I don't think I want to."

"What do you mean?" I asked. "Aren't you in pain? Doesn't it hurt?"

"No," Avy replied. "It feels... good. It feels right. I feel like it wants me as much as I want it. Like I can hear it, asking to be set free."

"How are you doing that?" It was Kelis' voice this time. She had wrapped a scarf around Xiao's shoulder and was on her feet, looking callously at Avy. "How did you activate the stone?" Suddenly, there was a weapon in Kelis' hand. Covered in red flowers; identical to the one her sister wielded.

"It doesn't matter how," said Kerrel, back on her feet. There were bloodied scratches up and down her arms, and a mean gash across her forehead that mirrored the fury painted across her face. "She dies. We take the stone. Or are you going to try to stop me again?"

"We can't interfere," Kelis protested. "Mother has a plan."

"Does her plan include someone who can harness the stone's power? If we next find mother in a pile of ashes, will you be glad you followed her request so blindly?"

Kelis looked uncertain, for the first time since her arrival, and though she had saved my life minutes earlier, there was no doubting her true allegiance as she unsheathed her sword.

"Finally," said Kerrel, as the sisters stood side by side with the blades inverted towards the ground like a pair of kunoichi.

As they prepared to attack, my attention turned to Avy, wondering whether it was too late to grab her by the arm and run. Our chances of escape were slim, at best, as I rose painfully to my feet. Kerrel had somehow caught up with us, no matter how fast we fled. And Kelis had seemingly disabled an entire squadron of police officers in just a few seconds. Then there was Xiao, who was still slumped against the wall, wearing a pained grimace as her arm hung by her chest. And Kang, who only now had scrambled to his feet in a daze. We would never make it. The odds were against us. It was hopeless. At least, until Avy spoke.

"Zeke," she said. "Stay behind me."

Something had happened to her, that much wasn't in doubt. But what manner of transformation would convince a librarian that she could face down two armed attackers was beyond me. And yet, I didn't question it. Didn't delay. Didn't worry. There was something, not in her eyes this time; in her voice. Her body language. Her aura. Whatever it was, I knew the best thing to do was fall in line, as I rushed behind her.

Instantly, the two attackers were on her. Kerrel came from the left, Kelis from the right. One sword low, the other high, in perfect unison. An attack clearly birthed of both harmonious thought and tireless practice. And yet, Avy avoided both attacks as if she too were telepathically pre-empting their movements and had rehearsed the dodge for days on end.

She sprung forward and spun between both blades, simultaneously landing her right fist and left foot on each of her attackers. Kelis took the kick straight to her abdomen. It was like she had been blasted from a cannon, as she was thrown against the wall much like her sister had been earlier. Kerrel, on the other hand, managed to nullify Avy's punch, negating most of its impact by catching her fist and countering by sweeping Avy's legs out from beneath her.

I recoiled as Avy landed with a thud on the hard ground, and found myself shouting, "Look out!" as Kerrel's blade came angling down towards her head.

I needn't have bothered, as Avy was out of the way long before the metal blade sparked against the stone pavement. Avy was back on her feet as Kelis re-entered the fray and both attackers' swords danced towards her once more. Watching her bob and weave so balletically was like watching an expertly choreographed Yuen-Woo-Ping action scene.

After delivering slash after slash and hitting nothing but air, both attackers finally retreated a few paces to pause their assault. Again, they didn't speak. Didn't whisper a plan in each other's ears. Didn't lock eyes or exchange a cursory nod of intent. They didn't even take their gaze off Avy to make sure the other was alright. Never had I seen two people operate in such perfect, rhythmic harmony. Then, they came again.

This time, Kerrel seemed to vanish entirely, and I found myself looking left and right down the alley to try to locate her. Avy lashed out at Kelis with a right hook, but seemed to place so much force behind the blow that she lost her balance and lurched forwards, only to find herself ensnared in a sleeper hold.

It was Kerrel who grappled her, having reappeared at some point without me, or Avy apparently, even noticing.

"Hold her still," said Kelis, taking a step closer and placing her palms on each of Avy's temples, obscuring each of their eyes from where I was standing. Then there was another bright flash, not as blinding as when Avy picked up the stone, but enough to force me into shielding my eyes.

When I lowered my hand, the sight frightened me enough to make me call out immediately.

"Avy!" I shouted, when I saw what had become of her. She had been frozen still with a look of distress carved on her face. No different than the statuesque police that still stood motionless around us. "What have you done?"

"Stay back, Zeke," said Kelis, threatening me with a gesture from her blade. "Just take the stone off her and let's go, sis."

"I'm not done here," Kerrel replied.

"Yes, you are," Kelis said, her eyes glowing briefly in that ominous, and unforgettable, emerald light that I had come to fear. It figured. The woman at the museum. The dog at the library. And now these two sword-wielding zealots. They were all connected. Connected by the stone. And connected in wanting us dead.

"Fine." Kerrel finally relented, as she reached around and plucked the stone from between Avy's unobjecting fingers. "It's nearly sunrise anyway."

As Kerrel's hand went to her pocket, her delight quickly turned to horror when Avy's hand shot out and grabbed her by the wrist. Life seemed to course suddenly through Avy's body again, as in one swift movement, she slapped the stone up and out of Kerrel's hand, took her opponent by the arm, and flipped her headfirst into the concrete.

"How did you break free?" said Kelis, wearing a look of similar disbelief to her sister.

"I don't know," Avy said honestly, as she caught the stone and retreated back to my side. "But you're not taking this."

"Enough!" Kerrel leapt back to her feet, growling like a bloodthirsty predator. "I'm going to–"

"Kerrel stop!" This time Kelis' fear was saved for her own sister, as she pointed down at the back of Kerrel's hand.

It was smoking, under a ray of thin sunlight that snuck into the alley between the walls of a few taller buildings. It was just a little at first, like a magnifying glass being held up to the sun over a newspaper. But as if it were a piece of paper, a flame licked its way across Kerrel's knuckles and her hand went up in flames.

She howled in agony, leaping first back into the shadows, then vanishing completely from sight once again in a blur. Kelis, now alone, quickly returned her sword to its sheath and raised both hands in surrender.

"What just happened?" I asked. Between the pain of my wound, whatever was going on with Avy, and a woman nigh on bursting into flames, my senses were scrambled. If things didn't start making sense soon, I was afraid my mind was going to wilt under the strain.

"Her time was up?" Kelis replied.

"Her time? What does that mean?"

"It doesn't matter. Just... Zeke, come here. Please."

"Why should he trust you?" Avy shouted. "You just tried to kill us."

"No." Kelis hissed. "I just tried to kill you. Your name wasn't on mother's list. His is. And he is who I'm talking to. So Zeke, please. Come here for a second. I won't hurt you. You've seen that."

She was telling the truth. I could see it. I could hear it. Though she seemed ready to spit venom at Avy, towards me she looked and sounded just as she had when the police arrived. Calm. Reassuring. Protective.

"It's alright, Avy," I said. "Just wait here a second."

"Zeke," Avy replied, reaching out to take me by the hand, then squeezing tight. "Don't."

It certainly wasn't the first time that night Avy and I had made contact, but it was definitely the first time it felt like she was acting out of more than just instinct or fear. It almost felt like she really... cared. Like she cared about what happened to me. And cared about not being close to me. It felt... empowering. Knowing she felt something for my safety. But it was also terrifying, knowing that someone I met just a few days ago, who was a mystery unto herself, had somehow become intertwined with my wellbeing.

"Trust me," I replied. "I'll be okay."

Slipping gently out of Avy's grasp, I took a few steps towards Kelis.

"Listen," she whispered, peering around me, perhaps ensuring Avy couldn't interpret what she was saying. "You need to get the stone away from that girl. Then get yourself away from her."

"Why?" I demanded angrily. "She saved my life. Your sister was the one trying to kill me."

"Kerrel is difficult to control. She has a temper. But it turns out someone dear to us was killed. And only now do I realise how."

Again, Kelis' eyes narrowed and flicked back and forth between myself and Avy.

"Avy hasn't killed anyone."

"You're wrong, Zeke. And you have no idea what you're travelling with."

"Then tell me!" I shouted.

"You, in your line of work, know how dangerous a little knowledge can be. Ignorance may be your only saviour. So I'm asking you, either take the stone from her and never let her touch it again. Or ditch them both and forget any of this ever happened. It's the only way you'll keep yourself, and your friends, safe. Are the lives of Xiao and Kang equal to this girl you don't know? Consider it."

I had no intention of thinking over anything she said. Until, of course, she mentioned my friends. I hated myself for admitting it, but she had a point. Kang. Xiao. They had already been through more than enough. What if things got worse? What if Avy was the magnet that kept pulling trouble towards us? What if the only way the three of us made it out of this was by–

"I have to go." Kelis derailed my train of thought. "I know you don't want to heed my words. That you'll need time. So take this."

My heart skipped a beat as her sword was suddenly curving through the air once more, but this time it flew up towards her own head, brushing across her scalp before being concealed again. She had cut loose one of her immaculately twisted braids, before cupping my hand and placing it within.

"What's this for?" I wondered.

"Protection. Consider it a gift. Keep it close to you. For when you find yourself in a tight squeeze. I can't always be there to defend you."

"Okay," I said, baffled by how a lock of hair was going to keep anyone safe. Before I could ask, Kelis' back was turned as she headed towards the street.

"You might want to get out of here too," she said, as she walked away. "The light brings more unwanted attention." She waved a hand at the frozen police officers as she weaved between them. "The authorities will want to know what happened. And I doubt you have the means to explain it."

A few seconds later, she was gone, leaving me to pick up the pieces of the encounter. The sisters had swung like wrecking balls through our night, leaving our group in dire of need of rest, salvation, and answers.

"Zeke," Avy said, in a voice doused with enough alarm for me to know that the drama may not quite have ended. "Something's wrong. I feel... faint. I... Argh!"

I rushed to Avy's side as she yelled in pain, casting my eyes down to her clenched fist. It was glowing, ominously, as she slowly unfurled her fingers to find the source of her pain. When she opened her hand, the stone pulsated wildly. Her palm was covered in black ash, arrowing out from the stone in the centre, as if a fire had been ablaze within.

"It burns," she said.

"Here." I extended my hand. "Let go."

"Are you sure? What if it burns you too?"

"I'm pretty sure it won't," I replied. I'd been carrying this thing for an entire day and it hadn't so much as twinkled under my ownership. "Just let it go. That is... unless you don't want to."

The moment was only fleeting, but I knew what I had seen. Hesitation. As I asked her to release the stone to me, she wavered. There was a part of her, whether she was conscious of it or not, that would rather not relinquish the stone. And no matter how small that part of her may have been, it gave me more than enough reasons to worry about what Kelis had warned.

"Okay." Avy nodded, then placed the stone in my hand.

Despite my confidence that it was safe in my possession, more than a few images of my hand melting off or exploding into pieces were drawn in my imagination. Thankfully, the reality was far less eventful. I took a quick look at the now regular-looking stone and pocketed it back inside my jacket.

"I think I need to sit down," Avy said, her legs wobbling like she might tip over at any second.

Taking her by the hand, I helped her to the ground. I had a million questions to ask, but Kelis was right about one thing at least. We needed to get out of here. Fast. And that meant rousing my team into action. I rushed to Kang's side, pulling him to his feet while trying my best to ignore the look of bewilderment on his face.

"Dude," he said, somehow out of breath though he had spent the last few minutes lying in a daze on the floor.

"Not now," I said, preempting his inquisition. "Help Avy walk. I'll check on Xiao. Then let's get out of this damn alley and somewhere at least a little safer."

To his credit, Kang didn't speak another word. There was no doubt he had thousands on the tip of his tongue, most followed by question marks, but he replied only with a nod before marching towards Avy.

"Xiao," I said, when I saw her using the wall to push herself into a standing position. "Take it easy."

"I'm fine," she replied. "Well, my legs are at least. You're the one losing blood."

I checked my shoulder for the wound I had all but forgotten about until now. There was blood soaking through the front of my jacket, and when I lifted it to check the damage beneath, a fresh dose of pain flushed through my body again. My grey shirt beneath had turned completely red with what seemed like enough blood to fill a bathtub.

"It's not so bad," I lied. Now wasn't the time. Getting everyone to safety was the priority. Nothing more, nothing less. "We need to get somewhere quiet, but where we can blend in. Like a cafe. Or a diner."

Xiao shook her head. "They'll have TVs. If we're on the news, we'll get made. I saw a laundromat a few blocks back. Could that work?"

"It's better than nothing." I reached for Xiao's hand, but she pulled away just as I made contact.

"I said I'm fine," she replied.

Whether she was still bitter from our argument, or some fresh offence I didn't know I'd committed, was unclear. Still, the effect was the same, as she picked up her pace and marched out of the alley.

I waited for Kang before following her, as he rushed up beside me carrying Avy on his back. "What are you doing?" I asked.

"Being a gentleman," he replied.

"A gentleman would have asked me first," Avy quipped.

"Whatever," said Kang, as he took off around the corner after Xiao.

"Perfect," I said aloud. Imagining what onlookers would wonder when they saw a girl with a makeshift sling, being followed by a guy with another out-of-sorts-looking girl on his back, followed up by another guy who could keel over from blood-loss at any second. "Just perfect."

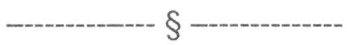

"You're an idiot," said Kang, as he helped me get my shirt over my shoulder.

In one of the first true strokes of fortune we'd had in hours, the laundromat was completely empty. There didn't seem to be any staff around either. The place was open twenty-four hours and completely self-serving. There was one camera, but Kang was absolutely certain it was more preventative than functional, listing the make and model as one he'd seen used in the past.

Our first priorities were to get in touch with Camilla, arrange transport of some kind to wherever her private jet awaited, pick up some food and find some medical supplies. The last point I made sure to emphasise, citing Avy's cuts and bruises as well as Xiao's busted arm as particular concerns, while keeping quiet about my own worsening condition.

Unfortunately, everything we needed required the one thing we were particularly short on. Money. To call Camilla, we needed a phone. And each of us had managed to either leave ours back at the hotel or lose track of during the chaos of the taxi crash. I was pretty certain mine was on the bedside table back in the hotel room, along with my passport and wallet.

Even if we knew where to go, we needed a way to get there. And taxis were out of the question, not just because we couldn't pay, but because we couldn't risk being recognised a second time by the next annoyingly observant driver.

Our last, and only, resort seemed to be a pawn shop across the road. And the second Kang and I were inside the dark and dreary store, my legs all but gave way as I clutched to him for support. It was then that he noticed my blood-soaked shirt. I knew the effects must have been showing on my face too, as my best friend looked at me with his eyes widened in distress.

"Hey," said the owner, a burly tattoo-faced man within an eastern-european accent, sitting behind the counter with his legs raised. "No dallying. Do business or go."

"Sure, we will. But, do you have a restroom?" asked Kang.

"Bathroom for paying customers only."

"Alright," Kang said, pulling my good arm over his shoulder and helping me towards the counter. "We're here to trade."

"Do you take gold?" I asked, straining as I tried and failed to reach for the chain around my neck.

"No," the man said. "No jewels. Only TV. And collect."

"TV and collect?" I looked around the store, wondering exactly what he meant. Certainly, it wasn't just any old pawn shop. There were no antiques, no jewellery and no old appliances like a kettle or toaster. Instead, the shelves were lined with toys, cards, comic books each preserved in plastic casings. The only exception was a counter in the corner which housed a few flat screen TVs and mobile phones.

"Ah," said Kang. "He only trades in collectables and tech. A man after my own heart."

"Well, sure," I replied. "But my All-New X-Men one-zero-one is in a frame on my wall. Along with everything else we own that might be useful right now."

"Oh, ye' of little faith." Kang reached into his pocket and pulled out his red sunglasses, sliding them across the counter as if he had just laid a brick of solid gold before the owner.

"What this?" the man asked. I had to admit, I was equally perplexed. "No junk."

"Junk?" Kang said in his finest accent, as if someone had just insulted his girlfriend. "This is far from junk my friend. And I would have thought a man of your repute, someone of such exquisite taste, would recognise a genuine real-world treasure when he saw it."

Kang looked back and forth at each of us, seemingly annoyed at the blank expressions he was faced with.

"Okay," he sighed, reaching for the glasses and flicking them open. "These are a pair of the very glasses that the great Godfather of the MCU, Robert Downey Jr, wore on the set of the third Iron Man movie. Two of a kind, but the only pair offered to the public. I won these at a private auction after the twenty-fourteen Hall H exhibition. The one where they showed the first Avengers sequel footage.

"So, my friend," Kang folded the glasses and slipped them into the shop owner's shirt pocket, finishing with a gentle tap. "You can take them off my hands for a mere... let's say two-thousand euros. My mentor funded nearly twice that for them, but I could just about stomach a discount on this fine morning."

The owner looked sceptically at Kang, before pulling the glasses out for a closer inspection. Whether it was the unnecessarily dramatic flavour Kang seemed to have added to his haggling speech, or the credibility his offer seemed to lack, the man clearly wasn't convinced. Twenty seconds later, he sat them back down on the counter and eyed us both a little more intently than he had previously. I thought our cover had been blown. He'd seen our faces on the news earlier, on one of the TVs around the store that were now playing episodes of One-Punch Man in a language I didn't understand.

"Two-hundred euro," he finally said, folding his arms as if his first offer were his last.

"Two-hundred!?" Kang shouted, far too loud for someone who had recently become a wanted criminal. "Are you insane? That is a genuine piece of history you have right before your eyes, sir. I simply cannot part with it for the breadcrumbs you have offered."

The man rolled his eyes. "Four-hundred then. And I let bleeding friend use bathroom and bandage for free."

The man was no fool, that much had been made clear. He knew I was injured and had likely determined that there was something altogether suspicious about the pair of us. The power of negotiation was his to command, as he placed the hard cash down on the counter.

"Kang," I urged, growing short of breath and beginning to sweat as much as I bled.

"Fine," Kang replied, snatching up the medical bag and money before dragging me down a narrow flight of stairs into an even smaller toilet cubicle where his, 'you're an idiot,' lecture had begun.

"Why didn't you just tell me about this back in the alley?" he asked.

"What difference would it have made?" I wondered.

"Well, you were the one I would have carried for a start. Could have spared myself some insults from Avy along the way."

"Fair," I said, as he dabbed clean my wound and wrapped a hefty bandage around my shoulder.

"Alright, it looks like the bleeding is slowing. But I'd say you need to get to a hospital sooner or later."

"What happened to 'Public places are a stupid idea.' Eh, Richard Kimble?"

"That was before your life was in danger. Better to end up arrested, or under attack by a magical monster, than dead in some pawn shop."

"I guess. Hey," I said, reaching out with my bad arm to test its strength, and struggling to raise it higher than my waist. "I'm sorry you had to lose those glasses man. Those must have been hard to part with."

"Huh?" Kang replied. "Oh, those. Prada."

"Fakes?"

Kang quickly clasped my mouth shut. "Ssh. Keep it down. And no those weren't fakes," he whispered. "Iron Man may not have worn them, but they still cost me like five hundred quid. That guy ripped us off. And I'm the one who's supposed to be a criminal?"

I couldn't help but laugh, though my arm faltered as I reached out for a high five. "Okay, so what now?"

"Now, I make a phone call," Kang smiled.

After helping me get my shirt and jacket back on, Kang and I headed back upstairs to confront the owner once more.

"Do you have a phone I can use?" Kang asked.

"Sure," the man said, placing an old Motorola flip-phone on the counter. "Fifty euro."

"What?" Kang replied. "For this piece of junk? And I only want to use it to make one phone call."

"No use. Only sell. Fifty."

I nudged Kang in the back.

"Seriously?" he said, handing over fifty of the euros he had only just acquired.

"SIM card free," the man said, with a smile belying his cruel business acumen.

"Great," said Kang, snatching the phone up and walking to the far corner of the store.

"Alright, we have a phone," I started. "But how are we–" I stopped abruptly when I saw Kang already tapping the phone digits, then placing it to his ear.

"What?" he said, as I overheard the ringing coming from the handset.

I was well aware of the seemingly limitless capacity of Kang's mnemonically-trained brain. But I knew for a fact that Camilla's number was not the same as when we were younger. So the fact that he could instantly retrieve it stirred me as slightly unusual.

"Nothing," I said, when I heard the muffled sound of a woman's voice coming from the phone. Kang looked poised to start the conversation, his lips parting to speak, when suddenly he froze. His body tensed and his eyes darted from side to side, as if he were nervous. "What's wrong?" I asked.

"Uh... you talk to her," he said, thrusting the phone into my hand.

"Okay..." I was too focused on preparing to haggle with my nemesis once more to press him on his erratic behaviour. "Camilla?"

"Well, well. Look who finally decided to get in touch," she said. "You'd think a trio of murderers like yourselves would perhaps keep your phones nearby."

"I'm not a–" No, it wasn't the time to succumb to her taunts. "Nevermind, we got sidetracked. Is your plane ready?"

"It's been ready for over an hour. I've called you a thousand times."

"I don't have my phone, Camilla. Anyway, forget about that. I need to ask another favour."

"Favour?" I couldn't tell whether she was laughing or scoffing at me. "Since when am I in the habit of doing you favours? We have a deal. This is a joint-venture to Pierceson, remember?"

"Yes, yes. I remember. But if you can't get us some transportation, we're never going to make it to the airport. Everywhere we go, someone seems to find us."

"Someone?" Camilla was always so quick with follow-up questions. "Someone like who?"

"I promise I'll explain. Or, at least I'll try to. But can you help us or not?"

Camilla sighed as if I had just asked her to run the London Marathon in her favourite pair of Jimmy Choo pumps.

"Fine," she finally said. "I'll send a car for you. Text me your address. And for the love of God, try to actually be there when it arrives."

"We will." I reached for the end call button, only to pause and press the phone back against my ear. "And Camilla," I said.

"Yes?"

"Thanks."

"You're welcome," she replied, before hanging up.

When the dated two-inch screen on the phone faded to black, I tapped the handset against my forehead in frustration.

"You okay dude?" asked Kang. "What is it?"

"I dunno. It's just... why is it that even after nearly being eaten alive, crashing a car and being stabbed, it's still accepting a favour from Camilla that seems like the most dangerous thing I've ever done?"

ACT VIII

THE CHELAE SCORPIONIS

'*Still, it was done at last, and the father hovered, Poised, in the moving air, and taught his son: "I warn you, Icarus, fly a middle course: Don't go too low, or water will weigh the wings down; Don't go too high, or the sun's fire will burn them. Keep to the middle way. And one more thing, No fancy steering by star or constellation, Follow my lead!"*'

For the longest time, I'd thought myself to be on the right course. I'm hardly comparing my intellect to Daedalus, Ovid wrote him to be a genius. No, it's his philosophy I chose to imitate. The 'middle course.'

My mum's mind would dance as she recounted vivid tales of miracle and wonder. Her eyes always came alive with awe, love and, more importantly, belief. Walking on water. A loaf of bread for a thousand. Water becoming wine. To me, they were bedtime stories. To her, they were irrefutable proof that the magical and the fantastic were, and always would be, a part of our lives.

I never had time for it. I humoured her, as best I could. The same way I would humour anyone whose opinion cultivated fiction, absent of fact. With science. Miracles were something to be explained, rather than marvelled. Mysteries required solutions, not romanticism.

Only as I sat opposite Avy, replaying the events of the past few days in my head, and coming up short of an explanation, did I realise the truth. I wasn't Daedalus at all. This wasn't the 'middle course' and I wasn't the aged and wise father. I was Icarus. I was the son. But unlike him, in my attempts to stay grounded, I had flown too low.

I'd spent a few paltry years studying the myths and legends of civilisations that had risen and fallen millennia before I'd even existed, and decided I had all the answers. And yet in just a few days, and faced with my first true enigma, it was painfully obvious that there was so much I still didn't understand. Events I had been so quick to dismiss as recently as the night before, I found myself contemplating over and over as my eyelids battled fatigue.

I couldn't escape the singular train of thought. The facts. The logic. Everything that had been my truth at the beginning and end of every day. What if that truth was a lie?

"Zeke?" It was Avy's voice that roused me. "Are you alright?"

"Yeah. Fine," I replied, squinting as I peered out the windows of the limousine Camilla had sent for us.

Honestly, the gulf in resources between her and us bordered on the ridiculous. Pierceson had nigh on unlimited funds available to him, but by these lavish standards, we were being kept on a relatively short leash. Making our way to the private jet she had at her disposal, in both assured safety and luxury, somehow felt like little more than her reminding us just who was in the driver's seat.

"He's not fine," said Kang, sitting beside me with his arms crossed in disapproval. "He needs a hospital, not an airport."

"Hospital?" asked Xiao, speaking more to Kang than me. "What for?"

Kang shot me a threatening glare. I knew it well. It was the same look he gave me whenever I got caught trying to hide something from our fathers. And the same look he used each time we were busted trying to convince Pierceson that we hadn't come back empty handed from one of his assignments.

"Show them," he nodded.

"Kang," I stressed, in an attempt to change his mind.

"Just show them. What's the point in making it home if you're half-dead by the time we get there?"

"Alright, alright."

He was right, I couldn't deny it any longer. I'd lost so much blood, I couldn't be sure if I was falling asleep or into a coma. And if I didn't tell the girls now, they'd find out when I fell unconscious anyway.

As I peeled away the shoulder of my jacket, wincing as each gruelling motion brought fresh suffering, I was greeted with contrasting reactions. Avy, dramatic and predictable, gasped and covered her mouth in shock. I couldn't blame her entirely, my shirt was soaked with so much blood I could give John McClane a run for his money.

Xiao, on the other hand, rolled her eyes and let out a sigh of vexation.

"Really, Zeke?" she said.

Her voice was devoid of any and all sympathy, but suddenly she was beside me, prying open Kang's makeshift bandaging and eyeing the wound intently.

"This is bad. This is really bad. What were you thinking? You should have told us. You should have–" Xiao seemed to catch herself before she vented any further frustration.

"Alright," she mumbled. "What can we do?"

"Let me try something," said Avy.

"Like what?" asked Kang.

"I don't know. I just... Switch with me, Xiao."

It was hardly the time to feel embarrassed, but as Avy shuffled up next to me in the back of the limo, I couldn't help but wonder what she thought of the sorry state I had ended up in.

"What are you–" Avy's hand was inside my jacket before I could ask.

She fumbled around for a few seconds, before her fist emerged, glowing faintly in the dimmed light. She unfurled her fingers, where the stone laid, pulsating in the palm of her hand. As if it were alive and under her command, responding to the touch of her skin and the rhythm of every breath she took.

"Hold still," she said, clasping the stone tight once more in her right hand, then reaching towards me with her left.

Her fingers brushed my shoulder, only a light touch at first. Then, her hand was over my chest, searching left and right until I could feel the faint pressure of her delicate hands over the puncture that was draining my life.

"There," she said, squeezing her eyes shut.

I wondered, for at least the first ten seconds, what she was expecting to happen. Was I supposed to feel more relaxed? Was it some mental exercise to keep my mind at ease until we could find a way to get medical attention? Or had she simply let the grandeur of tonight's events carry her away?

It wasn't until I felt the warmth in my chest that I realised something really was happening. It wasn't hot, not this time. This wasn't the scolding pain of being stabbed or subsequent gnawing of agony I had felt ever since. No, this was gentle and soothing. Like slipping into a running bath or taking the first sip of freshly brewed coffee. It felt... good.

Quickly, I forgot the ache of the injury. And it wasn't just the pain that dulled, either. My fatigue evaporated, as if I had just woken from a day long slumber with the morning sun stretching through the blinds. And as I clenched my fist, my arm felt strong again. Like the fresh pump of adrenaline after finishing an intense workout.

"What did you do?" I asked, as I lifted my shirt and found myself lost for words.

"Okay... what!?" said Kang, as he poked at the flesh where my wound had been. "Did you just heal him?"

She had. She really had. Gone was the torn flesh. Gone was the rushing blood. And gone was any sign that I had ever been injured to begin with. Not a bruise, scar or solitary cut remained. It was unfathomable. But perhaps most surprising of all, was how unruffled Avy seemed by the ordeal.

"How did you...?" I wasn't quite sure what to ask.

"I don't know," she replied. "But I just... knew. I knew what to do. As if, I'd done it before."

"But how?" said Kang, now searching Avy up and down as if the answer would present itself. "How did you do it? How did you do any of it? The healing. The fighting. The light. How?"

Kang's previously inquisitive tone suddenly had an accusatory edge to it, forcing Avy to shrug defensively.

"I don't know," she protested. "I still don't remember anything you said happened at the library. In the alley, I went for the stone because...because... Zeke was in trouble. It was just instinct. I guess. And after that, I remember the fighting and I remember feeling afraid. But that's it. It's not like I planned to do those things. Or even knew I could. I just... did it."

"So you just knew how to go all Michelle Yeoh on those chicks?" Kang remained unconvinced. "You must have at least–"

"Kang!" Surprisingly, Xiao came to Avy's defence, cutting him off before he could make any further allegations. "Enough. She doesn't know what's causing it. We don't need to have this out now."

"Yes we do," Kang shouted. "And what makes you so sure she doesn't know anything?"

"Because she told me," Xiao replied, in her usual stern but controlled manner. "While you two were off playing nurse together."

"And you believed her?" Kang was livid. I could understand why. The intensity of the last few days was making us all crazy, but all of sudden he seemed to be blaming Avy for the insanity that was swirling around us. "Am I the only one not buying the whole mild-mannered librarian act? We just had a bunch of monsters try to kill us. How do we know she isn't one of them?"

"Maybe because she protected us!" Now, Xiao was angry. "And we don't even know if it's her, or the stone, or whatever, that is making us a magnet to all this crazy shit. So why don't you get a grip and keep your idiotic opinions to yourself."

"I'm not being an idiot. We could have run anywhere in this town, but we ended up at her library. And every time she touches the stone, something crazy happens. Just her, nobody else. Are we just ignoring that? Coincidence? I don't buy it."

"Not true," Xiao shook her head. "I haven't held it yet." Finally, Kang stopped yelling. But only so that we could look at each other for long enough to determine whether that really was true or not. "That's right," Xiao continued, before either of us could respond. "You can wipe those dumb looks off your faces, because I know you haven't given me a second thought since the two of you got your hands on that stone. Sorry to intrude on you and Camilla's private discovery. But while Avy and I have been busy keeping you alive, you two have been acting like you have some God-given right to that thing."

"You're right," said Kang. I figured Xiao's outburst had brought on the same realisation in him that it had in me. That for whatever reason, we really had been taking Xiao for granted. I know I'd thought about little other than the credit we would get for bringing this discovery back to Pierceson and the mystery surrounding it.

I figured Kang would take the chance, before I could, to apologise to her and thank her for everything she had done so far. I was wrong.

"Give her the stone then, Zeke," he said. "Let's see if this thing turns her into Wonder Woman too."

"Ugh," Xiao scoffed. "You need to grow up, Nathaniel."

"Why? Are you afraid?"

"What? No."

"Then take it."

"No."

"Because you're one of them?"

"One of what?!" Xiao's exasperation was fast-approaching. "Have you lost your mind? Fine. Avy, give me the stone."

"Are… are you sure?" Xiao's demand clearly took Avy by surprise.

"Yes. Give it to me. Let's see what happens."

The situation had quickly unravelled beyond any of our control, but I wasn't about to let things go from bad to potentially worse. I felt terrible just knowing how Xiao felt about this whole mess, so the thought of how pissed she would be with what I was about to do next wasn't worth thinking about. Instead, I skipped the thought-process and dove straight into the action.

"No," I said, snatching the stone from Avy's hand before Xiao could get a hold of it.

"What are you doing?" Xiao said.

"I don't know," I replied. "Saving your life, maybe? We don't know how this thing will react to you. You're not a monster. Kang is just projecting. He doesn't mean it. About either of you." My eyes flicked to Avy, who seemed to be losing the fiery light in her eyes by the second. "But we really don't know if this thing will react to you. What if it is a female thing? The last thing we need is you passed out at a time like this. I promise you, we'll investigate this. But not right now. Right now, we just need to keep our heads and get on that plane. Has everybody got that?"

I was hoping for at least a nod of acceptance from everyone, but before we could even settle into an awkward silence, the limo came to an abrupt halt and the door swung open.

"Finally," came Camilla's autocratic proclamation, followed by her invasive eyes ducking through the door. "About time you misfits got here. Now, where is that lovely stone you promised me?"

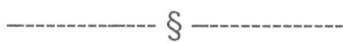

I was never the best cook. The microwave got me through most of life's troubles. But every now and then, I would try to help my mum out by attempting to mimic her kitchen sorcery. It rarely ended in success. Nine times out of ten, I'd be left with a mixture of burnt ingredients at the bottom of one of her favourite saucepans. And no matter how many times she would tell me, I would never heed her advice.

"Let the pan soak. Don't tackle it straight away. These things take time."

And every time, fearful of being caught in failure once again, I would immediately take a metal spoon to the pan and try to fix as much of the damage as I could before it was discovered. To this day, her cupboard was full of ruined pans scratched and scathed by my folly.

As we boarded the flight that had been prepared for us, our group felt like one of those pans. And Camilla, well, she was the spoon. Carving away at what little cohesion we had left.

"You haven't lost the stone, have you?" she prodded. "Is that why you still won't trust me to handle it?"

"No," I growled.

"Okay... then perhaps you got someone else inadvertently killed? Is that it?"

"No, Camilla."

"Then why in the heavens are you three moping around as if we're flying to a funeral? You led me to believe this was the discovery of a lifetime,

Zeke. And now you seem disinterested. I can still cancel this flight, you know?"

"No," I shouted. "Nothing has changed. This just... isn't a good time."

This time, Camilla looked past me to the others, as she marched up the steps to the aircraft by my side.

"Ah," she mused. "Your trump card."

"Excuse me?" I knew so much better than to engage her, but I was also becoming painfully aware of how easily I kept getting drawn in by her machinations.

"You do this every time. To everyone. At some point. You open that big mouth of yours, let that venomous tongue off its leash, and regret it soon after. Don't tell me you've alienated the both of them."

"Zeke didn't do anything." It was Avy who leapt to my defence. Well, it was more an attack on my ally than a defence. "It was Kang who did all the talking."

"Dear Nathaniel?" Camilla gasped mockingly and placed her hands on her cheeks. "He simply doesn't have it in him to defame the good reputation of others. Especially us of the fairer sex. He's a slave to our whims you know?"

"Oh yeah, what would you know?" said Avy. "You haven't been through what we have."

Camilla stopped dead in her tracks at the top of the stairs and looked down on Avy with eyes like an eagle that had just spotted its next meal.

"I'm sorry dear," she said. "I may have spoken out of turn, but if you'll do me the courtesy of reminding me just who the hell are you? And why you think you can talk to me as if you're the one doing me a favour? As a matter of fact–" Camilla swung on me now. "Give me one good reason why I should let this random side-chick aboard my plane in the first place, Zeke?"

"Ugh," I protested wearily. "This is getting tiresome. It's not even your plane, it's LaGuerre's. And don't act like you're doing us a favour for nothing. This is an exchange. So Avy comes, or nobody does."

"You really think you're in a position to threaten me?" Camilla scoffed. "May I remind you that you're one authority tip away from a pair of handcuffs."

"What's the hold up?" said Xiao, as she pushed past Avy and barged between Camilla and I. "We don't have time for this."

"She's right," said Camilla, her eyebrows raised. "So what is she to you? New crush?"

"No." I repeated once more, slightly embarrassed by how quickly I had answered.

Camilla rubbed her chin and switched her attention to Kang. "Don't tell me she's yours, Nathaniel?"

"What?" Kang looked twice as ashamed as I. "No... I– Can we just get on the plane?"

"Fine." Camilla sighed as she finally headed aboard. "Keep your secrets then. But if you aren't going to tell me, perhaps you should at least tell each other..."

Ten minutes later, the plane was in the air. And honestly, despite the number of first class trips I'd flown with Pierceson's credit, this was by far the most luxurious flight I'd ever taken. There were only nine or ten seats, but each of them had a lavish leather finish of such comfort that it was no surprise Xiao was asleep before the wheels had left the ground.

Kang had already inspected the minibar and skulked off to the back to sulk, while Camilla disappeared into the captain's cabin to conduct some private 'business' with the pilots. That left just Avy, sitting at a table of four by herself, with her head in her hands.

Following in Kang's footsteps, I helped myself to a quick sip of Captain Morgan's, along with a hefty dose of my own pride, and slipped into the chair opposite her.

"A little advice," I started. "Maybe don't pick a fight with Camilla. Maybe don't speak to her at all actually. She'll take tiny bites of you until die from blood loss."

Avy sat back in her chair, looking back at me with eyes that sagged weightily for the first time and a smile that was clearly just for show. "I'll keep that in mind."

"Speaking of blood loss, I owe you a debt. Thanks. I know that's probably not enough, considering you've saved my life three, four... maybe even five times now."

"That's okay." Avy's cheeks went a little rosy, then quickly her hands shielded her face once more. "But like I said, I don't really know what's going on. What *is* going on, Zeke? What's happening to me?"

"I don't know." It was the truth. "But I promise we'll figure it out."

"Alright," she nodded.

"You uh... you didn't say much back there."

"With Camilla?"

"No, not her. I meant in the car. With Kang."

"Oh." Avy's eyes went to the window. As if she were searching for anything but me to lock eyes with. "Yeah, well, my dad always said, 'if you don't have anything nice to say...'"

"Ha," I smiled. "My mum says the same."

To my surprise, Avy's eyes did swing back to me as she spoke. "You didn't say much either. Is that because you agree with him? Because you think I'm some kind of–"

"You're not a monster." This time, though my reply was quick, I was confident in what I wanted to say. "You're a person, caught up in something strange like the rest of. And... you're kind of my hero these days."

"Hero?" Avy smiled and this time I believed it. "This time a night ago, I was trying to remember which aisle was which in the library."

"Well, for what it's worth, you're still a terrible librarian. But I'll let it go on account of the mystical powers."

As Avy and I shared jokes, I realised it was the first time we'd really laughed together. Away from the madness. Away from the others. And away from being at odds with one another. For the first time, it felt like I was just talking to the girl I liked. And for the first time, I hoped she felt the same.

"So," she said, her guard seeming to drop further by the minute. "Does your mum know you're off galavanting around the continent?"

"She practically packed my bags." I found myself smiling again. "As soon as she saw what a good shot I had."

"Shot? At what?"

"Life."

"I don't know what you mean," Avy shook her head and frowned. "You wouldn't have a life with her?"

"Not the life she wants me to have, no. Where I'm from isn't... easy. Or safe. Not for people who look like me."

"People like you?"

"Yeah, me. The ones who aren't rich. Or privileged. Or white."

"Right." Her expression softened.

"Look, if I'd stayed at home, who knows where I'd be now. My mum already lost a husband and daughter to the poli– to the streets. I don't think she could stomach losing anymore. And.. I'm sorry," I caught myself before my emotions overwhelmed me. "I'm turning this into a pity party."

"No, don't be sorry," she said, and I could've sworn I saw her hand reach for mine before retracting. "I asked, you answered. I'm grateful. So... Now you work for the world's foremost archaeological expert?"

I had to admit, I was impressed by how delicately she changed tact. It was almost Camilla-esqe.

"Yeah. It's a long story, but he gave me a chance for a proper education. The chance to read, write and speak with the best of them."

"Ah, so that's why you're so well spoken," she said with a smile. "I wasn't exactly getting London street vibes."

"And how would you know what a London street-kid sounds like? Don't go judging a book by its cover."

"Clearly. I've learnt my lesson," she said, her eyebrows nearly stretching so high they could have leapt from her forehead. "Especially when I'm surrounded by so many books and covers all day long."

"I see what you're getting at." I nodded. "I've learnt my lesson too."

"I'm not convinced you have," she jovially replied. "But you still have time to make it up to me. By getting me out of this mess. So I can get back home. I'm suddenly longing for my dad, childish as that probably is."

"Believe me, I feel the same. My mum makes the best desserts you've ever had. Whips something up every other evening. I've lost so much weight being away, but my sweet tooth really misses it. Say, you said your dad had a journal about a lot of this kind of stuff right? Do you think he would have any idea what's going on with all this?"

"No way," she shook her head. "My dad is a myth and fantasy fanboy. If he knew about something like this, so would I."

"Oh really," I laughed. "Sounds like someone I'd like to meet some day."

Avy rolled her eyes. "Believe me, I'd trade his warhammer collection for a bowl of your mum's pudding any day. Speaking of which..."

Avy rubbed her stomach suggestively.

"Hungry?" I asked. "I saw some food up at the counter. And there must be some chocolate around here somewhere, right?"

"Hell yes," she replied, rubbing her hands together like a child in a dessert bar.

After rifling around the cabinets for a few minutes I returned, not empty handed, but unable to hide my disappointment as I laid a few snacks down on the table.

"Fruits? Nuts? Cheeses?" said Avy, as she turned over each item.

"Sorry," I replied. "I forgot Camilla is in charge here. She usually only eats healthy crap. You sure you don't have the magical ability to turn cheese into chocolate too?"

"If only," she said. "Anyway, I thought you didn't believe in magic?"

"I don't. But I'm starting to wonder if I've been approaching this all wrong. We're archaeology students. We know more about all of this stuff than ninety-nine percent of the people who could have been dropped into this situation, but the whole time we've been running away from it all. We should have been using what we know to give ourselves an advantage, whether it's real or not doesn't really matter. All I know is, I'm going to smooth things over with Xiao and Kang, somehow, and make sure nothing else surprises us."

"Okay," said Avy.

"Okay?" That was all she had to say after I pretty much admitted that I was going to start dealing with this like a mythological crisis.

"Yeah, okay. I believe you. And I'm with you. Let's figure this out. I know you don't mean me when you say 'we,' but this is my life's work too, you know? Still, there is one thing." Avy's face grew serious and she clasped her fingers to rest them beneath her chin. "One burning question I have for you."

"Alright, I'll bite."

"Nathaniel?" she half-whispered.

I couldn't help but burst into laughter. It wasn't the first or last time a girl had asked me, but for some reason the combination of her quizzical look and the way she made sure nobody else could hear her, had me in hysterics. Even she couldn't fight the infectious giggles as I tried to compose myself.

"That's what's bothering you?" I asked.

"Yes. Everyone suddenly started calling him Nathaniel!"

"You didn't really think his name was Kang, did you? Skin white as a paper. Eyes leafy like a forest."

"Well... I don't know. That's what you all called him. That's what he called himself! So what is his name then?"

"Nathaniel." I repeated, putting her out of her misery. "Nathaniel Richards. You probably wouldn't get it. He's–"

"Oh!" Avy looked like she had just had a revelation. "Kang the Conqueror. I get it. They have the same name."

My mood had never sobered so fast. "You know who Kang the Conqueror is?"

"Yes. I do. Kang, the time traveller. Battles the Avengers. First appeared as Rama-Tut in Fantastic Four. Didn't I just tell you my dad was a huge geek? Comics are a type of book too, you know? And they aren't just for boys either."

"Dammit. You can't ever tell him that. Do you have any idea how long he's waited for someone to get it? Seriously. If you ever tell him, you're pretty much signing up for a professional stalker for the rest of your life."

After another hour of speaking with Avy, and despite how much I was enjoying sharing the details of our contrasting but somehow aligned careers, I couldn't fight the call of sleep any longer. After settling down in the row of seats in front of her, she didn't need to see my wide open mouth and chin full of drool after all, I must've nodded off fairly quickly. When I awoke, feeling partially refreshed, I could hear Avy's voice behind me. I would have turned to check on her, but when it became clear who the other participant in the conversation was, I held still and listened intently.

"What are you trying to say?" Avy protested, clearly ruffled by something Camilla was accusing her of.

"Don't play coy with me?" Camilla pressed her. "You may have my ex-colleagues fooled, but this little act of yours won't work with me. So keep batting your eyelids, glossing those lips and twirling your hair all you want. Sooner or later, the truth will come out. And when I drop you off on the nearest street corner, I know you'll probably feel right at home."

"Camilla," I shouted, having heard about all I could stand. "That's enough. Leave her alone. You wanted to work together with us, right? Well Avy is part of the package. Deal with it."

"You are unbelievable," Camilla replied. "You barely trust me enough, someone you've worked with for years, to even turn your back while you tie your shoelace. But you're letting this complete stranger in on your findings. Just tell me why?"

"Because she's wrapped up in the same mess that we are. That makes her one of us."

"Mess? You're referring to the murders? What does she have to do with that? Was it her?"

"No." I sat down beside Avy and spoke more softly, hoping Camilla would do the same. "Listen. Since we last met, some women tried to kill us and a bunch of other things we can't explain happened."

"Can't explain?" Camilla grabbed the mug of tea that was rattling on the table and took a long sip. "Such as?"

I didn't want to gift Camilla any more information than she needed to know. She was almost as sceptical as I was when it came to the supernatural. But being laughed at was a cheaper price to pay than having her constantly wondering just what I was so afraid to share.

"Monsters," I said, in as plain a voice as I could muster.

"I'm sorry?" she replied. "I misheard you."

"No you didn't. Some monsters tried to kill us. More than once. And I've a good idea of what kind."

Camilla didn't reply. Not at first, anyway. She ran her long nails up to the fastener in her hair and tightened it, before taking another even longer sip of tea.

"I see," she finally said. "Go on."

"Really?" I questioned. "No remark? No put down? No systematic disassembling of my intelligence."

"Oh, I have a lot of disassembling to do, Ezekiel. But I'll first need to know the extent of whatever madness this girl has led to possess you. So, for the next few minutes, I'm humouring you. Go. On."

"Alright." I looked at Avy, who admittedly was also eyeing me like I was a few electrons short of an isotope. "There was a woman. At the museum. She killed Ealing and she tried to kill us. Her, I'm not sure about. But the monsters she set on us. I was looking at them like something I couldn't understand before. Some trick, or game, or misdirection. I was so busy trying to figure out how we were being deceived, that I didn't stop to think about how familiar they were. I recognised them. I recognised them all. Avy, can you describe the thing you saw at the museum? You vaguely remember it, right?"

"Kinda," Avy replied, looking to the ceiling and squinting. "It was like a dog. But bigger, with bright green eyes. And, I know this is gonna sound crazy, but it had two heads instead of one."

"Oh, for Christ's sake," Camilla sneered. "Zeke, please tell me you weren't about to spout anything as ridiculous as this nonsense."

"But that's just it." I slammed a hand down on the table. "That's exactly what I was going to describe. And that's exactly why it doesn't matter if we were hallucinating or not. We all saw the same thing. That's how myths and legends are formed. By two people believing and agreeing that the same thing happened. No matter how ridiculous or fantastical."

"Right... so you're really sticking with that?" Camilla asked. "A two headed dog... a hellhound?"

"Not just a hellhound. I didn't remember until I finally put my Pierceson School of Historical Arts hat back on and started playing this all back in my head. But at one point, she actually called it by name. Orthrus. That's what she said."

"Orthrus?" For once, Camilla sounded more intrigued than doubtful. "Father of the Nemean Lion? Guardian of Geryon's cattle? Brother of Cerberus?"

"Yeah." I couldn't help shrugging as I replied. "Maybe."

"Well," said Camilla. And I knew she was about to try and explain something by the way she switched her attention from staring at me to cleaning her fingernails. "If mythology is suddenly your cypher, Orthrus was killed by–"

"Heracles." I wasn't in the mood to listen to her tell me things that we both knew I was well aware of. "During his tenth, and originally final, labour. Club to the heads. Or an arrow to the hearts. Depending on your source. What's your point?"

"My point is, how does a dead dog end up in your story?"

"Like I said, the how isn't important right now. Only the what. And it's not the only example. There's more."

"Such as?"

"The women who attacked us. One of them, well, first I just thought she was sadistic."

"She was," said Avy, with a shiver. "Anyone who licks blood off a samurai sword has to be, right?"

"A sword?" Camilla's nose wrinkled as her face expression grew stern. "You mean, like a katana?"

"No," I replied. "It was shorter, like a wakizashi, and covered in red flowers. She kept tasting blood from it. She even told me she was hungry. And when she spoke to me back at the hotel, it was like... I couldn't concentrate. Like I was confused or... hypnotised. I think she was a Lamiai."

"A Lamiai?" said Camilla, frowning as she reached again for her mug.

"Yeah. It's kind of like a–"

"I know what a Lamiai is, Zeke," she snapped.

"Well I don't," Avy replied.

"Of course you don't. Remind me why you're here again?" Camilla breathed a long and heavy breath. "Lamiai were women who used trickery and illusions to deceive and seduce young men. Then, they would eat them."

"Eat them?" Avy gulped. "Like vampires."

"Yeah," I replied. "Same myth, different cultures. Always winds up with someone being eaten though."

"And that's why she burst into flames!"

"Okay, that's it" Camilla said, rising too quickly from her seat and spilling tea over her hand. "Dammit. Enough is enough. I've indulged the two of you for long enough. If you don't want to tell me what's really going on, fine. But just remember I'm taking as much risk as you are here."

"Excuse me?" I couldn't hold back. Sure, she was doing us a favour, but risking as much as us? "Are you serious? We nearly died, Camilla. More times than I can count. We've been protecting this artefact that I'm letting you take credit for, and you think that just because you made a few phone calls and got us a flight that it makes us even?"

"Yes, Zeke. Yes I do. Or have you forgotten that you're actually fugitives now? And try not to overlook the fact that this jet is owned by my boss, a direct competitor to yours, whose ire I'm coveting by gifting this discovery to you and Pierceson. If this doesn't pan out, at best my career with LaGuerre is done and at worst, I'm an accessory to murder."

"You're exaggerating."

"The hell I am. You know what, think whatever you want. And don't trust me with your secrets. Trust your new friend. The one you know nothing about, with the fake story and the fake name."

"Who are you calling a fake!?" said Avy, squaring up to Camilla so close I was afraid a fight could break out any second.

"Really?" said Camilla. "Avare Pendragon? You sound like a comic book character. Yeah, that's right." Camilla pressed her finger into Avy's chest. "I looked you up. It wasn't hard to figure out you came from the library that got destroyed. I see your lies for what they are and this little innocent act of yours won't work with me. It's pathetic."

"Stop it," I said, diffusing the situation by taking Camilla by the arm and easing her away. "And don't think I can't see what you're up to either. Always the same game, trying to drive a wedge between us wide enough for you to slither through. It won't work. For once in your life can you just stop trying to play us? Maybe you've been away so long, you don't realise we've put your games behind us."

"Oh really," she replied, a little too quickly for my liking. "Kang doesn't seem to think so."

"What's that supposed to mean?"

"Camilla!" Suddenly Kang was behind her, slamming his empty glass down on the table as his eyes burned with urgency. "Not now."

"Why?" she replied. "I asked you to tell them months ago. But you're afraid of them, aren't you? Well I'm not."

"Tell us what months ago?" I asked, already fearing the worst.

Camilla took Kang by the hand and threaded her fingers through his. "Kang never quite renounced me like you did. And we've rekindled our friendship. Without you.. so you see, Zeke, I haven't been away long, after all. Actually, it's like I never left."

There it was. I wasn't sure whether I had known it was coming or not. There were so many emotions, so many thoughts, running through my head. The only thing I knew was that Camilla had done it again. The same thing she always did.

"Zeke, listen," said Kang, his voice almost a whisper.

"Son of a–" Xiao was suddenly awake, and up against the window cursing in fury. "Camilla, you lying little–"

"What is it?" I said, leaping into the nearest seat and sliding up one of the window blinds. For just a second, I didn't know what I was seeing, my blood was rushing and there was so much to take in. But as my eyes fixed on the enormous latticed tower in the distance, I couldn't even summon enough rage to yell. It had become all so... predictable.

"I thought we were going to London?" said Avy. "Why are we in France?"

"Because Camilla lied to us," I replied. "Again. Paris is where her mentor lives. Professor LaGuerre. She's bringing us and the stone to him."

"What!?" Camilla yelled, feigning ignorance, as she took a look for herself. "That can't be! We're not supposed to be here. I saw our course myself."

"Save the theatrics," I sighed, scowling first at Camilla then turning my attention to Xiao. "You know he's probably waiting for us at the runway, with a team of security ready to pry this thing from our fingers. Imagine that?"

For the first time I could remember, Xiao looked more angry with herself than me.

"Fine. I get it. You were right," she said. "Scorpion."

ACT IX

THE THESSALIAN FRACTURE

'My comrades, hardly strangers to pain before now, we all have weathered worse. Some god will grant us an end to this as well. You've threaded the rocks resounding with Scylla's howling rabid dogs, and taken the brunt of the Cyclops' boulders, too. Call up your courage again. Dismiss your grief and fear. A joy it will be one day, perhaps, to remember even this. Through so many hard straits, so many twists and turns our course holds firm for Latium. There Fate holds out a homeland, calm, at peace.'

Okay, maybe the journey hadn't been quite that bad. I hadn't sailed past Scylla or outsmarted a Cyclops, and Virgil wasn't likely to be penning any poems about me anytime soon. But I had been pursued by some kind of nightmarish beast and had a bloodcurdling woman try to slice my arm from my shoulder. And just as Aeneas longed for the shores of Italy, I found myself wondering if we would ever reach the safety of London at this rate. Given we were hunched together in a taxi, enroute to one of LaGuerre's homes, it certainly seemed unlikely.

"What happened to your fancy limos?" I asked, nudging my boot probably a little too hard into Camilla's ankle as she sat opposite me.

"Ow. Zeke, I am on the phone," she protested, before bringing her heel down onto my toes. "For the last time, this is not my doing."

"Sure," I nodded sarcastically. "You agree to take us to London, but we miraculously run out of fuel halfway there. Then we're forced to land in the city of your benefactor, who just so happens to have a car standing by, ready to take us to his home. It's all just a coincidence, right?"

Camilla was doing her very best impression of an exasperated victim, in her attempts to mimic the frustration the rest of us were actually experiencing. She had been, supposedly, leaving message after message to LaGuerre's assistants attempting to ascertain exactly why we had been diverted. To no avail of course. But I had been fooled and manipulated by her so frequently in the past few days, I'd decided I was done letting her get away with it. It was time everyone else started recognising her for the liar she was.

"Why wasn't the fuel checked before takeoff?" I demanded.

"It was," she replied, angrily cramming her phone into her purse. "Something strange is going on?"

"You're damn right about that," said Xiao, swivelling around in her seat in the front by the driver. "You wouldn't let us in the cabin. So we could see for ourselves this magical fuel shortage."

"I didn't want the pilot to know who was onboard," Camilla replied.

"Cut the crap. We're not buying it."

"Good. Because I'm not selling it. Listen to me, you bunch of ungrateful freeloaders." Suddenly, there was a defensive ferocity about Camilla that had been lacking until now. "I don't care what you believe. But here's what's going to happen. Any minute now, we're going to pull up to Mon Reve. And there is every chance that LaGuerre is going to try to take the stone from you or make some kind of deal. So under no circumstances are you to show it to him, or even talk about it. Accept his hospitality. Eat. Drink. And change out of those disgusting clothes. Buy time until I can get us another flight. Do you understand?"

Truthfully, I didn't.

"You want us to believe you don't want to give the stone to him?" I asked. "That you wouldn't prefer to claim all the credit for yourself? And hang us out to dry?"

"Didn't we come to an agreement? Some of us more begrudgingly than others?"

"That's never stopped you before," I replied.

"You've never been on my turf before," she snapped. "Do as I say and we'll be back on track soon."

"Right..." I turned to Avy, who had spent the fifteen minute journey sitting in silence beside me.

She offered only a shrug in reply, either disinterested by the conversation or, more likely, still upset by how things had deteriorated aboard the plane.

Xiao seemed to be cautiously watching the street names and signposts as we travelled, leaving just Kang paying any real attention to Camilla's instruction.

"Well?" I said, raising my eyebrows as high as I could at him. "What do you think, Nathaniel?"

"Really?" he scoffed. "I knew you were going to do this. It's why I didn't– Actually, no. No, I'm not getting into this. Let's just do what she says and get out of here."

"So you do believe her," I replied, nodding my head slowly. "Figures."

"Enough," said Camilla, preemptively cutting off any argument we were about to have. "We're here."

From the outside, the building was surprisingly modest. Each of Pierceson's estates were either lavish stately homes or pristine, high-spec new builds. LaGuerre's residence, however, more resembled a warehouse or factory that had been restored. There were rows of vehicles, though none of them particularly caught the eye. Most were functional, jeeps and saloons, while others were more specialist in purpose, like trucks and forklifts.

It wasn't until a pair of men, bearded, suited and whispering only to Camilla, led us inside and up numerous flights of stairs, that the remarkable secrets of the property came to the fore. Despite our collective reluctance to be there, I could see everyone's eyes darting with intrigue and curiosity between the doorways of the rooms we passed. Each one seemed to house a different wonder.

There were aged sculptures, sealed in airtight glass. Authentic-looking weaponry hanging from mock-warriors. Eight-foot high ceramics were fastened in place by iron bars. And stone tablets, with everything from lettering and numerals to fine art were laid upon thick pedestals. It was as if LaGuerre had commissioned a museum, dedicated to his own historical triumphs of discovery.

"This place is incredible," said Kang, reaching up towards the frame of one of the many paintings that lined the corridor walls. "Like his own Sanctum Sanctorum."

"Don't touch anything," hissed Camilla, her eyes narrowed like a cat as she looked back on him. "Everything is alarmed, so keep your hands to yourself. If you want to learn something while you're here, use the control panels. If you break or damage anything in this building, monsters and police are going to be the least of your concerns."

It was true, each work of art seemed to be near a touchscreen device of some sort that would prompt us to tap for more information. Dozens of them, or more, at each turn. LaGuerre had certainly spared no expense in presenting each of his treasures, nor in flaunting his knowledge of them. It was nothing like our own benefactor. No, Pierceson wasn't one for flair or presentation. Most of his finest vestiges were on loan to museums, or secured in private vaults, the locales of which none of us were privy to. There would often be one or two of his favourite pieces, sitting in a spare room at one of his private residences. But none of it was for public consumption. The only Pierceson works you would expect to find on a shelf were one of his many publications.

"What is this place?" I asked. "A gallery?"

"Something like that," Camilla shrugged. "You think we just frivolously throw money around at jets and hotels? It's all carefully budgeted and affordable, because of ventures like this."

"Let me guess," said Xiao. "You charge people a small fortune to come and spend five minutes with your wares? How noble."

"Nobility isn't a business model," Camilla replied, as she slid apart a pair of doors and turned to face us. "Now if you've finished with your latest bout of jealousy... we're here." Beyond her, was a lounge equipped with all manner of state-of-the-art audio and video gadgets, along with a bar, kitchen and dining area. "These are the guest quarters. There are bedrooms with ensuites at the back. If you need food or rest, get it now. I don't plan for us to be here long."

"And where will you be?" asked Xiao, who seemed reluctant to venture any further into the room.

Camilla was already pulling the doors closed as she replied. "Figuring out where our fuel has disappeared to. And don't bother trying to go anywhere, the guards will be out in the hall most of the time."

Without another word, she was gone. Leaving the four of us standing idly, examining what appeared to be our home for the foreseeable future.

"Great," I said. "Guess we're prisoners then. Well, we should probably discuss–"

"I'm going to bed," said Xiao. "Wake me if Camilla comes back. Not before. I want to be alone."

Just as quickly, she turned on her heels and disappeared beyond the back of the room. Following suit, though without even a token word or nod,

Kang also headed away. If his mood wasn't clear enough, he stopped only to grab a bottle of Wray and Nephews along with a single glass before he too was gone. With just Avy and I remaining, it seemed pointless to try and put on any further displays of leadership.

"You alright?" I asked her.

"Yeah," she meekly replied. "But I kinda want some time to myself too. My head is spinning."

"Right." My eyes sunk from Avy to my own shuffling feet. "Of course."

I didn't bother watching her sidle away. It would just let my desperate hope, that she would change her mind or turn back, build to a higher level from which to pile crushing despondency down on me. Instead, I took a seat at the kitchen counter and let my head sag into my hands.

"Hey," Avy called, surprising me as I turned to find her lingering at the exit near the back. "Camilla's right about one thing at least."

"Oh yeah?" I sighed, wondering what more damage our common foe could have caused. "What's that?"

Though it lacked conviction, Avy managed a smile.

"You stink. Take a shower."

And while hers may have been forced, the relief from the loneliness I felt was genuine enough to make me smile back.

"Thanks."

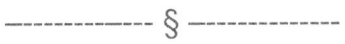

Admittedly, the shower made me feel much better. Having private facilities was a blessing, given the almost black colour of the filthy water that flowed down between my toes. It was as if I were back in early high-school and returning home after a game of rugby in the pouring rain and ankle-high mud. Thankfully, I didn't have to listen to my mum berate me for getting dirt everywhere. But the memory did make me at least clean the shower room after I was done. A part of me always felt like no matter how far away my mum was, she could always tell if I left a mess behind me, and would be waiting to pinch me by the ear when I returned.

As I headed back into the bedroom, I was close to jumping out of my skin when I saw the darkly dressed figure perched on the edge of the bed. "Holy shi–"

"Now, now," said Camilla, wagging a finger at me. "Aunt Claudette would be furious if she heard you blaspheming like that. Especially when you're such an infidel as it is."

"Don't talk about my mum," I said, grabbing my trousers off the bed and returning to the bathroom. "What do you want?" I yelled, not so loud as to disturb any of the others, but loud enough so that she would hear me in the bedroom.

"I'd like to be civil, for a start," she yelled back. "Come and sit down, I've someone on the phone for you."

"I am being civil. I'm trying to put some clothes on."

"Just take the phone," she said, shoving it into my hand, as I re-entered the bedroom.

"Hello," I said, putting the phone to my ear. "Who's this?"

"Aw," the voice said. "You sound pissed little bro. Did I interrupt summin' between you and the missus? Sounds like you were about to seduce her?"

"Sherelle?" I said.

"Ezekiel," she replied. "Didn't realise we were being all formal an' shit."

"How... how did you know I was with Camilla?"

"Erm, don't flatter yourself Bookz. Me and Cammy talk every week. You just happened to be in the neighbourhood. Does that mean you two are..."

"No," I snapped. "Absolutely not."

Sherelle cackled loudly. "Sure bro. Okay. Just don't take the whole hard to get thing too far yeah? She won't wait forever."

"Can you... can we not do this? Wait. Did she... what did she tell you?"

"Nothing..." Sherelle replied. "Should she have?"

Camilla rolled her eyes at me. It was fair enough. She probably wouldn't go as far as to tell my sister any of the insanity I'd told her. But in my defence, this was a total ambush.

"No," I said. "Just making sure you're getting the truth. Can't trust a word she says you know?"

"Bro," she said, and I could hear her sigh through the phone. "Please don't be that guy. Okay, she's a bad bitch, no doubt. But she's also one hundred percent legit at what she does. Same as you. Just because she moved on, don't make her a villain. Let the woman live her own life. You don't own her."

"Urgh." I threw my head back. "You have no idea what you're talking about. She–" I paused to look at Camilla, wondering if she could hear both sides of the conversation. "Look. I know that. You're right. I'll... try to be better."

"That's all it takes."

"So... is there something else I can do for you? I love you sis, but it's not the best time. I'm right in the middle of that work I'm always bragging about. And didn't we just talk about surprise calls?"

"I know, I know. In my defence I didn't know you were gonna' be there. But while I've got you, are you sure you're alright? You seem on edge. Last time and tonight."

"I'm okay, Relle. You don't have to worry. Trust me."

"And you'd tell me if you weren't, right?"

I paused, probably for a little too long.

"Of course," I said. "We do right by each other."

It wasn't a total lie. I was trying to do right by her. I just couldn't be sure I was going about it the right way.

"Always," she replied. "Listen, Bookz. You're not perfect. Nobody is. But you *are* too hard on yourself. You're doing great. You're doing exactly what I wanted you to do. What I knew I couldn't do. I made the choice to be in here and keep you out there. Not you. You made a mistake. But you've already paid for it. Stop punishing yourself. Just keep doing your thing, okay? Shine."

"I will. I promise. We'll talk more soon."

"And one more thing," she said.

"Yeah?"

"Wear a glove."

"Oh for fu– goodbye."

I hung up the phone and tossed it back at Camilla.

"That sounded fun," Camilla said, continuing to hover instead of leaving.

"Do you mind?" I snapped. "I'm getting dressed. Some privacy would be nice."

"Oh please," she scoffed. "I'm not interested in anything beneath your clothes, Zeke."

"I suppose not. You've got Kang for that."

For once, rather than snappily replying, Camilla seemed to pause for a few seconds to consider.

"I really don't want this to turn into one of the talks where we jab at each other until one of us, and let's be honest it's usually you, loses their temper. Can we just... talk? For once? Like we used to. There's a lot to discuss."

"Besides the fact that you've been secretly conspiring with my best friend?" I pondered, as I pulled the shirt over my head and buckled my belt. "What else is there? And what are you talking to my sister about anyway?"

Camilla shrugged.

"Girl stuff. But don't try and change the subject, Zeke. Kang mentioned that you had some trouble with the police," she said melancholily.

"Back in Cyprus. Said they had you pinned at one point? Is that why you're being coy with Sherelle? You're protecting her?"

"So?" I knew what she was getting at. Camilla was one of the few non-family members that knew what happened to my dad and sister. But these days, that was just another detail I wish we no longer shared.

"So, that can't have been easy for you to stomach. I know you don't want to talk about it. And I know you feel guilty that Sherelle chose you over her own wellbeing. But your Father would want you to–"

"Stop," I said. Cutting her off. She was right, I didn't want to talk about it right now. Least of all with her.

"Okay," she replied. "I get it. But if you ever do need to–" I stepped back into the bedroom, dragging my jacket back over my shoulders, and started searching for my shoes, which seemed to interrupt her. "Ugh. You are unbelievable."

"What?" I wondered.

"You're really wearing those clothes again? I keep the wardrobes stocked with perfectly good attire, in all different sizes. What was the point of the shower if you're just going to put those rags back on?"

"Actually, I'm wearing one of the t-shirts. But I would rather die than wear underwear that wasn't bought by me."

"Or your mother," she smirked. "What about the rest?"

"Please," I scoffed. "Plaid trousers and a dinner jacket? That's your taste, not mine."

"Fine, fine. Do as you wish. Look, I came to tell you that it's not safe here. And that I didn't betray you. This time."

"Is that so?" I said, slumping into the desk chair opposite her. "You didn't know we were short of fuel?"

"We were not short of fuel," she sharply reiterated. "LaGuerre forced the pilot to land here. Which means he knows about the stone. And he knows one of you has it."

"You didn't tell him about it?"

"No. Of course not. You think he would let me charter you a flight to London if he knew it was to deliver something to his lifetime enemy? Don't be moronic."

"Alright." I leant forward in my chair until just a metre or so separated us. "Say I believe you. Why wouldn't you just give it to him? You work for him after all. This seems like a win-win for you."

"Urgh!" Camilla half-groaned, half-shrieked. "You are so tiresome, Zeke. For once in your life can you just accept that I am trying to do the right thing? I promised to take you to London, and I *will* get you there. If you let me."

"Out of the goodness of your heart?"

"Tell me. Honestly." Camilla's tone sobered. "Have I ever broken a promise to you? Ever? I said I would get you to the airport, and I did. I said I would get you out of Cyprus, and I did. Do you remember what I promised you, back at the Iapetus? It was Kang's birthday and we–"

"Just finished forcing Pierceson to watch 300. He hated it, of course. And I told you my sister was being moved to a different prison. One it would take mum all day to get to by herself. So you promised you would send a car for her every week. Out of your own pocket."

"Promises mean something, Zeke. I never break them."

I turned my head away, before I responded, trying to avoid the emotion in her eyes.

"I know. I guess that's why you never promised to stay with us, right?"

Camilla sighed this time. Almost sounding defeated. "Is that why you hate me? Because, yes, I've hurt you. I've taken advantage of you. And occasionally I've made you feel like shit. But you've done things just as hideous to me over the years. And I still– I still don't hate you. I never could. We're... family. So why?"

"I..." Briefly, there was guilt. I had been unfair.

After all, she was right about a great many things. As Xiao had so rightly pointed out, Camilla and I were too similar to pretend otherwise.

Still, it passed.

I didn't need guilt. I knew exactly why I felt the way I felt. And the reason Camilla incensed me so much was because it felt like she had forgotten it all so easily.

"I don't hate you, Camilla," I started. "But I can't forgive you either. Can't be around you. We *used* to have something. We *used* to be family. Not just us. You, me, Kang. We were going places. Together. And you threw it all away. So you could do it all yourself. Did you even consider Kang and I? Did you even think about what that would do to us? Did you even wonder whether we would have gone with you?"

Again, Camilla seemed uncharacteristically lost for words. "I... would you have? Come with me, I mean. Would you have come with me?"

I stood up and strode over to the bottle of water on the desk, taking a long sip. I didn't realise this would be so difficult to talk about. And I didn't like revisiting these memories either.

"Doesn't matter now," I said. "You asked. I answered. We're done."

Camilla came and stood next to me, staring until I turned to face her, then placing her palm on my cheek.

"Is that why you're so cut up? About Kang and I? Look, on the plane I was just trying to rile you up. You know how I get. He and I... we're not. I mean, you and me... we can always–"

"No." I batted her hand away. "That's not it, actually. This thing with Kang. You're just using him."

"Oh my God." Camilla took a step back, then looked me up and down as if I were a lower form of life. "Are you serious?"

"Ah, whose blaspheming now?"

"Don't change the subject. I can't believe you can be so juvenile about this. You think I'm using him to get to you?"

"I never said that."

"Grow up, Zeke. Kang and I never needed you to complete our friendship. And honestly, since he seems to have grown up and you haven't, he's probably a much better friend than you anyway. He's smart and sweet. And—"

"Stop it. I can't hear any more of this. And Kang isn't any of those things. He's emotionally immature, has a weak spot for women and is desperate to make up for a childhood of rejection. And you're exploiting that for some gain or other. Most likely to steal information on us."

"I don't believe it." Camilla shook her head.

"Believe what?"

"He was right about you. He was actually right. All this time I was pressuring him to tell you. I thought it would help the three of us move past all this. But he said this is how you would react. And he was right. He was absolutely right."

Camilla pushed by me and was at the doorway in seconds.

"Where are you going?" I demanded.

"I told you. We need a way back to London. And I'm going to get it. I don't have time to sit here and suffer through your constant accusations. You can stay here and find another friend to turn on. But, oh, wait, you're running out of those, aren't you? Goodbye, Zeke."

Part of me wanted to storm after her. To grab her by the arm and tell her she was wrong. That this was her doing. That her lies had spun me around so many times I didn't know which way I was going anymore. But the other part of me couldn't. The rational part. The logical part. The part that knew she was right.

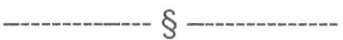

I sat for at least another twenty minutes. Alone. On the bed. In silence. Wondering how it had all gone so wrong. How I had fallen out with the people I loved the most. How I had let Camilla get so deep under my skin. And how, when we were being chased by monsters and myths, I had still ended up as the bad guy.

Finally, after going over it all in my head more than once, I decided there was little else to do besides making amends with my friends. Xiao was my first stop, she was in the room opposite mine. Before I risked knocking, however, I pushed the door gently ajar until it was just wide enough to see her. As I feared, she was curled around a pillow, fast asleep. And as much as I wanted to speak with her, waking her was certainly not the correct way to begin an apology.

Instead, I checked for Kang, but quickly found both his and Avy's rooms empty. They weren't in the lounge either, as I searched the guest area high and low for any sign of them. Finally, as I began to actually worry about their safety, I slid open the front doors to ask the guards if they had seen either of them. That too came to no avail, with neither guard being at their post to answer. My panic quickly subsided however, as I saw the opportunity presenting itself.

If the guards weren't here, that meant that we were free to explore some of the surrounding rooms. And no aspiring archaeologist would let a trip like this pass them by. Kang certainly wouldn't, so I was certain if I checked the next few rooms I would find my friend poking around. Most likely trying to discover some epic fantasy tale etched on ancient stone.

But after poking my head in and out of the first few rooms, it wasn't Kang that I bumped into first. Instead, in the centre of a room lined with row after row of books, it was Avy I found. Standing idly as she gawked at the towering collection.

"I actually feel a little silly now," I said. "I was searching for you, but I should have known I'd find you in a library."

"Sorry," she said. "I saw Kang leave, so I ran out to tell him to come back. But then I stumbled onto this and… there are just so many."

"Yeah." I wanted to sound scornful, but it was hard to deny the majesty of collections like this. "LaGuerre is probably the only person in the world who is more obsessed with books than my mentor. It must have taken decades to assemble this. And I know for a fact this is just one of his properties."

"This room is nearly as big as my dad's library. I'd love to spend a few days here. Or... years." Avy turned to me, momentarily breaking free of the spell the selection seemed to cast on her. "Do you think there is anything about the Ten Thunderbolts in here?"

I shrugged. "It's possible. But it would take forever to sift through all this information. Unless..." I searched left and right until I found what I was looking for, a small touchpad attached to one of the book cases. "There. She said you don't touch the collections, right? That means they must at least be summarised here somewhere."

Avy touched the pad, then began to swipe through page after page of contents menus. Dozens, then hundreds, then thousands of entries. Each one referencing a different text.

"Hold on a second," she said, as she began to arbitrarily select one article after another. "Camilla Winnett. Camilla Winnett. Camilla Winnett. Every single entry is by her. There's no way she could have compiled all this information alone, is there?"

"Absolutely not," I replied. "No doubt his junior apprentices did the heavy lifting. But it's just like her to take credit for other people's work. That's half the reason we're stuck here to begin with. Let me try a search."

I began by searching for the Ten Thunderbolts, which only brought up a loosely associated set of results that mostly referred to various accounts of Hephaestus, God of the forge, and his weapon craftsmanship. I tried a few other queries. Zeus and Prometheus. Zeus' Thunderbolt. The Death of Zeus. None of it produced anything meaningful enough to help me narrow down the search.

"You are so cute," said Avy, chuckling.

"Excuse me?" I replied. I'd love to pretend she was complimenting me on my good looks, but I knew when I was being mocked.

"Sorry. It's just... the way you search for things. It's all very... Pierceson. Isn't it? Official textbooks and quoted sources. I bet that's how he teaches. You almost expect the information to find its way to you. Just like the night I found you in my library."

"Oh, so you remember that now, do you?" I said, trying to stifle her laughter. "Well, what do you suggest, oh great chronicler?"

"Well, for a start. Take a look around. Do you see any Pierceson-style translations or codexes? No, these are all original texts."

Curious as to where she was going with this, I stood by and watched as Avy switched to an alternate keyboard and began to type Zeus, only using a different set of characters.

Ζεύς.

It looked more like the traditional Greek alphabet and when she tapped search, hundreds of results were displayed. Far more than during my paltry attempt.

"Okay. That was pretty cool," I said. "Since when do you speak Greek?"

Avy nudged me in the ribs. "You've been underestimating me since the moment we met. You didn't think I was a librarian. Let alone the manager. Why is that? Do I not have the look?"

"Well, no. You look too good to spend all your time with books."

"Too good?" she asked.

Suddenly I was aware that those lengthy lashes of hers were batting at me, causing my nerves to tingle.

"Check this out," I said, doing my best to change the subject as I wiped a bead of sweat from my brow. "The dates. They get relatively modern by Greek poet standards. Can you search for the Ten Thunderbolts in modern Greek too."

"Sure," said Avy, thankfully returning her attention to the work. "My closest approximation anyway."

"There." I pointed to an entry near the top as the new results started scrolling in. I could at least recognise the names of Zeus and Prometheus. "What's that one?"

"It's called, the Twilight of The Gods." Avy looked at me, ominously. "It's written by someone called Metabus Volsci."

"That's a pseudonym."

"It is?"

"Yeah." Secretly, I was thankful for an opportunity to claw my way back onto level footing in this bout of research. "King Metabus of the Volsci. It's from the Aeneid, I think. I can't quite remember the details, but long story short, he tied his daughter to a spear and threw her across the river."

"That's gruesome."

"She survived."

"I'm not sure that makes it okay. Anyway, why would somebody use that name?"

"No idea. See what it says."

"I can read it aloud if you'd like?"

"Sure. Go for it."

"The Twilight of the Gods," Avy started, after clearing her throat. "Despite the venerated and unending breadth and depth of his power and the grand battles of years past, Mighty Zeus had never faced war of this ilk. Ironic, the same strife beckoning his own rise to power would too be the origin of his downfall. Can even an All-Father, who raised sword to his own sire, expect not the seeds of rebellion to sow within his progeny? Once sparked, everlasting is the cycle. As Titans fell to Gods, so would Gods fall to Demigods.

"But Great Zeus despised one thing, above all others. Moreso even than treachery, he loathed defeat. His God-kin fell by the dozen. Brothers and sisters. Sons and daughters. Till only a handful remained. Their battle all but lost, Zeus turned to those he had cast out for salvation. First, the dread mother. And her brood. Vicious harpies, bloodthirsty chimaera and insidious gorgons. Foes he had before conquered and condemned to the shadows, he now sought to restore to light. So, his ranks swelled once more. And Great Olympus stood firm against siege.

"But decades of war brought closer neither victory nor defeat. To end his half-breed scions, Mighty Zeus turned to the greatest of betrayers. One he still feared to trust. But one he knew could bring an end to conflict. He sent for Prometheus. Prometheus, The Fire-Bringer. Prometheus,

Champion of Man. Prometheus, Son of the Piercer. Together, they rent Demigod flesh from bone, dispatching them back down to the Earth whence they came. And into hiding.

"Finally, his war was won. But not without toll taken on the All-Father. Weakened to the point of almost mortality, Great Zeus gathered his kin. He meant to name his successor, decreeing that he must leave Great Olympus, and see out his mortal days. The cycle must break, for while he remained King, his home would know not peace. Alas, before choice could be made, Mighty Zeus was betrayed. A deathblow dealt to the All-Father; a bite from the very hands he fed. He had not time to name the snake, only a moment with dying breaths to halt a murderous lust for power.

"The final act of the All-Father saw him strike his ten remaining allies. A thunderbolt to the heart of each, sapping them both of knowledge and Godhood. The once Gods, now closer to mortal than immortal, they ten were hurled from Great Olympus. Into the world of man. With them, ten thunderbolts flew. And ten times the Earth was scorched. Each one, sealing the power of a God away, forever. Never to be found. So they may each see out their days in peace. And that the murderer might never regain such power and sit atop Great Olympus' throne."

A cold silence swept between me and Avy. The once wonderous library had become a tomb of forbidden knowledge, the likes of which only the members of my group could probably fathom the reality of. A reality that I was quickly playing over in my head as Avy stared blankly at the end of the page.

"So..." she eventually said, lifting her head to lock eyes with me. "That's the end of the story."

"Yeah," I muttered. Nearly a minute passed, as I felt my mind churning over the details in an attempt to digest them. Or perhaps I'd already digested, and simply didn't care for the taste. "What?" I asked, when she refused to look away.

"Nothing," she replied. "It's just... you look like you're thinking about something."

"Do I?" Of course I was, but thinking a thing and saying it were two different courses of action with very different implications. Instead, I found myself on the defensive. "Oh. Well... you look like you're thinking about something too?"

"Maybe I am. Maybe I'm just thinking, 'hey, I wonder what he's thinking about?' So why don't you tell me what you're thinking and I'll tell you what I'm thinking?"

"Alright," I said. Realising that I wasn't actually the one that the story had the grandest implications for. "If this story is true, and I'm not saying it is. It's just a story, remember. A myth. But... if we were to, hypothetically, say it were true. Then, hypothetically, the thunderbolt wouldn't actually *be* a thunderbolt. It's actually more like a container. A vessel. For the powers of a God."

"Okay..." Avy managed to sound both worried and impatient. "You... still haven't told me what you're thinking."

"I'm getting there, okay. Let me do my process. So... the stones, hypothetically remember, don't actually grant power. They... restore it. To its owner. Now, obviously, nothing happens when I touch the stone. Because I'm not a God. Right?" My mouth started to dry as we quickly closed in on the conclusion I was trying to avoid verbalising. "But. When you touch it. It activates. Because... you know, hypothetically, you could be a–"

"God?" Avy frowned at me, the same way my mum would when I had just tried to convince her a lie was the truth. "You think I'm a God? Me? A few days ago you didn't even think I could be a librarian. Now you think I'm a God?"

"No," I said, waving my hands to dismiss the idea. "No. No, no, no. No way. Of course not. Come on. That would be ridiculous."

"Good." Avy seemed to breathe a sigh of relief. "Good."

"You're more like... a Goddess?"

"Zeke!?" she exclaimed in irritation.

"What?" I protested my innocence. "It's hypothetical, remember?"

"I am *not* a Goddess."

"I'm not saying you are. I'm just reading the story, same as you. And you're no idiot, so I know you came to the same conclusion."

Avy threw her hands in the air and stomped towards the exit.

"This is crazy! Since when do you believe any of this stuff?"

"I don't. Well, I didn't. But you have to admit, we're seeing an awful lot of patterns start to emerge. Too many to be coincidence. And I'm still not clear on a lot of things that happened, but the one thing I do know is that you saved me. You healed me, Avy. My injuries are gone. I may not know what's going on, but the only realistic way to figure that out is to follow this trail through to its conclusion."

Avy halted at the door and sighed. "If you eliminate the impossible, whatever remains, however improbable, must be the truth. Spock."

"Yeah." I nodded. "Although it's Sherlock Holmes, technically."

"Ugh." She ran her fingers through her hair and rubbed her scalp frantically.

At first I thought she was just frustrated, but soon she grew short of breath and her eyes began to dart around frantically.

"I'm not anything special," she said. "I'm just me. You believe me right? I know Camilla said some things. And that you probably–"

"I don't care what Camilla says." Slowly, I placed a hand on each of her shoulders, hoping to calm her down. "I know you're not lying."

"Thank you."

Thankfully, it did seem to settle her somewhat. Her bright golden eyes looked so soft, I thought they could melt at any moment, before she rested her head on my chest.

"Still… you are a little weird."

"Weird? Weird how."

"Well, for a start you seem to keep forgetting who I am. Then remembering ten minutes later."

"Right." She looked up at me, wearing a self-deprecating grin. "Sorry about that."

"It's fine. At least you seem to remember who Spock is."

"My dad loves Star Trek."

"Did I mention he sounds awesome? Besides, I've been best friends with Kang all my life. I'm used to the weirdness. You're in good hands, Wanderer."

"Wanderer?"

"Avare. Your name. It means wanderer, right? In Turkish."

"Yeah." Once again, Avy sounded like she had forgotten something important. Or at least as if she had only just remembered it. "You speak Turkish?" she asked.

"Of course," I said. "You've been underestimating me since the moment we met."

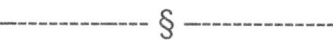

Avy and I sat in the lounge for another half an hour, still waiting for Camilla, or Kang for that matter, to return.

"I can't believe there isn't a single bar of chocolate in this whole place," said a deflated Avy.

Her mood had calmed further since the panic attack she had suffered in the library. For her sake, I ceased bringing up our findings in hopes of better discussing them with another member of my team. If they ever spoke to me again.

"I would even take a chocolate-chip cookie at this point," she continued. "Or a pain au chocolat. Why don't they have those? This is Paris, right?"

"Don't worry. I'll find you some chocolate," I said. "I promise. Honestly, if I could get us back home, my mum would whip us up something with a snap of her fingers."

As I readied myself to poke more fun at her, Kang finally came stumbling back through the door.

"Where have you been?" I asked him, feeling well within my rights to pose a few questions this time.

"Checking this place out," he replied. "Don't tell me you haven't?"

"I would have told someone where I was going first. Lime Soda, remember. You know, so we have a plan. And also so they don't think I'm up to anything?"

"Oh, I see." Kang took a few steps closer to me. "You think I was off with Camilla? Believe it or not Zeke, I spend ninety-nine percent of my time with you. A statistic I'm considering changing in the near future."

"I wasn't accusing you of anything." Truly, I didn't want to discuss it in depth in front of Avy, nor did I want to start a fight. "Actually, I just wanted to say to be careful."

"With what?"

"With her. Think about it. Camilla has been tracking us somehow. Arriving where we do. No matter how far we go."

"You think she's using me? Don't you think I've thought about that?"

"Yeah. But she's smart, remember?"

"Yeah. And I'm smarter, remember? Anyway, this can wait. I need to show you something. Come to the window."

That Kang had something more important to discuss than the Camilla-shaped wedge that was driving us apart was both a relief and cause for great concern. Eagerly, I followed him to the window, which he had already swung open as he scoured left and right.

"What are you looking for?" I wondered.

"Ah ha," he exclaimed, pointing to the right, then yanking me forward by the shoulder. "There. You see that?"

"See what?" I asked, brushing away his overly tight grip on my shoulder and squinting at the branches of a tall tree as it occasionally shed one of its bronze leaves. "It's a tree."

"Seriously?" he said. "You're doing this on purpose. To make me look crazy in front of your new girlfriend, aren't you?"

"Doing what?"

Kang sighed. "There, dude. On the branch. The bird." He was right. There definitely was a bird perched on the branch of the tree, only I had no idea what the significance of it might be. "You don't remember, do you?" He pointed once again. "That's the same kind of bird we saw back at the hotel."

"The sex hotel?" said Avy, her arms crossed in disapproval.

"Listen," Kang said, wisely ignoring her. "Outside the window. We saw it. Blue bird. Blue wings. Blue feet. Blue beak. Blue everything."

I looked again. The bird did appear blue, but the sky was growing darker by the minute as evening descended upon us and it was difficult to confirm any more details about the bird at this distance.

"Dude," I started. "I don't know anything about birds. Isn't it possible to have the same species of bird in Cyprus and France?"

"Maybe," said Kang. "But that's not the point. That thing is unnatural. What if that's how these monster women keep finding us? Think about it. They found us at the museum when all of Ealing's research was a secret. They found us at the hotel when nobody knew we were there. And they found us in the alley even though we were halfway across the city. You want to talk about someone spying on us, I think those birds are the problem."

"Kang... are you drunk?"

I could smell the rum on his breath, and though he had a pedigree for being able to handle his liquor, I had to wonder. There was a chance this weird bird obsession was just part of his need to deflect from our current mess with alcohol and conspiracy theories.

Kang's face was stern, however, expressing just how serious he was about this theory. And I wanted to take him seriously, particularly as this was the first conversation we'd had in a while that wasn't an argument. But in the corner of my eye, I saw Avy battling desperately to overcome the smirk that was threatening to spread across her face. Seconds later, she burst into laughter. Contagious laughter, apparently, as quickly I found myself smiling in Kang's face.

"Oh, okay," he said. "I get it. Laugh it up. It's all just a big joke, right? Well I'm glad you two are so happy while everything else is falling apart."

"It's not that," I said, stopping Kang as he pulled away while attempting to regain my composure. "Just hold on a sec."

"We're sorry," said Avy. "We're not laughing at you. It's just, with what we've just been reading, a magical tracking-bird actually doesn't seem all that scary anymore."

"What's so funny?" said Xiao, as she emerged from her room, yawning and stretching.

"Kang is wasted," Avy laughed.

"I am not. Xiao, maybe you'll listen," said Kang, probably getting ready to voice his bird suspicions once more, only to be interrupted by one of the doors to the hall sliding open.

Camilla was standing behind it, a fresh outfit and hairdo refreshing her since our last chat. I guess she hadn't been so busy getting us another flight after all.

"Hey," said Kang, taking a few steps towards the door. "I'm glad you're here. I need to show you–"

I raised an arm to halt him before he could take another step. Something was off. Though she was styled to her usual degree of chic, the look on Camilla's face betrayed a different mood to her arrival. Briefly, Camilla shook her head, before taking hold of the second door and sliding it the rest of the way open. Behind her, another figure loomed, as she stepped aside and made way for him to stride into the room.

Rarely do I find other people intimidating. I'm six-foot plus and built well enough to stand toe to toe with men twice my age. But it wasn't his physical stature that made this man imposing. No, there was something else about him. The way he tapped his gold studded cane on the floor tiles as his suede shoes slipped silently closer. The way he brushed his silver moustache as his head nodded between each of us. The way his dark, almost black-hole-like, eyes examined us as he unbuttoned the jacket of his plaid, burgundy blazer and settled onto the couch.

One thing was clear, as he made himself comfortable and rested his cane on the glass coffee table. He owned this room. He owned everything in it. And probably everything outside it. And right now, it felt like he owned us too.

"You must be Ezekiel," he boomed, his bassy words like cannons firing into my ears. "Welcome."

"The pleasure is mine," I replied, a droplet of sweat running beneath my arm and my heart rate multiplying by the second. "It's an honour to be your guest. Professor LaGuerre."

R.A.CRAWFORD

ACT X

THE MOTHER OF MONSTERS

'Nothing so evil as money ever grew to be current among men. This lays cities low, this drives men from their homes, this trains and warps honest souls till they set themselves to works of shame; this still teaches folk to practise villainies, and to know every godless deed. But all the men who wrought this thing for hire have made it sure that, soon or late, they shall pay the price.'

After seeing LaGuerre up close in person, for the first time, it was easy to confuse Sophocles' musings about the nature of man with Pierceson's own observations of his longtime rival.

'The man cares nothing for the story,"' Pierceson always said. 'His truth lies only in the material. The monetary.'

It only took a glance at him to see that, on face value at least, the claim was accurate. LaGuerre oozed wealth. He smelled earthy, like an inviting log cabin in the woods, as if he were sweating cologne. Of course, he wasn't sweating. No, despite my heart chugging like a locomotive, the Frenchman was serene, sliding one of the coasters closer to him on the table as he looked over at Camilla.

My eyes followed his hands, inadvertently, as I counted the gold rings that looped each of his fingers. They looked heavy and striking. Some were fierce animals, like lions and wolves. Others housed dark gemstones or were engraved with crests. And when he reached out a hand to accept the glass of cognac that Camilla had so hastily poured for him, his sleeve slipped down his arm and revealed row after row of thick chains and bracelets.

There was an exuberance about him that Pierceson lacked entirely. My benefactor was modest, at best. Maybe not in his words or works. But his appearance rarely belied his brilliance, or his own relative affluence. Shelf-bought shirts, secondhand ties and decades old footwear were commonplace in his wardrobe, while the closest thing he wore to jewellery was a metallic buckle on his belt.

"Have a seat," LaGuerre said, nodding at the couch opposite him while he took the first sip of his drink. "All of you. You're my guests."

As requested, I slid onto the middle of the sofa, as Avy parked down on my left and Kang shuffled in to my right. Xiao, only slightly surprisingly, didn't budge an inch.

LaGuerre tutted, then, much to my relief, laughed.

"Camilla warned me about you," he said, his voice jovial despite the slightly sinister rasp that was buried within. And there was something both charming and unsettling about his provincial accent. "Watch out for Xiao. She's a rebel against authority."

"I've no problem with authority," Xiao said, her tone more measured than I'd normally expect. "I just don't care for false pleasantries."

LaGuerre was still smiling, though he stopped to scratch the brown skin on his hairless head. For whatever reason, watching the warm light bounce of his scalp made me think about how young LaGuerre looked. Like Pierceson, he had to be in his sixties or seventies, that much I knew from the dates of his early publications. But, if you could count being bald as one and a silver goatee another, there were little to no other signs of decay.

His skin was smooth and unwrinkled, while his jacket bulged slightly at the arms each time he pulled his glass closer. He lacked the gauntness and languid range of motion that made Pierceson appear so much older and less mobile. Whatever LaGuerre was doing with all the money he was making here, it was certainly keeping him youthful.

If my mum had been there, she'd be blushing, nudging me in the ribs and whispering in my ear that, 'black don't crack.'

"False?" he said. "I may have an agenda, but there is nothing false to be found here. You're welcome in my abode. Just as your mentor is. Only difference is, you actually accepted my invitation. He never does."

"It wasn't much of an invitation," Xiao replied. "You grounded our plane."

"Did I?" LaGuerre's conviviality seemed to subside, as his eyes rounded accusingly on Camilla.

In all the years I've known her, I've never seen Camilla dip her head so apologetically as she did then. As if meeting his gaze would be punishment enough. As if she dare not face the consequences of accepting his ire. Eventually, after lingering too long for anyone to remain comfortable, he turned his attention back to us. Though there was still time for Camilla to shrug questioningly at Xiao, as if she had just been thrown under the bus.

Xiao was right about one thing though. It was time to stop being toyed with and figure out exactly what we were doing here.

"So what *is* your agenda?" I asked.

"Discovery, of course," he replied. "The three of you left behind quite the trail of mysteries in Nicosia. Or should I say, the four of you." His dark eyes rolled towards Avy. "I don't believe we've had the pleasure."

Before she replied, I felt the warmth of Avy's skin against mine. Her fingers curling around my wrist. I could feel her trepidation, her fear, and against my usual ascetic instincts, I took her by the hand and held her palm tight.

"Avy," she said. "Avy Pendragon."

"Ah." LaGuerre's eyes fixated upon her. Just as I thought he might accuse her directly of something, he seemed to relax once more, resting his tumbler atop the coaster and reclining into the cushions in his chair. "It's quite the wonderful name. Tell me, do you know the story of the Pendragons?"

"You mean King Arthur?" Avy asked.

"And the Knights of the Round Table," Kang added. "Every kid knows their story. There was a great cartoon about it in the nineties too."

"The Knight of Justice?" LaGuerre nodded. "Excellent story. Poorly animated. No, I'm not speaking of the Knights. You see when you remove the romanticism, there is a point to every myth and every legend. People don't tell stories just to entertain, they tell them to reveal something. A hidden truth. A lesson."

"And what does King Arthur reveal?" I asked.

"King Uther," LaGuerre corrected me. "Uther Pendragon. Not a well known King, but didn't he leave quite the legacy? You see, he used magic, from Merlin himself, to disguise himself as his enemy. Why? For a woman of course. He appeared to Igraine as Gorlois, her husband, and conceived with her an illegitimate child. And that child should have been a misfit. An outcast. But instead, they were one in a million. From Uther's monstrous deeds, came the once and future king. One amongst all who could step forth and pull a magical sword from a magical stone. Isn't that something? An ordinary sword in the hands of one, a weapon of immense power in the hands of another."

Avy was squeezing my hand so tight, I could barely feel the blood circulating.

"What was your Father's name, Miss Pendragon?" asked LaGuerre, his sonorous voice growing more sinister with every syllable. "I don't suppose he gave you something just as special, did he?"

He knew something. I wasn't sure what or how. But he knew something about Avy and he wanted her to admit it.

"Avy's father was just a librarian," I said, stepping in where she had become frozen.

"Of the library that you destroyed? After fleeing a murder scene?"

"How do you know that?"

"Isn't it obvious," said Xiao, pointing at Camilla. "She told him."

"It doesn't matter how I know," LaGuerre said. "What matters is that the four of you are in trouble. And I am in a position to help."

"We don't need your help." Xiao came and stood by the three of us. "We just need to be on our way. You're not getting anything out of us."

"You think me a thief?" LaGuerre held his hands up, protesting his innocence. "A liar? A cheat? That I would copy and steal your mentors' work. No, no. I am a businessman. You can give Pierceson his credit and his dues. Post his name in your memoirs and hold a conference in his honour. I merely ask that you have the good financial sense to keep it here, with me. Where it will have purpose."

Telepathically, or something at least using the approximation of telepathy that Kang and I had developed, we knew to look at each other. And I knew what he was thinking, just as he must have known what was on my mind. LaGuerre's tongue may have been lined with silver, but his eagerness had given the game away.

"Keep what here?" Kang said it before I could.

For just a fraction of a second, LaGuerre hesitated, before slipping back into character. "Whatever Ealing gave you. Whatever you are so desperate to carry home."

"You think he gave us something?" I said. "We're not even sure what he was working on."

"I think you do. I think you're harbouring something more valuable than you know what to do with. And I think you should tell me the truth."

"If you are looking for expert liars," said Xiao. "You'll find none here. Except your favourite apprentice of course. Maybe you shouldn't be so quick to believe everything she tells you."

LaGuerre sighed, exhaustedly, before downing the rest of his drink and rising to his feet.

"Very well," he said. "Play your games. We'll talk again before you leave. Let's hope that by then, you've decided to become more… cooperative."

He buttoned his jacket and swept his cane up off the table, stepping closer to me and extending one arm. As I reached out to meet it, he clamped down on my wrist, with far more strength than I had been expecting for a man of his years.

"Be mindful, Ezekiel," he whispered, pulling me in close. "When you escape a whirlpool, it's easy to lose track of which way is home. Remember, the thorn from the bush one has planted, nourished and pruned, pricks more deeply and draws more blood."

Before I could reply, he was smiling again and patting me on the shoulder, before doing the same to Kang and Avy, then settling for a courteous nod with Xiao. Not long after, he was gone, disappearing into the hall as Camilla stood waiting to slide the doors shut behind him.

"Hey," she said, a half-whisper half-shout. "We are leaving here first thing tomorrow. Be ready."

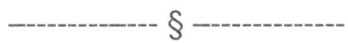

The night seemed everlasting, as heavy rain draped the windows and winds rattled the glass. There was little chance of sleep. I kept playing over what LaGuerre had said. *The thorn from the bush one has planted.* I knew the saying well enough. It was Maya Angelou. Though my mum had repeated it so often during my school years, that I could be excused for thinking the words had always been hers.

Was he talking about Avy? She would never betray us. Not after what we just read. Not after finding out that she could be... but then, did she only just find out? There was still so much about her that I didn't know. Her name... it did sound fake. And that story LaGuerre told, about Arthur and the sword. He was drawing parallels. But why? For my benefit? That meant he suspected her of something. Or wanted me to suspect her of something. What if she wasn't telling me the whole truth? What if he, Kang, and Camilla were all right?

No. I was letting him get in my head. The only way he could have known all those things is if he had someone spying on us. Even Camilla hadn't seen Avy use the stone. He was just trying to use the breadcrumbs of information he had to misdirect us for his own gain. So he could get hold of the stone and make another fortune at our expense. He had no idea what the stone was, so there was no way in hell I was going to let it fall into his–

My concentration broke when the door creaked open.

"Avy?" I wondered.

"You'd like that wouldn't you?" said Kang. "A girl sneaking into your room in the middle of the night?"

I breathed a sigh of relief. Though the fact that I felt relieved not to see Avy right now was another confusing matter. "You can't sleep either?"

"Not with all this going on." Kang sagged down onto the bed beside me. "This is a mess, Zeke."

"I know."

"I feel like we're on the Orient Express or something. Like we can't trust anyone."

I shook my head.

"We can trust each other," I said. "And Xiao."

"Right." Kang nodded.

"And Avy."

Kang stood up from the bed, rubbing his temples.

"No. We can't. She is lying to us, Zeke. Even LaGuerre can tell that."

"Lying about what?" I said

"I don't know!" Kang was pacing back and forth in the room. "About something."

"That's the best you can do? Avy is on our side. She's saved my life and yours."

"She's just been saving herself, dude. She saved you so you would buy into her story even more. Can't you see that? Your new girlfriend is going to get us all killed with her magical powers or whatever it is she does. We can't trust her."

"But we can trust yours?" I said, rising to accuse him. "Your secret girlfriend who you've been conspiring with behind our backs for who knows how long?"

"Camilla isn't conspiring against us, Zeke. And she isn't my girlfriend."

"Right. Because you're always interested in women for their intellect. You have no idea what she's after dude."

"I do know. She isn't interested in our secrets. She's interested in me. In friendship. We're not together. But dude, she's lonely. She missed me. She missed us. And what's really dumb about all this, is that I know you feel the same. You just won't admit it!"

Kang placed his arm on my shoulder, but I swatted it away.

"Wake up, Kang! She's playing you."

"Wow. So this is it? How you really see me?" Kang's face was a picture of revulsion. "No woman could ever really be interested in pathetic little Nathan, right? The only reason any woman would ever want to be my friend, is to get to you."

"I never said that. You're putting words in my mouth."

"Oh, you're not saying them, but I know you're thinking them. And I know what this is. It's jealousy."

"Jealousy?"

"That's right." Kang stepped so close I could almost feel his beard brushing against my chin. "You're jealous, because you always acted like it was only you two who had something special and now you resent us both for excluding you. You're the one who needs to wake up. I'm not your geeky little sidekick anymore, Zeke. She can talk to me because I have matured into someone who people actually like. Someone who listens to what she has to say instead of judging her. And you, on the other hand, have matured into a dick."

I'd never wanted to hit Kang before. Not really. When he was acting up, or getting in the way or generally being Kang, sure I'd think about shutting him up. But this really was the first time I'd wanted to hurt him. My fist was already balled, ready to strike him in that square chin of his, and make him regret ever speaking to me that way.

But I couldn't. No matter how badly I wanted to, I couldn't do it. Not because actually perpetrating the act would make him exactly right. But because he already was. Whether it was a trick or legitimate friendship was irrelevant. Kang knew I would never accept it, simply because it was her. And I had run out of evidence to suggest otherwise.

"Kang," I said, speaking even as I attempted to figure out what I wanted to say. "I–" Before the words would take shape, the room went dark.

"What now?" whispered Kang. "A power cut?"

"Maybe," I replied, just as quietly, reaching for the bedside lamp and flicking the switch, to no avail. "Everything's dead."

"This is bad. We gotta get out of here."

"Right. Why are we whispering though?"

"Because you never know who is listening," Kang said.

"How true," said a voice from the darkness, as the lamp seemed to turn on by itself, and three dark figures stood not three feet in front of us.

"Shi–" Kang tried to shout, but instantly one of the figures was in front of him, clamping her hand over his mouth and forcing him back against the wall. I watched him grimace, as the woman held him steady with just one hand, and when I turned back, another of the figures was directly in front of me. Her blade at my throat.

Like Kang, I wanted to cry out in fear. The only thing that stopped me, was that unfortunately, I recognised the three figures. The three women.

The one keeping Kang suppressed, was the same psychopathic murderer that confronted me back at the hotel. Thick and curly blonde hair. Hungry brown eyes. And that impudent and ruthless smirk on her face. Kerrel, that was her name.

I knew he was in more danger than I was. The woman in front of me looked identical, the same brown eyes, a tad softer maybe. But her hair was different, long dark braids twisted into a bun, and a smile that was somehow... reassuring, despite the icy steel of her sword against my skin. Kelis. The one that had saved me from the police in the alley. She hadn't seemed to want to hurt me then and there was something about her that made me feel almost safe even now.

Almost. Because the third woman, standing motionless behind them. Her hair, mouth, cheeks and even her nose might have been obscured by a dark head wrap, but those eyes were symbolic enough. Those uncanny, inhuman emerald green eyes.

"You," I said, not bothering to discard the contempt I felt for the vile woman. "You're the one from the museum. You murdered Ealing."

"And Vinter," Kang wheezed, Kerrel now simply pressing one hand against his chest rather than his mouth.

"If you only knew why," said the woman, her voice deeper and coarser than someone of her petite stature should sound.

"Because you–" I realised I was shouting when Kelis shoved her hand over my mouth, and the emerald eyed woman had one finger pressed to her lips.

"Please," she said, still motioning for us to hush. "We don't wish you harm."

I raised my eyebrows, as Kelis uncovered my mouth, and kept her weapon ready. "Could have fooled me."

"Release them," she hissed.

"But mother," said Kerrel. The emerald-eyed woman silenced her with a wave of her hand.

Mother. This was the one they had been referring to before. The one who had given them orders to find us. She had been pulling the strings since that night at the hotel. And, somehow, despite us travelling across countries and seas, she had found us again.

"This place is not safe," she said, stepping closer towards me as her two accomplices sheathed their weapons and I backed up beside Kang. "We must go."

"We?" I said.

"Why would we go anywhere with you?" Kang demanded. "So you can take us to another alley and kill us there?"

"Please," said Kelis. "We aren't trying to hurt you."

"This time," Kerrel added, her eyes still wide with desire.

"On this occasion," said the woman. "We share a common enemy."

"LaGuerre?" I wondered. "You don't want him to have the stone." The woman nodded. "Why?"

She took another few steps closer, until we were eye to emerald eye. Until I could see the pale lime tint of her skin. Until I could see the thin veins bulging beneath her pores. Until I could see that there were no whites or pupils in her eyes. Just an endless tunnel of green light. Until I was certain that whatever this woman was, she wasn't human.

"The why is unimportant. Just know that he will kill you both, and your friends, before he lets you leave with the stone. My only offer is that you leave with me and I promise you no harm. Take it or leave it."

Again, I found myself staring at Kang for answers. I found none as he returned the gesture, a blank look of hopelessness. Of confusion. Of wondering how on Earth we ended up in this mayhem and if it would ever end.

"Alright," I said.

"Good," she replied, as her eyes scanned me up and down. "Now where is the stone?"

"That wasn't part of the deal," Kang warned.

The woman's eyes grew narrow. "But you still have it?"

"It's safe," I replied. Which one of us had the stone was just about the only card we had left to play. And both Kang and I knew better than to reveal our hand before we even knew the true stakes of the game.

"Very well." She nodded and stepped towards the doors, somehow extinguishing the lights with a flick of her fingers. "Girls. Retrieve their friends. You two stay close to me."

I didn't like the idea of leaving Avy and Xiao in the hands of the two other women. After all, the four of them had tried to kill each other the last time we met. Then again, there was little I could do but entrust our escape to them. The idea of relying on this murderous woman for anything made my stomach churn, and I kept seeing Ealing's death playing through my head on repeat. But even though I abhorred her, there was something about LaGuerre. About the way even Camilla seemed to shrink in his presence, that made me certain he was not someone to be trifled with. The only way I could stifle the implications of it all was to concentrate on figuring out a way to keep the stone from them both.

I couldn't see the woman's feet beneath the long dark robe she was wearing, but she was fast. She seemed to glide across the floor, monitors and lights flickering out when she passed them, as she swept out into the hall and turned into what looked like a dead end. Another swipe of her hand later, and a bookcase was sliding out of view to reveal a flight of stone steps down into the darkness. When we followed her to the bottom, somehow Xiao and Avy were already waiting.

"Zeke!" Avy shouted, as she barreled into me, throwing her arms around my neck.

I did the same, pulling her in close until I found the emerald-eyed woman's eyes upon us.

"Are you finished?" she asked.

"What the hell is going on?" said Xiao, who had both arms pinned behind her back as she was trying to wrestle free. "Tell this vampire bitch to get off me."

"I think she's technically a lamiai," I said.

"I don't care. Get her off."

"For the hundredth time," said Kerrel. "I'm not trying to hurt you. Stop fighting."

"Xiao," said Kang, pulling her away from Kerrel's grip. "Calm down. We'll explain. Is your arm okay?"

"It's fine," said Xiao. "Now start explaining. Because you are not–"

"Alright enough!" shouted Kang. "Please just let us get out of here first."

"Quiet. All of you," The emerald-eyed woman held her hands out, waiting for everyone to be still. To be silent. "We are not alone."

"No," said a resounding voice. LaGuerre's voice. "You are not."

The woman clicked her fingers and each of the lights above our heads burst into life one by one. Soon, the cold stone room had been sprinkled with blue light. Enough light to see LaGuerre, leaning forward on his cane, and the security personnel flanking him.

"Well, well," he continued, sweeping one hand beneath his jacket to unbutton it. "The mother finally shows herself. And in my own secret passage no less. Don't you know it's rude to show up uninvited?"

"Fear not," said the woman. "We'll be taking leave of this place shortly."

LaGuerre laughed, slowly and in a manner devoid of any actual humour. "You can all leave, as long as we keep things cordial. And you hand over the stone."

The woman turned her back to us, her emerald-eyes glowing wildly.

"Run," she shouted.

"This way," yelled Kelis, as she started back up the stairs. But her path was quickly blocked as a loud crack echoed through the chamber and the bookcase slammed shut.

"How unfortunate," said LaGuerre, tapping the gold foot of his cane against the stone floor to create another loud crackle, as if he were striking with a sledgehammer. "You've chosen the unpleasant way."

The third time he slammed his cane against the ground, his guards unfolded their arms and stepped forward. Then all at once, and in the blink of an eye, they weren't guards anymore. There were no more black suits and ties. No more scowls and beady eyes. No, before us stood four creatures plucked straight from common myth. Or from nightmares. And unlike all the aberrations that had happened up until now. The dog. The women. The stone. I knew that this time, there was no ignoring, and no rationalising what we were facing.

On LaGuerre's left and right were two bulky animals, wrapped in dark fur and leather hides, wielding gigantic double-axes. Their wet snouts puffed smokey air as their cloven hooves trampled upon the stone towards us. The only thing more ferocious than the serrated weapons they brandished were the pair of curved horns that twisted away from their scalps and felt as if they were targeting us.

"Mother?" said Kerrel. "What now?"

The emerald-eyed woman took a step back, then reached a hand towards Kerrel. "Blood," she demanded.

Quickly, Kerrel drew her blade and swept it across the woman's palm, slicing open the flesh. The woman was unruffled, returning her attention to the threat in front, as she squeezed her lacerated hand into a fist until blood leaked down from her wrist. The dark liquid pooled into a circle on the floor, bubbling as if it were being boiled. The stench was powerful, though it didn't smell like blood. It was more distinct. Repulsive and almost acidic, like... urine.

"He always smells," said Kerrel, pinching her nose.

"Shield your eyes," the woman said, as she leapt aside and the pool burst to life. Heeding her warning, I threw my guard up just in time as blood splashed over the walls and ceiling. A deafening roar shook the room and when I finally lowered my arm, the blood pool was gone. In its place, was a towering beast, almost brushing its head against the roof of the cellar. Its golden fur was splattered with dark crimson blotches and its thick mane was frayed at the edges, but there was no mistaking it. It was a lion.

"Exit," said the woman, brushing the back of her fingers against the monstrous lion's fur.

It roared again in response, shaking the walls and forcing me and my friends to cover our ears, before turning and dashing towards the back of the room. Kelis dragged Avy and I aside, as the lion charged up the stairs and smashed head first through the bookcase.

"Go!" shouted the emerald-eyed woman. "We will hold them here. Now!" she yelled again, when she saw each of us still paralysed by fear.

"Come on," said Xiao, taking Kang by the arm and ushering him up the stairs.

Following her lead, I reached for Avy's hand and pulled her along behind me, as we bolted back up into LaGuerre's warehouse-estate.

"Like you said," Xiao continued. "Talk later. Run now."

"My thoughts exactly," Kang replied.

Xiao led the way, twisting and turning along the route we had taken upon arrival. The exit was only just in sight, when the adjacent wall burst apart and the lion came crashing through. And it wasn't alone. Atop the mighty creature, was another minotaur, skewering it through the chest with its pointed horn, before leaping down and fixing its attention on us.

"Back," shouted Xiao, immediately spinning about and darting back the way we came.

Twice I glanced back, checking whether the creature was pursuing us, only to find it raising its axe high above its head.

"Move!" I shouted, grabbing Avy and leaping to the side just as Kang shoved Xiao in the back and hit the deck.

No sooner had we landed, did the minotaur's deadly axe come spinning through the air and sink into the wall between us.

"Are you hurt?" I asked Avy, as I stood up and used the wall to steady myself.

"No," she said, already on her feet.

"Zeke!" Kang's voice dragged my attention away from her. "It's coming. Run!" The minotaurs giant axe was lodged against the doorway, trapping Xiao and Kang in the hall they had landed in, as the creature plodded menacingly towards us. "We'll find a way around."

"Alright," I shouted. "Meet us in the courtyard."

"Go!" said Xiao, her eyes darting back and forth between us and the nearing creature.

"Come on." Avy grabbed me by the arm and pulled me towards the opposite hall. "This way," she said, moving so fast and pinching my arm so tight that I felt like a child again, being hauled along by my mum.

She spun me about, as she backed into one of the rooms and dragged us behind one of the shelving cabinets. With one finger pressed to her lips, she slid down onto her haunches and opened her palm towards me.

"The stone," she whispered. "I need it."

My gut wrenched as she asked. "We can't."

"What?" Avy looked furious with me for the first time I could remember, her brow a storm of disapproval and heartache. "You can't be serious. After all this, now you don't want me to have it? I can't believe you would–"

"Avy. Quiet," I said, pressing my finger to her lips this time. "It's not that. I don't have it. I thought it would be safer for me not to, while we were here at least."

Avy managed to look both relieved and disappointed at the same time.

"What do we do?" she asked, her golden eyes trembling.

I pulled her in close and held my breath, as the sound of the beast neared. The taps of its hooves, each one louder than the last, made my heart skip every other beat. I held my breath, the minotaur so close I could hear its grizzled breath on the other side of the cabinet and smell the sweat of its leathery hide.

"The stone."

I wasn't sure if the voice was in the room or in my mind. It was muffled, almost like a growl. And there was something not human, almost... animalistic about the way the sound vibrated around my head.

"Give us the stone," it said again.

I hadn't taken a breath for over a minute, only finally exhaling when a hairy fist drove through the cabinet, sending shards of wood splintering over me, and clamped around my neck. As the minotaur's hefty thumb pressed down on my throat, I quickly lost the strength to try and wrestle him away. My eyes sunk to Avy, wondering if she would at least flee for her own life. But she wasn't running, or panicking or weeping. She was staring defiantly back at me and for just a brief second, I could have sworn I saw a greater amber glow in her already bright eyes as she shot into action.

Shoulder first, she crashed through the cabinet, taking the minotaur by surprise as she slammed him back against the wall. I gasped for air as I was knocked free, scrambling to my feet to see if Avy was still alive as another grotesque roar reverberated around the room.

The minotaur was pinned against the wall, as Avy somehow matched it for strength. The creature was trying to reach for her face with one arm, but she had a tight grip on his wrist, fighting him with everything she had.

Unfortunately, it didn't take long for the tide to turn. The minotaur drove its knee into her stomach, causing her to lose her grip before raising both hands and bringing them down towards her head. She caught his fists, but gradually he was forcing her down to her knees. I don't know whether it was instinct or just outright fear for Avy, but something made me launch towards the minotaur, grab hold of his arms and try to help her force him back.

I closed my eyes and strained with every ounce of strength and every muscle in my body, as I tried to push against the creature. Deep down, I knew my meagre resistance was worth little to her, but I couldn't just watch and do nothing as she put herself in danger for me yet again. But just as it looked like the minotaur was going to bring his fists down and pommel her over the head, his arms began to rise again.

"We're doing it," I said.

"You're doing nothing," said another strained voice.

I opened my eyes to find Kerrel next to me, the triceps in her dark athletic arms tensed as she drove the creature's fists back towards the ceiling.

"We're doing all the work. Girl," she said, clearly ignoring me and talking to Avy. "When I say, push him back with everything you have. Then I'll finish him off."

Avy nodded, as both women seemed to relax a little and the minotaurs' fists dropped closer to us. I knew I wasn't adding half as much strength as either of them, but I wanted to help them even if it was just a little. I bent my legs, feeling the crushing weight of the minotaur against us, and waited for Kerrel's signal.

"Now!" she shouted.

Alongside the two of them, I exploded into action and pushed back against the minotaur. As his arms were blown away, back over his head, Avy turned and tackled me to the ground. Kerrel on the other hand, had wasted no time drawing her sword and burying it deep in the neck of the minotaur. The creature didn't have time to cry out in agony as it sagged to the floor.

"Thanks," I said, as Avy helped me back to my feet.

"You're welcome," said Kerrel.

Ignoring her, I checked each of Avy's hands.

"How did you do that?" I asked, unsure exactly what I was checking for. Glowing light, magical symbols. At this point, nothing seemed out of the question. "Without the stone I mean?"

Avy grimaced. "Zeke, you do remember I have absolutely no idea what I'm doing? Right?"

"Not bad," Kerrel said, as she wiped the blade against her thigh. "For a... what are you again?"

"You're not going to drink that?" I asked, as she returned her sword to its sheath, and examined the blood on her hands.

"This?" she said, with disgust. "This isn't even real blood. All here is not what it seems. Though it looks like you're finally starting to realise that."

She nodded back at the ground where the minotaur's corpse should have been. In its place, there was only a black tie, just like the ones the security guards had been wearing.

"I don't understand," Avy said.

"And you don't need to. Let's just get out of here so I can find mother."

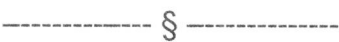

Following closely behind Kerrel, we hurried out to the courtyard, only to find an even more chaotic scene awaiting us. Kang was waiting in the back of one of the pickup trucks, while Xiao sat angrily wringing her hands against the steering wheel. The emerald-eyed woman was standing beside their vehicle, one arm hanging limply at her side as dark green blood dripped to the ground, and the other arm cradling a puncture wound in her abdomen.

"Mother!" cried Kerrel, as she left us behind and sprinted to the woman's side.

Opposite them, stood LaGuerre. Still calm as ever, he was smiling as he pressed his cane into the neck of Kelis, who was laid out on the ground in front of him.

"I think this is as simple as I can make this," LaGuerre said. "The stone stays here, or the gorgon dies. Decide quickly, dread mother."

Avy and I finally reached the truck, and the emerald-eyed woman turned towards us as we arrived. There was a gash across one of her glimmering eyes, eyes that even with their demonic appearance, looked pained.

"Can you revive him?" Kerrel nodded in the direction of the oversized lion, laying motionless against the caved-in wall at the front of the warehouse.

The woman shook her head. "I'm out of blood."

The pair looked desperate, as the woman directed her attention to me instead.

"Is the stone safe?" she demanded. I glanced briefly inside the vehicle, then nodded. "Good. Return to your plane. I will ensure he does not follow."

"Mother," Kerrel protested. "You're weakened. Deimos will kill you."

Deimos. She called him Deimos. As in, Deimos master of terror. Deimos, the son of Ares. Deimos, the God. LaGuerre was a God.

"Make sure they arrive safely," said the emerald-eyed woman.

"I'm not leaving you," Kerrel protested.

"You will do as I command." The emerald-eyed woman ran her fingers across Kerrel's cheek, before taking a few steps towards LaGuerre.

"You're on the wrong side, boy," LaGuerre said, his voice projecting across the courtyard, reaching us like a thunderstorm. "You will be betrayed again and again, whenever you trust them. And your master, he betrays you too. He's fooled you into thinking he is chasing knowledge. And that I desire nought but wealth. But this is about neither. It's about power. And you mean to hand it over to a monster."

"Enough," said the woman. "Release my child and face me, coward."

"You?" LaGuerre cackled, and the darkening sky seemed to echo him. "You are nothing. A pet loose from her leash. It's time I wipe you from this Earth, like my Grandfather did your husband."

The winds circled as the two of them prepared to face off, a showdown between two powers I couldn't understand. It felt like we were interrupting just by watching them, but I couldn't take my eyes off either for even a second. At least until Kerrel took me by the arm, nearly breaking it as she yanked me towards her.

"Listen up," she said, as if we were comrades. "My sister protected you. You owe her. And mother protects you still. When Deimos goes down, I want you to get them both out of here. Understand?"

Truthfully, I didn't, but for once my blank stare didn't elicit anger from her. Her eyes didn't burn with rage and fire. They were soft. They were afraid.

"Please, Zeke," she begged.

"Alright." I nodded, moved by her sudden show of emotion. "I promise. But what are you going to do?"

Kerrel smiled and drew her blade.

"Protect the ones I love," she said. "Same as you."

In one quick motion, Kerrel drove the sword through her own chest, then collapsed in a lifeless heap. Before she even hit the ground, the emerald-eyed woman had spun and charged towards her, screaming. As she knelt in a pool of Kerrel's violet blood, she howled at the sky like a grieving mother.

But LaGuerre was still standing. He was still laughing too.

"It looks like your whole family is going to die today," he jested. "I'll at least let this one go if you just hand over the stone now. Though I can't promise you the same. The world has enough true monsters in it."

I wasn't exactly sure what Kerrel had expected to happen, until the emerald-eyed woman began to reluctantly dip her hands into the pool of blood. She spread her fingers and her lips began to move, silently. She was chanting something, something the rest of us couldn't hear. Then the blood began to boil, turning to steam as it rose into the air. And when it had plumed into a red cloud all around her, she clasped her hands together, causing it to disperse.

"Disappointing," said LaGuerre, when nothing happened. "It seems you're too weak to even summon another–"

Before LaGuerre could finish taunting her, he was bitten in half.

The lion laying dormant by the warehouse had sprung to life, making quick work of the courtyard between them, and clamped its jaws around him. No sooner had it chomped on its prey, did the lion also begin to fade. Its skin turned to water, and the water turned to blood, as it melted into a puddle on the floor.

For a moment, I thought the emerald-eyed woman would be next. But rather than fade away, she swayed back and forth, before finally collapsing. She fell flat on her back, lying in a pool of Kerrel and the lion's blood, while Kelis laid still unconscious just a few metres from her.

"Did everyone else just see that?" said Kang, as the winds calmed and the stars grew brighter in the sky once more. "Seriously. Did everyone else just freaking see that?"

"We saw it," said Xiao, annoyed at either Kang or, more likely, the entire scene. "Let's get out of here."

"Right," said Avy, clambering up into the back of the truck, before extending a hand to me. "Zeke, let's go."

The sensible thing to do was to take her hand and jump up into the back of the truck. To leave behind the madness, and the monsters, and the Gods. It was the smart thing to do. The easy thing to do. But it wasn't the right thing to do.

Kerrel had just given her life to save us. And to save these other two. The same woman that wanted me dead had begged me to save her family. She wanted to save them even more than she wanted revenge on us. And no matter what they were, even if they were really monsters, I wasn't.

"Help me with them," I said, as I waded quickly through the bloodstains.

"What are you doing?" asked Kang.

"I promised to take them with us."

"So what?"

"Promises mean something, Kang. Now help me."

"This is insane," Kang protested "Xiao, would you talk some sense into him?"

Xiao looked unhappy. She always did. But I knew what she would do before Kang even asked. With a heavy sigh, she threw open the door and leapt down from the truck.

"Come on you two," she said to Kang and Avy. "Get them in the truck."

The four of us, including the still half-reluctant Kang, worked quickly to load the woman and Kelis into the back and a few minutes later, Xiao was speeding us away from the warehouse and back towards the airport.

"This is a mistake," said Kang. "They're murderers."

"I know," I replied, trying to suppress the acknowledgement that he was absolutely right. "But we might need them again."

"They might try to kill us again."

"I know that too. But I couldn't just leave them."

"Why not?" asked Avy, her bright eyes probing for answers.

"Because," croaked the woman, apparently conscious, as one of her emerald eyes slid open. "He doesn't believe in breaking his promises."

"Is that right?" I said, leaning in a little closer to her. There was something less chilling about her at this distance. Something altogether more... human. And I thought I finally knew why. "And how would you know?"

The woman closed her eye again, and there was something about the shape of her face beneath the cloth masking it that all but confirmed what I was feeling. A change in her expression.

"Honestly, I figured you already knew," she replied.

"Unfortunately," I said, as I reached down towards her. "You've always been able to pull the wool over my eyes."

"Zeke," said Avy, causing me to briefly recoil. "Be careful."

Heeding her warning, I reached carefully around the woman's neck and pulled at the cloth. As it began to unfurl, I loosened each corner, then lifted it over the top of her head.

"Holy shit," I said, as I stared at her face. I couldn't help exclaiming, even if on the inside I already knew.

Her skin may have been faint-green and her eyes like emeralds, but the rest of her face I could recognise anywhere. The sharp cheekbones. The slim nose. But more than anything, those perfect white-teeth, glinting up at me as she laid there... smiling.

"It can't be," said Kang. "Camilla?"

ACT XI

THE PIERCER'S SON

'Let no one think me a weak one, feeble-spirited, A stay-at-home, but rather just the opposite, One who can hurt my enemies and help my friends; For the lives of such persons are most remembered.'

How did I become so blind?

I'd always known Camilla was dangerous. But I'd always assumed her power lay in her words. Her wisdom. In all the time I'd known her. Worked with her. Eaten with her. Lived with her. And more recently, hated her. How had I never once suspected that there was something else, someone else, beneath her mask.

I hadn't always disparaged her. I wasn't Euripides, painting some misogynistic picture of a weak and feeble woman, where I was the sympathetic hero and she, the tragic villain. When we had been close, I embraced her strengths. When she led, I followed. And the admiration was mutual. I thought everything changed only after we split. But in hindsight, it was clear I never really knew her. Or at least, the person I thought I knew was a lie.

"We're here," said Xiao, as she sent the truck into an unnecessary handbrake turn, rattling each of us around and pulling up beside the private hangar.

"Help me up," Camilla wheezed, clearly still feeling the effects of the wounds she had suffered. I reached out a hand, before hesitating and leaning back away from her. "What? Don't tell me that you're scared of me now? Haven't I always been terrifying to you?"

I didn't rise to her taunt. We were way past the old rivalry that I had spent so long embroiled within, unable to see the forest from the trees.

"Where is the plane headed this time?" I asked.

"Where do you think?" she replied. I didn't answer, instead trying my best to remain harsh with her. "London," she added. "Cambridge."

"How can we be sure?"

"Zeke." She sat up this time, wincing and groaning as she fought against the pain. "I didn't just risk everything to–"

"Alright," I said, taking her by the hand and helping her move. "I believe you. But you betrayed LaGuerre to help us. How do I know you won't do the same again?"

"I didn't betray him," she protested. "You're still not seeing the big picture, are you?"

Before I could mull over what she meant by that, Xiao was around the back of the truck, opening the tailgate.

"You never worked for LaGuerre," she said. "It was all just a front. Wasn't it? For Pierceson? He sent you to him."

When Camilla nodded, it felt like someone had just kicked me in the gut. All this time. All the hatred, and the second-guessing and the paranoia. After all that, we had been working for the same man all along.

"I know you have questions," Camilla said. "And I will answer them, I promise. But right now, we need to get in the air. Fast. LaGuerre... Deimos. He will not be far behind."

"Wait," said Avy, hopping down from the truck. "Am I *really* losing my mind? Did he not just get bitten in two by a giant ten-foot lion?"

"He lives," Camilla snapped. "We can only hope to hinder him. No means I possess can kill a God."

"Okay," Avy said, biting her lip. "So we're really sticking with the God thing. Great..."

There were a lot of unravelled threads to tie, but Camilla was right. There was no sense in waiting here. With Avy's support, I helped Camilla limp towards the plane, while Xiao and the still silent Kang dragged Kelis over their shoulders.

"I take it, we have fuel this time?" asked Xiao.

"Yes. I was a fool before," Camilla replied, as she stuttered up the steps. "We always had fuel. But Deimos is the God of Terror. He can make us see things. Our nightmares. And our fears. And I... feared going to him. Now you know why. Even I can't see through all his illusions."

Her words were doleful. Whatever her true nature might have been, Camilla's affection for Kerrel was real. Her loss was real. Which made it even more startling when we rounded into the aisle and found a familiar face waiting for us.

A tall, dark-skinned woman, standing with her hands on her hips. At her waist hung a short-sword, the scabbard painted with blood-red flowers. And her face... other than the shaved sides of her head and spiked mohawk, she was the spitting image of Kerrel or Kelis.

"Kerrel?" I said, confused as to how she could be here.

"Mother?" she cried, rushing to Camilla's aid.

"I'll explain later," Camilla said. "After you get us in the air." The woman looked at me, through one eye, her second covered by an eye-patch. "It's okay. They're with me." Camilla opened her palm and gestured at the woman, then at me. "Ketra, Zeke. Zeke, Ketra. There, you're introduced. Now go. I need someone in the cockpit I can trust this time."

I helped Camilla into one of the seats, as the other woman grudgingly headed off to seal the doors, then disappeared into the cockpit.

"Ketra?" I said, pointing a thumb as I took a seat opposite. "Just how many of them are there?"

"It's complicated," Camilla replied.

"Uncomplicate it," said Xiao, as she slipped into the seat beside me.

"Fine," she sighed, before casting her eyes up at Kang, where he was loitering further down the aisle.

The emerald-green glow had faded and back were the, admittedly less vivid, cerulean eyes of the Camilla I knew.

"I can explain all this, Nate," she said, her voice trembling slightly. "You don't have to be afraid of me."

Kang looked sheepish, holding his distance before adding, "Then you better start explaining."

"I second that," said Avy, as she parked herself into the seat beside Camilla, glaring at her.

"Clearly, I'm not who you thought," Camilla started. "And I'm not *what* you thought."

"Clearly," Xiao repeated.

"But now that you've seen so much, you must at least be starting to put the pieces together. Am I right, Zeke?"

I was listening to every word she said, but yes, I was quickly trying to assemble the data gathered in my subconscious to cross-reference with everything we had seen. Her appearance in the museum, the two-headed dog, the lion and the trio of wicked women.

"I think so, yeah," I finally replied. "You're Echidna. The Mother of all Monsters."

Camilla rolled her eyes. "So dramatic. And a little insulting. That word, monster. That was a curse given to us by Zeus. And used by every mortal since to brand everything they fear or don't understand."

"So what are you then?" asked Avy.

"Does it matter?" Camilla shrugged. "Part Nymph. Part Deity. Part mystery. Many parts. And many myths. Only a few truths though."

"And the other monst–" I managed to catch my tongue before the insults could continue to roll. "The other women. Like Kelis. You created them?"

"Yes." She nodded proudly. "They're my family."

"Okay," said Xiao, scything through the revelations. "That explains next to nothing. All this would make you hundreds, or thousands, of years old. Get to that part. And get to whatever is going on."

"Of course," Camilla sighed, and her brow wrinkled as if she were searching for the right words to use.

Words that could possibly explain everything we had seen.

"Zeus is dead," she finally said. "Everything you've learned about. Every myth, legend and fairytale has some truth in it. The Gods were real. Their powers were real. Their deeds were real."

"Were?" asked Xiao.

"Yes, *were*. The reason we live in the world as it is now, the reason Gods don't soar down from the sky in chariots, the reason they have become three-thousand year old poems instead of stories on the evening news, is because Zeus was murdered. By one of his own kin. And the last thing he did before he died, was to cast out the remainder of the Gods. There were only ten left, by the time the war had run. But he sent them down to Earth, powerless, where they have lived ever since."

"The Ten Thunderbolts," I said. "I get it now. The story Avy and I read. Metabus Volsci. That was you. You wrote it. It was first hand experience."

"That was an old alias. I had to take on something new, so–"

"His daughter," Kang mumbled from afar. "He threw her across a river, on a spear. Her name was Camilla. Nice new alias for you."

Camilla dipped her head. I hadn't seen her look this embarrassed in... actually I'd just never seen her this embarrassed.

"Wait?" said Xiao. "What story?"

"Back at LaGuerre's," I said. "We found a myth in his library. It said the Gods were at war with the Demigods. And that Zeus called upon his old enemies for help. One of them was her, Echidna. The other was Prometheus."

Xiao rubbed her tired eyes. "That explains Ealing's statue at least. Of Zeus and Prometheus. They united against a common enemy."

"Yeah. And that's why Zeus was depicted so worn down. They had been at war."

Xiao actually looked relieved. And I had to admit, finally starting to put together a few of the pieces was just about the closest thing I was getting to catharsis.

"Okay," Xiao said. "So the stone. What is it?"

"Power," Camilla said. "Zeus stripped the Gods of theirs. But that kind of power cannot simply be thrown away. Or destroyed. He sealed it here on Earth."

"So you're saying inside the stone... is the power of a God?" Xiao cocked her head sceptically. "Even after all this, that seems like a stretch. You're sure it's not just some cursed artefact or magical remnant?"

"Don't believe me?" Camilla rapped her nails on the table, before angling her body towards Avy. "Then what exactly do you think she is?"

Avy didn't object, or profess her innocence like she had done before. Instead, she looked wary. Not of Camilla, but more of Xiao and I, as her eyes flicked between the two of us.

"She can't be a God," said Xiao. "Or a Goddess or whatever. She isn't even supposed to be here. She's just a librarian who we happened to bump into while we were running. Running away from you, I might add."

"Coincidence is uncommon," Camilla replied. "Providence however. That is inescapable."

"Wait," said Zeke. "You think destiny or fate brought her into contact with the stone?"

"I think, that the stone has found its way to one of only ten people in the world that can harness its power. Call it whatever you like."

"Nobody is asking the important question." Kang finally stepped a little closer, though he seemed to be addressing the group as a whole rather than just Avy. "Which Goddess is she?"

Many questions were burning through my mind, not least about the plausibility of any of this information, but that particular query had been chief amongst them. But one thing I was certain of was that part of me was afraid of the answer. Still, I looked to Camilla to see if one was forthcoming.

"I don't know," she shrugged. "I wasn't there at the end. Believe it or not, I wasn't part of Zeus' private counsel. By the time I knew something was amiss, Olympus was already crumbling. I barely survived myself."

Xiao was already shaking her head disapprovingly. "How convenient. You must at least recognise her!?"

"No." Camilla remained patient with Xiao, she usually did. Despite how much Xiao clearly despised her, she always saved her malice for Kang and I. Well, in hindsight, mostly just me. "Does she look like much of a Goddess to you?"

"What do you mean?" I said, ignoring the fact that, yes, Avy did look pretty spectacular to me.

"They don't appear as they did before. They look mortal. You think Deimos was always an old Frenchman?"

"That brings me to my next question," said Kang, this time leaning over the table but still avoiding eye contact with Camilla. "You're claiming you still work for Pierceson. Like you're some kind of Revolver Ocelot style double-agent. First of all, shouldn't he be all depowered like she is? How was he summoning minotaurs to kill us? And second, how did a... how did someone like you enter his employ?"

"That was just a taste," she said. "Deimos was a God once. And he still possesses fragments of that power. Those were mostly illusions and phantoms, though they still packed a punch. Imagine what he could do if his true strength were restored."

"Deimos?" asked Avy. "Which God is he again?"

"One of the sons of Ares," Kang replied. "The God of Terror. Which is apt because I nearly terrored my pants back there a bunch of times."

"Yes," said Camilla. "He's... very powerful. For years I'd thought he would catch me. And kill me. He's ruthless, like his father. And he would have killed us all if we had spent any longer there. Which is exactly why I was trying to avoid coming here in the first place."

Kang didn't seem to be listening. He had finally lifted his head and was looking directly at Camilla. "And my second question?" he said. "How did you get into Piercesons life? Into our lives?"

Camilla looked stumped for the first time, erratically scratching her head. She and Kang had reversed roles as she shied away from him.

"Please," she said, looking at me for support. "Can we talk about this later? I need to rest."

"Alright," I said. For once I really did feel sympathy for her. Kang was pressing her for something that, it seemed, would break her heart to reveal. "But you're the one not asking the right questions, Kang. There's one more." I rested my elbows on the table and looked into Camilla's eyes. "Deimos wanted the stone for himself. But he seemed equally desperate to keep it from Pierceson. Why? What does he think an old historian might do with it?"

Camilla opened her mouth to speak, but closed it again when no words came forth. She waited another few seconds before finally saying, "Something tells me you already think you know."

―――――――― § ――――――――

"Xiao," I said. "How's the arm?"

"Surprisingly okay," she said, wringing her wrist. "Not broken after all I guess. Why?"

"Because, we need a plan," whispered Kang, as he huddled close to Xiao and I, near the back of the plane. "And at this rate, it's going to involve kicking some ass."

"Like what?" asked Xiao, ducking her head back around to the aisle to check if any of the others were coming.

Kelis had finally awoken, and begun tending to Camilla's wound. While Avy had headed into the restroom just a few seconds earlier, giving the three of us our first chance to speak alone in what felt like days.

"Pierceson knows," I said.

"Knows what?" Xiao replied.

"Something, at least. If Camilla works for him, he must know about the stone like she does. And that means he sent her not only to find it, but to make sure LaGuerre didn't get his hands on it first. Now I don't know whether he's another monster or God or what. But to be entangled in all this, he knows more than he has ever let on to us."

"Again," said Kang. "Plan time."

"Okay." Xiao leant in even closer. "I say we play it dumb, just like everyone else has been doing to us. We don't mention anything about any of this until we force him to reveal his hand. Only when we're sure that we can still trust him, do we make a move."

"Right," I replied. "But what is that move, exactly?"

"I don't know," Xiao protested, throwing her hands in the air. "I'm making this up as I go along. I don't have a plan for dealing with Gods and monsters and whatever-the-hell else is after us."

"Alright, I get it." I knew Xiao wanted to play things safe, but sitting and waiting for something to happen didn't work so well for us with LaGuerre. "But I have another plan."

"I'm listening," said Kang eagerly.

"We give the stone to Avy."

"What?!" he yelled. "Are you insane?"

"Quiet," I said, as both Xiao and I pushed him back against the wall. "Hear me out. The more she touches it, the greater her powers seem to grow. The first time she passed out but the next time she was fine. If we let her hold it again, maybe she'll even start to remember who she is and what exactly we're dealing with."

"No." Kang was back to whispering. "It's a bad idea *because* we don't know who she is or what she can do. Or what she has done in the past for that matter. Back in the alley she said she felt like the stone wanted her. That doesn't sound ominous to you? For all we know, you could be unleashing some insane evil Goddess like Hera or Adestria."

"I'm not sure Goddesses are inherently good or evil, Kang. Besides, there's just as much chance she could be an Aphrodite or an Artemis. Someone who could help us. After all, she's been helping us all this time."

"Listen to yourself bro. You're fantasising about what she might be. You're missing the reality and you're missing the point." Kang made sure each of his next words was accompanied by a poke into my shoulder. "We. Don't. Know. It's too much of a risk."

Every conversation with Kang seemed to be an argument at this point. It was as if he would rather put us all in danger than risk executing any plan that I came up with. Especially if it involved Avy.

"Even if you don't trust her," I said. "Can't you just trust me?"

"Again, no." Kang was finally calm as he replied. "You didn't even tell us about this whole Goddess thing. You and Avy have been on your own secret adventure since this all started."

"Stop it," said Xiao, too quietly to slow me down.

"You know what," I said. "Maybe you should just head back in there and get back to conspiring with the murderer that you've been sleeping with."

"We are not sleeping together!" Kang protested.

"Enough!" Xiao shouted loud enough that even Ketra, in the pilot's cabin, would have heard. "Just stop it. Both of you. I am so sick of this. You two are best friends. We're *all* supposed to be friends. Bury whatever this is, before it buries us."

"What's going on?" All three of us turned rapidly to find Avy loitering in the end row.

"Nothing," I squirmed. "We're just trying to figure out what to do next."

"Right," she said, nodding solemnly. "Can't have some evil Goddess overhearing all your plans. I get it."

She turned to leave, and I desperately wanted to reach out and grab her by the hand. But I let Kang's glare get the better of me, foolishly allowing her to skulk off alone.

"Listen up, both of you," said Xiao, when Avy was out of sight. "Neither of you are thinking straight. So when we land, you follow my lead. Understood?"

I waited for Kang to nod, before doing the same.

"Good. Because if we're going to avoid being outsmarted yet again, at least one of us needs to start trusting the others."

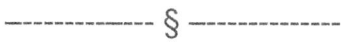

Though it had quickly become the normality, the silence during our descent into Cambridge was deafening. Camilla and her entourage, I was reluctant to call them children, kept pretty much to themselves, only informing us of where to go and what to do as we landed. There was no limousine waiting for us this time. Instead, a seven-seater taxi swept us up and headed for Pierceson's estate. The Iapetus, as my dad used to call it.

Xiao regularly made eye contact along the way, directing nods at Kang and I, most likely in order to make sure we weren't considering deviating from her bare bones of a plan. Kang completely ignored me, and everyone else, barring Avy who he still managed to regularly side-eye from across the vehicle.

Avy herself had muttered only a few words. Though she hadn't entirely recoiled from me, she seemed largely absent whenever she did speak. As if she were an android, spouting automated responses regardless of which questions I posed. There was no escaping the fact that each time we seemed to be drawn to one another, that bond would quickly be challenged and eroded soon after. As if I were being constantly forced to choose. Kang or Avy. Xiao or Camilla. Camilla or Avy. Kang or Xiao. It was unending. And exhausting.

Finally we pulled up at Iapetus. Previously, I had felt either relief or joy each time I arrived here. It either spelt the end of a long excursion or the start of a new one. On this occasion, it felt like neither and both all at once.

That didn't make it any less of a marvel to behold. A towering stately home, forged by stone and centuries past. Most impressive was the colossal sculpture just inside the gates. A mighty figure, a long spear in his hand aimed menacingly down at the gates. Iapetus himself. He was a Titan, the brother of Cronus. And a deadly combatant. The name came from the Greek Iapto. To wound, or to pierce. Which no doubt had made the figure so attractive to Pierceson to begin with.

Xiao led the way up the stone steps, taking care not to slip on the moss, then buzzed as she stood beside the great oak door that towered over her.

"Zeke," said Camilla, as the others each headed up before us. Since her wound had been tended, her skin had turned from the pale lime back to its usual rosy vibrancy. She looked just like the Camilla of old, not the inhuman murderer that lay beneath. "About Ealing."

"Just don't," I replied. "You shouldn't even get to mention his name."

"It's not what you think," she replied, reaching for my hand. I don't know whether it was because of her actions, or the revelation of her origin, but I quickly recoiled from the idea of touching her, placing my hand behind my back. "Oh come on, you don't have to be afraid. It's still me. We've known each other for a long time. That hasn't changed."

"Everything has changed," I said.

She backed away as her shoulders sagged. "Okay. But... Ealing. He wasn't who you think. He wasn't on our side."

"Our side?" It felt like the gravest of insults. We might both be working for Pierceson, but if each of our actions had proved one thing it was that we most definitely weren't on the same side.

"Pierceson's. The second I showed up. Ealing realised what he had. And he would have killed you, me and the others to stop us from taking it."

"That's ridiculous."

"It isn't, I promise you that. Before I attacked, he was calling you. I figured he had already spoken to you, but maybe he just left a message. You should listen to it. You'll see I'm telling the truth."

Camilla didn't bother waiting for me to reply, heading up the steps towards the estate, just as the doors opened wide. One of Piercesons many assistants, Julie I'm sure her name was, welcomed us inside and was quick to direct us straight through to the study.

I call it a study, but every room in Pierceson's estate was so homely that they could pass for a hotel. He may not have cared much for extravagant displays and indulgent possessions, but the man had an eye for interior decor. Finely hung velvet curtains. Pristinely kept persian rugs. Even the sofas and armchairs were more luxurious to recline in than any bed or pillow I had slept on during our travels.

Julie stood aside as we passed under the archway that led into the snug wooden room. The rasp of flames licking against stone bit my ears from across the room, where a tall brown-leather chair was parked opposite the fireplace. As I tiptoed further into the heat, it didn't take me long to notice the steaming mug on the tall coffee table, or the elderly hand reaching out to grasp it.

"Sir?" I said, vying for his attention against the coiling flames he was admiring.

The old man turned his head, as he sipped from the mug. When he finally pulled it from his lips, a familiarly vibrant smile was left behind.

"Zeke?" Pierceson said, his voice as frail as ever. "For a moment, I looked up and saw your father."

Pierceson rested his mug down on the table, then pushed down on the arm of his chair with one hand.

"Here," I said, reaching out to help him. "Let me."

I dragged him up to his feet, where he quickly straightened his purple robe, then wrapped both arms around me and patted me on the back.

"It's good to see you," he said. "Julie informed me of all the requests you made. Then I read some of the news in Nicosia. Something tells me we've much to discuss."

"You could say that," Camilla said, as she stepped into the room behind Kang and Xiao.

"Oh." Pierceson's expression turned severe, as he glanced only briefly at Camilla, before returning his attention to me. "This is... unexpected. I suppose I have some explaining to do." I simply nodded, not bothering to suggest what an understatement that was. "Come, all of you. Sit."

"Sir," said Kang, as he dragged his feet and similarly embraced the old man.

"Nathaniel," Pierceson said. "Tell me I don't have any debts to settle in your name this time?"

"Nah." Kang flashed a smile, a rarity in the past few days. "Just watch out for that freeloader, Ben Ecclestone. He's been spending your hard earned cash like crazy these days. Or so I've heard."

"I see." Pierceson sounded sceptical. "Xiao, my dear. Are you well?"

Pierceson nodded courteously, as Xiao bowed in response. "Sir. I'm well, yes. And yourself?"

"As well as someone my age could be, thank you."

Finally, he stood in front of Camilla.

"It's been a while," he said, clasping her by the hands. "But you're a sight for sore eyes."

"Thank you, sir," she replied.

It took a while for Pierceson's attention to fall from Camilla and land at the doorway, where Avy was still standing idly beside Julie.

"Who do we have here?" he asked, releasing Camilla and ambling over towards her.

I hadn't noticed it until now, but a pool of sweat was forming beneath each of my armpits, while my forehead was wet enough to leave a stain when I wiped it with my sleeve. Even though I was standing beside the fire, I knew it wasn't the heat. Xiao's plan was to act as if everything were normal. And that meant not making a big deal out of Avy's presence here. Depending on what Pierceson wanted, revealing her identity could put her, and potentially us, in danger. Instead, I opened my mouth to introduce her, only to be beaten to the punch.

"She's an assistant of mine," said Camilla. "Well, technically she's LaGuerre's assistant. But he's come to trust me with most of his assets."

"I see," said Pierceson, seeming to recoil at the mention of LaGuerre's name, with his interest in Avy diminishing in parallel. "Welcome."

"Thank you," Avy said, nervously.

Other than asking her not to say much, I hadn't been able to prepare Avy for any of this. But she was no idiot. Forgetful, perhaps, and a little out of sorts at times. She was still more than capable of covering her own tracks and falling in with the rest of us. In fact, I was far less concerned about Avy remaining anonymous than I was by the fact that Camilla had just fabricated her identity to protect her.

"So," said Xiao, eager to move on. "Camilla still works for you."

Pierceson gulped visibly. "Yes. But before you harangue her or myself. We needed to deceive you. LaGuerre would never have gone for it if it hadn't been believable."

There was at least some part of me that believed that. My mind raced back to the first time I had seen Camilla and LaGuerre together. He was parading her beside him, at an art exhibition in Korea. I had lost my temper completely. I called her things that would have my mum praying for my mortal soul, in full view of him, and only now was I realising how I'd played my part in the deception to perfection.

"But why?" asked Kang. "What did you need so badly from LaGuerre, that made you give up one of us? With all due respect, sir, we were best friends. And you tore us apart."

Pierceson slumped back down in his chair, rubbing his head of scruffy silver hair. "It wasn't a decision I made lightly, believe me. But you must understand, LaGuerre cannot be trusted. There are some things that simply must not fall into the hands of men like him."

"Such as?" Kang may not have been in his usual wise-cracking mood, but he was back to his probing poker-faced best as he matched wits with the wisest man either of us had ever known.

"Nathaniel, you know as well as I do the lengths some supposed historians will go to for their own gain. And they don't care about what or who might get in their way. For decades, I've stopped people like him from obtaining things that would make them a scourge to the world. And we've now reached a point where LaGuerre is at the very apex of that line. I did what I did because it was the only hand I had left to play. If there were any other way, I wouldn't have–"

"You should have told us." Kang wasn't letting up. "You kept putting us in danger with all these secrets. We deserved to know."

"I would never knowingly put you in any danger," Pierceson protested.

"So you didn't know about Ealing? About what he had found."

"Kang," I said, realising he was gradually overstepping as he grew more emotional.

"No," said Kang. "I'm curious. Did you know what you were sending us into?"

Pierceson shook his head, more in apparent frustration than to dispute the claim. "Ealing had been lying to me for years. He was keeping research from me. Research that he and I had started together. But I knew he wouldn't be able to get to the bottom of it all without my help. Ealing's best work is in the field, not the lab or the library. He needed keen minds to finish the work. I wanted the three of you to provide them."

"So you delivered us to him?" asked Kang. "Hoping he would take the bait." Pierceson nodded. "You were both using us."

"Using you?" asked Pierceson, his voice stern and his wrinkled skin amassing around his forehead, as he looked irritated for the first time. "Aren't you getting ahead of yourself? This apprenticeship is mutually beneficial. I ask the work of you, and in return you have the power and reach of my resources at your disposal."

It was as close to, 'don't bite the hand that feeds you,' as I had ever heard Pierceson express. He was the interrogator when one came to visit him here, and clearly he didn't care for the reversal of roles. Still, Kang's bold stance had at least revealed one thing. Just like Deimos, he wanted what Ealing had. And though he hadn't yet asked for it, or mentioned it directly, that meant he wanted the stone.

"Perhaps we should all get some rest," said Camilla. "We've done our fair share of travelling these last few days and I could use a hot bath. And some dinner. Then we can debrief you on all of Ealing's findings."

Pierceson nodded. "I agree. We dine at six. I'll have the chefs prepare that duck I'm sure you're still fond of, Camilla."

"Sounds fantastic." Camilla smiled and curtseyed like a giddy young girl, before leading the way out of the room.

"Not so subtle," whispered Xiao, as she poked Kang on the way up the stairs.

"Sorry," he replied, "I'm just getting tired of all the cloak and dagger."

"Me too," I said. "But I think Xiao is right. Unless he asks for the stone, we shouldn't confront him about it."

"Alright." Kang nodded.

"Nice work back there dude." I patted him on the back to make sure he knew I wasn't being sarcastic. Unexpectedly, he returned the gesture.

"Thanks."

"Okay enough," said Camilla, when she reached the top of the stairs. "If you're done congratulating each other on successfully wasting time, I suggest you think long and hard about your situation. Sooner or later, he will demand the stone from you. And when he does, I sincerely hope you give it to him and get back to your regular lives."

"Regular lives?" said Avy, her voice rising. "There is no regular after this!"

"Calm down," I said, taking her by the hand, only for her to pull away this time. "Avy we'll get to the bottom of this tonight. That I promise."

Camilla rolled her eyes. "You aren't in charge here, Zeke. There's only so much you can do. Have you ever known Pierceson to not get what he wants?"

"Maybe not," I said dismissively. "But he isn't the one holding the cards this time. Besides, you could have told him everything already. But you didn't. You lied. For Avy. Why?"

"I promised him the stone," she said, turning her back on us and starting down the hall. "I didn't promise him any of you."

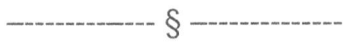

I'd stayed in the room a hundred times before. The double bed. The dusty bookcase. Even the squeaky door hinges. They were all endlessly familiar. Only this time, and for the first time, it didn't feel like home. The four walls seemed narrow. And my head felt like it would hit the chandelier each time I stood up. I knew it wasn't time that made it feel this way, I hadn't grown much since my last visit. No, there was simply something different about this stay. Something that made me feel... trapped.

As the door squeaked open and I looked up, I knew I was about to find out exactly why.

"Evening," said Pierceson, pushing the door shut behind him. "I hope I'm not disturbing you."

"Not at all," I said, sipping the last of the water from my bottle and setting it aside. "What's up?"

"I have something I wish to discuss before dinner. Something I thought you might understand better than the others."

"Of course," I replied, as he lowered himself into the chair opposite me. "I'm sorry about Kang earlier. It's just... wait till you hear about all the things that we have–"

"Is Ealing dead?" The way he cut my sentence in two with such an enormous question caught me like a sucker punch.

"Wha... what do you–"

"Michael. Did he die?" Pierceson was stone-faced. "The news seems to think so. They seem to think you're responsible too."

"I... I don't know what happened to him." Lying seemed harder now than ever. There were a hundred thoughts racing through my head. Did he already know the answers to his questions? Had he visited any of the others before me? Was he waiting for me to corroborate their stories? There were too many variables. "He was in bad shape when we last saw him."

"I see. That's... disconcerting. What was he working on?"

"You don't know?" I asked, trying desperately to fend off his assault and buy time to think up a countermeasure.

"I'm asking you." Pierceson's eyes were locked on mine, his gaze like fire burning my irises.

"He thought he had found something. He wanted us to–"

"Where is it?"

Another rapidfire question. To keep me off my game, off-kilter. "Where is what?"

"What he found, Zeke." It felt as if Pierceson had known exactly how each part of this conversation would go before he even entered the room. "Where is it?"

"I don't know."

"Does Camilla have it?"

"What?" Of course Camilla didn't have it. We wouldn't be having this conversation if she did–

"Does Avy have it?"

"Avy? No." Shit.

It was a cleverly worked trap. I hadn't given Pierceson nearly enough credit. There was a reason he was so good at his job and that I had been under his tutelage for so many years. He didn't just ask excellent questions, he asked the right questions. The questions that put him on the shortest route to what he wanted.

"You're getting better at this," he smiled. "But I think it's time we were both a little more honest with each other."

"Alright," I said, standing up and taking a deep breath, as he did the same. "You know exactly where we've been and what is going on. Don't you?" He nodded slowly. "So you're after Ealing's findings too? It was Camilla that killed him, did she tell you that too? Don't bother pretending you don't know what she is."

"I won't," he said, his voice somehow bolder and lacking the frailty I'd become accustomed to. "But do you know what I am?"

It was my turn to nod, warily. "A God. You want the stone to restore your powers. Just like LaGuerre did. Or Deimos, I should say. And I know that he would have killed us to get it. Are you any different?"

"Zeke." Pierceson did genuinely look offended by the accusation. "You really think I would? That I could? After all this time? All we've been through? I think of you as family, son. I made sure you had an education after your father passed away. And made sure you were off the streets, when your sister was incarcerated. You think after all that, I really want to get rid of you? Why do you think I sent Camilla to protect you? To escort you back here?"

"Protect me?" I found myself laughing out loud. "She killed Ealing. She tried to kill all of us."

"Don't be ridiculous. If she frightened you, it was only to stop you from becoming further embroiled in this matter. She cares deeply for you, Zeke. Whether you believe it or not. As do I. And all I want is the stone. After that, you're free to go as you please. Although I'd very much like us to continue working together."

"Really?" I said. "I guess that depends."

Pierceson smiled, as if I had said something amusing. "On what?"

"Which God you are? If you're one we can trust." His smile grew wider, until he had to cover his mouth and chuckle. "What's so funny?" I asked.

"Son," he said. "In some ways you haven't changed. You're still the same headstrong child that your father raised. Still reacting to everything around you. Never getting out in front of the mystery and using that head of yours to solve it first. I am no God, Zeke. To tar me with their brush is a little… insulting."

Then, and only then, did it hit me.

"The statue," I said. "The Ten Thunderbolts. Zeus called for help. First from the monsters. Then from a Titan. You're him aren't you?"

I found myself backing away, creating distance between him and me.

"LaGuerre wasn't warning me about Avy or Camilla betraying me. He was warning me about you. You're not a God. You're a Titan. Like Iapetus, the Piercer. You're his son. You're Prometheus."

R.A.CRAWFORD

ACT XII

THE PALLAS CLOAK

'The race of gods and men is one, and from one mother we both draw our breath. Yet all the difference in our power holds us apart, so that man is nothing, but the brazen floor of heaven is eternally unshakable.'

Unshakeable. Pindar couldn't have sung it more plainly. A man and a God couldn't have been further apart. And Pierceson wasn't even a God. He was a Titan. The past week had been one revelation after another, but this... this was something unfathomable.

"Zeke." Xiao's voice dragged me away from the spiralling thoughts that were like quicksand threatening to drag me down to some depth from which I might never return. "Kang's here now. What did you want to tell us?"

As Kang dragged a chair up beside the bed, where an impatient Xiao and disinterested Avy were sitting, I wrestled with each burden, attempting to shuffle them into some meaningful order. I'd had nearly two hours alone to contemplate what Pierceson had revealed to me, and decided I needed to share not just that, but the confirmation I'd pursued since.

"Alright," I started. "This is going to sound ridiculous. But who cares. Everything is ridiculous now so contesting it is getting pointless."

"Sure." Kang nodded. "There's pretty much nothing you can say at this point to surprise us."

"Good." I sighed a deep breath. "Because Pierceson is Prometheus."

Despite Kang's proclamation, a stunned silence did follow my announcement.

"What?" Avy was the first to shake her head in disbelief, her face a model of scepticism. "How can that be? The person who has been teaching you for your whole life is Prometheus? And you didn't even know?"

"Figures," Xiao replied, almost mockingly. "Their best friend was Echidna and they didn't notice that either."

"Hey," I objected. "You know you failed to spot this too, right?"

"We need to get out of here," said Kang.

"Why?" asked Xiao. "So what? He's Prometheus. Avy is supposedly some kind of Goddess. And there are a bunch of monsters sleeping down the hall. What difference does it make at this point?"

"Don't you get it?" Kang was scrubbing his forehead as if there were some invisible stain he couldn't rid himself of. "Someone stabbed Zeus in the back. To try and take his throne. He made the mistake of trusting an enemy he had condemned and it came back to haunt him."

"You think Prometheus turned on him again?" Xiao wearily rubbed her eyes. "Why?"

"The same old why. The endless cycle of betrayal." Kang stood up and began to pace around the room. "I say we wash our hands of this. Give up the stone and be on our merry way."

"I don't think that's a good idea either," I said. "Pierceson also… made me an offer. He gets the stone. And we carry on working for him."

"I'm struggling to see the negatives of that deal to be honest."

"It's not that simple, dude. Earlier, Camilla told me that before she killed Ealing, she found him trying to call me. So I called my operator and managed to retrieve my voicemails. He left me a message."

"What did it say?" asked Avy. "It's more bad news isn't it?"

Holding down the redial button on the phone unit by the bed, I waited for the loud speaker to switch on. "I'll let you decide."

A few seconds later, the robotic voicemail recording was reading out a number, before it began to play the last message I had received.

"Zeke." The voice belonged unmistakably to Ealing. "I wish I had taken the chance to tell you all of this face to face, but I wasn't exactly sure why Pierceson sent you. Or what you already knew. But something is coming after me. Something powerful. Maybe it's already here. And I don't know if I'll survive to tell you, but you need to know the truth about your mentor. About all of us.

"The Ten Thunderbolts are real. And they will turn the wielders into weapons of immense power. I know this is going to sound crazy, but Pierceson isn't what you think. He isn't even Human. And he is older than you can imagine. We have been fighting a war against his kind for thousands of years. And if he gets his hands on this power, he will throw the world back into chaos.

"So you must be mindful of him, Zeke. Everything he says is a trick. A ruse to gain your trust. He fooled me into trusting him once too. That's when I find out why it has taken so long to track down just one of these thunderbolts. It's because Pierceson already has–"

Just like the first time I listened, Ealing was cut short by the operator declaring the end of the message.

"I assume this is when Camilla attacked him," I said.

"Pierceson already has what?" asked Avy.

I slumped down on the bed and threw my head back onto the pillow.

"I don't know. But he made it pretty clear that Pierceson getting the stone would be bad news for everyone. And now that I know he's Prometheus, I can't say I feel all that differently."

"And if we run," started Xiao. "We're potentially putting more than just ourselves in danger." I nodded in reply. "Well... he could still be lying. It seems like he lied to us when we first met him. And now he wants us to take whatever his side was against Pierceson. How do we know which one to trust?"

Xiao made a good point. Ealing had stopped short of revealing his own identity, other than the fact that he was Pierceson's foe. Was he yet another God on his own quest for power? We were caught in the middle of a power struggle that started two thousand years before any of us were born. Anyone besides Avy that is.

"Let's ask him," said Kang, who had been quiet again up until then.

"Say that again?" I mumbled.

"That was the plan right? We don't reveal anything until Pierceson plays his hand. This is all the information we're going to get. We still have the stone. He doesn't. It's now or never. Let's confront him. If we don't like his answers, we leave."

"You think he's just going to let us leave?" Xiao protested.

"I don't think he has a choice. He would have to take it from us by force. At which point I think it would become pretty clear which side he is on."

"Or he could just have Camilla kill us and take it."

Kang shook his head. "She won't do that."

"She's been trying to kill us all week, Kang."

"No. She has been trying to take the stone from us." Kang sounded fed up. I could hardly blame him. Having to defend the woman who had been hunting us was probably taking its toll. "Other than that she *has* been protecting us."

"Ugh," Xiao groaned. "She's been trying to protect the stone. Wake up! Have you fallen so hard for her that you can't see that? She's an *actual* monster."

"Xiao," I said, making my voice loud enough that neither could speak over it. "That's enough. It doesn't matter what Camilla is. I'm with Kang." I made a point of looking at my best friend and waiting for his eyes to meet mine. "I don't think she'll hurt us."

The briefest flicker of a smile brushed Kang's lips.

"Alright then," he said. "We find out what he wants. Directly. Let's do this."

Xiao rolled her eyes as Kang opened the door and marched out.

"This is going to be a disaster," she said. "You know that right?"

"Well if things go south," I replied with a grin. "You still have your trusty pocket knife right? You'll just have to rescue me again. You're getting pretty good at it."

Xiao patted her jacket pocket reassuringly. "Unless you can knock him out with your awful sense of humour, I'll have to."

As Xiao followed Kang out the door, I turned to check on Avy, only to find her brushing past me and heading after them.

"Can't win with her right?" I said, chuckling away. "I'm too serious. I'm not serious enough."

"I guess," said Avy, as she reached for the creaking door to hold it open.

"Wait." My feet moved faster than my thoughts, skipping across the room as I reached out and took Avy by the hand. "I have something for you."

I reached into my pocket and pulled out two small foil-wrapped chocolates I'd found in the kitchen.

"No thanks," Avy said with a sigh, as her head lowered and angled away from me.

"Hey wait," I ducked my head to try and get her attention. "You've been after this for days. What's wrong? You know you can tell me."

"Can I?" she said, her head shooting up and revealing an unfamiliar glower that I hadn't seen before. "I'm supposed to tell you everything, am I? But you and your friends can huddle together in the corner and talk about *me* behind my back?"

"That wasn't... We weren't..." I didn't know what to say.

I wanted to tell her it wasn't true, but even that wasn't being completely honest. And any other time, I would have simply lied to her. But I couldn't do that either. At first I thought it was the guilt that stopped me, but in reality it was far simpler than that. It was simply because she was... Avy. I didn't want to have to lie to her.

"Avy," I tried again. "We were just... Kang and Xiao didn't want to–"

"Don't pass the blame," she shouted, pulling her arm free of my grasp. Her golden, lambent eyes, like torches in the night wind. "You act like you're on my side, but I know you don't trust me either."

"That's not true."

"It is!" Avy was yelling now, her emotions coming to the boil like one of my mum's iron teapots on the hot stove. "You like it when I help you. When I make you feel safe. But I've seen the way you look at me. When you're thinking about the stone. Or when Camilla or LaGuerre talks about what they think I am. It's the same look that Kang always has. You two are no different. You only trust me when it's convenient for you. And I'm sick of it. Who is there to make me feel safe, Zeke? Who here actually cares about helping me?"

"Avy, please." I said, reaching out for her once more, only for her to recoil and back into the doorway.

"I don't care whether you give the stone to Pierceson or Prometheus or whoever. After tonight, I'm going home. I don't want to be a part of whatever this is anymore."

Before I could reply, she was gone. And by the time I closed the door behind me, she was stepping off the bottom of the staircase and heading towards the dining room. The room where Pierceson, and our collective fate, awaited.

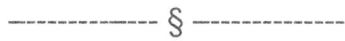

Everyone was already waiting, as I stepped into the dining room. There was an empty seat waiting for me at the end of a long oval-shaped table. On the nearest left seat sat Kang, as he helped himself to the food that had been prepared. Nervous eating was a staple of his childhood that he had only recently mastered, but the occasion looked to be getting the better of him.

Next to him was Camilla, already having carved halfway through the succulent piece of duck. I wondered if the pair of them had taken any time to discuss the fact that Camilla was actually an ancient creature rather than the young woman we had been fooled by. But Kang's rigid body language made it clear enough that he still wasn't ready to speak with her.

On the right hand side, Xiao was in the next closest chair, nibbling on some salad as her eyes darted around the room. She was no doubt making herself aware of the fastest routes out of here and taking note of anything that could be used as a makeshift weapon.

Beside her was Avy, neither eating, drinking or doing anything at all. Her chin was resting on her knuckles and her eyes never rose from the table. And though I knew that the most important thing for any of us right now was to escape this room unscathed, I couldn't fight the distressing notion that this might be the last moment I ever got to spend with her.

"You're late," said Pierceson, from his seat at the opposite end of the table.

"Sorry," I replied. "There was a lot to think about."

"Was there?"

Pierceson's eyebrow arched up towards his wrinkled forehead as he took a sip from the broad glass of wine in his hand. He looked first at Kang, then Xiao, both of whom had certainly sat at this end of the table to distance themselves from him.

"I would have thought that between the three of you, you could have made a decision by now. You're smart enough not to fall at the final hurdle."

It was beginning to feel like every move I made played further into his hands. Like he already knew how all of this was going to go before we even set foot in his home.

"Why do you want the stone?" I asked. Kang had wanted us to be forward. To stay on the front foot and stop waiting for answers to come to us. I don't think I could get any more direct than that. "What happens if we give it to you?"

Pierceson looked annoyed by the question. No, not annoyed. He looked disappointed.

"Does it matter?" he replied.

"It does." I refused to take a seat at his table. As if remaining standing somehow gave me an advantage. "What's the difference between giving it to you, or Deimos?"

"The difference, Zeke, is that you work for me. And that if you don't hand it over–"

"What?" Kang stood up too. "What are you going to do? Kill us?"

"Nathaniel, calm down." Pierceson made a lowering motion with his hand. "You're overreacting. I would never do anything to–"

"Quit lying to us." It was Xiao's turn to throw down her cutlery and take a stand. "If we decide to turn around and walk straight out the door, what happens then?"

Pierceson closed his eyes and shook his head. "That would be... regrettable."

"Then why don't you just take the stone from us?" I demanded, sensing an opening. And as I suspected, this time Pierceson didn't offer an instant rebuttal. "You can't, can you? That's why you need us. Or Camilla. Or anyone else. You can't touch the stone."

Pierceson finally smiled. "Now you're getting better at deduction. That damned Zeus and his enchantments. He prevented beings like myself, higher up the food chain, from accessing it. A mortal can hold the stone. But only a God can wield it."

"Then it's useless to you," I said smugly.

"Yes. It was. Until of course, you brought the very thing I needed to unleash its power wandering through my doors."

His eyes rolled towards Avy, who was now sitting up attentively and meeting his calculating gaze. I pushed my chair aside and started towards Avy.

"Leave her out of this," I cried. "She isn't–"

Suddenly my legs wouldn't move. I stood paralysed for a few seconds, as the chair slid back out from beneath the table, before I was thrust backwards into it. Kang and Xiao too, were both sitting again. I couldn't figure out why until I looked under the table and saw a thin wisp of lime light, encircling their feet, then noticed the same strange energy ensnaring mine.

Camilla. I looked further beneath the table and saw her hand reaching outwards, her fingers outstretched as a cloud of light bounced between her long nails.

"Please," she said earnestly. "Don't fight this."

"As I was saying," Pierceson continued, speaking directly to Avy. "I think the two of us can help each other, dear girl."

"Unless you're offering me a flight home, I'm not interested," Avy said defiantly. "There's nothing else you have that I want."

"On that, I might be able to change your mind." Pierceson raised one of his thin, frail looking wrists, then snapped his fingers.

The snap was so loud, it sounded as if a grenade had just gone off in the room. In an instant, the centre of the table was set alight, burning in a perfectly controlled bright orange square for a few seconds before being snuffed out just as quickly. In the middle of the blackened shape, was a clear bowl, stacked with jewels that sparkled as they caught the evening light and the flicker of the fireplace embers.

At first, I didn't understand the purpose of the flamboyant display. Yes, Pierceson could conjure flames from air, he was Prometheus after all. And yes, he was the owner of riches and artefacts from all over the world. I just didn't know what relevance any of that might be to Avy. Until I saw her face that is.

Her golden eyes were as wide as I'd ever seen them, almost radiating warmth and light as if they were glowing. No, this time they actually *were* glowing. Shining. Her lips had parted in a gasp and one of her hands seemed to be involuntarily reaching towards the bowl. I'd seen that look of desire, of hunger, on her face only once before. When under siege by a minotaur. She admitted to me that she wanted the stone. That she needed it. And even though I didn't have it on me at the time, that look had terrified me.

"What are those?" I said, both knowing and fearing the answer.

"As I said," Pierceson replied, rising from his chair. "You've brought me the very things I need. The last stone and someone to wield it. Because the other nine stones... I already possess."

Shit. Pierceson was never looking for the first stone. He wanted to complete the set. Whatever he was planning, he needed all ten stones for. If I had any doubts about giving up our stone before, that was an ominous enough reason to keep it from him at all costs.

"They won't let you keep the stone," said Pierceson. "Will they? They only let you hold it when they need you to protect them. But I offer one to you freely. You need only reach out and take it."

I wish I could say that Avy looked torn, but if anything it looked like her mind was already made up. She was pressed right up against the table, looming over the bowl of jewels, taking one deep breath after another. Only her trembling hand seemed unsure of whether or not to plunge her fingers inside and accept his offer.

"Avy don't," I shouted, wrestling against the magical restraints. "Please. Don't listen to him. He doesn't want to help you. He just wants to use you. He's the reason you've been in danger all this time."

"Am I?" Pierceson waved his hand, causing an amber stone from the bowl to levitate upwards until it dangled tantalisingly before Avy's yearning eyes. "Or is it simply that you haven't had the means to properly defend yourself? And that they have prevented you from even discovering who you truly are? The answers are right in front of you. You need only reach out and grasp them."

Avy finally looked at me, apologetically. With the eyes of someone who had already made their decision.

"I'm sorry, Zeke," she said. "But I need to know."

Her hand shot out, decisively, and wrapped around the jewel. Then another flash of light threatened to blind me. And it wasn't just the light this time. The room shook, audibly, as the sound of glasses and plates smashing caused me to flinch and my chair scratched back and forth across the wooden floorboards.

When the light finally faded, Avy still stood at the table. But it wasn't the Avy I knew. Again there was the glow of searing hot light, as if radiating from every pore on her skin. And again her eyes glinted like a cauldron of smelt gold. But this time, the changes were physical too.

She was bigger. Not taller, but more robust. Her usually supple arms were lean with muscle and her shoulders stood broader than before. Most notably, her hair had changed. Her dark-brown hair had thickened, doubled in length and crackled with electricity.

"Avy?" I said, foolishly. As if it could have been someone else. But when she didn't answer, I didn't feel quite so foolish anymore.

"Ah. There you are," said Pierceson, as if he had just laid eyes on an old friend after years apart. "It's easier to recognize you now, Athena."

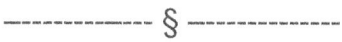

Athena? Avy is Athena?

It was unbelievable. It was amazing. And it was terrifying. All at once.

"How do you feel?" asked Pierceson.

"Better," Avy said, her voice unusual. Somehow both deep and delicate at the same time. As if the words were spoken by two seperate people.

"And your memories?"

Avy grunted and held her forehead. "There are... fragments. It's difficult to–"

"Give it time," Pierceson said, taking her by the hand. "For now, we must work quickly. Retrieve the final stone from them, so we can be on our way."

"On our way?" Avy asked, still combing her hand through her own hair. Then flexing her arms and examining her palm as if it belonged to a stranger. "To where?"

Pierceson nodded acceptingly.

"You've been absent a long time. But little has changed, Athena. The fighting never ceased. Zeus may have won the battle, but never the war. And ever since his demise and selfish decision to divide your kind's power, I have been forced to single-handedly hold his enemies at bay."

"Holding who..." Avy trailed off as she began to question him, lowering her hand from her head and balling it into a fist. "Demigods," she said, hotly.

"Yes." Pierceson pointed to the window. "They have plagued my existence, seldom allowing me a moment's peace. And stripping away the few comforts I have found. But I have a plan to stop them. Once and for all. And I need your help to do it. So, will you help me? I know all that they have taken from you too."

This time, without hesitation, Avy nodded. "Yes."

"Excellent. Then you must take the final stone from them. We'll need its power."

Quickly, Avy turned away from Pierceson and stood beside me. With one kick at the leg of my chair, she spun me around to face her and leant forward until we were at eye level. I assumed she was about to demand the stone, but instead her eyes simply lingered.

"Avy," I said, my voice a half-whimper. "Don't do this. You're playing into his hands."

She didn't bother replying, instead reaching a hand inside my jacket and clawing around inside the pocket. When she found it empty, she switched to the other side, then patted me down all over in search of it.

"Of course," she laughed, a little too threateningly for my liking. "Lime soda, right?"

I didn't know whether she was asking or mocking me, but I stayed silent nonetheless. Waiting and watching to see what she would do. As expected, she went to Kang, giving him the same invasive search treatment she had me. And coming up short.

"Ugh," she exclaimed, grabbing Kang by the collar and lifting him and his chair from the ground. "Enough games. Where is it?"

It was Kang who assuredly smiled this time.

"What's the matter?" he said. "Don't tell me you mighty Gods have been outsmarted by mere mortals?"

"You think this is funny?" Avy said, thrusting her hands out and jettisoning him against the wall. His wooden chair smashed into pieces, leaving him clutching at his arm on the ground.

"Avy!" I shouted. "Stop!"

"Don't hurt him," yelled Camilla, urgently. "Nate, just tell her where the stone is! You don't have to go through this."

"Yes, Nathaniel," said Pierceson. "Tell her. And this will all be over with."

I looked at Kang, checking to see whether he had some new idea or instruction he wanted me to follow. But even through whatever pain he was in, he lifted his head and shook it defiantly. I swallowed against the lump in my throat and fixed Pierceson with the most resentful expression I could manage.

"Go to hell," I said.

Pierceson let out a disappointed sigh. "Fine. I wish it could have been different. Athena, make him talk."

Avy nodded as she dragged Kang back to his feet and pulled his hand away from the forearm he was cradling. The broken wood had pierced his skin, and blood had begun slithering through the hole torn in his sleeve.

"I always knew we couldn't trust you," Kang said, as Avy took hold of him around his fresh wound.

"Congratulations," said Avy smugly, as she clamped down on him. "You're prophetic."

Kang let out an agonising scream, as she applied pressure. It must have been excruciating. Avy was impossibly strong, I knew that much already. So there was no way he could withstand that much agony for long.

I wanted to cry out and help him, but I knew that wasn't what he wanted. It wasn't the plan. Whether it was the change in Avy or the danger of whatever Pierceson had planned, Kang had reneged on his desire to wash his hands of this whole situation. His reluctance had become resolve.

And so he would have to endure the pain. After all, there had to be a limit to how far Avy would go. She may have been much more than the person I thought she was. She may have a past and history that I couldn't comprehend. But I was still certain of one thing. The present day Avy. The one I had spent the past week hiding and running and laughing with. She was still in there somewhere. And she wouldn't cross a line she couldn't return from.

Kang slumped to his knees as Avy released him.

"Finished already?" he said, trying his best to insert some bravado despite his heavy panting and the tears welling in his eyes.

My friend was always resilient. A childhood packed full of rejection and social outlying had ensured that. It had helped him develop a hard shell that could shrug off both verbal and physical attacks, all the while forging a man both comfortable with his own quirks and malleable enough to adapt to new and present challenges. Kang might have been afraid, but he was no coward. And not one to be picked on.

"Let him be," said Pierceson. "I can't have you further injuring one of my prized students."

"What about the stone?" said a confused Avy.

"It's time we tried a different tact." Pierceson nodded resolutely at Xiao. "The girl. Kill her."

"What!?" It was Camilla who protested first. "No. You said you wouldn't–"

"Silence." His voice was like thunder, striking the air from Camilla's lungs. "They won't talk. So they will understand consequence."

For the first time since her transformation, Avy looked hesitant. Still, she turned away from Kang and put her boot on Xiao's chair, easing it away from the table. Somehow, Xiao remained unflustered.

"Stupid," Xiao said, looking at Avy with the same disgust that Sisyphus would a rock. But as her head fell towards her lap, shaking resentfully, I realised she was cursing herself rather than Avy. "I actually thought you were... that we might be friends."

Avy had her back to me, so I couldn't see her face. Only her arm as she reached out and placed her hand around Xiao's neck. Xiao didn't try to break free, instead closing her eyes and waiting for what came next.

"Avy!" I cried, jerking my body back and forth as I tried to break free. "This isn't you. You don't want to do this. Please!"

Seconds that felt like an eternity ticked by until finally I could take no more. I opened my mouth to scream, to order them to stop, when suddenly my arms and legs came free of the magic that bound them. Before I could wonder why, Camilla was across the room, squeezing Avy around the arm.

"If you harm a single hair on her head," Camilla said, her words directed at Avy like daggers. "I will summon every child of mine on this earth to hunt you down. So if you're not the monster they think you are... let her go."

Avy looked at Camilla, challengingly. It felt like the two women were sizing each other up and would come to blows any second. Until Avy finally let go of Xiao and shook free of Camilla's grasp.

"I won't do it," Avy said. "I won't kill for you, Prometheus. I won't let you manipulate me. Whatever your game is, you'll have to do it without me."

Avy extended her arm over the centre of the table, then dropped the jewel back into the bowl. As the sound of the coloured stones clinking together rang around the room, I expected Avy to change back. To revert to the petite dark-haired librarian that I could no longer hide my affection for.

I couldn't have been more disappointed that she didn't.

"Well," said Pierceson. "If you want something done..."

He clenched his fist until his knuckles set aflame, as if it were a burning gauntlet of embers. It was the first time I'd truly been terrified of the old man. The first time it was clear that we weren't dealing with a mortal man, but an ancient creature that could incinerate us with a wave of his hand. So when he raised his arm and opened his palm, I knew I had to intervene.

"Wait," I shouted, standing up and stepping in front of Xiao. "Just wait a second." I helped Xiao up out of her seat, then reached inside her jacket.

"What are you doing?" she asked, as she leaned cautiously away from me.

"There," I said, wrapping my fingers around the smooth circular object inside her deep pocket.

I pulled out my hand and loosened my fingers, unveiling the stone in my palm.

"When did you...?" Xiao looked confused.

"Sorry," I replied. "I should have told you. Here." I thrust my hand towards Pierceson. "This is what you want, isn't it?"

The old man smiled haughtily and pointed back at me. "Camilla. If you could do the honours."

Camilla, still wearing a deploring frown, relieved me of the stone and tossed it dispassionately into the bowl.

"Perfect," said Pierceson, snapping his sparkling fingers once more, and causing the bowl to vanish. "But time is short. And I've wasted enough of it with this game."

His fingers snapped again and this time, in a wisp of smoke and fire, it was Avy that vanished.

"No!" I shouted, futilely reaching my hand into the fading fumes. "What did you do to her?!"

"She wasn't being cooperative," Pierceson said gratingly. "Attachment to mortals can be a grave weakness. Trust me, I know. For years it's stopped me from achieving what I set out to do. But no more. I'm ending this war today. And I'm going to need her to do it."

Pierceson turned away from us, shrugging off his silk robes and stepping hazardously close to the fireplace. He took in a long breath of air, then blew on the flames until they grew as high as the ceiling. Strangely, it didn't feel hotter. As if the fire were an illusion or my imagination was playing tricks on me.

"You'll have to excuse us," he said, one foot stepping onto the flames and beginning to burn. "But truly, I thank you for all that you have done. Camilla, take them home. Then join me."

Pierceson never looked back, receding further into the flames as they absorbed him. It took only a few seconds for his entire body to crisp and wither. When there was nothing left but ash, the flames abated until, finally, they went out.

"Shit," said Camilla.

"Where is he going?" asked Kang, still cradling his wounded arm.

"And where did he take Avy?" I asked.

"Does it matter?" Camilla growled. "You'll never see her again. Nobody will."

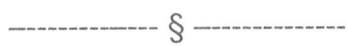

"Where?" I demanded.

"One of his secret locations," Camilla replied. "Somewhere underground. You'll never find it."

"What's he planning to do?" asked Xiao.

"Does it matter?"

"I just nearly died trying to stop him!" Xiao was suddenly shouting at the top of her voice. And for once, she had every right to. "Of course it matters."

"Okay," said Camilla, holding up her hands in appeasement. "I'm sorry. What I meant was… I don't know."

"You don't know?" I said, my own anger beginning to bubble "You don't know!? How can you not know what he's been planning? You've been working with him all this time!"

"Back off." Camilla shoved me in the chest and turned away. "I haven't been working with him, I've been working for him," she said dejectedly.

"What's the difference?" Kang asked, showing a little more compassion than I thought she deserved.

"The difference is… that he asked me to bring him the stones. That's it."

"In exchange for what?"

"For… it's complicated." Camilla's voice had grown so atypically shy and retiring, it was as if she were facing a tribunal. "He was going to bring someone back for me. Someone important. Someone I lost."

Surprisingly, Kang didn't react. Not negatively anyway. Instead, he placed a reassuring arm on her shoulder. "Do you at least know what he has been up to until now?"

"Partially. It's as he says. The war against the Demi-Gods never truly ended. But without the support of the Gods, Prometheus has been fighting them alone all this time. He spent lifetimes, several of them, battling them back. But their numbers only multiply. In this life, disguised as Pierceson, he was actually in hiding. None knew of his identity.

"But somehow, someone found out who he was. And ripped that life of peace away from him. That's when he approached me. I, too, had been living out multiple lives. Peacefully. With people I learned to love."

Camilla's eyes glanced quickly at each of us.

"He needed someone who could move around unnoticed. So he made me an offer I couldn't say no to. To track down the last few stones for him. It's taken me years, and I had to give up many things, many people, along the way. But I tracked each of them down. All he ever said was that once he had all ten he would have the power to end this war once and for all. I don't know how. But whatever he has planned, it's going to happen soon."

'To end this war once and for all.' I don't know how, but every inch of me knew that whatever Pierceson... whatever *Prometheus* meant by that, it was bad news.

"You have to help us stop him," I said.

"Stop him?" Camilla started by drying her eyes, before gesticulating angrily towards me. "What is wrong with you three? Since the moment this started, you keep putting yourself in the middle of this. First for discovery? And now over some misplaced sense of responsibility? You are *not* heroes. Get that through your thick skulls. This isn't a comic book. And it doesn't have a happy ending. So for once in your lives can you just listen to me and *go home*. Let this conflict play out without getting involved. Like you've done for your entire lives. Like everyone in the world has done for their entire lives. Let. It. Go."

"We can't," said Kang.

"Why?" Camilla pleaded. "Why can't you just go home and be safe?"

"You know us too well to ask that," I said. "Pierceson taught us to see things through. So that's what we're gonna do."

Camilla sighed wearily. "Ketra. Kelis."

She had barely finished uttering their names, yet somehow the two women were in the doorway already.

"Mother?" they both said, lowering their heads subserviently.

"I'm leaving," Camilla replied, brushing past her two accomplices and heading for the front door. "Ensure that our three guests make it home safely. They're no longer welcome here."

"You can't just kick us out," I said, following until Kelis placed a hand of warning on my chest.

"Please don't," she said. "Mother just wants you to be safe."

"Yes, Zeke," Camilla added. "And if you weren't so stubborn you would see–"

Camilla stopped short of admonishing me. Her attention spinning quickly towards the door as she held the handle. Then her eyes widened in distress as she leapt backwards and threw both hands up in front of her. A paling of emerald light sprung up in front of her just as the door caved in. The wooden debris bounced off Camilla's wall of light, protecting her from harm, but it offered no such protection from the figure thundering through the carnage and charging towards her.

Before Camilla could react, a woman was crashing shoulder first into her chest, sending her tumbling into the stair railing. Kelis and Ketra leapt instantly to her aid, putting themselves between their mother and the armed intruder looming in front of them.

And what a woman she was. I'd never seen anyone like her, not this side of a movie screen. She wore black sandals and a skirt that was made of shimmering metal that more resembled armour. And though she wore a black hoodie no different in style than my own, the material looked more like chainmail than cotton or leather.

More imperious than what she wore were the items she held. On her right arm hung an enormous round mirror-like shield, while in her left hand she gripped the handle of a thick double-edged sword. The kind that ancient Greek hoplites would have carried. It was as if she had stepped straight out of one of the paintings that adorned Piercesons walls. I was so distracted by it all, that it wasn't until she looked over at me, flicking her long braid over her shoulder, that I realised who she was.

"Vinter?" I wondered, trying desperately to reconcile the warrioress before me with Ealing's ill-tempered aid. The same one I thought had died with him back at the museum.

"Lewis," she replied, in her Scandinavian accent. "I bet you're wishing you'd left the museum when I asked you to."

R.A.CRAWFORD

ACT XIII

THE LERNEAN FRENZY

'Anybody can become angry — that is easy, but to be angry with the right person and to the right degree and at the right time and for the right purpose, and in the right way — that is not within everybody's power and is not easy.'

Vinter had been sullen the first time I met her. And the second, for that matter. She never seemed to want us anywhere near their research. Or near Ealing for that matter. None of it made sense to me back then. Such hostility between peers who were pursuing the same end seemed pointless. But now, as she lifted her blade to aim at Camilla's head, her rage seemed anything but pointless.

Camilla had murdered Ealing. Murdered Kincaid. And she had most certainly attempted to murder Vinter too. So as the warrior gritted her teeth and inched her toes forward, her rage bordered on contagion. I could feel it infecting me too. As if I could breathe it in or swallow it. It was pulsing through my veins and seeping from my pores.

It was the wrong time to succumb to this kind of fury, I knew that. But as Aristotle warned, choosing the right time for anger wasn't always within our own power. For the first time, I wanted Camilla to pay. To suffer.

Why shouldn't she be held accountable for all she had done. All of this was her fault. Every hardship we had suffered. Every wound. Every fear. It all came from her. And I hoped that Vinter would make her feel every ounce of pain we had one hundred times over.

Vinter lunged forward with her blade, but in an instant Ketra and Kelis were upon her. Every time I had seen one of Camilla's abettors in action, it was a fright to behold. But this time, the roles were reversed as Vinter made short work of them.

Kelis' eyes glowed as she readied that blinding and paralysing light of hers once more.

"Cover your eyes," I shouted to Kang and Xiao, as I turned away.

But there was no flash this time, and when I turned back to the fight, Vinter had Kelis' head flattened against the wall with her shield. Kelis slumped to the ground as Ketra pounced from behind, but Vinter caught her by the wrist and halted her in her tracks.

"I'm not here for puppets," said Vinter, just before she drove Ketra's own blade through her chest.

Both women laid motionless at her feet as Vinter took three steps closer to Camilla.

"You shouldn't have done that," Camilla said, her voice sharp and cold as an icicle.

"Don't weep for them," Vinter replied. "We know you'll just make more. You see, this isn't real loss. Real sorrow. You have no idea what it means to mourn one you truly love. One who loves you back. There aren't any more Michaels. He didn't deserve what you did to him. And if I can't at least make you feel that, then I will make you suffer enough pain to compare."

Vinter launched at Camilla, only to receive a green energy burst in the chest that blasted her through the staircase and into the study. Camilla pursued her, screaming in anger as the sound of walls, tables and glass smashing filled the house.

"Zeke." Xiao grabbed me by the arm. "This is our chance."

"Right," I replied, jogging towards the door and ducking through the hole in the splintered wooden door from which Vinter had made her entrance.

I took the stone steps in one leap, before taking a second to gather my thoughts. We needed a car. Pierceson didn't drive, but he still had a garage, usually filled with at least three or four cars that his chauffeurs used to ferry him about.

"This way," I said, finally turning back to see Kang milling about at the bottom of the stairs. "Dude. What are you doing? We need to go. Now."

"What about Camilla?" he asked.

I looked up at the house, as flashes of jade filled the windows on the first floor, blowing each of them out.

"What about her?" said Xiao.

"Vinter wants to kill her!" Kang was yelling at us, as if we hadn't understood exactly what was unfolding behind us.

"They'll kill each other at this rate," Xiao replied, circling behind him and shoving him away. "And if Camilla does survive, she has orders to kill one of us. Remember?"

"So we're just going to abandon her?"

Admittedly, my desire to see Camilla burn had subsided marginally since we exited the house, and whether or not she would or could survive the encounter was beginning to nag at my conscience.

"We're not abandoning her," I said, squeezing Kang by the shoulder. "But we can't exactly help her either. What we can do is get far away from here and come up with our next move. This isn't our fight."

Kang pulled away from me and turned back towards the house. He lingered there for another ten seconds or so, not quite ready to rush in and not prepared to step away, like a child unsure of which parent to run to.

"Alright," he said, his shoulders sagging. "Let's just–"

Kang was drowned out by the crash of stone exploding away from the house as a body came tumbling through the front wall. She was thrown another twenty metres away as her fall was finally, and unfortunately, broken by the towering Iapetus statue in the centre of the courtyard.

The sculpture was split in two as Camilla laid, writhing, in the rubble and cradling a bloody gash on her forehead. When she finally managed to raise her head enough to lock eyes with us, there was scarcely a moment for her to catch a breath as Vinter came bounding out through the breach in the wall. In one leap she covered the distance to Camilla and dove through the air like a javelin to bring her heel down on Camilla's chest.

Camilla howled in agony as she spat blood and futilely attempted to wrestle herself free.

"Hurts doesn't it?" Vinter taunted, as she screwed her heel further into her victim. "Not so tough when your enemy is prepared, are you? Life in the shadows has made even you a weakling."

Vinter raised her sword high above her head till it glinted in the late orange sunlight.

"I'm not going to kill you yet," she said. "First I'll take your limbs. Then we'll see what next takes my fancy."

"Stop!" yelled Kang.

"Quiet," Vinter shouted back. "This has nothing to do with you. And anyone who comes between her and I is going to get the same treatment."

Kang was right. Camilla really was going to end up dead at this rate. And though I could feel anger building in my heart once more, this time it wasn't reserved just for Camilla.

I was mad at Vinter too, for only showing up now when everything had spiralled so wildly out of control. I was furious with Kang, for letting me spend all this time hating Camilla alone. And I was mad at Xiao for... for... I didn't even know why. But all that rage had boiled up at once, until I was overflowing with the need to take action. My fingers itched with intent and my legs trembled with anticipation until I finally I took flight.

Kang was still yelling something at Vinter, enough to keep her attention away from me as my feet compelled me closer. Before I knew it, I had slammed shoulder-first into Vinter, putting every inch of my six-foot frame into a challenge robust enough to knock any human from their feet.

But Vinter clearly wasn't human. And she didn't move. Without even bracing herself, she had taken the full brunt of my tackle and remained undeterred. With an irritated grunt and a shrug of her shoulder, she sent me tumbling to the ground.

"You idiots," she said. "Why are you wasting your time trying to save her? You know what she's done. What she is. Why help her?"

"Because I *do* know what she is," I replied, pushing back to my feet, though my knees wobbled like gelatin. "She's my friend. And I won't let you kill her."

"Well," said Vinter. "It's a shame you can't stop me then."

"Wanna bet?" Xiao's voice took Vinter by surprise, coming from right beside her.

I hadn't noticed her either until she was right in Vinter's face. Xiao had always been quick and nimble, but most of all it was her cunning that came in handy. Like Diana Ross in the supremes, she regularly upstaged Kang and I by thinking outside the box and being generally brilliant. So I shouldn't have been surprised to see her get one over on Vinter so easily too.

Rather than aim at the woman, or whatever she was, Xiao slid across the turf and landed on her back at Vinter's feet. She glanced quickly at

Camilla, who laid beside her, then reached out with one hand. Her palm was slick with blood, as if someone had sliced clean through the flesh on her hand. Camilla reacted instantly, clasping Xiao by the hand and sending a wave of emerald light pulsing down her arm.

The ground around their heads split as if an earthquake had just hit, caving in until a crater large enough to devour a car had been formed. A grizzly and inhuman snort echoed from within the tunnel, followed by the quickening stamp of hooves against the stone.

"Shit," cried Vinter, as she leapt a dozen feet backwards.

From the hole emerged a nightmarish boar. It was eight-feet tall, covered in shredded fur and armed with two enormous elephant-like tusks that looked sharp enough to skewer anything they touched.

The beast hurtled towards Vinter like a train, shaking the ground as it stomped across the courtyard. For a second I wondered if Vinter might simply be torn to shreds, but again she astonished me. Planting her feet wide, she lifted her arms and clamped the beast around the tusks, halting it dead in its tracks. And she wasn't done.

As if that feat weren't absurd enough, she took a step forward, pushing the beast back. Vinter grunted as she unleashed the raw power in her legs, and the veins in her arms bulged, ready to explode, as she strained against the boar's mighty tusks. A few seconds later, the beast's feet were dangling in the air as she heaved it above her head, twisted like an olympic hammer throw competitor, and heaved it through the window of the house.

I'd seen a lot of insane things in the past week, but I'd never imagined such impossible strength.

"We're dead," said Kang, as he backpedalled towards me.

"Helping her was your idea," I said, as I turned to check on the girls.

Xiao was yanking Camilla back to her feet, but they both wore a look of similar pessimism as Vinter fixed her attention back on them.

"Come on," I said. "We have to help them."

Before we could even get near them, Vinter had closed the distance on us. With one swing of her shield, she sent both Kang and I crashing back to the ground, then took off towards the girls.

Without hesitation, her blade came arcing down towards Camilla's head. Xiao was paralysed by the speed of Vinter's attack, and clearly Camilla had expended the last of whatever magic she wielded in summoning the gigantic boar. She was spent, and the blow would have cleaved her in two if she wasn't shoved aside at the last minute.

Kelis, sporting a blood-soaked brow after being clattered by Vinter earlier, rejoined the fight at the opportune moment. She stepped between Xiao and Camilla, shoving them both aside and took Vinter's attack head on. The sword sliced down through her shoulder, only halting when Kelis raised her own blade to fight it.

Still, there was no way she could survive much longer. Vinter's sword was halfway through Kelis's chest and, at this point, even removing the blade would spell the end for her.

"No!" shouted Camilla, when she sat up and saw the injury.

"Mother," Kelis winced, her eyelids shut as if she were already passing on from this life. "Your eyes!"

Belatedly, I realised what Kelis meant as her eyes flew open once more. I shut mine just in time to avoid the blinding light. Even through my eyelids I could feel the intensity. It lasted longer than ever before, but was eventually brought to an end through screams of agony.

Everything went dark once more. And I opened my eyes to see Vinter still on her feet. She was neither injured nor turned to stone. Instead, she had her shield raised over her head, likely shielding her from the attack. Poor Kelis, on the other hand, was laid out on her back. Her eyes finally shut for good as Vinter shook her sword free of the blood.

"No!" Camilla howled. "What have you done?"

I wasn't surprised to see her anguish. Kelis was supposedly one of her offspring. Her own flesh and blood. But it wasn't until I turned towards her that I noticed it wasn't Kelis she was looking at. Beyond Vinter, and past

Kelis's fallen body, was Xiao. She wasn't moving, not even breathing. Her hands and feet were locked in place. Even her eyes were still. A blank stare, devoid of intent. Devoid of life.

She had been turned completely to stone.

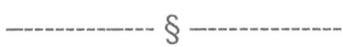

I couldn't quite bring myself to react. I willed my body forwards, but it didn't move. I felt as paralysed as Xiao looked. Even the screams of fury I could feel building in my lungs wouldn't escape.

"Xiao?" I finally said. More a whisper than anything else.

This... this can't be. She can't... Xiao can't.

"Vinter!" Kang shouted in my stead. "I'm going to–"

"What have you done?" Camilla once again demanded, this time more in fury than despair as she rushed towards Xiao and ran her fingers frantically over our friend's frozen face. "What have you done!"

"It was your friend's fault," Vinter replied with a nonchalance that set my pulse racing. "This is Kalypso." Vinter tapped her shield with her blade. "It keeps the holder safe from anything. Even magic. Xiao was in the wrong place at the wrong time when it reflected. You all did this. Not me."

"We did this?" Finally words bounced off my tongue again. "We did this!?"

"Why did you get involved?" Vinter said. "This has nothing to do with you. This is between me and the monster. If you had just let me deal with her. I could have been halfway to Prometheus by now. Rescuing your other friend."

"Don't try to act like you're the hero here," said Kang, the disgust in his voice reaching its apex. "You're no better than either of them. You're heartless. And you're a murderer."

"Give me a break," Vinter replied. "This is the problem with mortals. You involve yourself in the matters of others. You think yourselves more righteous, valliant or wise than all those around you. This war started because of you. And continues each day you delay us."

"Shut up!" I screamed. "Just shut up. You don't get to lecture us about–"

"What. Have. You. Done?" Camilla had finally stopped facing Xiao.

Now her attention was fixed solely on Vinter. And it was clear there was only one thing on her mind. Her eyes glowed, no, they burned with fiery green light. She panted like a frenzied animal circling its prey. And she was squeezing her fists so tight the knuckles went pale and blood oozed from her palm.

With a single thrust of her arm, she summoned Kelis's fallen sword to her hand and without pause, drove it into her own abdomen. Camilla refused even to flinch as she pulled the sword clear once more, tossed it at Vinter's feet, then wiped the thick blood across her own hands.

"Another summon?" said Vinter. "You're getting desperate, monster."

Camilla didn't respond, instead slamming both her palms to the ground and letting out a lung-busting scream. It was so chilling I nearly screamed, covering my mouth and shielding my eyes as a gale of crackling green wind and otherworldly energy threatened to blast me from my feet.

The air crackled and fizzed as if we were amidst a storm called forth from Camilla's fingertips. Even Vinter had planted her sword to brace herself against the raging force until, finally, the storm spread out around us and we stood unharmed within its eye.

"That's it?" said Vinter, claiming her sword from the splintered earth and resting it assuredly upon her shoulder. "A flicker before the flame goes out? I expected more."

Camilla had slumped down to her knees as she panted in exhaustion. As if the last of her power had been expelled from her body. Her green skin was almost pale white and it looked as if her lips and cheeks had cracked and broken. When she finally lifted her hand to point a finger at Vinter, her wrist sparked and caught fire.

She turned and examined her palm as the flames spread down her arm.

"I'm done here," she said, sounding frustrated. "But it's too late. I've petitioned for your death, Vinter. And my child has answered."

Within seconds, the blaze had spread to Camilla's torso and begun to burn brighter until it consumed her from head to toe. A flash of crimson sparks later, she was gone.

"Is she…" I couldn't quite bring myself to say the word aloud. "Did we just lose both our friends?"

"This can't be happening," Kang replied.

I swung on Vinter, ready to bury her under a fresh tirade of vitriol and fury. But she wasn't paying us any attention, nor was she celebrating Camilla's death as I had anticipated. No, Vinter's eyes were uneasy and she had raised her shield in expectation as the cyclone around us faded.

"Get behind me," she said, when she finally fixed on one direction in the storm.

"Why?" I demanded.

"This isn't over."

The last thing I wanted was to be anywhere near Vinter, but as I too searched around for danger, I realised she was right. The storm wasn't fading at all, it was being absorbed or extracted. The violent winds were drawn towards the point directly in front of Vinter, as if they were being inhaled by a giant.

"Something's coming," Vinter said, when all that remained was a single pillar of dark fog, obscuring the entrance to the courtyard. Her voice sounded wary. Maybe even a little nervous. And as I peered through the gloom, I really could see something there.

A towering silhouette dipped forward, parting the mists and bringing with it a deep, bassy, rattling that grew louder by the second. Then a head pushed through the fog and reared in front of Vinter, looking down on her from the long neck upon which it hung.

It only took me a few seconds to identify the serpent-like creature. An enormous head, the size of the entire boar that had attacked Vinter earlier, dangled before us. Its forked tongue licked slowly across its scaly lips, which were stained in dark maroon and crimson. Its eyes didn't twinkle like the other beasts, but they bore the same, if slightly diminished, emerald green that had haunted us since the museum. And they were fixed, unblinking, on us.

A Hydra.

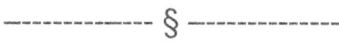

Vinter's feet inched backwards as the Hydra examined her, when suddenly the creature's mouth shot open and let out a chilling wail.

"Don't breathe it in!" yelled Vinter, as we were showered with thick saliva. But it wasn't the liquid she was warning us of. A dark purple vapour hissed out of the Hydra's mouth, surrounding us until the air was a violet haze.

I held my breath, ensuring that none of the potentially toxic gas entered my lungs. There was hardly any dividing myth from fact at this point, but in the second labour of Herakles, the Hydra's blood and breath were poisonous. So I wasn't taking any chances. There weren't many deaths I could think of any worse than being eaten alive from the inside. Still, there was only so long I could go without oxygen and if Vinter didn't make her move soon, that fate would be inevitable.

Fortunately, she took a step closer to the Hydra. As if she had finished weighing up her opponent and was ready to strike. That Camilla had summoned such an enormous creature to begin with was unfathomable. But

I still had confidence in Vinter's ability to slay the beast. After all, she had easily dealt with everything else that had been thrown at her.

I spoke too soon.

Before Vinter could make one of her bone-crunching lunges towards the creature, from within the fog a second silhouette loomed and lunged. It snapped ferociously into position, a long spiked neck uncurling until another head hung beside the first, identical in every way. It wasn't long before a third head swooped into formation, followed by a fourth and a fifth, and soon after there must have been a dozen heads or more surrounding us.

Both bewilderment and fear kept me from counting them exactly. But one thing I was certain of was just how low our odds of surviving this encounter had fallen. Whether Camilla had meant for this thing to kill just Vinter, or all of us, our fate seemed entirely dependent on the warrioress's ability to fend off this monster.

"Run!" she finally said, risking inhaling its pernicious breath and confirming that even she was no match for a multi-headed Hydra.

I turned to find Kang already ten metres or so ahead of me, his feet eating up the ground towards the house as if he were amid one of the sprint finishes that ended most of our cardio sessions.

I chased him down as fast as my feet would carry me, never chancing a glance back to see why Vinter hadn't overtaken us yet. No, she told us to run and that was exactly what I had planned. Unfortunately, Vinter did bypass us shortly after. Only she wasn't running. Her body sailed through the air and crashed into the stone steps at the foot of the house, demolishing them under the force of her impact.

"Are you alright?" Kang shouted, leaning over her without quite helping her up.

Vinter didn't answer. I reached out a hand to help her as I arrived, but she swatted it away in revulsion. Instead she yanked her shield from the stone and wiped away the blood that trickled down her arm.

"Get inside," she said. "I have an idea."

A small part of me felt guilt, as Vinter watched our backs while we retreated inside the house. She was doing her best to protect us. Minutes after the two of us had condemned her and branded her a murderer. In truth, she had every right to her revenge over Ealing's death. And though I was loath to admit it, this Hydra attack was proof enough that our wellbeing was no longer top of Camilla's wish list.

As Kang burst into the mansion, he banked into the study. I followed him, only to lose my footing when a section of the wall caved in. One of the Hydra heads came crashing towards us, with Vinter trapped and flailing between its jaws. I half-expected to be crushed under its weight, as its neck lashed back and forth, but Vinter managed to turn the tables, prying open its jaws and grappling with the creature. Straining her entire body, she managed to wrestle the Hydra onto its side just as several pursuing heads darted into the room.

The entire house shook under the force of the Hydra being flipped onto its back, as each of its multiple necks twisted and tangled around each other in chaos.

"This way," yelled Vinter, beckoning us as she limped towards the door.

Her right leg was soaked in blood and she had so many cuts and bruises across her arms and neck, it was a miracle that she was even still conscious and standing, let alone fighting.

Vinter practically shoved Kang and I across the room, as the Hydra once again forced its way into the remains of the already razed dining room.

"Get down," Vinter said, as she drew her sword and shield once more. "And hold your breath."

"What are you going to do?" asked Kang, as he ducked down regardless.

"Just... trust me."

I huddled down beside Kang as Vinter, now the only thing standing between us and the multi-headed monster, stood bravely face to face with certain death. The Hydra heads were almost taunting her, many of them probing left and right for an opening, as Vinter twisted her shield rapidly left and right to deny them. When she failed to present them with a clear opportunity to strike, each of the heads shot their mouths open at once, hissing loudly as the violet mist filled the room. With nowhere left to run and only so long we could realistically hold our breath, it felt like the end was closer than ever.

But only when the toxin had completely surrounded us, did Vinter finally surge into action. She spun, launching her sword towards the extinguished fireplace behind us, and continued her spiral motion to come down atop Kang and I, bringing her hefty shield down as cover.

I couldn't see anything besides the few centimetres that the shield left uncovered beside our feet, but what happened around us was as clear in my mind as if I had witnessed it with my own eyes.

The clang of Vinter's metal sword striking the fireplace coals. The deafening cacophony of the raucous explosion that followed. Wind and heat battering us and the flash of bright swirling flames smothering Vinter's shield as it eclipsed the fiery tornado swirling around us.

The gas from the Hydra's jaws had been ignited. And now everything around us was suffering in flames. I kept expecting to be hurled away by the force of the explosion or a tendril of fire to creep beneath the shield and turn us to ash along with everything else in the room.

But Vinter held the shield steady and unmoving against the flames licking at us and the raging inferno outside. She mentioned that it reflected magic. So maybe the flames were being bounced off of us too.

There were howls of agony, as if a wild animal were being skewered. It was both traumatic and cathartic, both because they were exactly the sounds I'd expect to hear from something or someone being burnt alive and because, at this point, it was either the Hydra or us.

Only when the ground shook under a mighty thud did Vinter finally relax her rigid stance and stand up tall, revealing what little of Pierceson's home there was left to speak of. The formerly stone walls were barely piles of rubble. Where there were once ceilings and both a first and second floor, I could see only the sunset sky through the parting smoke.

Piles of wood still burned in isolation all around the grounds, but in the centre was a grotesque spectacle of almost vomit-inducing horror. Only having seen the monster when it still breathed allowed me to identify what remained. A charcoaled mass of twisted scales and appendages. Worse was the smell. That of roasted flesh and searing organs. The intense ammonia in its blood-soaked remains made my nostrils flare in disapproval and eventually even Vinter turned away from the mess.

"We should go," she said, her speech noticeably more calm and measured than before.

Only when I noticed the slight stagger in her gait and the trembling of her fingers as she retrieved her sword from the flames did I realise that she wasn't calm at all. She was exhausted.

"Are you alright?" I asked.

"Oh, suddenly you care?" she remarked. "Someone will have noticed this whole place going up in smoke. We should be gone when the authorities arrive."

I couldn't argue with that. There was no explaining any of this to the police or a fire brigade.

"Kang. How's your arm?" I asked.

I was certain Kang must have heard me. It was silent but for the sputter of embers flickering around us. But he was still staring down at the mangled Hydra body, gravity in his sharp eyes.

"Kang?" I probed, only to be hushed as he pressed a finger urgently to his lips.

"Do you hear that?" he said.

Rather than question him, I stayed quiet as he'd asked. Listening intently to the silence. Only it wasn't actually silent. Not entirely. Aside from the flames, there was wind. Blowing through the non-existent walls of the house. Then, somewhere in the distance, there was a rattle. A train, maybe, passing us by. But much closer than that, something was stirring.

A rustle. Or more like... burrowing. It grew louder and louder until I was certain that neither of us were imagining it. Only then did I notice it. The smallest of twitches across the Hydra's body. It could have just been the wind, but then it happened again. And again. And the burrowing grew louder and louder.

Then, in one violent jolt, the scattered Hydra remains parted and one very much alive head stabbed towards us. Its teeth were only inches from my face, and I could taste its acidic breath. But before its jaws could clamp shut, I was flying backwards across the rubble.

I landed awkwardly on a pile of stones and clutched at my abdomen where I had been struck hard enough to knock me from my feet. Vinter, with that monstrous strength of hers, had forced me out of the Hydra's path. And she had paid the price for it in full.

She hadn't so much as stopped the Hydra, as the creature had stopped to take a bite out of her. Its teeth had sunk deep into her shoulders and waist, and only the weight from her sword pressed against its jaw saved her from being bitten utterly in half.

Vinter growled in agony, then slipped her blade free and drove it into the Hydra's right eye. The creature recoiled, flicking its tail around wildly as it writhed and wriggled out of the room. It was more like a serpent now, a single remaining head atop a long streamlined body that had somehow survived the rain of fire.

"Zeke," Vinter whispered, before collapsing. She fell flat on her back, as I rushed achingly to her side.

I could feel Kang poised over my shoulder as we both stared down at her quickly emptying eyes. He didn't need to say it. I didn't need to say it. We both knew. And Vinter did too.

"I'm here," I said, raising her head. "Why... why did you do that?"

As life continued to leak from her wounds, Vinter placed her blood-stained fingers around the back of my neck.

"Michael was always telling me to be better," she wheezed. "I'm sorry about your friend. At least I could save *you*. Now, you get to make it up to me. Prometheus. He means to destroy my kind. And just like today, mortals will fall as collateral. Find him. Stop him."

I nodded, without even considering the magnitude of what she was asking.

"We will," I replied.

"Here." She pushed the sword into my hands and tried to sit up further. "Sword. Shield. Armour. Take them."

"But–"

"Take them," she yelled, coughing blood onto my cheek.

Though she was just about still alive, taking Vinter's weapons and armour felt too much like looting a corpse.

I still had so many questions to ask her. About Ealing. About Camilla. About Prometheus. But the scratching of scales snaking across stone drew closer too rapidly for me to risk waiting any longer.

"Come on," said Kang, as he pulled me up.

I shoved the hefty sword into his chest. It felt like carrying a dumbbell, and wielding both it and the shield seemed impossible for one person. Together we raced through the wreckage until we found ourselves hiding beside the remnants of a kitchen island.

"What now?" I whispered.

"Quiet," said Kang. "I'm thinking."

"Think faster," I replied, as the scraping reached the room we were in.

At this range, I could hear the Hydra breathing as it stalked us. It surely knew we couldn't have gotten far and seemed intent on making sure there were no survivors.

"Come on," I saw Kang mouth, as he crept around the counter and beckoned me with a wave of his hand. The Hydra's tail had barely rounded the corner as we tiptoed by it and back towards the front of the house.

"Okay," said Kang. "I have an idea. But you have to draw its attention."

"What?" I said, surprised by Kangs sudden desire to split up. "What are you going to do?"

"Kill it. Of course."

"But Kang–"

Before I could talk him out of it, he was already sprinting away, hurdling over a section of the collapsed staircase and out of sight. And while I had little intention of following through on his ill-conceived plan, the hiss of the Hydra turning back this way gave me little choice over whether I would be its prey or not.

By the time I had made it back to the front door, I knew the Hydra had laid eyes on me. It's hissing had risen to a shriek and I could hear debris being bounced and crashed out of the way as it slalomed after me. The stone steps into the courtyard were only a metre or so away, but my instincts told me there was little to no chance of making it to the bottom as the creature bore down on me.

Instead, I spun and raised Vinter's weighty shield to fend off the fangs I could almost feel on my neck. When the Hydra's teeth pounded against the metal, it felt like I'd been thrown from a motorcycle. My legs buckled and I rolled helplessly to the ground, losing my grip on the shield and striking my head against a rock.

Dazed, I looked up to find the Hydra lowering its head once more. It seemed primed to zip towards me, only to have its head severed at the top of the neck before it could pounce. Kang, leaping from the piled rubble above, had brought Vinter's sword down, straight through the creature.

"Kang?" I said, unsure of how hard I had hit my head and whether I could be hallucinating. "Did you just–"

"Slay a Hydra?" he replied. "Hell yeah."

Kang pushed the head aside, causing it to roll down the stairs as he strode confidently towards me.

"Dude. What the hell even made you do that?" I wondered. "That was insane."

"I... I don't really know." Kang's uncertain expression told the true story of bewilderment he was admitting. "It was like something just came over me and I had to attack. To go on the offensive. I just really wanted to kill it."

"Well... thanks. Only problem is...." I pointed towards the body that had begun to flail around once more. "It's a Hydra, Kang. If you cut off a head."

Kang gulped as his mettle faded. "Two more grow in its place."

While I was glad to be alive, Kang's tenacity had only taken things from bad to worse. The Hydra sprouted not just a second menacing head, but a new pair of legs. It stomped furiously towards us, as if it were taunting us knowing that we were out of ideas.

"Zeke," Kang said, nudging me with his elbow. "I'm sorry about all the fighting. We're smarter than this. I... wish we could have used our heads to solve this sooner."

"Me too," I replied. "Glad you're here with me at the end though. Even if it's a gruesome one."

Kang smiled. "I really wish Vinter had spared one of those women you had protecting you."

"That's it."

Kang had brought a memory crashing back to me, like a tidal wave engulfing a wayward surfer, that had me reaching around inside my jacket pocket.

"Protection," I said, glancing down at Kelis' body. "Kang, get behind me and cover your eyes."

"What?" he replied.

"Just do it!"

As Kang shuffled in behind me, and the Hydra towered before us, I pulled out the strand of braided hair that Kelis had gifted me that night.

Please work.

I held the hair up in front of me as the Hydra dipped its head and plunged towards us. I closed my eyes in fear, and hope, unwittingly squeezing the hair with my fingers. As the patterned braids hardened into cold scales, the darkness of my eyelids was awash with magnificent light.

It lasted just a second before a sharp sting pinched the flesh on my hand and whatever I was clutching wriggled free. I opened my eyes to see a short grey snake, shirking away as I examined the puncture mark its fangs had left beside my thumb.

"Zeke," said Kang, holding me by the back of the head and craning my neck to look at the Hydra. "It's a freaking miracle, dude. You did it".

The enormous two-headed Hydra was now little more than a statue, frozen in time in the centre of the courtyard. Not unlike the Iapetus statue that stood there until earlier.

"Holy shit," I said. "We actually did it."

Kang spun me around and grabbed hold of me, jumping and spinning us around in jubilation. I laughed too, astonished that we had somehow not only survived the Hydra, but defeated it.

But as we turned, my adrenaline subsided. Over Kang's shoulder I could see a second figure, far lesser than the Hydra but no less statuesque. And this one was proof that all this was no miracle. It was magic. And it had cost us dearly.

"Kang." I pried him off and nodded in the direction of the petite statue.

His glee was erased, as the two of us remembered the true cost of what had unfolded, then dragged our feet towards the miserable sight.

For all our fighting over Avy and Camilla, or Athena and Echidna, or whatever we were supposed to call them. Neither of us had been able to protect the one girl who had been there for us throughout this whole ordeal.

"Xiao," I whispered, sweeping my fingers over her petrified cheek. "She's gone."

ACT XIV

THE VIPER'S PROGENY

'The bravest are surely those who have the clearest vision of what is before them, glory and danger alike, and yet notwithstanding, go out to meet it.'

Had I been brave at any point on this journey? Had I made a single move that put the safety of my friends, my family, above my own. Or above the need to procure the wretched stone. Even when Avy was in peril, I wanted to protect her because of my feelings for her. By Thucydides account, bravery was not a quality I possessed.

Xiao was different.

At every turn, she had seen the declining odds. She had seen the threats. She had seen treachery and villainy up close, and met them head on each time. I was alive because of her. Kang, Avy and even Camilla were alive because of *her*. And in the end, when she was in danger, I had been too busy keeping our team in disarray to lift a hand in her aid.

If I had been brave enough, maybe it would have been different. Brave enough, not just to fight, but to accept my own flaws and mistakes. Brave enough to use the intelligence I'd been blessed with to change our fate. To change Xiao's fate.

Finally I was thinking clearly. Clearly enough to feel the regret of being too late.

"We have to move her," Kang said urgently.

"Where?" I wondered. "Where are we even going, Kang? What are we even doing? How can we even–"

"Shut up." Kang's ferociousness caught me off guard. "Shut up, Zeke. We're not giving up. Let's just get her in one of the cars and figure out our next move."

"Are you okay?" I asked, knowing it was impossible that he could be. Between Camilla turning to ash and Xiao turning to stone, he'd just lost two best friends in one swoop.

"I'm fine," he growled, as he spread his feet and took hold of Xiao by the waist.

Stepping warily in front of her, I reached out an arm, stroking my fingers gently beneath her outstretched forearms. Her once leather jacket sent chills through my fingers, as if I'd grabbed hold of an ice-pack. I tried desperately to avoid her gaze, but my eyes wandered from her waist to her eyes once more.

I swallowed, and suppressed the tears I could feel welling in my eyes, as I stared into the now empty void of her pupils. There was nothing there. Not even the vaguest hint of consciousness. Of pain. Of life. Her eyes were empty. As if her soul had been frozen along with her body.

"Lift," said Kang.

"Right." I nodded.

I bent my knees and thrust my weight beneath her, as Kang did the same, expecting tiny Xiao to simply glide off the ground. I'd lifted her plenty of times before. She was so headstrong, and forever asking for a boost or leg up to force her way into places she shouldn't be. And she had always been as light as I'd imagine a ballerina to be.

"Shit," I said, feeling the strain as we bore her weight between us and managed just a few steps before I was forced to readjust. "Wait," I gasped, easing her back to the ground before I lost my grip.

"Why are you stopping?" Kang demanded, even as he sweated and panted more heavily than I.

"She's so heavy," I replied. "She isn't just frozen, Kang. She's been turned to solid stone."

"So?" Kang was dusting down his hands and preparing to heave her up once more.

"So we're never going to get her very far."

"And you want to just leave her here?!"

"No, dude. I don't. I'm just saying– look can you just calm down. You're clearly upset about–"

"Upset?" Kang screamed. "Upset!? I'm so far beyond upset, Zeke. Every single day since we saw that damned stone has gone from bad to worse. This is a nightmare that just won't end. Avy is gone. Camilla is dead. Xiao is petrified. We've lost *everything*."

I thought really hard for something clever, or reassuring, or even melancholy to say. But none of it would help. Kang's furor was almost visibly melting him, as the vein in his forehead bulged and he rested his hands on his knees to catch his breath.

"I don't freaking believe it," Kang cursed, as he barged past me and marched back towards the estate.

"What?" I said, searching the ruins for whatever he had taken issue to, until I happened upon the small creature perched atop the remains of the stone steps.

A bird, but not just any bird. Its feathers were ocean blue. As was its beak and, at this close distance, it's unblinking cerulean eyes. It was odd-looking to say the least, but more odd was that again, somehow, the same unnatural creature was stalking us.

I wondered at once whether I had been wrong to ignore Kang each time he had mentioned it. After all, it was unlikely, or impossible, to encounter the same extraordinary breed of creature in three seperate countries. But while I considered what its presence, a third time, could mean, Kang had already decided on what he would do.

"I'm so sick of being followed," he said, reaching down to hoist Vinter's sword up off the ground and drag it with him. "Camilla summoned you to spy on us, didn't she? But all you do is watch. Were you watching when Deimos nearly slaughtered her? Were you watching when Vinter nearly carved her to pieces?"

When Kang was just a step away from the bird, he strained audibly as he forced the sword above his head and held it ready to strike.

"Were you there when she burned away into nothing!?" he cried.

Kang wavered for just a moment, before swinging the sword down where the blade sparked against the rock and lodged itself within.

The bird had slipped easily away from his strike, and landed swiftly on his shoulder, just an inch from his face.

"That would have been a mistake," said a laidback voice.

Kang's eyes grew so wide, I worried they might pop out from his head and end up on the ground.

"Did you…" he started, his attention fixed on the bird. "Did you just talk?"

"Yeah," said the bird. "When someone takes a swing at me, you better believe I've got summin' to say about it."

For the next minute or so, I didn't utter a word.

I'm not sure why, but even after embracing all of the insanity of the past few days, a talking bird was something my mind simply refused to process. Kang must have been suffering from a similar bout of disbelief, as he stood motionless with the creature perched on his shoulder.

"Are you finished being dumbstruck," said the bird. And I could've sworn it rolled its eyes too. "You cut the head off a giant snake, but you're afraid to talk to a little birdy? You two got some serious issues."

"So you *can* talk?" Kang finally said.

"Okay," said the bird, flapping its wings to blast away from Kang and glide effortlessly through the sky. "Clearly, you're not the brains of this operation."

It soared across the courtyard until it reached Xiao's frozen body, circling her once before touching down on her wrist, and fixing me with a prying stare.

"Problem is," the bird said to me. "I'm not convinced you are, either."

"Get off her," I cried, waving my hand towards them, suddenly feeling provoked by the way it casually rested on the friend I had barely begun to mourn. "She isn't some statue you can just trample on."

"Would you chill out," the bird replied. "I'm not gonna shit on her or anything. I'm trying to do you two a favour. And from the looks of how badly you've cocked things up, you need all the favours you can get."

"You want to help us?" I asked, making sure to scoff sceptically. "As if we'd trust you. You've been watching us. Spying on us. Going wherever Camilla summoned you and relaying our every move to her and her boss. Just because she's gone doesn't mean we're on the same side now."

"Wow," the bird said, raising one wing over its face in mock disbelief. "You two really are in the dark, innit? I haven't been watching you. And Camilla didn't summon me, you idiots."

"Then who did?" Kang asked, as he drew closer, a bewildered frown still ingrained on his face.

"Someone I thought I might never get to meet again. Until recently. You three actually got my hopes high for a while there. But you just couldn't stop bitching between yourselves. So now you've gone and nearly pissed it all away. Lost the only thing that was gonna stop this war from bubbling to the surface again."

"Avy," I said, before the bird could say any more. "You weren't watching us. You were watching her."

"Bingo," it replied.

"Wait. I get it now. You're... Athene Noctua."

"The owl of Athena?" Kang added.

"You're finally getting it," the bird said. "Shame you only started playing when the game was over. Friends call me Nox, by the way."

"What friends?" Kang scoffed.

"Well... you two clowns now. I guess."

"You don't look like much of an owl. More like a... blue jay."

"You scholarly types," the bird shook his head. "Only trust what you read. And only read what you trust. Surely by now you know everything isn't the way you imagined?"

"Okay," I said, worried that our supposed new friend might lose interest if we didn't get up to speed fast. "Nox. Do you know where Avy is?"

"Not exactly," Nox shrugged his tiny shoulders. "I know the place old P-boy has taken her. I just don't know where that place is."

"But there's a way you can track Avy directly, right?"

"Sure. We can just hit 'find my phone' on her laptop and it'll take us straight to her."

"Really?" I said, so optimistically it took me a few seconds to realise how desperate, and idiotic, I sounded.

"Of course not," Nox yelled. "Do I look like a tracking app to you?"

"Then what good are you?!" Kang shouted. "I thought you said you could help us."

"You're right." Nox nodded. "And I'm gonna help you first with two bits of advice. One. Stick to using your inside voice and that big brain of yours. Because honestly, you're not very intimidating. And if a tiny bird says you ain't intimidating, then really you couldn't scare a hiccup out of a baby. Two. And this is the big one. Stop touching that damned sword. It's making you crazy."

"The sword?" asked Kang. "How do you mean?"

"It's called Herja." Nox looked back and forth between us, only to quickly throw his head up in irritation when we offered no response. "You mean you don't even know who she was? You two are like Terry and Allen."

"Wait. Did you just reference The Other Guys?"

"Damn right. Vintage Wahlberg and Ferrell. But don't change the subject. Vinter. She was the demi-Goddess of fury, ya know? Her sword, Herja, is like a beacon of anger. It fueled her. And any mortal who goes near it, let alone touches the bloody thing, will get caught up by all that rage pretty fast. That's why you, a fanboy bookworm from Cambridge, thinks he's Leonidas of Sparta every time he picks it up."

It actually made more sense than I first realised. When Vinter showed up, her presence alone nearly drove me into a frenzy. I was on the verge of diving in to attack Camilla with her. And when Kang had taken hold of the weapon, he was suddenly rushing off to attack the Hydra.

Kang and I both checked out the sword, where it was lodged in the stone steps, and took an uneasy step back.

"Cute," said Nox. "Listen, I got a plan to fix this mess you've made. But seeing as I'd given you way too much credit up till now, this next part is definitely gonna' blow your little minds."

I gave Kang a nudge in the arm, gaining his attention as I nodded confidently at him. When he nodded back, I took a long breath and readied myself.

"As long as it helps us find Avy. We can take it. We can't lose all three of our friends today."

"Yeah…" Nox rubbed his beak against his wing. "About that."

"About what?"

"Well… it ain't easy to explain. But if we wait for a bit, you'll see for yourself."

"See what?" Kang demanded, embodying my growing frustration. "If you know something about our friends, just spit it out."

"Right. Well… the thing is–" Before Nox could finish, his tiny head began darting to the left and right as if alerted by some new danger. "Ah bollocks," he said.

"What?" I asked, spinning aimlessly around, wary of just what new myth could spring to life to compound this awful day.

"You don't hear that?" he replied.

A few seconds later, I could finally hear what Nox was so concerned by.

"Sirens," I cursed. "Police sirens."

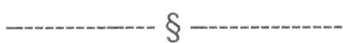

"Try and stay calm," Kang urged.

Ironically, after doing his best impression of a bubbling cauldron of rage earlier, he'd been back to his level-headed self. I, on the other hand, found that maintaining my composure had become a futile struggle.

"I am calm," I replied, doing my utmost to bury my resentment.

"No. You're not. For a start, you need to sit still. It looks like you're trying to escape."

"We *are* trying to escape."

"No, we're not. We're trying to *think* of a way to escape."

I sighed in defeat. Kang was right. The only way out of this was to use our heads.

In my defence, staying calm while being held captive inside a police station wasn't exactly a box I'd tick on my list of skills. Since the police cars had pulled up outside the estate, it had been a series of repeated sledgehammer blows against the wall of composure I was trying to hide behind.

First, they had slammed me head first into the gravel. Next, they cuffed me so tight I could feel the skin chafing and cutting away at my wrists. Their barrage of questions left us without any time to provide answers, before forcing us into the back of their car and shuttling us back to their station.

Of course, I didn't exactly have a half-decent explanation for any of it, even if they had been willing to listen. I'd even contemplated whether getting Nox to do the explaining for us could have bought us some time, by dazzling them at the sight and sound of a talking animal. But, typical of our luck, he had disappeared back into the skies and was nowhere to be found by the time their tyres screeched to a halt.

It wasn't far from rock-bottom, but I knew that Kang still feared things going from bad to worse if I couldn't control myself. We both knew how easily I could be antagonised, given how passionately I hated the police.

Growing up where I did, my parents always had to be wary. Being in the wrong place at the wrong time had gotten friends and family of ours arrested, shot, beaten. Or worse. And when you were as poor as we were, working late nights and earning extra pennies in bad or disreputable neighbourhoods always put my parents at high-risk of getting caught up in someone else's wrongdoings.

When you're a young black family, trying to make ends meet, every single action you ever take bears the weight of risk versus reward. And with plenty of people who looked just like us and lived right beside us, wading knee-deep through the waters of whatever illegal enterprise was keeping them afloat, the risks just kept getting higher. While the rewards only got slimmer.

But my dad always refused to succumb to those types of prejudice. On either side.

"The police aren't our enemy," he told me every day. "And the people in our community, tarring us with their stereotypes. They aren't our enemy either. Our only enemy is our situation. And we have the means and ambition to change it."

He was right. Things eventually turned around. He got a job as a security guard at a museum. On the recommendation of a friend. Walter Summers. Kang's old man. They'd only met because the bulk of my parent's income was spent making sure I went to a decent pre-school. It took an hour and a half to get there every day, but it was worth it.

I was slow to do pretty much everything as a child. Didn't walk until I was three. Didn't talk until I was five. Without the extra attention that school gave me, who knows when or if I would have ever caught up with other kids my age. But even more importantly than that, it was where mine and Kang's parents met.

Kang's family had moved to the Greater London suburbs since his dad took a job in the city. And luckily, our parents had become close friends too. Close enough for my dad to accept that job as the one and only handout of his life.

The rest was sheer old-fashioned elbow grease and the daily grind, as it wasn't long before he climbed the career ladder, eventually getting into the good graces of the museum's owner. Pierceson, of course. A few years later, he was head of security for both Pierceson and his various real estate all around the city. My mum was always proud of him, but even she was speechless when he moved us up and out of the neighbourhood, to a house in the city.

He had been right all along. Our situation was the enemy, and he had worked hard to defeat it every day of his life. And mum would tell him every day that his story was an example that every man, woman or child would be proud to have as their own.

But my dad's story would have no happy ending.

One evening, when he was responding to a broken alarm going off at one of the buildings under his management. He was shot. And killed. Not by a criminal. Or in the crossfire of some firefight.

No. My dad was shot and killed by a policeman. A policeman who was never convicted of his real crime. A policeman who had arrived on the scene and mistaken an unarmed black man, wearing a security badge, for a criminal.

My dad was right about everything. But not everyone treats their situation like their enemy. Not like he did. Others let their situation define them and react accordingly. Those people are my enemies too. Because I can't trust them. Just like I can't trust anyone who points a gun at me.

"Can we get a phone call?" asked Kang, when the officers that arrested us finally returned to the booking room. "Each? We're legally obligated to notify someone outside the station of our arrest. So you might as well let us speak to them ourselves, otherwise I'll make sure to call my solicitor instead of my parents."

I would have laughed, were I in a slightly better mood. Kang had spent no end of time poking fun at his mum, and the myriad of procedural police and crime dramas she sunk her time into. Clearly, however, his indisputable memory had recorded most of what he'd heard. And I bet he was more than a little grateful to have some of it come in handy for once.

After the officers eventually agreed, they unlocked our cuffs and escorted us to the phones, with Kang nodding for me to go first.

"Who do we call?" I asked, wondering if there were actually any chance of us finding someone, or something, that could explain us out of all of this.

"Don't worry about that," Kang replied, placing a reassuring arm on my shoulder. "Zeke, there may not *be* a good way out of this. Either way, I'll use my call to reach my parents. At the very least, they'll get us bail and a lawyer. Just use your call to get your head right."

"Kang." Admittedly, I was a little lost for words. "I'm... glad you're here with me."

"Well, believe it or not, I wish I was elsewhere. But I'm glad you're here with me too."

It took me another thirty seconds to slow my breathing and prepare my thoughts before picking up the phone. I briefly considered calling Sherelle. After all, nobody could understand my current predicament better than her. She'd know exactly what to say. And what not to say. How to act and keep a cool head.

But I decided against it. In fact, it was the very definition of a terrible idea. The first thing that would happen, if Sherelle heard I was locked up, was that she'd berate me. She'd lay into me, ask me how the hell I let this happen, and wonder why I couldn't just keep my head above the surface like I was supposed to.

Worse than all that, however, was that she would blame herself. She'd wonder if her example had forever damned me, if somehow our continued contact had been detrimental to me and if she should have just removed herself from my life entirely. It wouldn't be the first time she'd suggested as much, but if dropped all this on her, it might be the last.

And with her locked away, unable to even lift a finger to help me, she'd slip back into her old ways. The anger, the violence and the hatred. No. I couldn't do that to her. I'd gotten myself into this mess and I'd get myself out. She needn't ever know that her 'shining knight' had proved to be nothing special after all.

Instead, I dialled the numbers with my eyes closed and waited breathlessly as the ring tone sounded four times without interruption.

Typical. Never in a hurry. If she were here right now, she'd say 'if you live your life in the fast lane, you never get to–'

"Good evening," said a cordial, overly-formal and slightly fluttering voice through the dated handset. It didn't sound like her. Not like she was at home, anyway. But it was her in the way she addressed strangers, outsiders, and other people she didn't need judging her.

I stumbled for a second. It had been over a month since we'd spoken directly, and hearing her voice, after everything I'd been through, brought a wealth of emotions tumbling back down on me.

"Is there someone there?" she said.

"Mum," I replied. "It's me. You don't have to speak the Queen's English."

"Z," she said. "What's wrong?"

"I... uh. I just–"

"Talk and taste your tongue," she said, sounding much more like the Jamaica born and bred that I knew, before I could delay any more.

It pretty much meant, 'think before you speak.' And for the first time since I'd been cuffed, I laughed.

"You still never say what you mean," I replied.

"I mean every'ting I say," mum said. "So what's wrong, likkle' Z?"

"Something has to be wrong for me to call?"

"Yeah," she quickly retorted.

"You make me sound like a terrible son."

"You're a *wonderful* son, Z. You're a *terrible* liar. And I know something's up. One, cos' this ain't your number. Two, cos' you're not bragging on and on about your latest trip. An alligator may lay egg–'

"But he's not a fowl."

It actually felt good to be finishing her sentences off for her again. It reminded me how whenever I quoted her, I was actually translating the many riddles buried within her latent patois musings. She may have left her homeland when she was just a teenager, and did a fair approximation of your everyday Brit, but in her mind she was still Kingston through and through.

"Everything's fine, mum." A lie or not, she didn't need to know the impossible details of how her only son got himself arrested. After what happened to my sister, I couldn't tell her where I was. Couldn't break her heart a second time.

"Just letting you know that I'm still away. Yes, things got a little out of hand. I lost my phone and a bunch of other stuff. But the job isn't over yet. So I'm staying to finish it. I probably won't be home in time for my birthday next week."

"You're sure that's all?" she asked, her words heavy with suspicion.

"Yeah mum, I'm sure. I'll tell you the full story when I get back."

"Alright. You give me notice though. You know they make me travel to get a good price on your favourites."

"No excuses," I replied. "Oxtail stew or I'm not coming. You pay whatever they ask."

My mum kissed her teeth loud enough to make me flinch even over the phone.

"You bringing anyone?" she asked.

If I could roll my eyes back any further, I would have.

"Mum, when was the last time I brought a girl round for dinner?"

"That's what I'm saying. Maybe I can call Camilla. You know she's the only one I ever liked. Ever since you two were this high, you–"

"Mum!" I had to cut short her rambling before she got any closer to the truth.

"Fine. I'm just saying, old fire stick easy fi' catch."

"Not as easy as you think," I replied. "Listen, I have to go. I promise you'll hear from me soon."

"I better. Zeke, have you visited Sherelle lately?"

"No," I replied. "But we speak."

"Good. I'm glad," mum said. "You should come with me. To see her in person. She's changed."

Sherelle had changed. She was less angry. Less impulsive. Less aggressive. But she was also very much the same.

Mum still didn't know it. She could *never* be allowed to know it. That Sherelle was entirely… innocent. That she was in prison, because I made a mistake. Because I was on the streets, in the wrong place at the wrong time. And that she took the fall for it all. Her criminal record and street cred made it all too easy for the police to take her away instead of me. Dirtying herself even further to keep me clean.

Mum could never know. The shame was mine alone to bear. I'd been round in circles, hating myself on and off for years. And only recently had I accepted that the only thing I could do now, was be everything she wanted me to be. To shine.

She could never know.

"She has," I mumbled. "She's doing great."

"Your lovely Camilla still sends me a car you know," mum said.

"I know," I replied. Unable to keep the pain of it all from washing over me and barely keeping the emotion out of my voice. "I'll see you soon. I love you mum."

"I love you too. But remember what your father say. No trouble trouble–"

"Until trouble, troubles you. I know. Bye, mum."

"Goodbye, likkle' Z."

Five minutes later, we were in a holding cell, having been through most of our processing. Kang's parents hadn't picked up, so we were waiting for them to get back in touch before answering any more of the officer's questions.

The inside of a cell was just as I'd imagined it would be. Cold. Empty. Devoid of life. We didn't know if we were being observed, so we kept mostly quiet beyond exchanges of small talk to keep each other's spirits up.

Doing nothing was oddly torturous. Kang's breathing suddenly sounded like a snoring giant, while the harsh metallic bench felt like I was laying on a bed of jagged rocks as time wore on.

"We're never getting out of here," I said, staring blankly up at the ceiling.

"Have a little faith," Kang replied. "My parents will check their voicemail... eventually."

"Eventually. Great."

"And with our luck, something crazy will happen before then anyway. All the police will turn into apes, or the building will melt into water, or you'll remember you're a God or something."

"A God?" I thought for a moment. "More like a Titan."

"Ha," Kang laughed, seemingly happy that he'd cracked me. "I knew it. Any second now, you're going to go all Magneto from X-Men, and bust us out of here."

"But he had Mystique helping him from the outside."

"Yeah well, he wasn't a Titan. What we need is–" The lights in the cell went out before Kang could finish his idea. "What the– Did you just use your Titan powers to turn out the lights?"

"If only," I said, leaping up and pushing my forehead against the bars to see what was going on. "It looks like the lights are out down the hall too."

The initial grunts and groans of the police officers bemoaning a power cut were drowned out by yelling and cursing as commotion broke out somewhere in the station. It sounded, at first, as if a hound had gotten loose and begun rampaging around the building. There was ferocious barking, followed by the sound of chairs, and tables and other equipment being clattered left and right.

But the more I heard, the more certain I became that the dogs weren't the ones causing the commotion. Their barks quickly turned to whimpers and the scurrying of their feet was muffled by a howl so grizzled it took me straight back to the museum in Nicosia.

"Something bad is happening," I said, stepping back and pulling Kang away from the bars with me.

The lights began to flicker down the corridor, until the single bulb swinging back and forth outside our cell switched on, casting a dull yellow glare over the figure who had appeared suddenly outside.

The panic of their swift appearance sent my heart racing, but it quickly subsided as the light fell still over their face, allowing me to glimpse their face for the first time.

And both Kang I knew those dark eyes, furrowed brows and golden skin anywhere.

"No way," said Kang. "Xiao? Is it really you?"

"Shut up," said Xiao, as her fingers jingled and eventually presented a key. She fiddled with the lock until the door slid open, then tossed them aside and stepped into the cell.

"How are you–" I tried to find the words. "When did you– We thought–"

"I said shut up," Xiao replied. "Just hug me you idiots."

Despite the uncharacteristic show of affection, which was forgivable considering she had been a stone statue only a few hours ago, this really was Xiao. After refusing to answer any questions and urging us to shut up a third time, she led the way out of the station via a backdoor, far away from the turbulence that continued to erupt within.

A minute later, we were outside and racing down the street. We must have run for nearly ten minutes straight until Xiao finally slowed and turned into an alley. A few twists and turns later, the three of us collapsed against a dumpster and slid down to the ground.

"Not that I'm complaining," said Kang, between breaths. "But why are we stopping?"

"Waiting," said Xiao, who had her head rolled back against the bins as she looked to the skies and panted. "For your friend."

"Our friend?" I asked, just as a blue feathered bird fluttered down into the alley and landed between us.

"You owe me," said Nox, as he brushed his beak with his wing. "I just bit a dog for you two. You know what dog tastes like?"

"Wait," I said. "That was you in the police station? Causing all that commotion?"

"Well it wasn't your old lady, that's for sure. Clearly, you should've called me instead of her."

"But we heard growling."

"Because feathers weren't gonna scare 'em', were they genius?"

With one wave of his wing, Nox ballooned in size until he was as big as a tiger. His feathers had turned to fur, and his beak became sharp fangs. He let out a blaring roar, before he shrunk back into a bird just as quickly.

"You're a shapeshifter," said Kang, his arms still raised in defence.

"Yeah," Nox replied, before leaning forward and coughing a blue ball of fur onto the ground. "Your keen observations are blowing my mind guys."

"And you fixed Xiao," I added.

"I told you she wasn't dead."

"No you didn't," said Kang.

"Well. I was about to, but those blues interrupted me."

"More like you ran away when we needed you."

"Did I not just bring your mate to find you?" Nox shouted.

"Forget it. How did he fix you?" I asked Xiao directly.

"He hasn't exactly explained that part," Xiao replied, brushing away the messy strands of hair that were stuck to her forehead. Probably to make sure Nox could see the scowl she was fixing him with.

"The last thing I remember is that bright flash and thinking I was done for," she continued. "Then suddenly I was awake again. There were police everywhere, but before they saw me I heard that little guy calling out to me. I thought I was going crazy. But then he told me all about you two, and Camilla, and the hydra. And his plan to rescue you. So, *bird*, I'd also like to know exactly what you did."

Nox sighed. "I've been trying to tell the lot of you. I didn't do anything. The spell wore off."

"I don't get it," I said. "Does the binding not last forever?"

"Oh, it's permanent," Nox replied. "If you're mortal."

"I don't understand."

"I told you it was hard to explain. And I told you all we had to do was wait. Which is what I did. Your mate here fixed herself."

"You're saying the spell wore off... because she isn't mortal?"

For the first time in the handful of years since Xiao had first sat in front of me in our ecofacts class, I didn't recognize the look on her face. That's why it had to be a look of terror.

"Not possible," Kang declared. "Of course she's mortal. She's Xiao. We know her."

"Like you knew your boss was a Titan?" said Nox, promptly shutting Kang up.

What Nox was saying was *impossible*. But there was something about the way he said it. Something about the way that Xiao herself, usually the first to refute any claim, had still yet to protest it. Something that made it seem... *probable*.

"Nox," I finally said. "If you think you know something, spit it out."

"Okay," he replied. "If you're sure you wanna' hear it."

Kang and I nodded in response, but Xiao seemed to have retreated further into her shell, like I'd never seen before.

"All this time, you figured it was me tracking you, right? But like I said, I'm here for Avy. So ask yourself this. Before you ever noticed me. Before you ever met that friendly librarian. If I wasn't the one leading her to you, then who was?"

The alley fell so silent, you could almost hear our collective hearts beating.

"Come on guys," Xiao eventually said, her voice trembling slightly. "You're not buying any of this, are you? He's saying what? That I'm... some kind of... monster? That Camilla sent me after you. That's bullshit. You know me."

"She's right," Kang added. "We know her. Her name is Song Xiao. Her father was Song Gang. She was born in Nanjing and her birthday is May 29th. We know her."

"You know what she's told you," Nox said. "Why don't you ask her something you don't know?"

"Like what?" Xiao demanded.

"Like the names of your childhood friends?"

"I..."

"Or your mum's name?"

"She passed away."

"When? How about your grandparents? What were they called?"

"They–"

"What year did you move to London? How did you celebrate your birthdays before you got here? When did you first become interested in archaeology?"

"Stop it!" Xiao shouted, covering her ears. As if the questions were deafening her. Torturing her. Soon her temper waived, and the courage in her voice wilted. "Just stop it. I'm not a monster. I'm not. Zeke. Kang. You can't believe any of this?"

"It sounds–" I caught myself before saying it. *Impossible? What is impossible anymore?* "Hard to believe. But Xiao..."

I hated myself before I'd even asked, and as I paused I saw Xiao's scowl return.

"Tell me you're not about to ask me something?!" she yelled.

"I don't want to," I replied. "But... do you actually remember any of the things he's saying? Xiao... what's the oldest thing you remember? And I don't mean a thing that you know. No facts. No events. I'm talking about you. Your childhood. What's your very first memory?"

Xiao shut her eyes tightly, as if she were trying to squeeze them hard enough to burst through the bubble of confusion now shrouding her mind.

As if the question alone was more difficult than any exam or interrogation I had ever seen her confront. As if, only now, she was taking a moment to consider herself before others.

Then, finally, she opened her eyes. And with a solitary tear dragging down her cheek, the bubble burst.

"It's you." She said, beginning to sob. "My first memory... is the two of you."

ACT XV

THE RIDDLIC THESPIAN

"Some say an army of horsemen, or infantry, a fleet of ships is the fairest thing on the face of the black earth. But I say, it's what one loves."

All my life, I'd had many motivators.

When I was a child, I wanted to emulate my dad. To follow in his footsteps and create something from nothing. When he passed, I wanted to take his place. To give mum all the things he ran out of time to give her. After that, it was an endless string of goals I had to meet. Needed to meet.

To be first in my class. To pass the next exam. To make the next enrollment. To beat Kang. To exceed Camilla. To keep up with Xiao. To fulfil my promise to Sherelle.

There was always the next task. The next discovery. The next success. And I thought, no. I knew. That the one motivation that brought them all to balance was my insatiable desire to win.

But I was wrong.

And only after being wrong so many times, after tasting failure so many times, as I sat contemplating that one line of Sappho's poetry, could I finally see what it was all for.

Love.

I loved what I did. But more importantly, I loved the people who did it with me. I loved my dad for everything he had done for us and for himself. And I wanted to be just like him. I loved my mum and wanted to grow into a man she could be proud of. I loved my sister, not because she had sacrificed so much for me, but because she had believed so deeply in me to begin with.

I loved Kang and his unrequited friendship that had changed my life. I loved Camilla, in so many different ways. Even when I hated her, I loved her. And I loved Xiao, even though she had only come into our lives relatively recently.

No matter who she might have been and why she was here, she completed us. And even in that harsh standoffish style of hers, I knew she loved us back. So I wasn't going to let any revelation come between us after we had come so far. The past didn't matter. It was just a road we travelled to become the people we are.

And more than ever I needed the help of the people I love. Because there was one more person in that category that needed saving.

"Xiao," I said, offering my hand.

We had left her to herself for almost ten minutes now, as she retreated further down the alley and slumped till her head touched her knees. But knowing that Prometheus was already executing whatever his master plan might be. Knowing that the police were out there looking for us. Knowing that it was now or never to make our move. We couldn't afford to wait much longer.

"We have to go," I added.

Xiao wiped her leather sleeve across her eyes, then lifted her head to bear her reddened face.

"You really want to go anywhere with me?" she asked. "I'm just some monster, Zeke. Designed to track you. To stab you in the back at the first chance I get."

"Do you really believe that?" I smiled. "Besides, you usually stab me in the front. I'm used to it. And if you think I'm going to abandon you based on finding out some weird shit about you, then you clearly haven't been paying much attention to how stupid I've been this week."

The tiniest and most reluctant of smiles cracked the very corner of Xiao's lips.

"I guess you're right," she replied, finally taking my hand and dragging herself up.

"Damned right I am. And if you're supposed to be a spy, you should probably stop saving my life one day. I owe you like ten times over. That being said, I could use one more save."

"What exactly are you planning this time?"

"A rescue," I said. "We find Avy. Take down Prometheus. And get you the answers you need?"

"Answers?" Xiao looked perplexed. "From who?"

"Camilla," I said. "She isn't dead. And I think… you're the one who can lead us right to her."

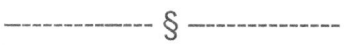

"I have so many questions," said Xiao, as the wind whipped through her hair. "But only two that come to mind right now. Why did Kang bring this disgusting blindfold from the sex hotel? And why do *I* have to wear it?"

There hadn't quite been enough time to bring Xiao completely up to speed before we'd taken off. Aboard Nox's back. The shapeshifting familiar had transformed himself into an enormous eagle, that Kang had likened to his favourite legendary Pokemon, Articuno. A comparison Nox hurried to take offence to.

The three of us had clambered up onto his back before he took to the skies and began soaring back towards the south of England. Despite being hammered by the elements and swallowing a three-course-meal worth of bugs, it was an incredible feeling to be blasting through the air.

"Camilla can't know we're coming," said Nox.

"How would she know that if I don't tell her?" Xiao replied, as she grudgingly let Kang place the blindfold over her eyes.

"You don't exactly tell her," Nox said, as he banked to avoid a large dell of trees. "You know how these clowns keep making fun of you because you're always so tired. Well, when you fall asleep, Camilla takes over."

"Bullshit," Xiao scoffed.

"Trust me," Nox said. "It sounds crazy, but I've seen it. At night. That emerald glow... you have it too. Xiao, you may not know it, but you've been Camilla's greatest weapon the entire time."

"That would actually explain a few things," said Kang, as he pulled the knot tight behind Xiao's head. "Zeke's laptop battery draining while he's asleep? Camilla's been going through our files. Our research. Finding out what we know, where we've been, and where we will be. Things we didn't even let Pierceson know about, like Ealing's stones. And whenever you storm off, which is a lot of the time by the way. When you left us at the hotel, that vampire lady showed up not long after."

"She was a lamiai," I corrected.

Xiao, for once, didn't offer a sharp riposte.

"So she can drive me like a puppet," she replied. "Great."

"How did we not notice this?" I wondered, shaking my head.

"Oh, please," said Nox. "You didn't even know Kang was talking to Camilla. There was no chance you were ever going to catch Xiao."

"Can we not make this about me?" Kang replied. "And now that we're talking about it, I did notice some discrepancies."

"Discrepancies?" said Xiao.

"Yeah. Like the fact that her other daughter, the one with snake-braid things, wouldn't hurt you in the alley?"

"She was a gorgon," I added.

"Whatever!" Kang shouted. "And then there was how nice she always was with you, even though you pretty much insult her every chance you get. She begged Avy not to hurt you when she was trying to take the stone from us. Then she completely lost it when she thought you were gone forever? She summoned a bloody Hydra to eat us. Why would she nearly kill herself to avenge someone who didn't mean the world to her? And let's not forget how your clearly busted arm miraculously healed itself."

"You had all those concerns and you never said a word!?" I shouted.

Kang shrugged. "I figured you noticed too. It all worked out in the end, didn't it?"

"I got turned into a statue, Kang," Xiao muttered.

"Then you came back to rescue us. Hey, she actually turned out to be our Mystique after all, Zeke."

"Technically, shouldn't I be Mystique?" said Nox. "I am the shapeshifter after all."

"How have you seen X-Men 2?" Kang asked quizzically.

"You think I just sit around perched on branches all day. I've got a life mate. Do you know how many times I've found Athena, only to lose her again? This girl has been wandering the earth for centuries with no memory. This isn't the first time I've caught up with her either. But the last two times, I've rushed in and frightened her. If she gets overwhelmed, then it all goes tits up and she ends up back at square one. Memory reset and all. Maybe some kinda' PTSD or summin'. This time I've been playin' the long game. Spent the past hundred years in this country following P-boy and his subjects around."

"You've been in England for a hundred years?"

"Thereabouts. Mostly London. That's where all the action is. Nothing like Hackney Empire back in the day."

"Guess that explains why you sound like you were born in North-East rather than Athens."

"What can I say? I'm a mimic. And the place grows on you."

"Okay, okay," said Xiao. "That explains the blindfold. I guess. But how am I supposed to find her?"

"You have to do what she does," Nox replied. "Only in reverse."

"See through her eyes? How?"

"Well, she's not my mum is she? I don't have all the answers. But it was a two-way radio for the others. You need to figure it out."

"Alright," said Xiao, lifting her head as her nose wrinkled in concentration. "Let's see if this is bullshit or not."

I glanced back and forth at Kang in anticipation, not knowing what to expect. Would she simply know where Camilla was, or would it be more like activating a homing beacon that would lead us to her? There was so much about all this that was the very antithesis of the way we had been taught. To make reasonings and logical deductions. Every step we took forced me to combat my rational stream of thoughts and supplant them with something altogether more... hopeful. More unexplored. And I had to admit, it was a little exciting.

But every time I did, I felt even more foolish every time it didn't work. A minute passed. Then another and another, until it became all too obvious that nothing was happening.

"Urgh," Xiao exclaimed, more frustrated than anyone as she tore her blindfold away. "Guys. This isn't working. I don't know what I'm supposed to be doing."

"It's okay," Kang said. "Let's just take a second and think. Thinking is what we do best, remember? I'm sure we'll come up with something. Nox, where are we headed anyway?"

"I told you," Nox replied. "London is where all the action is. Whatever old P-boy has planned, that's where it will happen. He has a lair there. I just don't know where to get in. If you can just pick out a landmark, or road or something."

Xiao looked deflated, as she rubbed her weary eyes. There had to be a way to help her connect with Camilla, I just couldn't think of anything I could do to help her get there.

"A lair?" said Kang. "You know, Nox, you haven't actually told us what Prometheus has planned for Avy. And how we're going to stop this supposed war he is going to reignite."

"Yeah." Nox replied. "Well, I've been trying to avoid that part."

"Why?"

"To keep you from turning tail of course."

"Just spit it out. We can handle it."

"Alright. You asked for it. He plans to unleash his old kin. The Titans. He's going to open up those prisons that Zeus sealed them in, and wage war on the Demi-Gods. And trust me, if Titans get loose on Earth again, the Demi-Gods aren't going to be the only losers around here."

Kang gulped. "Maybe you *should* have kept that to yourself."

"You think? Trust me, Titans are bad news. Prometheus has lost the majority of his power over centuries of constant battles and defeats, but he's still Godlike. A full-strength Titan is like a whirlwind of chaos and destruction. It will be like opening Pandora's box all over again."

"And you think we can stop him?"

"Don't be stupid mate. You can't, but Avy can. If we restore her powers properly this time. She can do it."

"Properly?" said Kang. "Is the stone not enough?"

"You forget what that stone is," said Nox. "Zeus's greatest weapon, a God struck by it is stripped of their power."

"Not a stone," I remembered. "A thunderbolt."

"Yeah. And you don't hold thunderbolts. You *throw* them."

"I held it before and nothing happened. It didn't react to me at all."

"Because you still thought it was a stone," Nox said condescendingly.

"What?"

"You ignored me too while you thought I was a bird. But once you start to believe in summin', everything changes. Right?"

It may have sounded corny, but he did have a point. We only started making progress when I learned to embrace the unthinkable. To stop thinking like... Pierceson.

"Okay, okay" I said. "I get the bolt and throw it at the girl. But why does he need Avy at all anyway?"

"No Titan, God or Demi-God can remove that seal. Only Zeus could do that. He was far more powerful than any of his siblings or offspring. But Prometheus thinks that with enough Godly power, say... ten Gods, he can at least break it. And since he can't touch the bolts himself, he needs someone who can to activate them."

"Why would Avy help him anymore? He took her against her will. And even as Athena, she wouldn't want to unleash the Titans."

"He doesn't need her to. When Avy touches the bolt, it sparks into life. One big explosion of power too big for her to control."

"Like at the museum," said Xiao.

"So he forces her to touch all ten bolts at once," Kang added.

"Boom," Nox replied.

"And what happens to Avy when that much power hits her?" I asked, knowing the answer would frighten me.

"Well she won't be opening any more libraries, that's for sure."

"Dammit," I said. "We have to find him. We can't let him use her as his weapon– Wait, that's it."

"What's it?" asked Kang.

I reached into Xiao's jacket and rummaged around for the metal object inside. A knife. Her knife. I'd returned it to her just before things had gone wrong with Vinter and Camilla, back at the estate. Fortunately, she still had it on her.

I'd taken a good look at it, before hiding it away. But only now, faced with all the new information about Xiao, was I thinking again about what I'd seen. The small butterfly blade was decorated on the handle. A collection of golden flowers. But for the colour, they were the same red lotuses that each of Camilla's kin bore on the weapons they tried to kill us with.

"Take this," I said.

Xiao's eyes widened, as she pushed my hand and the blade away.

"Why?" she said. "I don't remember anything about that, either. So it's probably part of this whole charade."

"That's just it, Xiao. You've had this as long as I've known you. It's the only thing I know that you've always owned. So someone must have given it to you. Kerrel and Kelis both had a weapon like this. Maybe now, it will help you remember."

Xiao's eyes softened, as she reached out her palm. And when I dropped the knife into her hand, it was like an explosion of energy. I would have slipped from Nox's back, had Kang not gripped me tightly around the arm and dragged me closer to him.

"The blindfold!" yelled Nox.

Kang quickly wrestled the mask back over Xiao's face, as her eyes gaped wide and beamed with scintillating emerald light. As he yanked the knot tight, Xiao's head started to swivel left and right, as if she were following the flight of a flock of invisible birds passing us by.

"Xiao," I said, taking her by her left hand while the knife in her right still bubbled like a cauldron of energy. "What do you see?"

"You," she said. "And Kang. And now… I'm not sure. You're younger. You're children. Playing in an arcade."

"Are there guns?" asked Kang.

"What?"

"Are the controllers guns? One blue, one red?"

"Yes," she nodded.

"It's Time Crisis," Kang said with certainty. "Are Zeke and I playing?"

"Yeah."

"Are the scores above two million, one-hundred thousand and eight?"

"How do you know this?" Xiao asked.

"We were twelve years old. At Namco World. Zeke and I had just surpassed the arcade's all-time high-scores. Those are memories Xiao. Camilla's memories. I think you're seeing what she's lived through."

"That means it's working," I said. "Kinda. You've made a connection at least."

"Yeah, well while I appreciate this stroll down memory lane," said Nox. "Get her to focus on the here and now."

"Right," I said. "Xiao, we need you to skip forward. To the present day. To find out where she is now. Focus on the things we know she's seen in the past week. The stone. Avy. Everything."

"Okay," Xiao said nervously. "I'll try."

Whether subconsciously, or whether it was just because she was afraid or lonely, Xiao reached out with both hands. And, instinctively, Kang and I both grabbed one each. I expected her to squeeze, as if she were in pain, but her petite fingers rested gently in mine as she bit her lip. Her head went from side to side, slower this time, almost as if she were walking down an aisle in the library searching for the right book.

"The museum," she said, short of breath. "I'm at the museum. I'm talking to you. No. You're upset. Angry. Camilla is talking to you. Now, I'm in our hotel. But... I'm going through your laptop. Searching. Your history. Your research. God, Nox is right. Except, this isn't me. It's her. She's using me to spy on you."

"Forget about it," said Kang, dismissively. He was right. The ramifications for Xiao were so great, and could derail her if she spent too long contemplating what it all meant.

"Right. Now... she's in the museum," Xiao continued. "And... she's hurting Ealing. And Vinter. She–"

"Don't linger," I urged, knowing only pain and disgust could come from watching many of Camilla's deeds. Her... *mother's* deeds. "Keep moving, Xiao."

"Yeah. Sorry. I... she's with us. You and me. Making our deal. Then... she finds her way to the hotel. Or someone does. I think it's that vampire lady."

"She was actually a lami–," I started. "Nevermind. Go on."

"Now... I think she's me again. When I stormed out of the room. Guys, she knew exactly where we were. All along."

Xiao's distress was tangible and rising, as she gripped me tighter by the hand.

"The plane," I said. "She took us on the plane."

"Right," said Xiao, taking a deep breath. "We're all there. On the plane."

"Then LaGuerre's," said Kang. "She fought him."

"Yes. We escape him. Then we come to London. To Pierceson. He takes Avy. And the stones. Then... Vinter is there. We fight and I get... I get turned to stone. Camilla... she's... touching me. Holding my face. Now there's blood. And mist. And flames. She's on fire. But it goes away. And now... now she's... I dunno. There's nobody else here. It's all white like... it's a tube station. She's underground. She... argh!"

"Xiao," I shouted, squeezing her by the shoulder to get her attention, as I prayed she was okay. "What happened?"

"I don't know. I lost it. I'm sorry. But it felt like... like I wasn't alone. Like someone else was watching me. I had to get out."

"It's her," said Nox. "She knew you were there. In her head. In her eyes. She's probably trying to connect with you."

"What if she makes a connection?" Xiao asked, warily.

"That's what the blindfold is for," Nox replied.

"So I have to keep this thing on forever?"

"Nah. Just until we find em'. Don't spose' you happen to see which tube station she was in? Otherwise we're gonna need travel cards."

Xiao looked disappointed in herself. "I don't remember."

"It's okay," I said. "There has to be a way to know."

"Maybe you know, but you don't know," said Kang.

"What's that supposed to mean?" Xiao asked.

"That's how it is for me. I remember things I don't know I've remembered. But I have a process. Here, take my hands."

I watched as Kang and Xiao joined hands, an almost too harmonious sight of two friends who enjoyed antagonising each other. Kang took a moment to get them breathing in unison before he finally spoke.

"My mind to your mind."

"Kang!" I shouted irritatedly. "A Vulcan mind meld? This isn't the time for jokes dude."

"You are such an idiot," Xiao exclaimed, pulling away. "If you're not going to take this seriously-"

"Wait," Kang shouted. "Just wait. Sorry, that's just how I always begin. I'm not messing around. I promise."

Xiao sighed and took him by the hands once more.

"I swear Kang, if you–"

"I get it," he said. "Just listen. You're back in the white room, remember."

"Yes. But I–"

"Don't try to picture it. Just look at your feet. What are you wearing?"

"On my feet? Kang, can we just–"

"What are you wearing?" Kang demanded angrily.

"Boots," Xiao whispered, perhaps slightly taken aback by Kang's sudden gravity.

"What kind of boots?"

"I dunno'. Black. Size three. Little gold strip on the back."

"Where'd you buy them?"

"Amazon. And don't you dare judge me."

"Already have. But what are they standing on?"

"The floor obviously."

"And what kind of floor is it?"

"It's a floor, Kang. Tiles. White tiles. Slightly yellowing now, I guess. In fact, this whole platform isn't all that white after all. It's old. And the lighting isn't great. But the ad boards are new. Digital. They're much brighter. If it wasn't for them, I'd barely be able to make out the sign... oh shit! It's Monument!" I could hardly remember Xiao ever screaming so excitedly.

"It's Monument station! Kang," she said, leaning in to hug him. "It worked. Is that... is that how your memory works? You visualise it all, piece by piece? Every little detail?"

Kang shrugged. "Yeah. First time I've ever tried it on someone else though."

"That was badass," I said, leaning in to make it a double hug.

"Alright, alright. If you're done acting like a bunch of tweens," Nox shouted, as he veered suddenly to the right. "Hold on tight. We've finally got a destination."

"I'm not just going to abandon them!" Xiao protested.

Nox shook his head. "You're not abandoning them. In fact, you're the only shot they've got. If they're going to get the drop on P-boy, they need Camilla out of the way. The last thing we need is her dropping another Hydra on em'. If we ditch that blindfold, you and I can lead her away."

"No," said Xiao. "I can't. We're a team. I'm not leaving you guys to face him alone."

"Xiao," I said, taking her by the hand. "It's okay. You've been protecting us this whole time. And... we need you to do it again. Now get out there and be a badass."

"Yeah. We'll be fine," Kang added. "I've got my WWXD bracelet on to remind me."

Xiao finally managed a smirk, followed by a trademark roll of her eyes.

"Oh please," she sniffed, as she regained her composure. "You can't do half of what I can do."

"Now that's the Xiao I remember," said Kang, as we both gave her a high five.

"Get Avy out," she said, as Nox readied his wings for takeoff. "Don't screw it up. And, please, don't get yourselves killed."

"We won't," I said. "Promise. But... Nox. I've been thinking. Once we hit Avy with that bolt, what happens to her? If she becomes Athena full-time? Avy is a real person now, right? She has a life, and a library and she even seems to have a dad, somehow, who must be worried about her. What happens to all that?"

"Her dad is a man who took in a wandering girl with no memory," Nox replied. "An Avare, in his tongue. Because that's exactly what she's been. Her life is a jumble of false names and identities. Neither of them are real. She may have made her way for the past decade or so, but Zeke, you have to accept that it's one or the other. Avy the girl, who gets used as a weapon and probably dies anyway, along with all of us. Or Athena the goddess, who maybe saves us all. You can't have it both ways."

Nox's words were hard to hear, and truthfully I wasn't ready to either accept or deny them. Instead, I simply nodded in acknowledgement.

"You'll do the right thing," said Nox, his wings beginning to shine with a dazzling blue light. As we shielded our eyes, he flapped and blasted off the ground. "You're a smart guy. You'll figure it out."

"Right. In that case, what are the odds that she just kills us once she has her powers back?"

"Don't be such a downer, she won't do that," Nox said. "But... just in case, take these. In case you need 'em."

Nox rocketed away into the sky with Xiao, leaving a mirror-like shield, hanging from the handle of a hefty sword.

"Nope," said Kang. "I'm not touching that thing again. I've hulked out enough for one day."

"Come on," I said, grabbing the shield and slinging it across my back. "You were actually kind of heroic back there. Almost worthy of the title, Kang The Conqueror."

"Do not bait me with comic book titles."

"Why? Is it working?"

"A little," Kang replied, as he grabbed hold of the sword and hauled it with us.

After climbing through the closed doors and barriers throughout the station, we finally made our way down to the track.

Kang had helped Xiao further revisit her memories before we landed, helping us to figure out exactly which direction we should head. We followed the tracks South, in near darkness, for five minutes or so before we finally came across the opening Xiao had described.

It would have been invisible, if we hadn't known exactly where to look. A small rectangular door, only waist-high. It was as black as the walls around it, and only the heat we could feel coming from beyond the door made me sure it was the right place.

With the edge of the shield, I caved the door inwards and crawled through into the stiflingly hot passageway. Kang and I shuffled through the dirt for another minute or so as it gradually opened up into an opening large enough to stand in.

It became swelteringly hot as we made our way further inside, through what felt like a tunnel illuminated only by a small flickering light ahead. When the tunnel finally ended, we were standing in a circular chamber with just a single candle sitting on a pedestal in the centre as its tiny flame flickered left and right.

"This can't be right," I said, throwing off my jacket and wiping away the sweat dripping from my forehead. "All this heat can't be coming from this tiny flame."

Kang held one hand up to the flame.

"The flame isn't especially hot either," Kang said, as he turned his attention to the walls all around us and coughed. "And this dusty old room looks like a dead end."

"Well," I said. "This candle is the only thing here."

"So?"

"So... touch it."

"What?" Kang sounded perplexed. "Why?"

"Because... Prometheus and fire. When he stepped into those flames back at the estate, they didn't burn him. His fire isn't just fire."

"Well... yeah." Kang sounded like he agreed. "But I'm not Prometheus. If you're so sure, you touch it."

"Fine," I said. "You big baby. I'll do it. But I take back that Conqueror stuff I said about you."

Not quite as boldly as I pictured in my head, I extended my hand towards the candle. After gently lowering my fingers over the flame and watching the smoke darken them, I pushed my hand quickly down into the luminous fire.

It didn't burn.

Though I could feel the flames caressing and probing my skin, there was no pain.

"See," I said. "Prometheus fire."

For once, Kang looked impressed.

"Okay," he said. "What now?"

"Well, now we just–"

I was cut off when the candle erupted into an explosive yellow fire, knocking both Kang and I backwards and off our feet. I screamed. Briefly. Or maybe a little longer than briefly. But it still felt short, relative to how loudly Kang was still screaming at the top of his lungs.

"Kang!" I shouted, placing both arms on his shoulders. "Kang! It's okay. Calm down. We're okay. We're okay. We're not burning. Look."

As he calmed down, I turned his attention to the chamber which was now awash with light as a column of orange flame burned brightly in the centre. The entrance we had followed inside had disappeared, leaving us trapped inside the circular room. And before either of us could question what the change meant, a voice with nearly enough bass to burst my eardrums rattled around the chamber.

"Voice the pretender's name. Embrace the burning flame," it said.

"You know," Kang started, as the column of flame licked at the air. "If I hadn't flown here on a cockney bird, I might find it weird that a fire is talking to us. But now, this doesn't even register."

"Voice the pretender's name," I said. "Some kind of riddle?"

"Makes sense," Kang mused, tugging at his beard. "Prometheus isn't always here right? It's only logical that he has a way to keep his enemies from getting inside."

Before giving us time to ask any questions, the flame burst towards us once more, raging around the chamber before uniting in the centre once more. This time, however, it no longer held the form of just a burning flame.

The fire weaved and wrapped its way around itself, forming shapes and lines as it intertwined. After a few seconds, it stopped moving and held its configuration to appear in the form of a figure.

"That was pretty awesome," I said, despite the continued fear of being burnt alive every time the flame moved.

"Speak the pretender's name," I repeated. "I think it wants to know who this is."

"Well that's easy," said Kang.

It was a fair assessment. The figure that had been burned to life in front of us, and almost flickered with life as the fire within pulsated, was arched forward with his shoulders wide as he carried the weight of an enormous globe on his back.

"Atlas," he said. "One of Prometheus' own brothers. So I guess we just say the name and a door or something opens. Right?"

"Hmm." I nodded. "Embrace the eternal flame. You have to put your hand in the fire."

Kang looked at me sceptically. "You mean *you* as in *we*, or *you* as in *me*."

"Hey, I went the first time. And you're the one who said it was easy. Go for it."

Kang mumbled something as he took a deep breath and stepped closer to the fiery mosaic.

"Damn dust," he said, coughing again as he waved a hand across his face. "Wait. What do you think happens if we're wrong?"

I was swiftly inspired to take a long look at the ground, which was covered in more of the supposed dust that was causing us to cough. As I swept my foot to the right brushing a layer of dirt to the side, I realised it wasn't dust we were stepping in at all.

"Actually," I said. "I think we might be breathing in people who have got it wrong before. Or whatever is left of them."

"Ah shit", said Kang, covering his mouth and panicking.

"Still sure about that answer?" I wondered.

Kang took another long and deep breath. He was standing just a few inches from the fire now, as he raised one hand and pushed it into the flame.

"Wait," he said, uncovering his mouth to reveal an awakening smile. "It's a trap."

"Yes," I replied. "We get it wrong, we die. That's how traps work."

"No, I mean it's a trap-trap. Look," he raised his arm and pointed a finger at the head of the figure. "I didn't see it before, but he has pointy ears."

"So?"

"So... he's wearing a cloak over his head. A cloak of a lion. It's not Atlas, it's Heracles."

"Holy crap," I said, more astonished at how close we might have just come to being reduced to ashes than how obvious Kang's correction had been.

"You're right," I said. "Heracles holds the sky up when he asks Atlas to pick some golden apples."

"And he has to trick Atlas into taking it back by saying he needs to adjust his lion cloak."

"Dude. You just saved us from being burnt alive. Okay. Heracles. Go for it."

This time, without as much ceremony, Kang raised his hand to the fire once more. But just as I saw his lips part, a jolt of both fear and realisation shot through me and I knew I had to cry out.

"Stop!" I screamed. Kang jerked visibly, my outburst taking him by surprise as he prepared to offer his answer. "Don't say a word."

"You scared the crap out of me," Kang said, as he panted. Short of breath from how much I'd startled him.

"It's a trap."

"That's what I said."

"No, it's like a trap-trap... trap. Whatever. We know it's a trap but who is it a trap for? Think about it."

Only as I thought about how obvious the answer had been, despite our brief slip up, had it dawned on me that yes this was a trap. But not one set for us.

"Prometheus wants to keep his enemies out, right?" I said. "But that's not us. Usually. His enemies are the Demi-Gods, Gods, and whatever else is out there that we don't know about. This trap is meant to keep them out. And something as simple as identifying Atlas from Heracles is hardly going to stump anyone. Especially people who know all about this kind of stuff."

"Okay." Kang nodded along, as he appeared to catch up. "Then this is something that Pierceson thinks a Demi-God wouldn't know and couldn't guess." Kang opened his arms out wide and shrugged at me. "So? Any ideas?"

I traced my finger through the air as I talked Kang through my thought process.

"Camilla came through here before us, right?" I eyeballed Kang, and he nodded along. "So he told her the answers. Or she was able to figure this out. I think this is something that people who are here for Prometheus can't answer. But people who are here for Pierceson... well they know things about him that his enemies don't."

"Okay, but the riddle doesn't leave much wiggle room here," said Kang. "Speak the pretender's name. And there's only one figure in the flames."

It took a moment, as it usually did for me to bounce ideas off Kang, but listening to him recite information always helped me unlock something I'd missed before. Luckily for us, this time was no different.

"Pretender," I said. "Kang that's it. Pierceson says that. Pretender."

Kang's eyes lit up as if I'd just handed him a freshly minted new comic to enjoy. Then he rubbed his chin once more, as he always did when traversing the streets of information in his head.

"They're actors," he said.

Pierceson, the figure, was a model of consistency and professionalism. The media knew relatively little about him, outside of his public pursuit of history and excellence. But like any man, and I could taste the irony having learned that he wasn't actually any man, he had his hobbies and interests.

Like us, he read comic books. Though he strictly preferred non-superhero mediums. And he was also an extreme connoisseur of spirits. Kang and I could attest to that, having snuck into his cellar and sampled his considerable collection of drinks on more than one occasion. But the guiltiest of all his pleasures was how much he enjoyed movies.

You could name just about any movie from any era, and he would have a strong opinion one way or the other on the narrative, script, or its effect on popular culture. But, again ironically, his least favourite genre was anything fantastical. Above all, he would despise B-grade period action movies that sampled mythology for cheap thrills.

Of course, Kang, Camilla and I loved those kinds of movies. Time and time again, we would force him to endure them. And each time, he would indulge us, only to end the experience full of contempt for not just the movies, but the actors who portrayed the heroes in them.

'Lousy pretenders,' he would call them, no matter what calibre of actor graced the screen. 'Pretending to be part of a culture they can never comprehend.'

"Actors," I finally replied to Kang. "This is Heracles. Or Hercules if you're a Disney or Kevin Sorbo fan. But we need to say who played him."

"Alright," said Kang. "I think I've got it this time."

With more confidence than either previous attempt, Kang lifted his hand into the flame and said, "Dwayne Johnson."

In reply, the flames burst to life once more, enveloping us in brilliant flames, before pulling back to the centre.

"We're still alive," said Kang.

"Yep," I replied.

"God I love The Rock," he added.

"Yep," I said again.

The column of flame appeared briefly once more, before exclaiming once again, "Voice the pretender's name. Embrace the burning flame."

"I guess we're not done," I said, as the flames swirled once more, then assembled into a new figure.

This time, the figure was staring off into the distance, holding one arm aloft with a rough-looking fiery sphere clutched in his hand.

"What's that in his hand?" I wondered, stepping closer to get a look.

"An apple?" I could tell Kang wasn't sure, his voice lacked the usual confidence of beating me to a deduction. "A golden apple maybe? It could be Paris of Troy. Judging the beauty contest. Played by Orlando Bloom."

"Urgh," I scoffed. "That's even worse than The Rock's Hercules. Maybe Pierceson had a point."

As I examined the fire a little closer, I found the same level of hidden detail that Kang had spotted the last time around.

"It's not an apple," I said. "And those aren't just flames coming off it, they're strings. It's a ball of yarn. This is Theseus."

"Ahh," Kang snapped his fingers. "Kills the Minotaur then finds his way out with Ariadne's string. And..."

"Played by Superman himself, in the Immortals. Pierceson really hated that movie," I said, as I reached my hand into the flame. "Henry Cavill."

Again the fire burst and swirled around us, until once more the flame spoke.

"Voice the pretender's name. Embrace the burning flame."

Kang smirked, as a larger figure than before formed above the pedestal.

"What's so funny?" I said. "Apart from the fact that we're naming actors to save the world."

"Nothing," he replied. "I just remember Camilla really digging every time Cavill took his shirt off in that movie. Which was all the time."

I half-laughed, half-sighed as I gave him a playful nudge towards the new scene burning brightly before us. "Let's just hope this is the last one."

The most obvious thing about the next figure was the enormous wingspan that rippled in flame across the entire chamber. But the wings weren't attached to a bird. Instead the creature had a fiery mane and four legs.

"It's Pegasus," I said.

"Yep," Kang agreed.

"But it can't just be the horse's name, can it?" I said, stepping forward, only to find Kang's hand on my shoulder, heaving me back.

"Maybe the owner," he said, pushing past me. "He was tamed by Bellaraphon, but made famous by Perseus as he grew in western popular culture. And in the end of Wrath of Titans, Perseus rides atop a black Pegasus to save the day."

Kang was already raising his hands against the fire and smiling back at me.

"You're sure about this?" I asked.

"Sam Worthington," he yelled, as the fire burst apart once more.

This time, the column of flame didn't appear and the fire receded back into the tiny candle that first lit the room.

"Is there anyone Pierceson hates more than Sam Worthington?" Kang asked.

"Probably not," I replied.

Kang and I stood in silence for a few seconds longer, and I was ready to ask him if he was sure about the answer again, when the candle finally went out. Without it, there wasn't a drop of light in the entire chamber and I found my hands reaching out for Kang just to regain my sense of space.

For over a minute, I fretted in complete darkness that we were destined to be trapped blindly underground for the rest of our lives, until Kang broke the silence with a moment of reflection that, admittedly, caught me a little off guard.

"Isn't this a little weird?" he said. "To protect something valuable to him, Pierceson used something that we love."

"Uhh," I fumbled, searching for an answer that wasn't the one he was looking for. "I guess it had to be something that someone like Vinter wouldn't know."

"Yeah... but.... those movies. We watched them together. We made him sit through to get a kick out of how much we knew he'd hate them. Those were good times, Zeke. Good memories. And, clearly, he still remembers them too."

Of course it was weird. And more than just a little. It was blowing my mind. Pierceson. Prometheus. Whoever he was. He'd just tried to have us killed. He'd been manipulating us all our lives. And he was bad news for arguably everyone if he got what he wanted. So why, despite all that, was a part of me wondering whether, actually, the two of us really *were* important to him? Whether he actually cherished the history we'd had? Whether he actually loved us like we were his own children?

"Those memories aren't real Kang," I lied. "We are just pawns in Prometheus' plan. Just like Camilla. And just like Avy. None of us meant anything to him. We just served to help him get his way."

"Right," Kang said, unconvincingly. "I guess there's probably no talking him out of whatever he has planned then."

"Of course not," I said, angrily, as the candle flickered back to life. "Now focus, Kang. It's time to end this. Are you ready?"

I waited for Kang's reply, as the tiny wisps of candlelight relieved us of darkness, and revealed a newly formed exit to the chamber. But instead of my friend's voice, a rasping grunt echoed through the faint light.

"Zeke?" Kang said, stepping closer to the candle. Close enough for me to see the look of horror glazed in his eyes. "Tell me that was your stomach."

We glanced at each other, knowing both that the sound came from neither of us, and that it was an all too familiar grizzle to be good news. We both inched backwards as a pair of emerald eyes loomed through the shadows and came to glare at us.

"Camilla?" Kang said gingerly. "Is that you?"

His question was answered as a second set of eyes appeared on the right. The growl built steadily until whatever was approaching puffed a gust of air towards us that blew the candle out.

"Othrus," Kang said, with a frightened gulp.

But before he spoke, a third pair of eyes blinked on the left, making six emerald eyes staring menacingly back at us.

"Uh uh," I gulped. "Not Othrus. Cerberus."

ACT XVI

THE EMBRACE OF THUNDER

"Come, weave us a scheme so I can pay them back! Stand beside me, Athena, fire me with daring, fierce as the day we ripped Troy's glittering crown of towers down. Stand by me - furious now as then, my bright-eyed one - and I would fight three hundred men, great goddess, with you to brace me, comrade-in-arms in battle!"

Avy. Athena. Whichever she was, I wanted– no, I needed to see her again. If it really was her. The Warrior. The Goddess. The same Athena that had helped Odysseus return home, then I couldn't help but grasp at the slither of hope that she could also help return our lives to normal.

That she could help Xiao conciliate with whatever she was getting through. That she could fix this spiralling Titan apocalypse. And that maybe, just maybe, there was a happy ending where her and I, and even Kang and Camilla, could all just go back to being ourselves.

I'd read Homer's epic, The Odyssey, a hundred times since I first learned to read and as recently as last summer. And if it really was all real, there was one important thing that tale had always made clear. Nothing was beyond her power.

"Zeke, move it!" shouted Kang, as his hand pressed down between my shoulders, almost causing me to lose my balance as I sprinted ahead.

As Cerberus lunged towards us, we'd barely managed to dodge his sharpened claws, which scythed into the wall behind us, and left the beast stuck long enough for us to make our escape. We rushed headlong into the light, and I had to keep reminding myself not to look back as the panting of his breath and beating of his paws grew louder to our rear.

"Wait!" Kang yelled this time, as his feet swerved to a halt in the turf.

When I panned around, he was looking up and down at a stone frame we had just passed under.

"A door!" I quickly recognised.

"Help me close it," he replied.

In tandem, we both barreled into the stone door that was ajar, summoning every ounce of strength and straining every inch of muscle as we heaved it shut. Cerberus' bright eyes were close enough to shade everything in my vision green, and his jaws were so near I could feel his snarling and wet breaths on my forehead, as we just barely slammed the door in his face.

"Close one," I said, gasping for air.

"I'm getting used to it," Kang replied, wiping the sweat from his face with his shirt. "Which is its own kind of scary."

As my breathing began to slow, I looked ahead into the cavern we had entered. Flames climbed the surrounding walls with a life and mind of their own, and steam hissed up over the edge of the footpath from the depths below.

"Out of the frying pan, as your mum would say," Kang said.

"What now?" I wondered, as I considered the ominous path ahead against the hellhound still drumming at the door behind us.

"Now," Kang replied. "You go."

"What?"

"You heard me. This door isn't going to hold. I know you have a plan for when you get in there, so I'll try and buy you time to do it. Give me that."

Kang was already relieving me of the shield.

"Are you sure about this?" I said, trying and failing to stop my voice from breaking.

"Dude, do you know who I am?"

"What?"

"I'm Kang the freaking Conqueror. I cut the heads off Hydras and face certain death. You go, I'll handle this."

"Alright," I said, finding a smile on my lips as I extended my hand for a fist bump. "You do have a plan of your own though, right?"

"Of course," he said. "I'm going to find a good spot to hide and stab him in the back. I'm not an idiot."

"Good," I replied. "Just checking."

At any other point on this journey, I would have been too frightened to leave Kang behind. I'd be afraid for both of us. Neither of us were fighters. Neither of us were regularly brave. And above all, neither of us were heroes. And yet, we'd faced down gorgons, hellhounds and lam... vampires. We'd fought vampires together. And lived.

So as I edged my foot out onto the smoking ledge, my second footstep followed more quickly. And each step after that came more rapidly and more confidently than the one that preceded it. There was no turning back, and there was no stopping me. No stopping us. Not now. It was all or nothing.

My walk broke into a sprint as I followed the path round and up, my nostrils burning and my head melting in the furnace-like enclosure, until I reached the opening at the top. The path suddenly widened into a mass clearing, the walls impossibly high and wide, with only a narrow bridge between me and the central enclave, all of which was surrounded by a moat of bubbling liquid flame.

I shook the hellish scene from my mind as my eyes were drawn to a pedestal in the centre, beside which a figure crouched with both hands placed down on the floor. I would've investigated him further, but my line of sight was drawn again by the flicker of orange flame closer still. Just across the other side of the bridge another figure was laying down on the ground, her wrists and ankles bound by restraints made of twisting fire rather than metal.

Avy.

Before I knew it, my legs had spirited me across the bridge and only stopped moving when they pulled me down onto one knee by her side. I'd feared the worst, that Prometheus had already used her to achieve his end and I'd find only a depleted human husk where the once vibrant Avy had been. To my relief, her hypnotic golden eyes were wide open and regarding me with something I hoped was relief.

"Zeke!" she breathed tentatively.

"Quiet!" I half-whispered with a finger to my lips. "And hold still."

"You came. You came to get me. I... I'm so sorry, Zeke. I never meant to... I should have-"

"Shut up for a second," I said, turning my attention away from her and up towards the figure ahead.

Prometheus. Earlier, I thought he was merely touching the floor, but now I could see more clearly. Both his hands were submerged into the cavern floor, and he seemed to be drawing magma and stone directly out of the ground. It was a sight to behold, but it wasn't him I was interested in. Between us stood a pedestal, and sitting atop it were all ten stones, just waiting to be claimed.

"Hey," Avy said, snapping my attention back to her. "Are you going to get me out of here or not?"

"Can't," I replied.

"What!?"

"Only you can do that. Just wait here and try to remember who's on your side when the time comes."

"Zeke. Zeke... wait. I'm scared. I don't want to hurt you again."

"You won't," I replied. "Whatever happens, we're in this together."

Avy kept calling me back, but my mind was already made up. There was only one way out of this, one way to save her life, and it certainly didn't involve any sneaking around. No, our escape plan was sitting right in front of me. I just had to convince the millennia old titan beside it not to burn me to ash before I could enact it.

Of all my mum's proverbs, there was always one that stuck in my mind. 'If you were born to be hanged, you can't drown,' she would say. She didn't exactly say it in those words, there were several layers of hometown colloquialism to decipher first. But the point is, it stuck with me because I never understood it. She believed in destiny. That we were all meant for something.

So for years I wondered if it was my dad's destiny to be gunned down needlessly. But only in the years following his death, did I begin to witness and understand the effects.

His death raised awareness of privilege and racism within our community and the institutions that were supposed to police it. It woke many of the youths in my area up, showing them that they had to work together to overcome their situation. And it even kick-started charities that helped raise money for under-privileged families across London. The same charities I donated almost all of the salary Pierceson paid me into.

His destiny was never to change lives as a security guard. It was so much more. So much greater. And it sucked. Because it took him away from us. And maybe even cost us Sherelle, who in a twisted irony ended up being one of the youths his message was unable to reach. Death has many consequences, and from his came a legacy that was so much more than it first seemed.

So, finally, I was beginning to believe that I too had a destiny. I still didn't know what it was, but I was certain that it didn't involve surviving everything I had up until now just to have some ancient evil snap his fingers at me and turn me into a pile of forgotten cinders.

And even if it was, there was no need to be afraid. Because I'd make sure Avy and the others got out of here, and that our story didn't have to end.

"Prometheus!" I said, striding towards the pedestal.

"Zeke," he replied, before even turning to face me. "Welcome. And you can still call me Pierceson, you know?"

"Aren't you surprised to see me?" I said, narrowing my eyes. "I had to get past your little flame test."

"My boy," he laughed. "You're one of the few people alive who actually *could* get in here."

Flexing his shoulders wearily, he pulled his palms from the ground and stood up. It didn't take long to notice how different he looked now.

Gone was the slowed and elderly pace he usually moved at. Gone was the thin sheet of pale skin, cracked and stretched across weary bones. And gone were the tired half-shut eyes.

In their place stood a reinvigorated creature pulsating with energy, his skin aglow like a molten hot blade ready to be tempered, and his eyes burning like a pair of flaming pyres in the night.

"Did Camilla let you pass?" he asked, his voice somehow deeper and more emphatic than ever. "I shouldn't be surprised. I've observed her over many lives, but never have I seen her forge so strong a bond, and in so short a time, as she did with the three of you."

"And yet, you still forced her to turn against us," I barked, edging my feet closer towards the pedestal. "I know you have something on her. Some promise to force her to do your bidding. How can you do that to her?"

"Does it matter? Is that why you're doing this, son? For her? And for that... librarian? For love? There is so much more out there, Zeke. So much more I can show you, now that you know the truth."

"So why didn't you just tell me?" I wondered, honestly, despite taking another step.

"I've wanted to tell you. A thousand times. But I could never know how you would react. It's the smart ones, you see, who find it more difficult to digest. But I underestimated you. I should have expected your potential. Should've known you'd grow beyond your station, just like your father."

The mention of him lit the fuse in my blood.

"Don't talk about my father!" I yelled. "And I'm not your son."

"No," Prometheus said. "But haven't we shared just as much? Haven't I helped you become the person you are today? Haven't I given you everything!?"

"Everything." I nodded, taking one long step that placed my feet before the pedestal. "Everything except the truth. Because you knew, deep down, that I would have to stop you."

"Please." Prometheus laughed, with a smile I'd describe for the very first time as sinister. "You're capable of a great many things, son. But how are you planning to stop me?"

"With this," I said, mettle and certainty coursing through my veins as I reached out and plucked one of the stones from the pile.

He shook his head. "It won't work for you, Zeke. You cannot wield the power of the stone any more than I can."

"I know," I replied, raising the stone high above my head. "But it's not a stone. It's a thunderbolt."

My instinct told me to squeeze the stone tight. To force out its power and bend it to my will. But I remembered. I remembered what Avy had said that night in the alley. That this power was hers, and she had felt like it wanted to return to her. And for the first time, that's exactly what I wanted too.

I loosened my grip, let my fingers glide over the warm and smooth surface of the stone, and focused on one thing. Avy. Her knowledge. Her strength. Her smile. And when I glanced back at her, and caught a flash of those golden eyes, I felt the spark.

A sensation in my palm both like searing fire and soothing water. The look of true astonishment in Prometheus' eyes told much of the story, but I had to look up and see the rest for myself. Crackling between my fingers, as if it were alive, like a restless lover yearning for their soulmate, was the electric blue glow of thunder.

As much as I wanted to savour the moment, of both the power and bewilderment on the old man's face, I knew the time was now or never.

"And you don't hold thunderbolts," I said, casting one final glance at Prometheus before turning towards Avy. "You throw them."

With my arm already pulled back, I let rip and launched the bolt like a javelin, barely bothering to aim. It didn't matter. The thunder cut through the air in an instant, striking the whole area around Avy with blinding azure light. From the ground, grew a pillar of thunder that blasted through the roof of the cavern and let afternoon light pour in from the sky, as the thunder dissipated in another bright flash.

Avy was up off the ground, only... she wasn't Avy anymore. Involuntarily, I squeezed my hand, only to find the stone already gone.

"No!" The cry came from Prometheus, who exploded into action in a burst of fiery rage. He brushed quickly passed me and towards Avy, only to tumble over as she vanished from sight.

"Zeke." Her voice was suddenly behind me now, as I turned to find her standing over my shoulder.

"Avy?" I still had to wonder.

This time her transformation was more complete. Not just her even brighter eyes. And not just her glowing locks. Even her clothes had changed. She was clad head to toe in armour now. Bright golden armour, befitting of a Goddess. And I could swear there was almost a hum in the air as she stood just a breath away from me.

"Athena," she replied, putting a dent in my faith. "Thank you. For restoring me."

"No problem," I said. "Does that mean you're... not going to kill me?"

"Zeke," she said, with a fake, mocking gasp. "Of course not. You still owe me some chocolate."

As she smiled, I laughed, finally releasing all the fear and tension I'd been suppressing.

"You're still in there," I said.

"I am."

"You don't know what you've done!" Prometheus interrupted. "You should have listened to me, Zeke. You should have–"

"Excuse me," Avy said, interrupting him to give me a comforting nod. "Let me just shut him up for a second."

The aura Avy was giving off was completely different to her earlier transformations. The air was practically singing, and the ground beneath us quaking, as she summoned her strength, then took off like a jet plane. She barreled into Prometheus and arrowed high into the air with him in her clutches, battering him against the cavern wall to begin their colossal battle.

I wanted nothing more than to watch her work, but my attention spun back around as I heard metal come crashing down behind me, followed by Kang's bruised and battered body. Trailing him was Cerberus, still very much alive and chomping at the bit.

And I was just about out of ideas on how to protect us, when a pair of blue wings descended through the hole in the roof and swooped down between us and the hellhound. Before Nox's talons could even reach the ground, Xiao leapt down from atop his back, ripped off her blindfold and rushed to confront the beast.

"Stop!" she yelled, raising her hand in imposition.

And on command, as if obeying the lash of its very master, Cerberus stopped dead in its tracks and bowed its head. Xiao took another step closer, as if tempting it to resume its attack, when Cerberus opened its mouth and licked her.

Not her fingers. Not her arm. Not even her leg. It ran one of its long tongues down the side of her face, then nestled its nose against her shoulder.

"Wow," said Kang, unsteadily rising back to his feet. "That's one of the cutest, and most disgusting, things I have ever seen."

"She saw him coming," said Nox.

"Saw someone else coming too," said Xiao, the slightest hint of emerald in her eyes as she lifted her haid to the sky.

A second bird soared through the opening, this one with odd metallic skin, a bronze beak, and a passenger aboard its back who's presence left me torn. As it always had.

"Xiao," Camilla gasped, as she slid gracefully down from the bird's back. "It's... really you. You're alive. I... I felt it, but I never truly believed--"

"That's close enough," Xiao hissed, halting Camilla as she inched towards us.

"Xiao. Please," Camilla pleaded, her eyes wide and passionate. "Let me explain."

"You've had years to explain!" Xiao yelled. "You're a liar. And a murderer. And you're–"

"Your mother, Xiao. I'm your mother."

"No," Xiao hissed. "You're... a monster. And I'm nothing like you."

"That word... don't let mythology fill your head with fear. They are the monsters. The Gods. The Titans. They manipulate my kind. And humankind. I've only ever done what I had to. To survive. And to protect the people I love."

"Like us?" said Kang. "A monster isn't what you are, it's who you are. Someone who tries to kill their own friends. Someone who gives up others for their own gain."

"Kang." Camilla's words lost their defensive edge and grew sombre. "Nathan. I'm... I'm sorry. I never meant to hurt you. And I never meant for any of you to get caught up in this. It's just... it's all been impossible. Leaving you. Serving him."

"Then why did you?" I demanded. "If you cared so much, how could you toss us aside so easily?"

"I do love you, Zeke. And you, Nathan. None of it was a lie. But I've lived a long time. And you're not the first ones I've loved. He promised... he promised to bring someone back for me. Someone who gave up everything for me. So I had to do it. I made a promise. And I always keep my promises."

"Camilla, look around," I said, pointing at the river of lava and the sound of Avy and Prometheus thundering around the cavern. "Is it really worth all this? You're going to let him unleash hell on earth just to bring someone back?"

"I have to, Zeke. If I don't see this through, then everything I've already lost has all been for nothing. Everything I've done. Everyone I've hurt. Losing all of you. I can't let it all be for nothing."

"You haven't lost us yet," I said, trying to meet her eyes. But she refused to look at me.

"They must have meant a lot to you," Kang said wistfully. "This person."

"More than you know," she replied. "But... not more than your lives. The mansion was an accident. I never meant for things to get so out of hand. So please, leave now. While you still can. While I can still protect you. Let's be on the same side."

"We don't need your protection," Xiao said. "And we're not on your side. Come on guys, we're done with her."

Before we could completely turn our backs on her, a ball of fire came tumbling out of the air, leaving a crater in the ground. Avy fanned the flames from her body as she rose to her feet, only to be taken by surprise as the floor beneath her burst open and the burning rock clamped around her.

Only, they weren't rocks. They were more like... fingers, attached to a titanic hand that had locked its grip around Avy and was squeezing the life out of her.

"What the hell is that?" I yelled.

"What the bloody hell does it look like?" Nox replied. "You don't know a Titan when you see one? This is what he's been here raising all this time. Using up half his strength to pull it from the depths of the earth where it was sealed."

"But it's... huge."

"Of course it's huge, mate. It's in the name. Now quit comparing sizes and help me get it off her."

Nox was already moving towards Avy, his feathers retreating into a coat of fur while his wings ballooned into powerful biceps. His now hefty fists pounded the ground as he bounded towards her, dragging his knuckles. He landed atop the Titanic hand and started trying to pry the fingers away from Avy.

As I watched him, in the form of a musclebound cobalt-blue gorilla, I wasn't sure what more I could do to help.

"Oi," Nox yelled, catching me off guard.

For some reason, watching him transform into a primate had again made me forget he could speak, so it took me a few seconds to regain my wits.

"What?" I asked.

"Quit standing around and help me get her free. Before he can force her to use the other stones."

"Enough!" The cry came from Prometheus, as he slammed down to the ground, both arms smoking with intense heat from his fingertips to his shoulders. "Step aside, all of you. Leave me to my business. It's no longer the work of mortals."

"We can't," said Kang. "We let you take Camilla away from us. You're not taking Avy too."

I shot Kang a smile, half-terrified and half-resolute, then in tandem we both raced towards Avy. Wrapping both my arms around one of the hulking fingers, I yanked back and tried to wrestle her free. With Nox and Kang's help, the index finger began to give and Avy's left leg slipped from its grasp.

"Fine!" Prometheus was yelling now, his seething fury burning up beyond his shoulders now to meet across his chest. "I tried to treat you like family, but now it's time to bring my real brothers and sisters back. I've worked for too long and come too close to let you stop me now. So if this is the fate you choose, then so be it."

There wasn't time for any of us to budge as Prometheus' hands came up and a towering avalanche of fire came tumbling towards us. The flames were so hot, I could feel the saliva in my mouth evaporating as my barren throat seized up and my eyes slammed shut. And all I could wonder was how badly, and for how long, it was going to burn.

But the pain never came.

"No!" I heard Kang's cry before I could force my eyes open again.

When I finally looked ahead, a smoking body stood between us and Prometheus, the shattered remnants of a barrier of emerald energy crumbling at her feet.

Camilla.

I hesitated, wondering whether Prometheus would try to hit us with a second blast while we were still stunned, but unfortunately for him, Cerberus was already leaping over our heads. He came down on top of Prometheus, tearing at him in ferocity and rage over the attack on his mother.

But as much as I wanted to see him torn limb from limb, he wasn't as important as... my friend. Kang was already down by her side, one arm beneath her head and the other patting out flames still flickering on the hem of her dress.

"Hang on." Kang's voice was panicked. "Just hang on."

"Nathan," she said.

"Just wait," he replied. "Just—"

"Nathaniel," she interrupted him, her voice barely registering. "It's okay."

"Camilla," I said, falling to my knees and taking her by the hand. "Why... why did you... why did you have to—"

"I'm sorry," she said. "For everything."

"Stop," I said. "This isn't—"

"I've lived a long time, boys. Long enough to know when it's the end. I... I've been an idiot. Fighting... for something that I lost. And never fighting for what I've gained."

"Save your strength," I said, lying a little to her. And to myself.

"Leaving the two of you was the hardest thing I've ever done. And the most stupid. I really did... really do, love you guys. And I'm glad I got to be on your side. One last time. Instead of being the scorpion that sinks you."

Kang was too busy wiping the tears from his eyes to reply, so I deputised for him.

"We love you too. I guess you do break your promises after all. When it's really worth it. Back at the hotel, you asked if I was a frog or swan? But we're more like turtles. You can sting our shell, but you can never sink us."

"I'm glad," Camilla sputtered, coughing black blood, and reached one trembling hand out. "Xiao. Make sure she survives."

I looked up at Xiao, wondering if she would simply keep her distance or turn her back on the whole affair. To my surprise, instead of the regular aloof and vigilant grimace she reserved for Camilla, Xiao's glassy eyes betrayed a look of what seemed like... anguish.

Xiao crouched awkwardly by Camilla's side, close enough to take her by the hand, but still distant enough to not confuse her grief with affection.

"Xiao," Camilla said once more. "I was... never a mother to you. To anyone. All I carried was hate, vengeance and a longing for things long past. It took me too long to realise that new love can just be as powerful as old. Don't live as I did. Angry about what went before. Be... better. Embrace what comes next. What you are. Be..."

As Camilla's words faded, I had an aching certainty that they were the last words I'd ever hear her say. And despite the chaos of Cerberus and Prometheus' brawl competing with Avy's struggling as she tried to break herself free, I could still digest nothing but the deafening silence of sorrow, between Xiao, Kang and I.

"Hey," Kang finally said, filling the void. "I think she would have–"

He was cut off by the swipe of Xiao, unsheathing her knife and standing upright.

"Hey, Xiao," I started, sensing her rage even before I caught the look in her eyes. "Calm down. Please. Don't do anything stu–"

Xiao swung her blade towards the ground in a downwards motion, extending it by three feet as it flipped from a knife into a katana instantly. The sword almost perfectly resembled the ones carried by Camilla's other children, as Xiao spun and marched away from us.

"Wait," I yelled. "What are you gonna..."

There was no stopping Xiao, as she broke into a sprint, leaped a startling ten feet in the air, then planted her blade deep into the flesh of the titanic hand that trapped Avy. Right away, the hand recoiled in agony, loosening its grasp around Avy as another finger uncurled.

Nox took advantage of the opening by latching onto the finger and pushing it all the way back until the knuckle bent unnaturally away from the hand, unfastening the other fingers enough for Avy to throw her arms out wide and break fully free from its grip.

She rolled away from the hand, grabbing Xiao by the arm and lifting her and her blade out of the Titan's reach.

"Thanks Xiao," Avy said, her tone both compassionate and confused. "Are you... alright?"

Xiao's eyes drifted back towards us. Though I knew she was looking more at Camilla's lifeless body than Kang or I.

"Can you make him suffer?" Xiao said, her voice erratic, like cracking ice.

"Yes." Avy nodded.

"I'll be alright once you do."

"Understood." Avy pursed her lips and let out a shrill whistle. "Noctue."

"Okay, okay," Nox said, ambling over to her. "You don't ave' to do that whistle thing. I'm listening ain't I?"

"I've missed you old friend." She brushed the backs of her fingers over his ape-like fur.

"Yeah. Been a long time, Theenie. But I see you've kept well."

"What's with the accent?"

"I'm a mimic, right? What can I say? You sound a little off as well."

Avy shrugged. "Turkish, I guess. I have been wandering around in Avy's human body for centuries. Remember? Now, help me kill this guy."

"Honestly," Nox replied. "I'm more of a lover than a fighter these days you know?"

Avy glared back at him, unimpressed.

""Alright, alright," Nox relented. "What do you need?"

"Something classic."

Nox smiled and leapt into the air, irradiating us with an eruption of blue light, as his arms stretched back into wings. This time, however, he was much larger and though the creature was mythical, I knew straight away what he had become.

"A phoenix?" I said.

"That's right," Avy replied. "It's time for us to rise again."

Leaping upon Nox's back, Avy extended both her arms and held them out expectantly, summoning both Vinter's sword and shield into each hand.

"Stand back." she ordered. "I'm ending this."

Without any further conversation, Nox blasted into the air and soared towards Prometheus. Cerberus laid defeated and aflame at the Titan's feet as the pair dived into him, knocking him flying across the cavern.

He tumbled across the ground for thirty metres or so before rolling back up onto his feet, raising his arm and firing several more streaks of flame at them. But Nox was too fast, banking and rolling through the air like a fighter jet as he closed the ground.

Prometheus took a second to ready another, more powerful blast, but he couldn't have noticed any sooner than I did, that Avy was no longer riding her companion.

By the time I relocated her, on the ground, hurtling towards him, Prometheus had already adjusted and poured a wave of flame directly at her. Despite the chances of seeing her melted away right before my eyes, I didn't dare look away. Not when I knew how determined she was to finish him.

As I should have expected, she raised the shield to deflect the flames. I could see her thighs and triceps bulging as she wrestled against the flame, taking step after step closer towards him. Closing in, as the fire splashed past her in streams of lava-like heat.

She was just a few metres from him when the ominous crack of the shield giving way caused me to flinch and grit my teeth. Avy took one look down at the failing shield, then pivoted out of the flame, brought her sword to bear, and sliced swiftly through the air.

Prometheus' head hit the ground before the flames had died down.

Avy puffed out a long breath that looked like both exhaustion and relief, then bent down and plucked his head from the ground. She held the severed appendage up by the hair, turning her nose up in revulsion.

"Is he dead?" I said, deciding to walk cautiously to join her.

"See for yourself," she said, turning the head to face me.

"Of course not," came Prometheus' voice, his eyes still open and glaring at *me* now. "This Olympian does not possess the means to kill me. None of them do."

"He's right," Avy replied, pointing her sword down at his headless body.

The blade glowed briefly, before a ray of white light shot down at the corpse and disintegrated it completely.

"But without a body," Avy continued. "You're going to have to put your plans on hold."

Avy headed back towards the pedestal, scooping the rest of the stones up casually and resting his head down in their place.

"Why don't you hang out here with your friend," she said. "For, let's say... ever."

With a second swing of the sword, she lopped all five of the giant Titan fingers off, and kicked them down into the bubbling flames.

"You lose, old man," said Kang, as he and Xiao arrived at the pedestal. "How does it feel?"

"You should have told us the truth," I added. "From the start."

"You're right," Prometheus replied. "I should have. Because now, it's not just me who is going to lose. You have no idea what you've walked into the middle of. Whose side you've taken. I tried to protect you from it all. All of the lies and betrayal that *her* kind is capable of."

"The only betrayer here is you," I yelled. "This, all of this, started because you betrayed and killed Zeus."

Before he replied, Prometheus stared at me, long and mockingly, and began to laugh. Not triumphant or maniacally, but quietly.

"Young, Ezekiel," he finally said. "Still only believing the parts of the story he wants to believe. The parts that are convenient to fuel his own personal narrative."

He paused, long enough to let the cogs in my head turn until they got stuck in the one possibility that I hadn't bothered to consider right up until that very second.

"Ah there it is," Prometheus continued. "You've finally realised, all too late, that I didn't kill Zeus at all. Athena did."

EPILOGUE

THE ATHENIAN TAPESTRY

"Hindsight is a gift. As Historians, we look upon the past. We weigh motivation against consequence, all in the context of the entire world's history. But hindsight is a lie. We all know through living out our own success and failure that knowledge is never absolute. We act and we react, only ever in control of our actions here and now. Using what we know to be true in one fleeting moment. It is only once we've acted, that we must deal with the fallout of our choices. And only then, when the results have won, does history record us. What we know becomes what we knew, and that added knowledge, for better or worse, will change us. And for those of us who thought ourselves content or unwilling to change, hindsight becomes a curse."

I couldn't have been older than seven or eight when I read my first Pierceson book. Those were the first words of his I ever saw written down, on the inside of the cover. Was it advice? A riddle? Or was it a warning? I had never been sure. Until now.

Until Avy walked into my life, I knew that myths and legends were just that. Fiction. Interpretation. Not real. It wasn't a feeling or hunch. I knew it. And that certainty defined how I lived my life. How I worked, how I studied, how I processed new information. I used it to explore history in ways that other students couldn't. That truth was my lexicon for understanding their world. And by extension, my own.

Avy and Camilla had changed all that. They had inadvertently revealed that my truth was a lie. And left me wondering if I could be so wrong about one of the only things of which I was so assured, well... What else had I gotten wrong in my life? What else had I misinterpreted so badly that my entire worldview was broken? What other core pillars of my life were unfounded?

But Pierceson was right. Next came the curse. And I felt it threefold.

Cursed once because as much as I hated to admit it now, I was happy. My life was good. It was rewarding, and it was fun, and, for the most part, I had everyone I needed around me. All that was over now.

Cursed twice because upon having my worldview shattered, I thought I'd found comfort in a new normal. A new goal. To help Avy. To help everyone maybe. To use my old knowledge in this new world. But even that was the past now, what I knew about Avy, no– Athena, was wrong. I'd gotten it all wrong.

And cursed a third time in finally arriving in a place of knowledge and now being too late to do anything about it. I thought rescuing Avy would be a new beginning. But I didn't even need her to confirm Prometheus' story to know that this was in fact, the end.

"He's lying!" said Kang. "Right?"

"Classic P-boy bullshit," Nox added.

"You didn't kill your father?" Xiao questioned. "You... couldn't have. Avy?"

Avy's shoulders sagged as she sighed. Her right hand glowed ominously as she rested her palm across Prometheus' mouth. When she removed it, his lips too were gone. Sealed from revealing any more secrets.

"Bothersome, young, mortal," she said, with a shake of the head. "And always meddling in affairs beyond your station."

"No..." Nox whispered. "You've gotta be kidding me? Tell me you didn't–"

"Quiet," Avy shouted, silencing him with a threatening wave of her arm.

"Why?" I hissed, with a venom I'd reserved usually for being on the wrong end of betrayal by Camilla, not for a girl I'd grown to–

"It had to be done," Avy said scornfully. "Zeus was old. And tired. And no longer worthy. He was ready to give up. To surrender to the Demi-Gods. He claimed our time was over and that it was time for the cycle of mortality to flourish."

"So, you killed him?" I said accusingly.

"Yes. Though... he saw it coming. Not from me, I was hardly the only one he'd displeased. But he knew enough to be suspicious, and so he'd set a trap. And when I struck, we were all stripped of our powers and cast out. I can still remember the surprise in his eyes before his thunder rained down. The moment he saw it was me. I was so close to him, it's no wonder I had most of my memories knocked out, leaving your precious little Avy to wander around all this time. But, thanks to you, I'm myself again. So there will certainly be no Titans. And soon, no more Demi-Gods."

I could feel my heartrate quickening, the riotous drumming in my chest as Avy's golden eyes probed us uncertainly. Like a tiger realising that their cage door had been left open.

"I'm tempted," she started. "To let the three of you walk. But the thing is, I'm taking these stones back to their rightful owners. And you all know a little too much. I can't have you flipping sides, or tipping off a Demi."

"Because you plan to kill them all?" Xiao asked, her hand still clutching her blade tightly enough that I knew this wasn't going to end peacefully.

"You can't," I intervened, admittedly without a plan. I realised all too late that my plan only went as far as rescuing Avy, not stopping her.

"I'm very sure I can," Avy said. "Who's going to stop me?"

"We will," Kang added. "If we have to."

"You see." Avy laughed mockingly. "I said I was tempted to let you be. But this is why I can't."

In a flash, Xiao drew her weapon as Kang lunged for Vinter's sword, planted in the ground nearby. Even faster, Avy extended both hands and held both my friends still, as if they were in the clutch of some invisible restraint.

The ground vanished from beneath my feet too, as I rose into the air and was pulled towards Avy along with them. She plucked the sword from the ground and raised it initially, and threateningly, in my direction before levelling it at each of Xiao and Kang.

"Wait!" It was Nox this time, landing between us and flapping a mighty gust of wind towards Avy. "You don't have to do this, Theenie. These are good people. They helped me find you. And they can–"

"I said quiet," yelled Avy, her eyes irradiating a burst of blinding light that forced my eyes shut.

When the light dissipated and I willed them open again, Nox had been reduced from his grand phoenix form, back into a tiny blue owl.

"That suits you better, little one," Avy continued. "If you harbour any desires of leaving this form, Noctue, I suggest you keep your beak out of my business."

After shooing Nox away with her hand, Avy stepped ominously in front of Xiao and smiled.

"Maybe you and I should pick up where we left off," she said.

"Go to hell," Xiao yelled, denying Avy the pleasure of witnessing any fear.

But having seen more than enough people I love hurt already on this journey, I had more than enough fear for the three of us.

"Stop," I said. "Take me."

"Zeke, no," Xiao protested.

"Take me instead. If you kill me, I promise neither of them will come after you. Just let them go and this will all be over."

"What the hell are you doing?" shouted Kang. "Don't be such a... you can't just–"

"Kang!" I shouted. "I'm trying to save your life. It doesn't have to be all of us. Just let me do this."

Kang looked at me, somehow fondly and angrily at once, before shaking his head.

"How brave," Avy said. "But do you know what bravery gets?"

Avy raised her eyebrows, but I had no idea what she meant. What she wanted me to say.

"What?" I whispered.

"Other people killed."

Avy pressed her sword forwards. But it didn't strike me.

Instead, I had to watch on in what felt like slow motion as her sword dipped into Kang's chest, twisted, then slid out covered in his blood.

Xiao's cries filled the cavern. I thought I'd scream too. Maybe I already had. But for the seconds that came after, as I watched his body spill out of the air and sag, unmoving, to the ground below, everything began to grow more and more silent.

It felt like a movie. Unreal. Unbelievable. Impossible. At that moment, and for the first time on this entire journey, I half expected to wake up, asleep on the couch or mid-flight, to find that this entire fiasco had been a feverish nightmare. I even found myself revisiting my earliest hypotheses, in that this all had to be some trick or illusion, or something else I didn't yet understand.

And yet, the rest of me, the logical side of my brain, was more certain than ever that this was it. Kang was dead.

"That's drained the life out of you," Avy said, stepping next in front of Xiao. "No pun intended. Maybe you're too numb to feel this one then?"

She was right. I barely struggled, barely even breathed, as she thrust her sword towards Xiao, who already had her eyes closed. I only felt the sense of greater awareness rushing back into me when the sword halted just inches from her chest, and hung unmoving in the air.

"No!" Avy said, her words straining, as if she were struggling against some unseen force. "I won't... I won't let you... kill... my... friends!"

"Avy!" I shouted, my strength renewed as we fell out of the air and I crashed down on my knees.

"Zeke," she said. "I'm trying to stop her, but... she's... she's too strong."

"No!" I said. "She is strong. But so are you. You've lived just as long as her. You're your own person. With your own life. You don't have to do what she wants. And you don't have to become her. You can just be you. You can be Avy."

Tears streamed down Avy's face as she twisted away in pain, yelling and fighting against herself.

"How!?" she screamed. "How do I fight her?"

"Put the power back!" Nox landed on my shoulder. "Just like Zeus did. Choose a container and seal her away."

"No!" Avy's voice grew harsh again. "I will not go back! This is our time. My time. I've waited centuries for this and you will not take it from me."

"Yes... I... Will," Avy said, contesting herself once more.

She raised the sword above her head, then stabbed it into the ground. The blade erupted in a cyclone of light, piercing the roof of the cave again and battering Avy's body with dazzling golden lightning. She looked as if she was being burnt alive as she convulsed and shuddered, her hand never leaving the sword.

She shrieked, one final and deafening time, before she was blown backwards away from the sword and slammed down on her back.

"Avy," I shouted, rushing down to check on her. "Are you okay? What happened?"

"I... I'm okay," she said, her eyes dimmed from goddess bright down to regular golden Avy lustre. "I channelled the energy into the sword. That power. Athena's power. It's trapped in there now."

"So you're not a goddess anymore?" Xiao asked.

She was sitting with Kang in her arms, tears already rushing down her cheeks.

"Does that mean Kang is..." I couldn't bring myself to say the words. "Does that mean you can't–"

Avy quickly pushed me away, rising to her feet and limping over to Kang. She placed one hand over the wound in his chest and closed her eyes.

I waited. I waited for what felt like an eternity. Like days and months and years were all falling off my life with every moment I spent watching absolutely nothing happen.

"No," Avy cried. "No. This has to work. There has to be something left. He has to come back. I have to bring him back. I have to–"

I wasn't sure if Avy's words were becoming more muffled and lost amongst her sobs, or if my mind was simply tuning out the insufferable noise of the world, shrinking in on itself to protect me from more pain.

"Avy," I said, attempting to force the words out before my lips were sealed forever. "It's not your–"

"Hey." A voice interrupted me. A voice both comforting in its familiarity and shocking in its timing. "What... what happened?"

At once, I dragged my chin from where it rested on my chest.

"Kang?" I said.

"Am I... am I alive?" Kang asked, his voice weary and uncertain.

"I... I think so," Avy replied. "You're... alive?"

"Ah okay, I'm not the only one who's surprised then. Good."

Kang patted down his chest, widening his eyes as he searched for his wound. Xiao, still cradling him, lifted his blood-soaked shirt to reveal his bloodless torso.

"You healed him," she said. "Without the stone. Without... the power."

"Maybe there's something left," Avy replied, turning her hand back and forth.

"Or maybe," Kang replied. "Maybe you're just special. With or without."

Suddenly, he swung forward, wrapped both arms around Avy and pulled her close. Xiao quickly followed, embracing Kang from behind and looking up at me with impatient eyes.

"What are you doing?" Xiao said. "Get in here."

"I..." For once, I realised there just wasn't anything else to say, so I knelt down and threw my arms around all three of them. I'd hugged Kang a thousand times before, but this was the first time in a long time that I'd really appreciated, and savoured, having my best friend in my arms. That Xiao and Avy were joining felt like the best bonus I could ask for.

"Tell you what mate," said Nox, breaking up our perfect moment. "You are one lucky bastard, you know that? Honestly, I wasn't even sure that would work. What with her just being a plain old librarian after all. No offence."

"None taken," Avy replied, breaking away and wiping the tears from her eyes.

"I'm Nox, by the way," he said, extending one of his dainty wings.

"I know." She shook him, comically, by the wing. "I'm Avare Pendragon. Nice to properly meet you. *And* for helping me seal her away. I have to admit, I'm a little surprised. Didn't you just spend centuries trying to get her back?"

"Yeah. I did. But... maybe I've been looking for someone who doesn't exist anymore. Maybe the person who has been walking all these miles in those shoes should get to keep wearing them. You're as real as they come. I realise that now."

Avy smiled. "Thank you."

"Don't mention it. Besides, I've gotten used to being alone anyway."

"Well, you're not alone anymore. You're with us now. Me, and these three lunatics who dive into ancient burial grounds to rescue people they hardly know."

Avy's attention switched to Kang and Xiao.

"Even when you threaten them. Even when you betray them. Even when they've had doubts about you from the start."

Kang shrugged. "Well when you put it like that... let's just say you're on your last life. To be honest, I've been through too much to process right now. We all have. I died, you know?"

"And I'm the daughter of a thousand year old shapeshifter," Xiao added.

"See Avy," Kang added. "We've all had one hell of a day."

"Camilla," said Avy. "I saw what she did. We wouldn't have made it without her. Beneath all her layers, she really was a good friend to you guys."

"Yeah," Kang said. "She was."

It was true, she really had come through for us when it really mattered. Just like old times. I still couldn't quite find the words to address what I was feeling for her just yet, so Kang had to settle for my simple nod and smile in agreement.

"She was really scary though," Avy said. "And I mean normal Camilla. She scared the life out of me."

Against all odds, Avy actually had each of us smiling and laughing. Something that just a few moments ago, I knew was impossible. But again and again, this girl seemed to be changing everything I thought I knew.

"And you," she said, finally addressing me. "You threw a lightning bolt at me. Not cool."

"Well, it did save your life," I replied.

"Very briefly, before turning me into a psychotic goddess of destruction."

"In my defence, you've been a little crazy since the night I met you."

"Well, that's something you're just going to have to learn to live with. Along with me being plain old Avy now. Is that going to be enough? After all you've seen?"

"Are you kidding me?!" I tried to stifle my laughter. "I've been waiting to kiss plain old Avy all week."

"Oh really?" she smirked. "Then don't keep me waiting."

As I leant in to kiss her, feeling her hot breath on mine for the first time, my heart and head spun like a tie-fighter in a nosedive. I brimmed with, first, anticipation as the moment closed in on me, but it was washed away just as quickly by bitter disappointment.

Not from Avy, of course. No, it was Kang's arm on my shoulder, dragging us apart as he began to crack wise with classically awful timing.

"I hate to break this up," he said. "But can we save the romantics until we're out of this Titan hole, away from the Prometheus head, and back to some sense of normality?"

"I think normal is pretty much over for me," Xiao replied. "Besides, there's still the question of the stones. Can we afford to just leave them here? Hoping nobody else stumbles upon them?"

"We *should* leave them here," said Kang. "They're not our problem anymore. All this started because I took one when I shouldn't have."

"Don't be ridiculous," Nox said. "You leave 'em' here and some poor sod will come along and start this whole show back up again."

"Then we destroy them," said Xiao.

"Do you even know how? Listen, there's still a war going on out there. Between Gods and Demi-Gods. This isn't over. Just because you want to sit on the fence, doesn't mean others out there aren't going to keep picking sides."

"Everyone relax," I said, my voice raised just enough to drown them out. "For once, let's all just stop trying to lead each other and do some following. This isn't our decision to make."

I took Avy by the hand this time, savouring its warmth just for a second, before giving her a gentle squeeze.

"What do you want to do?" I asked.

Avy took a deep breath, as if she were taking a moment to absorb not just the insane scene around us, but each of the events of the past week behind us.

"Okay," she finally said. "There are ten stones. Ten Thunderbolts. That means nine other people like me. Well, eight people and one asshole in Deimos. What if some of them are lost, like I was? Lost and alone."

"You want to meet them?" I asked.

"Maybe," she replied. "But first, can we get some chocolate? You promised."

"Sure," I said. "My mum makes a mean chocolate tart."

That's it.

Another year, another story. I first started TTT way back in 2017 to try a few things like First-Person POV, Urban Fantasy and context-switching between this and other projects.

And while I can't say I'll ever take this scenic route to the finish line ever again - I'm forever grateful to all my beta readers and supporters who helped me get this passion project over the line.

In particular it's my first novel where I've poured tons of myself and my culture into the main character (so no apologies if he's dislikable, I can't help it). And equally important to me was taking the chance to explore Greek Mythology. It was always my favourite subject at school, not to mention the one I was best at. And whenever I regret not following the path of writing sooner, it's often my days studying Classical Civilisations that I find myself looking back on.

But life isn't about regret. Just like Zeke eventually realises - you move on from the past and loosen your grip on the things you thought you knew. Only then do we get to grow and open ourselves up to exciting new experiences.

And above all - thanks to my kids for always keeping my brain stimulated and the creative juices flowing. And to my wife for putting up with the sounds of endless keyboard tapping and always pushing me to be my best. I couldn't love them anymore if I tried.

I hope you've all enjoyed the ride.

And I hope to see you all on the next literary adventure too!

Printed in Great Britain
by Amazon